THE HOUSE THAT SAMAEL BUILT

RUBY JEAN JENSEN

DID YOU EVER SEE EYES LIKE THAT ON A LITTLE BOY?

Tara said musingly as she looked up at the painting she had just uncovered. It was the portrait of a child, and from it, the eyes—large, fiery, yellow—glared at her like something from an old horror movie ...

"They are kind of glary, aren't they?" Amy replied. "But," she continued happily, "this will be a lovely place to have my baby. This was a child's room. And look, there's a peace sign on the painting. That's a very good omen, isn't it, Sherwood?"'

Sherwood looked for a long while at the vertical bar with the inverted V on the bottom of the painting."

"That's no peace sign," he finally said. "It has no circle around it, and it was made a long time ago. No, it's no peace sign, Amy. It's the sign of the devil."

To three special cousins: Lon, Jerry, and Orlie McCool, who at one time would even do the dishes, for a ghost story.

First Printed 1974 in the United States of America

Published by: Gayle J. Foster, Carrollton, Texas

Library of Congress Control Number: 2021922037

Cover art: SelfPubBookCovers.com/ Shardel

❀ Created with Vellum

PROLOGUE

She stood by the coffin, which was held in place above the prepared grave, and heard only the drone of the minister's voice as he spoke the last words.

Hot, strong, Nebraska wind swept her long hair across her face, obscuring the vision that tears did not. She raised a hand slowly and pushed the hair back and looked at the other grave, the one so tactfully covered with a carpet of too-green artificial grass. And the large double stone. Though she saw only its gray, granite back she knew the words by heart. The names. Her father, and now her mother. Both so near to her, as they always had been, yet so far away. Forever gone.

Her mother had said, "I cannot live without him, Tara," just three weeks ago. And even then she knew that her answer, "Not even for me, Mother?" was useless because her mother had been ill for a long time before the sudden heart attack that had taken the man she loved, and the hand she reached out to Tara was very thin, and trembled. "Oh, Tara, Tara, Tara," she whispered. "I pray for you a love like ours—and the blessing of a child like you."

Tara looked up at the people who stood around this new funeral, and saw their eyes upon her, and knew that each one wondered why no tears fell from the eyes of the daughter of the woman who was being buried. They did not know—how could they? They who shed tears for someone who had been but a friend, an acquaintance. They could not know that when you can't cry, you hurt. And you keep hurting, hurting, hurting.

The man who stood behind her touched her arm, grasped it, and pulled her away, back toward the long black car that had driven her to the cemetery for the second time in recent weeks.

"It's over," he said, sounding relieved. "Let's get in out of this heat."

He had ridden with her because there were no close relatives and because she had been dating him off and on for several years. He had considered them informally engaged even though she had never said yes, or even maybe. In her numbness now he had taken over and handled almost everything, and for that she was grateful. But she didn't speak to him until they had reached the small living room of the only home she had ever known.

Accustomed hospitality forced her to ask, "Would you like something cold—tea—something?"

"No thanks."

They were standing just inside the door, and he spoke as he always had, in the voice that always demanded and received. Except with her. Sometimes she wondered if that was the thing that had kept him coming back since their high-school days.

"You can't keep living here now," he said.

She looked around and felt the emptiness, heard the vacuum of silence left by loved ones gone.

"It's not worth much," he said, a critical eye disapproving of small rooms and old furniture that hadn't cost much to begin with. In comparison to his large family home it was nothing. "It wouldn't bring more than five thousand— junk and all. We'll sell it and you can marry me now. Your mother doesn't need you anymore and you can't stay here alone."

He was right about that. She couldn't stay. To be here hurt far too much. The memories were in her heart. She couldn't stand the house. Not even the few old photographs of happier days.

"There's no point in waiting," he said again. "Maybe a six-month engagement just to give Mama a chance to do her thing with the wedding arrangements."

Tara opened her mouth to say bluntly that she had never said she would marry him, but sighed instead. She did want children and a home, and so far all the men she had dated seemed to see only her face and figure. What did love really matter?

I pray for you a love like ours ...

. . .

OH MOTHER, Dad, her heart cried silently, and in answer to Albert she shrugged, accepting.

He turned her to him and placed a tight, cold kiss on her lips. She wondered vaguely if there was any real love or passion in the man.

"Good," he said on his way out the door. "I'll let you know later about the rings. I know I can get the family rings for you. With your looks and my blood the folks will be pleased with our children."

When he had gone she looked at her left hand. She had worn a few well-padded class rings there, but nothing important. She thought of the large house where he lived, and knew she would be expected to live there too, just another one of the family treasures.

She crossed the room and sat down in her father's old chair and ran her hand along the cracked plastic upholstery, and suddenly she was thinking, what have I done? Even for the security of a home, yes, even for the kids she wanted, would she settle for a man she didn't love?

The thought of lying in Albert Smith's arms even for one night was too much.

She leaned to one side and picked up the telephone. Her daddy's best friend would handle it. The sale of the house and furniture, and all that which Albert had called "junk." The money would cover hospital and funeral expenses. She wanted only what she could carry with her, because somewhere there had to be something for her.

Somewhere, something.

CHAPTER 1

Tara stepped from the rain into the crowd under the awning of the news shop and wiped the water from her face, pushing her wet hair back so that she could see. On the sidewalk she had walked with her head down, as most of the others walked, trying to duck out of the pounding rain. The loosely woven shawl she hugged to her shoulders dripped water onto her feet and down the wet legs of her blue jeans. In one hand she carried a black valise, and in it was all she had brought with her. Even her last seven dollars. She had never before been so wet and miserable and she wondered now if Albert had been all that bad. At least in his house, as his wife, she would be dry and comfortable instead of stranded in San Francisco with not even enough money for another week's room rent.

Soaked, smelly bodies crowded in out of the rain and nearly trampled her down. She moved over to lean against the small counter behind which stood the man who sold newspapers.

"Something for you?" he asked grumpily, "or you just looking for a dry spot?"

"I want a newspaper," she answered. She placed the valise between her feet to protect it and dug into the pocket of her jeans for change.

"What one?"

"The one with the most want ads."

He gave her the San Francisco Examiner.

She asked, "Does this entitle me to stand here long enough to look at the ads and see if there are any jobs available?" The frown was deliberate. She could be just as grumpy as he.

He looked her over, from her dripping red hair to her dripping shawl, and shrugged.

She spread the newspaper on the counter and thereafter ignored him. She needed a job, needed it so desperately that she didn't know what she was going to do if she didn't find something. Quick. She wondered how far her experience as a small-town librarian would take her. Probably about as far as the nearest waitress job.

She looked at the "waitresses needed" list and discovered that it wouldn't even take her that far. Experience necessary. Experience. *Experience.*

She heard the man yell, "Go on, get out of here, you hippies. Go somewhere else to park out of the rain!"

She looked around to see that he was waving his arms, herding them like cattle.

One girl caught her attention. All she could see among the mass of people was a small, thin, white face with huge, hungry-looking eyes. She was backing away from the newsman with the waving arms. Then she turned and looked out into the rain with an expression on her face that made Tara forget the paper and the want ads. A child lost? With nowhere to go but out into the rain. She didn't look more than fifteen years old.

Tara thought she had seen it all during these past few months of her search, on this trip that was turning out to be a mistake. But the homeless, rain-soaked child being herded back into the rain was something she wouldn't have believed.

The girl didn't notice that she was being watched. She moistened her small, pale lips as if to gather her nerve, and stepped out from under the awning. Tara saw that she wore an old sweater, bagging with water, and a thin dress that clung to a huge, round belly.

Astonished, Tara stared. So young, and pregnant? Nowhere to go except into the rain? Her age though—the youthfulness of her face was probably misleading. She might be older than Tara had thought.

The girl turned toward her then, and for a moment returned her stare. A tall, gaunt man followed behind her. A man typical of the hippie parks, with long hair and a beard that nearly covered his face. All but his nose, and his eyes. The eyes were cut sideways at her, watching her as closely as she had watched the girl.

Tara returned his look, wondering where she had seen him before. On the street, or in a park? Well, she had looked into a lot of eyes that could have been his. He reminded her of Abraham Lincoln, maybe—something about the shape of his nose, and the hollowness of the cheeks above his beard.

Tara turned back to her paper. For a while she couldn't see anything but the face of the pregnant girl. The newsprint blurred and the words she read she had to read again, and still the face of the girl remained foremost in her mind. Surely she was one of those tiny girls who always look younger than they are. But even so, compared to her Tara felt ancient at twenty-three.

The rain was coming down harder, and dusk was falling. In another few minutes it would be dark and she would be worse off than she was at the moment.

She gathered the newspaper into a roll and stuffed it into the valise, then faced the sidewalk. There was a small doughnut shop up the street. A cup of coffee and a doughnut wouldn't take much of her money, and it would help fill the terrible emptiness in her stomach, warm her up, and dry her off a little. It was worth walking two blocks for.

People pushed by her on the sidewalk, almost all going the other way. Very few people wore shawls. Her information about the flower children of the West Coast had been slightly off. A desperate illusion, a search for a better world. They kept pushing by, going somewhere she didn't know about, just long-haired people who seemed genderless.

She wiped rainwater out of her mouth and mumbled aloud, "Snow in Nebraska was never like this." At least she had had sense enough then to stay in out of the worst of it.

When it was possible she walked under overhanging roofs and awnings, and under the third one she found herself brushing back her hair to look slightly downward into the young girl's eyes again.

She had unknowingly walked in to stand right beside her.

A tiny smile trembled on the girl's lips. "Wet, isn't it?" she said. Even her voice had a childish ring to it, sweet and high pitched.

"Yes," Tara answered, aware of the contrasting deep, soft tones of her own voice.

The tall, full-bearded man was still with the girl, standing just behind her, and his eyes were just as watchful as they had been under the other awning.

Impulsively, Tara said to the girl, "I was just going down to the doughnut shop for coffee and a doughnut. Won't you come with me?"

The girl's eyes lighted as if she had been offered a rainbow. "Doughnut? You mean you really—want—us to eat with you?"

Tara glanced at the man. His cheeks were sunken too, so much so that they were visible under his beard. In fact, he resembled Abraham Lincoln more than anyone she had ever seen, except his eyes seemed hard and cold. She thought he was smiling, but she wasn't sure.

"Why not?" Three doughnuts and coffees wouldn't cost but three times as much as one. Anything to get some food into that starving girl. "Come on, it's not much farther."

They stood back to let Tara lead the way, but she soon found she had to slow her steps to allow for the girl's awkwardness.

At the coffee shop the man held the door and Tara took the girl's hand to help her over the threshold. She didn't look as if she would even be able to see her feet well enough to know where to place them.

Tara had been half afraid that the owners would ask them to leave, but she saw the shop was nearly filled with wet and dripping customers.

"Looks like we'll have to stand up," she said as she moved to the cash register to order and pay for the food.

The girl was silent when she got her doughnut, looking at the sugary ring in her hand, nibbling on it as if to make it last forever.

"I'm called Fox," said the man. "What's your name?" Tara glanced up to see that he was nearly over her. His cheeks looked slightly puffed out with the entire doughnut. She watched him chew it three times and swallow. "Fox?" Well, at least that was to be expected. Anonymity. What else? In self-contempt she said, "Just call me Flower-child."

He laughed as if he knew it were just a gag of some kind. "Are you cold, Flowerchild?"

She had been shivering under her shawl for hours, and she couldn't quit. Even in this overheated room. "I thought California was supposed to be sunny."

"You mean you never heard of the West Coast rains? Where are you from, Flowerchild?"

"Nebraska."

"You're putting me on."

"What makes you think that?" she asked indignantly.

"Not Nebraska. Corn-fed girls would never take off and come out here to stand around in a shawl. Not even the ones with flaming red hair and witchy green eyes like yours. Where are you really from?"

Tara glanced at the girl nibbling her doughnut. The man was obviously flirting, yet the girl didn't seem to notice at all. Or didn't care.

"Back East, then," she said, and carefully closed her mouth. She wasn't prepared to open up her past life and tell this stranger all about it.

"What in the hell are you doing here in that stupid shawl?"

She retorted, "What are you doing here without even a shawl? To say nothing of a hat or umbrella."

He leaned closer to her and pulled his beard, saying in a faked and throaty drawl, "I've got this to protect me." When she drew back and frowned slightly he said in a normal tone. "Would it help if I told you my name is really Eldon?"

"Help me what?"

He straightened and raised his shoulders in a shrug. "Well, like say, be friendlier?"

"Drink your coffee before it gets cold," she said, and to her surprise he obeyed without comment.

She found herself wondering about him, if he perhaps could be the girl's brother. The girl was still nibbling her doughnut in ecstasy, and then with a low "*yummmm*" she stuffed her mouth full and ate it down. The temptation clearly had become too much. When that was finished she looked at Tara, wiped the sugar from her mouth, then carefully licked each finger.

"Come home with us," she said.

"Home!" Tara cried. "You mean you have one of those?"

The man, who had by now finished his coffee, laughed shortly. "Sure, home. There's this tree we got, Flower-child. At least you'll have shelter."

"Then what are you doing here in so much rain?" She was trying hard to imagine a tree as a home, and came up with a tree house such as she had once during her childhood.

"We came to get some bread," the girl answered.

"But there's no grocery store in this direction for another two blocks."

The man laughed again. "She means *bread*, Flower-child. You know, I believe you are from Nebraska after all."

The girl offered helpfully, "That's really money."

"Oh." Of course Tara had heard that one, it was just that the expression had slipped her mind for a moment, as most of their strange words did.

The girl's hand touched her. "Do come with us. The fellows will welcome you. We're a real family, you know." Tara looked down into the girl's eyes, wondering if she really lived in a tree. Perhaps in a tent underneath it? "You have a family?"

"Just a very small one. There's room for one more."

"True," said the man. "We'd love to have you along. You can come look us over, anyway, and leave if you don't like us."

Six dollars and some change left in her valise; rain pouring from a sky that had gone black since they'd come into the shop. But mostly, a very young, very pregnant girl who called a tree "home." Tara felt that she had done some impulsive, perhaps very foolish things in the past few months. This could hardly be worse. At least it promised shelter from the rain on a night when she really couldn't afford a room. She had to stop somewhere and figure out what to do. She had already decided she wouldn't make a decent flower child even if such creatures still existed. She had learned that she liked warmth and the security of a job. Even her old job in the tiny Smithville public library looked good. Even marrying dull, insensitive Albert Smith, rich son of the richest man in Smithville, was beginning to look good, drawing her away from the beckoning of another world.

But in the meantime, there was tonight, and her reluctance to give in and call Albert.

"Okay," she said. "Thanks for sharing your tree. I hope it's waterproof. Are you sure the others won't mind?"

The man's hand touched her back and withdrew as quickly as had the girl's. "No. Why should they? And don't worry about the guys. I'll just slip them the message that you're my woman and they won't bother you."

That gave her a start of surprise, a slight feeling of curiosity at the ease with which he mentioned it. She wondered if he were teasing.

The girl was smiling, waiting. "Please come with us," she said. "It's the least we can do after you sharing with us."

Tara decided that the man, Eldon, Fox, or whoever he was, had been putting her on with his own private little joke. It was hard to tell with so much beard on his face, and his middle-parted hair hanging forward, obscuring most of his face. He opened the door and the girl went out, holding onto him for support, and after a moment of indecision Tara gripped her valise to her midriff and joined them.

Once started, she followed with no misgivings, walking slowly, tense from hoping that the girl wouldn't slip and fall. And in the silent walk her thoughts wandered back and became occupied with the past three months. She had found nothing in her travels to make her say, "This is what I left home in search of." She had found no man of whom she could say, "This is the love my mother wished for me." She wondered how she could get back home when she had less than seven dollars.

And she wondered if the library's board of directors would give her back her job.

After several long minutes she and her companions left the crowds and walked in grass, under dripping trees. Darkness had closed around them, and for the first time, she felt a sudden panic at having done this thing, having come away from the crowds because a very young girl had an innocent, appealing face and had aroused her sympathy.

Where were they really taking her? What kind of fool was she?

She stopped so suddenly that he bumped into her. He muttered something, and the girl stopped too, turning to look at them.

"It's just a little farther," he said. "See the light over there."

Tara squinted through the rain and saw a tiny fire that was protected by a roof not much larger than the fire itself, and around the fire crouched four figures. Though it was hard to tell, at least three of them were men. The other a girl? At least one was beardless.

Slowly she moved on.

The roof over the fire was a rusty piece of sheet iron balanced by four sticks stuck into the ground. Eldon, or Fox, ducked down and pulled Tara with him into the group that surrounded the fire. Every pink-tinged face that stared at her looked cold and miserable beneath its surface heat. No one smiled.

"Hey," Fox said, "meet Flowerchild."

They kept staring at her, then one of the guys, whose face was nearly covered with hair, turned small fire-reflecting eyes on Fox.

"Is that all you two brought?" he demanded in sharp, staccato words, an accent somewhere from the far North.

"Yeah."

"For Christ's sake, man, we can't eat her. We ain't cannibals."

"Sherwood," Fox said in a voice patiently imploring, "I couldn't get anything."

The pregnant girl had laboriously lowered herself to a sitting position on the ground, her legs bent beneath her belly like a frog's. As she pulled up a blanket from near the fire and wrapped it around her, she said, "She bought us a doughnut. A real doughnut."

The other girl spoke up, groaning. "Oh God! Do you have to say things like that? I'm so hungry I feel like somebody's got his foot on my stomach."

The man called Sherwood demanded of Tara, "You bought doughnuts? What with?"

"Uh—money," she said.

"Money! How much you got?"

"I have about six dollars, and some change."

Sherwood reached out his hand. "Christomighty, that'll feed us a couple of days. Give it here."

Tara saw the waiting faces, and knew that if she didn't willingly hand it over they'd probably take it anyway. Immediately she considered the selfishness of the thought. They did need food. Especially the pregnant girl.

"It's all I've got," she said, opening her bag.

"That's all right," Sherwood said. "You can eat with us." The moment he had the bills in his hand he leaped up. Tara saw that his feet were bare.

"Come on, Giles, Fox, Leon."

"Hell, Sherwood," Fox answered, holding his hands to the fire. "I just got in."

Tara watched him, wondering how she could ever have thought he resembled Abraham Lincoln. Just because he was tall and stooped, had a full beard and sunken cheeks? Well, the whine in his voice totally ruined the image.

Sherwood paused, his face in shadows, but his eyes as bright as a cat's eyes. "Come on," he said in a voice swift, hard and commanding.

Tara saw by the way Eldon moved then that he was used to taking orders from Sherwood. She sat still, watching them disappear into the darkness beyond the fire. The name "Eldon" seemed appropriate, and incongruously, so did "Fox." To her they suggested a weak but sneaky cunning. Like a shadow he was gone, a part of the darkness and the rain, trailing in the paths of the leading shadows.

Tara moved closer to the small fire, feeling stupid and naive. She had given her last penny. She didn't even have money to call home for help. Ah, but wouldn't Albert gloat if she had to call him collect, with a dime borrowed from a policeman! She knew he'd take her back, though— knew it the way an escaped convict knows that prison will take him back. And if someone had pointed out to her then that going back to Albert, feeling as she did, was unlikely to make either of them happy, she would have answered scornfully, "Oh, *Albert* will be happy, all right."

The pregnant girl said, "That was so sweet of you, Flowerchild."

"My name is Tara."

"Oh that's a pretty name. I'm Amy, and this is Leda. You don't have to be afraid of the guys, you know. They're okay. Sherwood is our leader. He takes care of us, and always will."

Tara looked from one face to the other. The girl called Leda looked dark and hostile; at least there was little friendliness in her face. She was staring morosely into the fire.

Amy's fine voice competed with the rain on the roof over the fire. She said simply, "I'm sort of knocked up."

Tara's mouth fell open in astonishment. A person would have to be totally blind to not see that, but the expression the girl used was too much, especially considering the tenderness behind the words. Tara blurted out, "You mean you're going to have a baby."

"Yes. A baby."

The other girl made some kind of sound and said to herself, *"Dumb."* A word carrying extreme contempt.

Tara didn't know which one of them she meant, but since Amy ignored it so did she. Tara looked around, and then spoke only to Amy. "But shouldn't you be somewhere? Shouldn't you have help?" She hesitated, wondering how people manage without money. "A hospital or clinic or something?"

Amy was smiling. "Oh no, Tara, this is the natural way, don't you see? This is the way our ancestors did it."

Tara closed her mouth and stared at the girl. Sunken eyes, dark circles. The girl moved, tried to stand up, and put one hand to her back. Tara rose swiftly to help her. The smile on Amy's face was pierced for a moment by a grimace of pain.

"Oh not *now*," Tara whispered frantically to herself.

Amy heard and smiled up at her. Taking a hand, she used the strength of the stronger, taller Tara to get to her feet.

"Don't worry," she said, "I'm only seven months. By the time the baby comes it will be spring again, and the rains will be gone. Don't you think spring is a lovely time to be born? He will be a boy. A strong, healthy boy. He will be our new leader, you know. For the whole world. Another Jesus. The world needs a living Jesus, don't you agree?"

Tara answered softly, deciding that her own convictions weren't needed at the moment. "That would be nice."

Amy pulled away. "The worst thing now is that water runs right through me, like it does this blanket. I keep having to go to the bathroom."

Tara looked around. "Bathroom?"

Amy laughed. "Well!"

Tara stood near the fire and watched the front-heavy girl waddle away, and looked in horror at the grossly swollen ankles which she hadn't noticed in the darkness of the walk through the park or among the crowds on the street. She had done a little volunteer nursing work, and knew that the girl should have help. She suddenly wished she had spent her savings on going to nursing school instead of seeing the country and trying to find herself, lost as she had been, but it was too late to worry about that.

Behind her, still seated by the fire, the other girl said, "*Dumb*," in the same scornful tone.

Tara looked over her shoulder and wondered silently if the girl was mentally challenged or something, but when the bright, fire-lit eyes raised and met hers, she saw that was not the case.

"Why do you keep saying that?" Tara asked.

The girl shrugged. "Why not? You think of a better word, you let me know, huh?"

Tara decided to ignore her. She watched the darkness for Amy. After a time the girl came slowly into view. Tara went to meet her and helped as best she could, though she had never felt more helpless. Finally Amy was down again, sitting like a Buddha.

Curiosity ate at Tara's thoughts. "Is this the best you have?" She motioned toward the tree above, which was far from waterproof. "I mean —don't you have folks?"

Amy merely smiled at her. But Tara saw beneath the smile something else which she couldn't identify. Sadness? Fear? Was Amy only pretending courage? Her face in the firelight looked even more thin and hollow, and in some ways she looked mature. Yet Tara suspected that she was less than eighteen years old. Very young. Perhaps very, very young.

Tara said, "When your husband gets back—"

Laughter interrupted her. The other girl, Leda, snorted scornfully. "Husband. Are you ever a kook. Where'd you come from? Flowerchild, my ass. Dumb!"

Tara glared at her, and quickly decided that she didn't like her one bit. "Will you shut up?"

Leda snorted again, but said no more. Tara turned her attention back to the pregnant girl.

Amy no longer pretended to smile. Gently she said to Tara, "Marriage is simply a formality. It's really not necessary."

"Oh yeah?" Tara answered, and to herself, my God, sixteen, seventeen years old, no folks, no husband, not even a roof. Thinking she's going to have another Jesus. Ankles swollen three times a normal size. My God. "You really should see a doctor."

"But this is the natural way," Amy said.

"It's the primitive way," Tara replied, trying not to sound as furious as she suddenly felt. "Your—the father of your child should—"

The interrupting snort came again from Leda. "Now I know where you came from. A haystack."

Tara stared at Amy, and Amy stared back, her eyes wide, and once again she said, "Don't you see this is the natural way?"

Tara hadn't felt she was that Victorian, yet she couldn't help the rise of revulsion in her throat. Not for the girl; for the girl she felt only a desperate kind of pity. In disgust she thought of the adult men, gone for food, influencing the mind of the too-young girl. Tara felt like getting up and walking away. If this was a sample of the new freedom, the new life, she didn't want anything to do with it. It was clearly only a shirking of responsibility. And somebody had to be responsible for the girl.

She knew she couldn't leave the girl tonight, and perhaps not at all before her baby lay safely in her arms. If she did leave, who would take care of Amy?

The men returned, looking like some kind of half-drowned animals, and by the fire dumped out packages of vegetables and meat.

"Her," Leda said, pointing a long, sharp fingernail. "Let her do the cooking for a change."

Sherwood switched open a knife that looked like a dagger and flipped it at Tara. When she gasped and pulled back, watching it quiver in the ground at her feet where the blade pierced through the trodden grass, he laughed, and was joined by so many others that Tara wondered if they were all mad. Fox draped his arm over her shoulders.

"You don't have to jump when Sherwood throws his knife, kid. It goes right where he wants it."

Tara glanced up to see that even Amy was smiling.

"Well," she said, "I guess peeling spuds would be better than sitting here doing nothing." She reached for the knife and pulled it out of the ground. Mud clung to its bright silver blade. Looking for a dishcloth and soap would be dumb indeed, that was obvious, so she held the knife under the rain until the blade was rinsed clean.

Someone dragged a blackened pot out of the shadows, and the stew was on its first legs. With the long-handled knife Tara trimmed the ends from the vegetables because the hairy leader of the group gave her fierce orders to not get knife happy and peel anything.

"Them's the vitamins," he said. "That's the—"

"I know," she answered, glad to do the interrupting herself for a change. "That's the natural way. Dirt and all."

"Ain't nothin wrong with the earth's dirt."

"Soil," Tara muttered. "For once you're partly right." Fox brought a rusted bucket of water from somewhere and dumped it into the pot. Tara tossed in the vegetables. They all sat back watching her, and she glanced round at them once and wondered who had fed them before she came along. Amy, she'd bet. Surely not Leda. She didn't seem the type, regardless of what she had said. Amy was the only one whom Tara could look at without cringing in revulsion. Even Eldon, Fox, who for a while back in the doughnut shop had seemed almost a friend in this world of no friends, had taken on the aspects of a total stranger. So thereafter she carefully attended to cooking the stew.

Dark, shadowed hands fed sticks to the fire, and Tara held the long-handled spoon dripping over the pot, waiting. No one spoke. Only the rain pouring steadily from the black sky above had any voice.

Finally, the leader asked, "Ain't it ready?" and at the same time snatched the spoon from her hand.

She had wondered how they would eat, and she watched in amazement as he scooped up a spoonful and smacked it down. Twice, three times. Then he handed the spoon to Giles. And by that method the spoon made its way around the silent circle and back to her.

Tara held the spoon for a moment, hating the thought of eating after all of them, or anyone, for that matter, but finally gave in. It was that or nothing. She scooped out a hot potato and held it with her wet, bunched shawl, and gave it her whole attention, letting Sherwood snatch the spoon without resistance. When the potato was cool enough to handle she peeled and ate it.

Three of the men and the one girl had gone to bed together, under a single cover, at one side of the fire. Amy too had lain down, alone, curled around the bulk of her baby. Tara turned her back to the four and tried not to hear their noises. She felt so revolted that when Fox attempted to pull her into his arms she shoved him away roughly, and would have slapped him bald if he hadn't caught her hands and held them.

Though she stretched back, he leaned close enough for her to catch his angry whisper.

"I told you I'd protect you, and I will, but you got to make the guys think you're my girl."

He was close to her side, warm, helping keep away the rain. She wondered just where he usually slept, and with whom, before she came along. Her whisper hissed as loudly as the occasional drops of rain that ran under the roof and into the fire. "If I have to be protected from anyone, I'll leave!"

"Hey," he said teasingly, "I was only trying to trick you into a kiss. Don't go. Okay? I promise to leave you alone, hands off, until you're ready."

She jerked her hands out of his. "As they say in Nebraska—don't hold your breath."

"Don't you like me at all?"

"I don't even know you, man, I just met you!"

"Oh. You're one of them that needs time." His shoulders twisted into a shrug of sorts. "*Old-fashioned* Flowerchild."

"My name is Tara, and I'm sleepy, so if you don't mind ..."

"Here. Feel free to use my lap for your pillow."

She faced him for a moment in the flickering firelight, her nose very close to his. "Which one do you belong with?" she asked, keeping her voice down so that no one else could hear. "Amy? Or do you usually join the gang?" The contempt was undisguised in her voice. From him came nothing but silence. After a moment she turned her face away.

And deliberately yawned.

He answered slowly, actually sounding serious for a change. "I know we're new to you. You've got mid-western morals, right?"

"Let's just say I do have morals."

"But hadn't you thought they might be wrong?"

"No, I hadn't."

"Don't you know a family marriage, one for all, all for one, in the natural way?"

"Natural! I'm sick of that word. I'm getting out of here."

She started to rise but he pulled her back.

"Tara, you need me. I'll take care of you. I promise. Stay. I fell in love with you the minute I saw you, and I've seen you several times whether you know it or not, and I'll wait. No force from me, ever. Just give us a chance. Stay. If you want to sleep by yourself, that's your privilege. Only, don't go."

The darkness, more than his pleading, stopped her. And Amy's eyes, turned upon her now in silent, animal begging. The security that had filmed her voice and words didn't show in her eyes.

Tara sighed, drew closer to the fire, and put her head and arms on her bent knees. Fox lay down near her, and was quiet. The rain beat on the tin roof, and the men and Leda on the other side of the fire finally were still and slept.

THE RAINS CONTINUED, and on the second day the stew ran out. The black pot sat in the rain, catching water in its unwashed bottom. The four men sat to one side and mumbled among themselves.

Tara tried to talk Amy into going to the county hospital. When that didn't work she tried another tactic, while the men were still in their low-voiced conference and Leda was curled into an afternoon nap.

"Would you go home with me, Amy? All I have to do is get to a police station to get a dime for a telephone, or have them call this fellow who wanted to marry me. He'd send money for us."

But Amy kept shaking her head. "Can't you understand what we're doing, Tara? We're starting a new world, really we are."

Tara drew a deep sigh. "Well then, good luck to you, Amy. I guess I'll go back to the old one. I've decided I rather like it." She hated to leave the girl, and she didn't want to marry Albert, but she couldn't stand the others and had to get away. She could alert the officials, she thought, and ask if a county nurse would check on Amy.

Then, to her surprise, Amy reached out a thin hand and grasped her shawl, nearly dragging it off of her.

"No," she whispered, her eyes large with desperation. "Don't leave me yet."

Tara didn't move. "Amy, this isn't for me. What are you afraid of?"

Tears filled the girl's eyes, but all she said was, "Please, Tara. Don't go yet."

So once again Tara discarded thoughts of calling on Albert Smith for money to come home. She decided to stay with Amy until the baby was born, or until she could talk her into seeking help, and by that time she might figure out exactly what she really wanted for herself.

She looked around and saw that the four men were gone. After food? She wondered how they managed without money or jobs. Rob some farmer's truck garden? Whatever they did in their absences, it was a relief to have them gone. She noticed then that Leda had gone also.

Sometime in the night a low-pitched voice woke her. She lay still, curled with her back to a dead fire, her damp shawl over her, and listened.

"Well, whatever the hell we do," was the answer to the first voice, "we got to get out of here." It was Sherwood's voice, and it held a note of something like alarm. Instinct warned Tara to be very quiet and pretend sleep. "But where the hell? *Where?*"

Giles answered, his irritatingly slow voice indicating a slow mind. "There's this house I know," he said.

"You know a house?" Sherwood interrupted, his rapid Northern accent even more pronounced with sarcasm. "I know a million houses. So what?"

Giles' slow words continued, answering with the patience of an old work horse. "This house I know, it's empty, but—"

"Well, why didn't you say so? Let's go. Where is it?"

"Oh, it's way back across the country, right next to Black Swamp. My aunt owns it. I remember her telling me about it when I was a kid and once she took me with her to see it—"

"Black Swamp? Where the devil is that, Giles?"

"I don't know which state it's in, but it's close to the Mississippi River, pretty much south, and the name of the town is Greenhill."

Sherwood groaned. "Two thousand damned miles. Holy hell, it might as well be in ... wait a minute! That may be the perfect place. You say it's empty?"

"Yeah. My aunt, see, she married this guy with a lot of money and when he died she found out she'd inherited this property. She went down to this little town and looked it over and decided to sell it. But nobody'd ever buy it, so it's still there, I guess."

"Do you think you could find it?"

"Yeah. She told me all about it, and I went down with her. Quite a ways out of town, I remember. There's this dumb little road that goes straight into a swamp and stops. And right there at the edge of the swamp is this old house. Practically a hotel it is, it's so big. Her property includes about a thousand acres, but most of it is swamp."

Sherwood kept mumbling. "Perfect. Perfect. Purr-fect!"

"But—" said Giles, and hushed.

"But what? Let's go. We can get there. No trouble now."

"But the house is haunted, Sherwood. Really haunted. Badly haunted. It's creepy."

There was a moment of silence, then both Fox and Sherwood laughed. "Great!" Sherwood said. "Are the local cornballs afraid of it?"

"I guess so."

"Perfect! Oh, man, that's really perfect!"

Giles didn't answer, and a moment later Sherwood said, chidingly, "Hey, you ain't afraid of a little ole ghost, are you, Giles? Anyway, you believe that crap?"

"Well ... that's why it never sold, anyway, my aunt said."

"Good. We're really in luck. Let's go get us some wheels. I know a guy. No trouble."

Their footsteps faded into the night.

After a while Tara got up and sat down against the tree, leaning back. The man called Leon had not been with them. She wondered what had happened to him. Leda had remained behind this time, and slept, alone, as if she were exhausted.

It wasn't long before Sherwood, Giles and Fox returned, three long shadows emerging from the pouring rain on the other side of the tree. With his toe Sherwood nudged sleeping Amy. She came up quietly and quickly, like an alerted animal, Tara thought.

"Get a move on," Sherwood said. "We're pulling out. We're shaking this crappy place." He looked at Tara. "You got to come too."

It was not an invitation, it was an order.

Tara frowned. "Where's the other one? Leon?" She didn't move. She didn't like orders in that tone of voice, as if she had no choice. Besides, she knew something must have happened.

"Just don't ask no questions. That's a rule around here. Just don't ask me no crappy questions."

Tara got up and stood still, watching them gather their possessions. A black coffee pot that was gray granite underneath the soot. The soup pot. The spoon. An armload of damp blankets. She watched the men move swiftly away, with Leda following. And she watched Amy move clumsily, pause and look back at her.

Sherwood glanced back at Tara, then slowed and spoke a short command over his shoulder at Fox. He paused, looked back, and waited.

"Come on, Flowerchild, hurry it up."

Amy said, "Please, Tara."

Tara could feel the urgency, and was puzzled by it, but she hesitated for only a moment longer, then got her valise, ducked her head against the rain and followed.

CHAPTER 2

The sign under the heavily leafed magnolia tree read *Yates Realty*. Sunlight rarely touched it, yet it had faded so much that it was hardly legible. The younger half of the Yates partnership looked at the sign from behind the office window and said, "We ought to have that painted so people can read it."

The other half, seated comfortably at his desk in the rear of the front office, answered, "They know what it says."

The secretary, juggling papers at a center desk, giggled. "As long as this is the only real estate agency in town there's nothing to worry about." Her voice was fine; a liquid, Southern one that seemed incongruous with her large-boned square face.

Mr. Yates said, "That's the way I figure."

But the young one remained at the window, looking gloomily at the sign, his hands limp in his pockets, a lethargy unsuited to the cool, early spring season, or a niggling worry dragging at his mind. It was one of those days when he didn't want to do paper work. He didn't even want to show a customer around. Of course there was no point in worrying about that because there was no customer to show around anyway. There never were a lot of customers, prospective buyers, at this end of the county. Just enough to make a comfortable living for each of the three people who worked in Yates Realty office.

He thought he himself might sometime take a crack at repainting that sign.

The secretary waved a piece of paper at him. "Do you know the rent is overdue on that Bishop place?"

Scott Yates turned from the window and looked at her. The lethargy was still in his mind. He had almost forgotten about renting the old Bishop place. "Overdue?"

"Yes," she said. "Ten days."

Ten days overdue. When there was rent to collect for an estate he collected it on time. "I forgot all about it," he said. "Maybe because I've never rented it before."

His father said, "Lucky to get one month's rent on that place. I'd forget it if I were you. The man probably just pulled out. I didn't figure he'd rent it another month anyway."

But that didn't satisfy Scott. "I wonder why he hasn't been in. If he left, what did he do with the keys?"

"Probably left them there," his father said. "The only time I ever rented it, about twelve years ago, the family left the key on the doorstep in plain sight."

Anna Lou said, "I guess they were in such a hurry to get away they just dropped it." Her voice was amused, followed by her original little giggle.

Aldon Yates chuckled in a lazy, slightly overweight way. "Well, I told them at the start that the place was reportedly haunted. I always told everyone I showed it to that it was haunted. In most cases that was enough. They didn't want it."

Yeah, that was his dad. Kill a sale, or a fee, with a lot of unnecessary information. Why tell interested parties a bunch of local superstitions that had their origins somewhere back in slave days? Something that had about as much reality and actual connection with slavery as somebody's imagination, probably.

"No wonder you never sold it," he said.

"It's not easy to sell a place like that with a history like that. When your grandpa still had the office, when I was a boy, four people died in that house. All but one in the family. I have to tell people it's not a healthy place to be."

"Smallpox, wasn't it?" Scott reminded him. He'd heard the old story so much that it no longer had any effect on his thoughts.

"Well, sho. Or something contagious. I don't know. I hardly remember it. But after that people got sick there. So if you want to unload it, it's just plain good business, I say, to pass on the superstitions rather than the facts. Tell them it's haunted, don't tell them it's poisoned. Somebody might buy a haunted house for the devil of it, but nobody is going to buy a poisoned one."

"I doubt if it's still contagious."

"Maybe not. But that's the reason I won't fool with it anymore. The land's not worth much. The swamp has taken most of it now. If the house rots down that's the business of the Bishops. I rented it once, I never rented it again. Almost sold it a few times, but saw no point in trying to rent it."

"It's too big for most renters anyway," Anna Lou said. "And the selling price the Bishops want is high for this area."

Anna Lou had been to the big city for a few months, and she liked to keep people reminded of it, but Scott only half listened to her, or to his dad. He was thinking of the man who had come into the office that day in February and asked to rent a house in an out-of-the-way location. He was an artist, he said, and was trying to get the unusual view of America, the out of way, the lonely. The natural. He didn't care if he didn't see a soul for months, he said. And after showing him several places he didn't like, Scott had finally taken him out the old dead-end road to the Black Swamp and the long-deserted Bishop house. It suited the man. He'd rented it without going through its uncounted rooms. He would live in the big kitchen, he said. It was all the room he needed. He'd paid the price, in cash, one month's rent in advance. And Scott hadn't told him all that silly stuff about it being haunted. Or poisoned. He hadn't seen the man since.

"What was his name?"

Anna Lou asked, "Whose name?"

"The man who rented the Bishop house."

Anna Lou crinkled papers a moment. "Uh—Fred Stowe."

"Yeah."

He should have remembered. People, names, places, were his business, but sometimes the names inch-wormed away. The person, the appearance, he remembered well. A man of medium height, quite thin, his clothes expensive but old, as if his fortune had come and gone. A man who would never stand out in a crowd. The only thing he had told Scott about his life, other than his profession, was that he had no family to speak of. He would be living alone in the house.

Could the man possibly have gotten sick?

"I'll be back," he said, and went out before they could ask where he was going.

He got his car from the tree-shaded empty lot beside the real estate office and drove down Main Street and out of town on Highway 32. The road curved gently through lush pastures where cattle grazed. It was good farmland, and sold for good prices. He had grown up keeping an eye out for land that might be turned over for profit. His dad's influence.

About three miles out of town a dim wooden sign on the left read *Black Swamp*. And beneath it someone had painted in crooked letters *dead-end road*.

It wasn't much of a road. A lot of tall weeds grew on each side and in the middle, the reaching, pale green of spring among the remaining brown of winter. All the land in the area was increasingly swampy, with the groves more and more numerous, becoming the forest of Black Swamp, on the left. To the right was more grazing land, but even that had spots of swamp settling between the high places. As his dad had said, the Bishop land was all turning to swamp.

The road curled for four miles and the last two of those miles were closed in on both sides by tall, dark trees whose trunks were nearly covered by vines. As his car moved slowly and quietly along the grassy road beside the swamp the message was passed from one frog chorus to another so that their voices were silent by the time he reached them. Behind him they struck up again, uncountable voices singing each in its own pitch and making of it a kind of music that was both eerily strange and hypnotically beautiful.

The house sat just off the road to the right, its boxlike hip roof reaching gray-green above the highest treetops, yet its ground floor sunk so low and so dark that the house was hardly noticeable until suddenly it was there, a monster in the forest, just out of reach of the plant-camouflaged water of Black Swamp. The road ended abruptly a few yards farther on, at the edge of the black water. Lost tourists, and kids out seeking thrills, had created a turn-around spot that encroached onto the narrow front yard of the Bishop house.

Scott pulled in and parked there, listening and looking.

For a while silence seemed a total thing, and then the frogs began to sing, voices high and voices low, uneven, uncoordinated, unwittingly creating their beauty.

The house, a large, squarish structure with no interesting features at all on the front, not even a porch, was so covered with vines that its sparse, narrow windows looked like hidden creatures' eyes peeping out. Every time Scott saw it he wondered why anyone would build a house in such an unholy location. The old rumor was that it had something to do with the runaway slaves that sought the dangerous refuge of Black Swamp. The first Bishop had turned them in for money. Scott didn't know. He hadn't paid much attention to its history. On the few times he had attempted to sell it he'd tried to find only the good points, which were the farm buildings, on higher ground back behind the house, that, like the house, were constructed of heavy, strong oak, and were nearly indestructible because they were far enough away from the swamp, and hadn't been eaten by creeping decay, like the house had been.

And of course there were also the several hundred acres of land that could be drained and made into good grazing land.

There was no sign of his renter. He pressed the horn, and waited. But the only result was that the frogs grew instantly quiet.

After a while he got out and walked gingerly through the vining groundcover around the house toward the garage. He always half suspected that the vines were something poison even though they had five leaves instead of the three leaves of poison ivy. They still had an evil, hiding look that he didn't care for. Evil and hiding like the windows of the house, peeping out from the growth of vines that covered nearly everything in its reach.

The renter's car was there in the twilight of the garage, visible beyond one garage door that was standing open, leaning, the top hinge broken.

Scott turned toward the back door of the house. The only difference between the front of the house and the rear was a tiny roof jutting over the back steps like a dirty, overgrown toenail. He knocked and called, but only the frogs answered, in their reverse way. Scott opened the door and pushed it back.

The interior was like the interior of any house that was over a hundred years old, seldom cleaned and aired, decaying and falling apart. Flatly, it stank like hell. He stood on the threshold of the long dark hall, then went along rough board floors to the door of the big kitchen where the renter said he'd be living. He squinted in. The huge, walk-in fireplace had a cricket sawing away, but otherwise there were no sounds of any kind.

"Anybody home?" he called, his voice bouncing and echoing hollowly against the dark beams of the ceiling and the smoked cave of the fireplace.

The stench was awful. He didn't see how anyone could stand to live with it. Either a draft of it was moving through the house and into the narrow rear hall where he stood, or it was something in the kitchen. Rotted food? Dead mice or rats?

Like the frogs outdoors, the crickets had gone quiet, and the silence was so intense that it seemed nearly physical. His footsteps, when he walked into the kitchen, thundered hollowly like the steps of a giant. He began to walk softly.

The kitchen was at least forty feet long, and nearly as wide, but whoever had built the house hadn't believed in windows. Two narrow slits, old-fashioned unwashed panes, kept the room somewhere between total darkness and a kind of watchful twilight. There was a coldness, too, that did not fit the warmth of the spring season.

Along the right wall old-fashioned flat-faced cupboards ran the length of the room, broken only by two closed doors. The cupboards had once been varnished, perhaps, but it was hard to tell. They had turned into the same dark, stained wood that filled the entire kitchen, ceiling and all.

In the center of the room sat a long table that looked as if it had risen from the rough oak floor. Long benches had been nailed to the floor on each side. The remains of a meal were on a plate on the table, and Scott stood frowning at it, for the half-eaten food was covered with green mold.

A wariness like the chill in the room crept over him and he stood without moving, his attention going from one end of the room to the other. In one corner, on the floor, were quilts and a pillow. He half expected to see the renter there, ill, but the bed had been neatly made. It looked flat, hard and uncomfortable.

At the other end of the room, somewhere among the loose stones of the huge fireplace, the cricket began a tentative sawing again. Scott's attention went there, and in the midst of old ashes he found a small metal support on which sat a blackened coffee pot. Everything was cold and dead. A fire had not been laid there for some time. The food on the table could be weeks old.

The car was still in the garage.

Scott turned back to the hallway, and the stench grew stronger. So it was not in the kitchen after all. The swamp invading, he told himself uneasily. The renter couldn't stand it so he had simply moved out onto higher ground, perhaps into one of the barns. That was the solution he was hoping for, yet when he reached the hall he turned on impulse to the left, away from the open door that led to the fresher air of outdoors.

The rear entrance hall was long and narrow and finally widened into a tiny room where, on the right, narrow service stairs reached up to second and third stories. He ignored doors closing off other halls, and small useless rooms, and continued on toward the steep stairway. Dark, dank, cold.

The stairs reached up, one almost on top of the other, to a second-floor landing similar to the one below, but darker. Doors opened off of main halls and old closets, and to the right another long, steep stairway went on to the third story.

Something lay sprawled, broken, on the bottom step of the stairs, the smell of rotting flesh coming up from it in waves that nauseated the stomach and sickened the brain.

Scott stopped, stared, seeing amidst the clothing a white face staring back at him, its mouth open as if it were emitting a soundless and perpetual scream, and in and out of that mouth crawled a forest of big black ants.

Now he knew what the sickening, stomach-crushing stink was.

He bent first to touch it, the man, the renter, the—he couldn't remember the name again—and then he drew sharply back, afraid that the flesh would come away in his hand. Dead? My God, yes, the man was dead. Stupid to try to feel the pulse, stupid.

Dragging his handkerchief from his pocket, he pressed it over his mouth and nose and began to walk backwards, his eyes pinned in horror to the man.

About ten feet away he forced himself to stop and view it objectively. The way the body lay twisted, he could have fallen down the stairs, breaking his neck in the fall. And the scream could have been from the fear of the fall.

Yet something had caused the man to leave his half-eaten lunch, or dinner, or breakfast, and go up the long, steep stairs to the third floor.

The cold moved through the hairs on the back of Scott's neck, and he turned and walked swiftly down the stairs, along the hall and out onto the spongy, vine-covered ground. He didn't pause to shut the door. The moment his feet touched the ground he began to run toward his car.

When his feet tangled in the vines, causing him to stumble, he stopped and steadied himself against a tree, his hand sinking in to the vines there. He was not even aware of them. Deep breaths settled his stomach. He tore away from the vines and ran on to his car, then drove as fast as he dared down the road, to the highway, where the bright sun was still shining, and returned to town.

• • •

THE CORONER and an ambulance were sent after the body. The police took the man's car and all his belongings.

When the sun went down a small knot of people gathered on the street in front of the Main Street Cafe.

"I allowed as how that would happen," said an old-timer who wore faded blue overalls on his skinny frame, his serious eyes peering out from beneath the brim of an old hat "Nobody ever lived in that house but died."

Scott, coming out of the cafe, heard him and stopped. He had to end talk like that if he intended to get the house sold, and he did plan to. "The man simply fell down the stairs, Jake. The police said the stairs had broken through. It was an accident."

"Don't matter," said Jake, his tone pessimistically unchanged. "He died."

"Dad rented that house out a few years ago and nobody died then."

But Jake was ready for that one too. He'd lived there longer than either Scott or Scott's father had.

"How do you know? If I recollect it proper they flat disappeared. Left the keys on the door stoop. What happened to 'em? I say the house got 'em. Or Black Swamp. Probably they run into the swamp just like them slaves did."

"They were migrant workers," Scott said, wishing he hadn't stopped to argue. "They were fruit pickers and harvesters on their way west, and Dad gave them a month's free rent for cleaning up the place."

"Did they clean it up?" another man asked.

"Well," Scott admitted, "not much. I guess it was too big a job. A lot of vines out there, and that's a big house. It must have twenty or thirty rooms. I've never even looked it over."

"Died," Jake said with flat obstinacy.

Scott walked away. He had a date that night and wanted to forget the house, the dead man, and the smell. Especially that godawful smell.

THE FOLLOWING morning he went to the office to tell his dad and Anna Lou that he wouldn't be in. And then he went to the Main Street Cafe, ordered a glass of beer and took it to the corner booth and stared into its foamy depths.

The man had been dead for two weeks or more. A simple accident, the police had told him.

Scott began to wonder about the tragedy that had happened when his father was a boy—the contagious disease that some people had called smallpox, and some had said was the plain work of the devil.

Scott had never listened to any of the junk about the house being haunted. He didn't believe that. But he had to admit now that the odds were unreasonable.

He took one drink of the beer, warmed by the absent-minded turning and cradling of his hands, and left it and slid out of the booth. If something about the house destroyed people he wanted to know what it was. Besides, he needed to get the renter's keys. There had been no reason to have duplicates made.

THE AWFUL, sickening smell was still there, and burst out at him like gas under pressure when he opened the unlocked front door. It stank in the front rooms and hall. He pushed the door open and left it, covered his face with his handkerchief and stepped softly across the threshold and into the front hall. The floor had been stripped of its rags. They lay against one wall in a long moldy roll. A couple of tapestries still hanging on the walls had turned gray-green with mildew. Once or twice in every two or three years, irregularly, a cleaning crew was sent out. But Scott suspected that they did as little as possible and hurried out because there were very few people around who didn't believe that the house actually was haunted. Though it was known in his books as the Bishop place it was locally known as the Black Swamp Mansion.

The original furniture was still in the house, covered by grayed and rotted muslin, and in some rooms it had been pushed into heaps in corners. In most rooms the rugs had been rolled, but in the second-floor bedrooms they hadn't been touched.

Scott stood at the bottom of the back stairs on the second floor and looked again where the body of his renter had lain, as if looking there would reconstruct the scene and tell him what had really happened. The cricket in the huge stone fireplace in the kitchen was still sawing, off and on, and the sound came thinly to his ears.

He noticed suddenly that the wind must have risen because faint waves of cold and warm air passed over his arms and there was a soft sighing, as wind among the trees. Well, good, he thought, wind would freshen the air in the house. But the back door needed to be open to create a good draft. He went down the steep stairs, remembering the man who had fallen, and holding the rail in a grip tighter than he ordinarily would have held it. Under his feet the stairs groaned and cried as if they were being tortured. The sound of the wind was rising and falling, sounding like someone breathing heavily, long, slow, deep breaths. A storm, he thought. Building up for a good one, probably.

He passed the doorway to the kitchen and noticed that the cricket had grown silent. Then Scott opened the back door and stepped out onto the tiny porch, and stared about him at the trees in the yard, the treetops in the swamp, and the blue of the sky. The air was so still it almost suffocated him for a moment. Not even a whisper of a breeze stirred among the vines.

He stood undecided, puzzled, and then he turned back into the house. The sighing wind had gone entirely. The house was as still as the swamp. He wished the cricket would get with it again, for company. The loneliness in the house was appalling. He looked at the opening of the small room where the service stairs were, dim and far away down the hall, and knew he should go open some doors to the main hall so that the air could move through the house. What little air there was. But he didn't.

"The keys," he murmured to himself, then went into the kitchen.

The food was still on the table, but the police had taken the bedding, and all personal belongings of the man. They hadn't looked for the keys, they'd said. It hadn't occurred to them to lock the house. Only a simple accident. They were in a hurry to get out, though.

Scott went to the first place that came to his mind—the long high mantle over the fireplace—and ran his hand through the moldy dust that had collected there. At the far end he found them: two long, old-time keys on a round ring.

Instead of going through the house to the front door, he went out the back, locked it, and walked around the house to the front door, pulled it shut and locked it. Relieved, he stood back for a moment to look up at the house. Its evil little windows looked down on him, and from somewhere deep within came a series of creakings, like small cackles of laughter.

"God!" he said, feeling his flesh pull with a slight chill. He laughed, amused at himself for letting a mere house, a manmade thing, get to him. Still, it was an ugly thing, this house, and looked slightly off level, as if it too were settling into the swamp. And that was very likely, and would account for the snaps and cracks that sounded from the old wood.

The frogs in the swamp had worked up to a high pitch, and Scott wondered about the cricket. He raised his hand in farewell and said aloud, "You can have it, old boy." The walls inside could rot with mildew, the vines outside could smother it and bear it down into a soggy pile of timbers, companions to the living roots in Black Swamp. He would never rent it again.

He turned his car around and drove away. He not only would never rent it, he would never even show it to a customer.

The image of the man stayed in his mind. Long dead, the report had said. He must have fallen down those stairs within a week or two after moving into the house.

He went back to the cafe for a cup of coffee.

Over at the counter a man reading a paper snorted loudly, unable to keep his opinion to himself. "Hippies! Long hairs! What they ought to do is string up every danged one of them."

The waitress answered good-naturedly, "What's the matter, Tom? Somebody's hair get in your coffee?"

Tom wasn't amused. The edge of the counter made a deep dent in his fat belly as he hovered over the newspaper. "Didn't you read this? Another family murdered, out there near San Francisco. A man, his wife, and a couple of hired girls. Tore the place all to hell, robbed the man's private safe, stole they don't know how much money. Cash. No way of tracing it, they say. Dumb man keeping money around like that. Used knives, they did, blood all over."

The waitress made a face and grunted. "I guess it pays to be poor sometimes."

"People like that would cut you up just to see you squirm."

"Did the police catch the killers?"

"No."

"Then how do they know it was a hippie gang?"

"One of them was shot and killed by the man. Long dirty hair, they said. Hippie. Like I said, they ought to string them all up."

Another man, at a table next to Scott's, said, "Haven't you heard? Nobody gets strung up anymore. It's not humane. You can murder whomever you damned please, and get by with it."

The waitress said, "Maybe not. Maybe God will take care of it."

"What god is that?" the man replied in soft contempt.

"Well," said somebody else, "everything has its opposite. Even evil. If you don't believe in God anymore, you have to at least believe in goodness, which is synonymous with God."

"I," the waitress said hotly, "believe in the old-fashioned God."

"Good for you," Scott said. He liked Mary. And he liked girls who were a bit of what was now condescendingly called "Victorian." That wasn't necessarily the kind he always dated, but that was the kind he wanted to marry. The waitress was young, but plump in a motherly way, a figure that went well with aprons and visions of cradled babies. And she had beautiful eyes and one of those rare, clear complexions. He had thought a few times about settling down and asking Mary to date him, but just hadn't gotten around to it. Someday, maybe. "Stick to your convictions, Mary," he said.

"I intend to."

The man reading the paper muttered something, shook his head repeatedly, and raised his voice. "They figure there must have been a gang of them, all right, to do so much damage. How're you going to find a half dozen creeps among all them other ones?"

"Like you said," the contemptuous one answered, sounding amused, "string them all up."

"Huh!" The paper rattled angrily in his thick hands, and then was thrown aside.

"You might as well not even read stuff like that," Mary said. "You can't do anything about it anyway, and all you do is give yourself an ulcer, Tom."

"Well, hand me one of them doughnuts and I'll feed it."

Scott watched for a moment as Tom fed his ulcer, and then he remembered that he was supposed to have been at the bank fifteen minutes earlier to help on the signing of a farm sold last week. As he went out the door Mary's voice called after him.

"Seems you're always leaving your coffee or beer untouched, Scott. Don't you like our cooking around here?"

"Love it, Mary," he answered without pausing. "Love it."

And faintly behind him came the voice of the sarcastic one. "Now that's what I call a diplomatic fellow, because you're the only hangout in town, aren't you?"

"What do you mean *hangout*?" Mary retorted.

"Cafe. Restaurant. Bar."

"It's *not* a bar—"

Scott went on, grinning. Just a guy passing through, he suspected. All the big-city ones were easy to pick out because of their inability to believe that a town could be so small and still be on the map.

Actually, it was bigger than it looked. Just because the highway went straight through the middle and became Main Street, because there were only two supermarkets, one hardware store, a couple of dress shops in sight, and, of course, the Main Street Cafe, didn't mean there weren't also a couple of thousand homes and a nice little park toward the south side of town.

Scott realized that he was defending the old hometown only in the back of his mind, and it wasn't accomplishing a thing. He started his car, turned an undisturbed U in the middle of the wide street and headed for the bank. He took his time, admiring the beauty and sweet fragrance of flowering trees along the street. That was one good thing about the south—nobody objected if a guy took his time.

CHAPTER 3

Tara didn't know where they were going, but it reminded her of a string of ducks winding through the rain the way the ducks had done on her grandparents' farm in Nebraska. The rain was coming down too hard to look into it. Ahead of her she saw Amy's wet shoes moving along, cloddy things on legs ghostly white and naked. And she knew that behind her walked Eldon, because his hand occasionally touched her shoulder, as if gently pushing her on.

To her amazement they soon came to a halt beside a long, late-model sedan. It looked dark, nearly black, under a faraway streetlight. There was nothing flashy or outstanding about the car, even though it was of a more expensive make than the average car. Her astonishment growing, she watched Sherwood unlock the front door, reach in and unlock the back, and then slide across the front seat to sit under the wheel. The overhead light made him look different from the way he had in the unsteady campfire. Hardly any of his face was visible from under the cover of long tangled hair. He looked dirty and unclean. Far more so than Eldon had when she'd met him.

He tossed the keys to Leda and said, "Open the trunk so they can put the things in there. Hurry."

Leda moved quickly, and the blankets, pot and even Tara's overnight bag were tossed into the trunk. Then Leda slid in beside Sherwood and gave him back the keys. Giles sat beside Leda, and Eldon opened the back door and gave Amy a push. Amy obeyed without a word. But when he pushed Tara, her astonishment exploded in a burst.

"Hey, wait a minute! What are you doing?"

Sherwood looked over his shoulder at her. "We're getting to hell out of this wet place. We're going to live in a house. Now come on, will you?"

But Tara pushed back against Eldon's hand. "I most certainly will not! Do you think I'm some kind of mindless idiot? I'm not going anywhere in a stolen car!" Now she had an idea where Leon was. In the jug. "No wonder you were in such a darn hurry!"

Sherwood turned, laying his arm across the back of the seat in a way that added to the blazing but silent threat in his eyes. "It is not stolen. We bought it a while ago." His eyes flashed upward toward Eldon. "Get her in here!"

Eldon pushed, but Tara held to the door, refusing to be forced. "Bought it! With what, may I ask? You didn't have a dime for a cup of coffee!"

Sherwood said angrily, but in a low voice, "Sometimes I don't think you got brain one, Fox. How'd the hell'd you pick a bitch like her?" His eyes darted back to pierce Tara's. "*Get in!*"

"No!"

Amy leaned toward her, whispering, "Please, oh please, Tara!"

The fear in her voice caused Tara to hesitate. She didn't understand it, and wanted to ask Amy why it was so important to her. Tara felt it had something to do with herself, and not Amy at all. Amy wasn't that afraid of the condition of her health, or the birth of her baby. But the fear was there, white and tearful in her face. She reached a hand toward Tara.

"Please."

Leda laughed. "Dumb!"

And then Sherwood drew a long sigh, and as if explaining to someone who actually was very stupid, if not completely retarded, he said, "Look, Flowerchild, Giles here, he's got this rich aunt. Well, she telegraphed us some money. She said we'd need some to get started on, see. She said we could live on her farm and grow them organic foods and stuff, you know, and get healthy." He laughed and glanced sideways at Giles. "Now ain't that right, old man?"

"Yeah, yeah," Giles said, looking around at Tara. "Plenty of money to keep us. She doesn't have anything else to do with her money because she's childless."

Eldon's hand had slowly tightened on her arm. He pulled her aside into the shadows and turned her face up into the rain, his fingers forcing her chin upward, and slowly his mouth came down to move over hers. She stiffened.

"Please," he said. "I want you to go. Amy needs you. I need you. It will be all right. Tara, I can't leave you here." And then, "You've got to. No choice. Keep quiet and mind what I say—you got to."

It was more than the words, more than the warning that hung heavily behind the words. It was Amy needing her, and an undercurrent in his voice that made her uncomfortable. She believed that it would be very unwise to refuse. "Trust me," he said. "It's much better this way."

Sherwood's voice called impatiently, "Hey! You can make love in the back seat. Come on, will you?"

Tara drew sharply away from Eldon. The suggestion in Sherwood's voice had sounded downright dirty, and she didn't like it. Eldon's hand continued to firmly hold her arm, and she let him push her into the car. Before the door closed, Sherwood had started the car and was pulling out onto the street.

The night flew by in swift glances of lights from all-night places along the road, and then there were longer and longer stretches of no light at all except the car's own yellow beams on the glistening pavement ahead. Tara had to admit that Sherwood could handle a car, as if at some time in his past he had been a chauffeur or a truck driver, or perhaps both. When Giles and Leda began to make love Sherwood ignored them, as if his pleasure was satiated by the smooth handling of the car over mountain curves. He sang along softly with the music on the radio. Jazz. Hard rock. Naturally. What else.

Tara turned her face away from the tops of the heads of Leda and Giles and leaned back against the seat, looking across at Amy, who seemed to be sleeping soundly. She felt Eldon's hand begin to caress her arm, and she pretended to be asleep, hoping he would stop with her arm, because if he didn't there would be a bloody battle in the back seat.

He did. She heard him sigh deeply in disappointment as he slid down to rest on his curved back. Within minutes he had gone to sleep, and so had Leda and Giles, her head on his shoulder. And after a time Tara too slept.

Sherwood's voice woke her. He was still driving, facing the glow of a rising sun, and obviously answering a question Tara hadn't heard.

"Soon as I find one, goddamnit, or do you want to sit on a cactus?"

There was no answer, and Tara glanced at Amy, who had turned and was looking out the window in a way that was pathetic and lost. Tara placed her hand over Amy's and squeezed, and Amy turned a quick and grateful smile toward her. The shadow of tears glistened in her eyes. In the front seat Giles stretched his arms high and groaned, and Leda sat up and looked around. Sherwood had gone back to humming along with the hard rock that still poured from the radio, clashing against a blue sky and the rising sun. Only Fox continued to sleep, slumped over against his window. He snored softly.

"You need a bathroom?" Tara whispered, her eyes demanding an answer, and when Amy gave a short nod, Tara told her, "I'll get you one." Then she leaned forward to look closely at the hair on the side of Sherwood's face. "Don't you have any feeling for anybody but yourself, Mr. Fuzzbox?"

His face flew around to glare at her. "You talkin' to me?"

"Yes, I am. I saw that truck stop, with those restrooms. Why didn't you stop?"

"And why the hell don't you shut up and stop buggin' me! I tell you, gal, I'm going to fix you up good one of these days."

"Well, first you stop and let Amy go to the bathroom, or we'll get out and hitchhike, and, buster, I mean it. You stop at the first place you see, and that sign says there's a place eight miles down the road—"

His arm came up in front of her face, stiff, pointing at Fox, and his voice, interrupting, shook with anger. "Fox, you keep that bitch of yours out of my hair or I'll—"

"Ha!" Tara said. "That would be a job for the Civil Defense, considering how much you've got."

"—or I'll—or I'll—so help me I'll cut her goddamned throat. What the hell you wanted with a redheaded freckle-faced bitch like her I don't know anyhow. I told you. I warned you, with hair like hers and eyes that unholy cat-green, it's hidin' more than you'll ever be able to handle!"

"I don't hide anything," Tara told him hotly, "and I'd rather have freckles than that stuff you've got."

The car began to swerve as Sherwood turned toward her, prepared to give her a backhanded slap. She stayed where she was, too close for him to get much done without first stopping the car. She knew he could beat the devil out of her if he really tried, but she wasn't about to back down. At least he would get an earful as long as she could talk.

"Don't you dare hit me, Fuzzbox!"

Eldon's arms grabbed her and pulled her back out of Sherwood's reach, and Sherwood was forced to give his attention to the car and the traffic. He breathed heavily with the anger he was trying to repress.

"You keep that cat-eyed witch away from me," he muttered through small, unwashed teeth. "I don't care if she is stacked. I'll unstack her so fast you won't know what she is."

Tara opened her mouth, but Eldon's hand clamped over it so fast and so hard that she could hardly breathe, and then his other hand grabbed her wrists and held them as securely as if they had been handcuffed.

"Sure, Sherwood, sure," he said amiably. "She didn't mean any of it. She's just got a little temper, that's all. Just bark, no bite. She won't bother you anymore."

Tara tried her best to bite the palm of his hand, but it was impossible. She groaned out her response then, hating Eldon for holding her and for talking in so subservient a voice to the revolting Sherwood.

From Leda, in the front seat, came a surprised, "Wow!"

When Sherwood glared for a moment at her she looked straight down the road as if she hadn't opened her mouth. Giles was looking out his window, as if he had been oblivious to everything. Beside Tara though, Amy trembled. And it infuriated Tara even more to see how intimidated they all were, how they blindly followed Sherwood like helpless little dogs, dependent on one person.

She yelled as best as she could under Eldon's hand, but when his hand pressed only harder and his thumb closed down on her nose she was forced to stop. She met his straight look over the top of his hand, putting all her feelings into her eyes, and receiving in return a warning shake of his head. She would have to be quiet, like it or not. Okay. But she had other ways, and since she had found out that she could needle Sherwood, that was exactly what she planned to do. She would show these people that he wasn't so great. He couldn't push everyone around.

Slowly, Eldon let up on his hand, and when finally he drew it away from her mouth Tara smiled at him as sweetly as she could. The responding surprise that came to his face was so quick and revealing that her smile turned to laughter.

Like a sigh of mutual relief everybody in the car, except Tara and Sherwood, began to talk, drawing attentions to other things.

"Great scenery," Giles said. "I always liked the desert."

"Yeah," said Fox. "Good driving, Sherwood."

"Want me to drive awhile?" Leda asked.

And from Amy, mostly to Tara, "I'm really not so uncomfortable. It's so much nicer here where the sun is shining."

To Tara's surprise Sherwood pulled in at the cafe. It was a small place, attached to a service station, and a sign read "restrooms." It had other things advertised there too, but Tara didn't look any further. Sherwood didn't turn off the engine. He reached into his pocket, pulled out some bills, turned around and threw them into Eldon's lap. His stare was hard, direct, and full of meaning.

"Feed 'em. Take 'em to the toilet. And wait. Keep an eye on her."

Eldon nodded and opened the door. Not until they stood on the hard-packed ground and the car roared on toward the town that was visible down the road did Tara notice that Leda and Giles had not stayed with them.

She looked up to find Eldon gazing helplessly from her to Amy and back to her.

"Well," he said. "Take her to the toilet, I guess. You won't run off, will you?"

Amy clutched Tara's arm and answered before Tara got a chance. "No, no. We won't, will we, Tara? No!" And then she was pulling, urgently.

In the small and crowded restroom Tara washed as best as she could with a paper towel. "Why don't we, Amy?" she asked. "I could take you home with me and you'd be safe."

Amy answered quickly and nervously, "What makes you think I'm not safe where I am, Tara?"

Tara considered the answer, aware that the statement had been spontaneous, and nearly subconscious. A slight feeling of chill, of warning, moved along her arms. "I don't know," she said seriously. "Something strikes me as being wrong. Doesn't it you?"

"No. Oh no." Amy shook her head and kept shaking it. "Sherwood is our leader, our protector. He won't let anything happen to us."

"You won't go with me?"

"Oh please don't go, Tara. Please. You can't even think about it. You just mustn't."

She sounded too frantic to be so sure of the security of the situation, and for a moment Tara felt trapped. Instead of the freedom and peace of mind she had been looking for she had found a prison. An emotional prison, because a very young pregnant girl needed her.

She smiled and touched the girl's cheek lightly with the back of her hand. "All right. Now stop getting yourself all upset, get cleaned up instead and let's go eat. I don't know about you, but I'm hungry."

She wasn't hungry though. She felt like a moocher, and she didn't like feeling that way. She ordered only toast and coffee, but enjoyed watching Amy eat a large breakfast of sausage, eggs and hot rolls. The food was very good, and the small place clean and quite popular, she noticed. She began to watch the customers. Beside her, in the low, plastic-covered booth, Eldon, like Amy, ate as if he were starved.

A truck, about half a block long, pulled in off the highway, entirely blocking the view of the road, and from it came two men who entered the cafe, sat at the counter and ordered breakfast. Within a few minutes a man and woman came in, travelers too, obviously, from the way they looked around and discussed where they would sit. Time slid by slowly and comfortably, and Eldon began to look out the window, a faint frown on his face. Tara wondered if Sherwood had left them for good, hoping that he had. But she kept her thoughts to herself and continued to sip her coffee and watch the customers.

Two more men came in, tall, clean shaven, hair styles a bit on the short side for the day. She particularly noticed their clothing. Tight western trousers and loose western shirts. Shining new. They didn't look as though they had seen much of the dust that was being blown about outdoors by the strong spurts of wind. One man was slightly smaller than the other, but both were loosely supple and well built. Tara's eyes left them and went back to the next people coming in—a family. They decided on a booth in the corner and the kids grabbed and fought over the two plastic-covered menus.

Tara noticed then the two western-garbed men had stopped at her own booth and with no invitation one of them sat down beside Amy and the other stood near him, waiting. Both Amy and Eldon paused to stare at the men.

The one who sat beside Amy leaned forward with an elbow on the table and said in a foul-breathed whisper, "For God's sake stop your stupid gawkin'! You'd think we was a couple of damned creeps." His head jerked sideways, directing, his small, glinting eyes hard on Eldon. "Take the car. Town's that way. Get a haircut and a shave and some clean clothes, for cripes sake. You look like a goddamned hippie."

Tara's amazement had quickly grown, deepened, and turned colors several times. The part about looking like a hippie was a joke, she thought, but Eldon didn't laugh. He moved fast, leaving his third cup of coffee nearly untouched. He grabbed the keys which Sherwood had handed to him and hurried toward the door. Tara looked back at Sherwood to see his eyes on her.

"What the hell are you waiting for? Get out there with him, both of you, and when you come back you be dressed proper. You're going to be Southern ladies, not bums in shawls. And no tricks now, sister."

Tara's surprise was still holding her tongue quite well. Mutely she slid out of the booth and stood waiting for Amy. Sherwood got up and moved to the other side, and Amy wriggled her large belly out of the narrow space of the booth and, grunting, rose to follow Tara.

They found that Leda was still in the car. The change in her was not so striking. Her hair was still long, but instead of dirty blue jeans and a discarded man's shirt she wore a dress of soft and clinging material and when Tara got into the back seat of the car she glimpsed one long, smooth, bare leg and a pair of new white sandals. Leda said nothing to them. The drive was rather fast and very silent.

The moment they reached the shopping district Leda said, "Pull over and let us out here. And hurry. Sherwood will want to be on the way as soon as possible."

Without answering Eldon pulled to a stop beside some parked cars and paused just long enough for them to get out. It was obvious who was in command now. Leda. "Hurry up," she said, watching Amy struggle along. They went into the first dress shop, and Leda took Amy to the maternity section and handed her over to a saleslady with a few words which Tara couldn't hear, and then she came back to Tara.

Tara didn't move. She wasn't at all sure she intended to be bossed about by Leda, and she held her chin high and let her eyes show her defiance. Deep within her the female part of her nature kept urging her to cooperate and get a feel of good clothes again. She was as sick of blue jeans as a person could be.

Leda stopped in front of her. They were nearly the same height, but Leda was very thin. Almost skinny. Tara's development would make her require a dress at least one size larger.

Leda's gaze faltered, and when she spoke she sounded unsure of herself. "Look, Tara. I didn't want this job of getting you outfitted any more than you want me to have it. I'm only here to pay the bill. Get what you want. But do get dresses, as well as pants and blouses and things. And underclothes, too. And sandals. That's all they have here, and we don't have time to stop anywhere else. Get a smaller bra, or something. Tighten them tits down a little, if you don't mind, and you'll have less trouble with the men."

"I don't have any trouble with the men," Tara answered, wondering if there were any end to the surprises.

Leda snorted lightly. "You will, baby, you will, if you don't watch it. Come on, let me help you, please."

Tara followed her slowly, thinking, looking at the back of Leda's head rather than at the racks of colorful clothing. What did Leda care if she had trouble with the men? It couldn't be concern for her, so it had to be jealousy. She considered the men hers. Yet it was obvious that she had shared them with Amy. Or was Amy really Eldon's girl? Tara stopped. She hadn't really thought of that because Amy had not seemed to be the least possessive toward Eldon, or any of them, so far as that went.

"What size do you wear?" Leda asked, pausing to look her up and down.

"Eight, usually. Depends on the prices and quality."

"Yeah, I know what you mean. Let's try the eights then, okay?"

"Okay."

Why not, Tara decided. She would note the bill and as soon as they reached wherever they were going she would get a job, pay for the clothes and her expenses, and as soon as Amy's baby was born she could leave. By that time she would have decided whether or not to stay on her own and roam the world a while longer—not as a flower child—or go back home and marry her rich fiancé. He might be a little teed off at her, but she knew he'd be waiting. Not because he was so very much in love with her, but because he considered her the prettiest catch in the county. He had never been wild about getting married. Not Albert. He plodded along as if he had forever to plod. So far their dating had run three years with no end in sight anyway. So she knew Albert would be waiting.

She bought two dresses and four pairs of pants and matching blouses, and enough underclothes to keep her for a while. It was done quickly and without waste of time, but Tara could see that Leda was nervous about the time anyway. She kept looking at the clock on the wall, near the ceiling.

"We just got to go," she finally said.

When Tara saw Amy again she saw a girl in a purple maternity dress. She was smiling, and her eyes glowed with the pleasure of pretty clothes. Tara had a feeling that Amy hadn't seen much of that in her life.

"Happy?" Tara asked.

"Oh yes! Tara, you're gorgeous."

"Thank you. You're rather a doll yourself."

Amy glanced down at her stomach, for the first time showing that it brought something to her besides love. "I'm afraid not now. I did have a rather good figure before. Not like yours, of course, but not bad either."

"You'll get it back."

Amy smiled. "I'll get more. It really doesn't matter that much about the figure part. I expect I'll lose part of my bust because I'm going to nurse him, you know."

Tara listened to Amy with part of her attention on the bill that was being totaled. Her part came to slightly less than three hundred dollars.

Leda led the way out, her arms loaded with bundles. Tara picked up the rest and followed.

"Don't you want me to carry some of that?" Amy asked.

"Just yourself, dear," Tara answered, and paused for Amy to go ahead of her.

When Leda looked back impatiently, Amy tried so hard to hurry that she looked very much like a duck under stress waddling along. Tara felt sorry for her.

Even though she was prepared to see a change in Eldon she still didn't recognize him. His face was thinner than she had realized, his nose larger, his chin sloping under. If he hadn't taken her arm she wouldn't have known him at all. His face, beardless, couldn't even be said to have character.

"The car's up this way," he said, "and across the street. We'd better hurry."

Leda answered irritably, "That's what I've been trying to do, lunkhead. We weren't playing games in there, you know."

Eldon didn't answer. They crossed the street and he unlocked the trunk. Tara saw that it was nearly full with bags and boxes of, she supposed, clothing. Eldon took from her the packages he hadn't offered to carry and stuffed them into the trunk. Within a minute they were on their way back to the cafe.

Sherwood and Giles were standing, waiting, behind a truck in the graveled lot. Sherwood opened the back door on Tara's side and slid in, and Tara had to move quickly to keep him from sitting on her lap. He seemed not to notice. Giles took his place in front, beside Leda, and draped one arm around her neck. Sherwood slammed the door and settled back.

"Get it going," he ordered. "What the hell took you so long?"

Eldon, however, held the car still, looking over his shoulder at Sherwood with a worried expression. "You want me to drive?"

"Yeah. Get it goin'."

Eldon kept looking back. His glance flickered to Tara, and to the arm in the western shirt that lay relaxed against her hip. Though she had moved as far away as she could without crushing Amy, still Sherwood touched her, seemingly unaware that he did.

"What are you waitin' for?" Sherwood demanded. He scooted down onto his back, folded his arms across his flat belly, put his head back and closed his eyes. "I drove all night, you think I don't ever need no sleep or nothin'?"

Eldon turned, gunned the car and nearly gave them all whiplash. He pressed it to its limit, gravel flew, and Tara expected a cop to materialize out of somewhere and give them a chase, but nothing happened. Sherwood said nothing until the highway sang smoothly under the tires. When he did speak his voice was surprisingly calm and even-tempered.

"Hold it down in town, boy. You want to be stopped for speeding?"

After a moment Eldon obeyed, as if he had thought it over and decided Sherwood was right. They maintained the speed limit as they moved through the small town. Not until they were in open country did he speed up again.

In the afternoon they stopped to eat a short snack. And Sherwood traded places with Eldon. Tara wished for the snoring back again, because the first thing Eldon wanted to do was give her a long, sloppy kiss. She turned her face away from the kiss, and faked a nap of her own. Sherwood, at the wheel, sang along with the radio as if no one else was in the car.

That night when Sherwood began watching for a place to eat, Leda began to beg. Leaning over him, with her arms around his neck, her tongue nuzzling his ear, she made her mouth ready for the kisses he turned on her occasionally." She whined like a baby, Tara thought with disgust.

"Make it a club, darling, okay? Do you know how long it's been since I've danced? Come on, darling, say yes. Don't I always do everything you want me to?"

"Ummm." He kissed her with a loud, sucking sound.

The whole thing affected Eldon in just the opposite way that it had Tara, and he began to want to neck again. Tara pushed him away. He was easy to push. He moved back, quiet, pouting.

Tara was glad when Sherwood pulled in at a place with flickering neon lights that said *Dining and Dancing*.

Most of the people there, she saw as they entered the long, dim, rustic hangout, were dancing, not dining. The rock band was so loud that talking was nearly impossible. When the waitress came to take their order she had to lean down while Sherwood shouted in her ear. Without asking what anyone wanted he ordered steaks all around.

The money, Tara thought, amounted to quite a lot, evidently. But it seemed a little odd because Giles' aunt had sent it but Sherwood was the one who handled it. But then, he was the leader of the pack. She had forgotten that for a moment.

Sherwood and Leda danced, and Tara found herself watching them with fascination. The man who seemed so repulsive before suddenly had a sexy grace about him that she couldn't take her eyes away from. He was one of the best dancers she had ever watched.

When Sherwood brought Leda back to the table he came around to Tara immediately, bowed slightly, smiled, and held out his hand, and Tara knew she would not refuse him. She wanted to dance with him.

She coordinated her movements with his, saw that his eyes roved over her body in a way that made her follow him as if he used some kind of magic. His hands didn't touch her, though they moved toward and away from her constantly. He danced about a yard away, a dance either so modem she hadn't caught up with it, or something of his own design. Other dancers began to move back to watch him.

When it was over Eldon was standing at the edge of the floor, waiting, ready to take Sherwood's place. And Sherwood went back to get Leda.

The music had slowed considerably, and Eldon drew her into his arms, his mouth close to her ear.

"You better watch that guy," he whispered.

She laughed, thinking he was jealous. "Don't worry, I might have enjoyed dancing with him, but he isn't about to do anything else."

"That's not what I mean," he answered. "A screw won't kill you."

She drew back and looked up into his face, but he was looking over her head, watching someone behind her. His eyes squinted under a faint frown.

"What does that mean?" she asked.

For a while he didn't answer then he said, "You just remember what I told you, that's all. And don't mention it. Don't even breathe it."

He looked too serious to be joking, but his remark and his answers were too vague to suit her. "I want to know what you mean."

He stopped dancing, and in the pause of music said casually, "The food's here. We'd better eat. Sherwood will want to be on the way as soon as possible."

Tara decided to shelve it for the time being. Let her mind ruminate on it awhile. They went to the table and sat down to large platters of steak and fries.

After that they drove straight through, with hardly a pause even for eating, night and day, changing drivers only for short periods. Tara had never seen anyone who could keep driving the way Sherwood did. Again she was sure he must have done it many times before, as a truck driver, chauffeur, something.

In a restroom once she asked Amy, "What kind of work did Sherwood used to do?"

"I don't know. I met him in San Francisco about a year and a half ago. That's all I know about him. The only time he ever mentioned work was once when he said he had decided to give it up." She giggled. "He said work was for ants and birds and bees and things of that nature. People ought to be above it."

Tara decided to pry a little since Amy seemed in a confiding mood. "Where are you from, Amy?"

Immediately Amy looked down at the floor, and she didn't raise her head. After a long period of silence she said quietly, "Here and there. I had a mother, but not anymore."

"Oh, I'm sorry. Who raised you?"

"Well—she did. Until I ran away."

"She's still living?"

"Her? You can bet your life on it! She'd sell her own— her own daughter to keep alive and have what she wants. Look, Tara, Sherwood said that in our family there's no past, see. So we don't talk about things like that."

"Yes, I see." Tara had only a vague idea, mostly from literature and news, of the kind of life some children led. But the pain in Amy's eyes brought it into focus so sharply that for a moment she lived it herself.

Amy looked up suddenly, her face bright with hope. "It's already better, you see, Tara. We have a home now. A real house. And we can raise vegetables and really live and my baby boy will have a real home." She paused, the hope fading, her voice lowering. "It is better, don't you see? I know you don't like Sherwood, Tara, but at least he never sold me to an outsider. Not to anyone."

"Yes, Amy, it is better." Tara's voice was strong and calm, accepting. She understood now what brought one girl, at least, into communal living.

The next day at about noon Giles stopped in Sherwood, a small town of about two thousand people. It had wide, quiet streets, tree-shaded walks, and a completely lazy, Southern atmosphere that brought an easy kind of peace to Tara as she looked around.

"Is this it?" Sherwood demanded, not sounding very pleased. "This dead burg?"

Giles stretched his neck and twisted his head, looking. "I think so. It's the right name, anyhow."

"Does it look familiar, for cripes sake, or don't it?"

"It's been a long time—I was only ten that year. But I think this is it."

Sherwood cursed a little, adding, "How're we goin' to find out, go ask the local cop?"

Giles didn't answer. Sherwood drove slowly through town and around a block and headed back.

"Well?"

Giles said, "If I saw the house I'd know it for sure. I remember it. It was big and brown with little windows and a lot of vines. Dark inside. Lots of rooms didn't even have windows. I'd know the house."

Sherwood sighed. "Can you remember how to get to it?"

"You go out of town to this road, see, and turn off there."

"Which side of town?"

Giles thought for a moment. "The west side. We faced the sun when we got groceries that evening. But we decided not to stay in the house after all because there was no stove or anything, so we came back to town to a rooming house."

Leda said, "Speaking of grub—"

"Later," Sherwood said. "We got to find the house. Then we buy groceries. Your eatin'-out days are over. From now on you cook."

"Not me," Leda retorted, and pointed a thumb over her shoulder. "Her. Let *her* do the cooking. I'm not about to."

Tara said, "I'd rather cook than lie around doing what you do all the time."

Sherwood, to Tara's surprise, tilted his head back and yelled with laughter. It roared in the car.

Leda slumped down to pout, and Sherwood drove slowly on through town and west again on the highway, still chuckling deep inside. Gradually he sobered, but Tara had a feeling that Leda had all at once become her enemy because of Sherwood's unexpected reaction.

"Which way off the highway did the road turn?" he asked.

"That way." Giles had leaned forward, looking for a road to the left. After a while he shouted with satisfaction, "There! See? Black Swamp, it says. That's it, bound to be."

"It just better be," Sherwood answered, his old grumpy self again. "What's that sign say?"

"Black Swamp. And dead-end road."

Sherwood laughed again. "You better believe it! Well, kids, we're on our way home. Wake up and look around." The road was narrow and rutted by rains, though solid enough on this sunny day so that only an occasional mud-hole threatened to mire the car.

"Frogs," said Sherwood. "Hear them frogs? There must be a jillion of 'em."

No one answered him. Even Leda had sat up and was looking around.

The trees began to close them in, shutting off the brightness of the sun. Leda shuddered visibly.

"Did somebody mention growing vegetables? In this?"

"We could eat frogs maybe," Sherwood answered. His spirits had risen considerably, Tara saw. But then he seemed to be an excessively moody person, constantly up or down. She had thought he might be on drugs, but she knew now he wasn't.

The trees dropped back suddenly in a small clearing and the house was there, a solid front of vine-covered wall. Small, dusty window panes peered out from under their creeping cover of vines. The car stopped, still in the road, motor idling. In the silence the frogs began again, the only voices, the only sound other than the soft throbbing of the car.

It was not what Tara had expected. She hadn't formed much of a vision of any kind, but what little had come to her was no match for what she saw. Just a few yards beyond the house the trees started again in a thick, dark clutter where the green of water plants broke away in places to show black reflecting pools. And the road did go straight on into the swamp, just as Giles had said it did, and near its end a faint circle made it look like a snake coiled near the water. Snakes. Tara's eyes followed the ground cover of vines that seemed to be everywhere.

"Hey," she said, "aren't we far enough south now for water moccasins? The cotton-mouthed variety?" She could practically see them writhing about in the vines, waiting for her bare ankle to sink within reach. She groaned faintly. She wasn't afraid of many things, but she had a phobia about snakes.

Sherwood's voice, slightly puzzled, came at her. "Moccasins?" As if the only moccasin he had ever heard of had been worn by an Indian.

Giles said in his slow voice that Tara was beginning to think was misleading, "She means snakes. Very poisonous. But very lazy, too, Tara. They keep out of your way if they can."

"I'll certainly do my best to let them. Meantime, how do I get to the door?"

Sherwood said sarcastically, "Like, say, walk?"

Giles was more understanding. "If you're thinking they're hiding in the vines, forget it. They'll be out there in the water. Stay out of the water and you'll be okay."

Leda spoke up suddenly. "I'm not going into that house. You expect me to go in that house? It's hideous. Compared to that house a poison snake is nothing. I'm not going in there." Her head jerked a quick nod back toward Tara. "Her, if she wants to get in, let her ride her broomstick. That house fits her like a pair of black gloves."

Even from the back seat Tara could see that Leda had folded stubborn arms across a determined chest. Sherwood gave her a long, hard, sideways look, said, "Meow, pft, pft," then silently turned the steering wheel and eased the car through the vines toward the garage with the sagging door. Everyone turned to look at the back of the house, except Leda. She held her position and stared straight ahead.

Sherwood opened his door and gave a crisp order. "Pile out and let's see if we can get in."

Everyone but Leda obeyed. Even Tara followed Fox out the door and stepped gingerly into the vines, curiosity drawing her on toward the house, a curiosity so strong that it over-rode her fear of snakes. She watched each step carefully, and was the last to reach the back door. Sherwood was using a small tool on the old rusty lock, and in a short time had the door open. Even Amy went up the steps ahead of Tara. At the porch, safely out of the vines, Tara looked back at the car. Only the rear of it showed, but she knew that Leda was still there, her arms folded across her chest, her eyes straight ahead, her mouth held so tightly it practically disappeared into her face.

Tara smiled in private amusement and stepped over the threshold into the house. She found herself against the wall of stink that came from somewhere, everywhere. Amy was turning back, her face pale. She staggered a little in her hurry toward the door.

Tara stepped aside to let her pass in the narrow hall, asking, "Are you sick, Amy?"

Amy put her hand to her mouth and nodded, mumbling, "But I'll be all right in a minute."

Sherwood was bawling orders, and his voice echoed as if inside a cave. "Open this goddamned place up! Clean out the dead rats! Christomighty! Is everything around here dead? Open them winders! Giles, is there any door but the back one and the front one? A house this big ought to have a dozen doors."

"I don't know. I don't remember."

"Well, find out, and go open the damned front door. Fox, open them winders. Christ, is this a kitchen? This is not a kitchen, it's a cave. Well, let's open it up. Come on."

Curiosity still pulling, Tara held her breath for as long as possible without exploding and walked the ten feet or so down the hall to the door through which Sherwood and Eldon had gone. She followed and stood looking at the kitchen. Huge. Unbelievably bleak and dark and colorless, as if any paint that had once existed had faded into the narrow, grooved boards that covered walls, ceiling and cupboards. She decided that it was a kind of ancient paneling that had once been varnished. On the left, two narrow windows broke the long wall, and ahead was the great mouth of the fireplace. She shivered in the damp cold. The house felt as if it were about twenty degrees cooler than it was outside.

She walked the length of the bare floor, past the picnic-type dining table and on to the fireplace and stood staring at it.

High enough so that she could easily walk into it without bending, black with ages of soot, cold with fires long gone, it gave her a feeling she couldn't define but which was very uncomfortable. She rubbed cold hands along cold arms and wished she had her jacket, but it was in the car.

"Is this the only place to cook?" she asked incredulously, walking back to look down at the table, and the plate of green mold that sat there.

Nobody answered. Both men were grunting over one window that wouldn't budge, and Sherwood was threatening to knock the "*bleep bleep*" out and be done with it. He didn't, however, but simply moved to the other window and began the same fruitless efforts.

Tara looked at the plate. A fork lay on it, and a knife. She wondered how many years it had been sitting there like that, but for some reason she didn't say anything. With a tissue from her pocket she picked up the thing and carried it to the fireplace and slid it far back into the ashes. She tossed the tissue after it and stood up, brushing her hands in distaste. A fire, she thought, would destroy whatever it had been.

A cricket, somewhere in the loose stones of the fireplace, began to sing a little, but stopped quickly and was silent again, as if it listened. Well, Tara thought, at least the fireplace didn't eat things. It certainly looked capable of it though. She backed away.

"Maybe it only eats people," she said aloud.

Sherwood kicked the wall below the window and came away cursing.

Tara said half in amusement and half in disgust, "Why don't you go ahead and knock it out as you said you would?"

Sherwood stopped and glared at her. "Just shut up for once, will you? You talk, talk, talk all the time." He waved the back of his hand toward the fireplace. "Get a fire built or something. Get something cooked."

"What? Crickets? Frogs? With poison-ivy salad?"

He held up his hand. "Hold it! Just hold it, goddamn it. I'll get you something if you'll just stop buggin me for a while."

Tara glared back at him. "For a guy whose personality can change into something almost human when there's music, you sure are a crab."

Instead of answering Tara, Sherwood turned his hard stare on Eldon. "What'd I tell you, Fox, what'd I tell you. You just better quiet her down."

Eldon started toward Tara, but she turned her back to both of them and looked into the fireplace. "Never mind! Just rustle me some wood, or buffalo chips, or whatever you can find that will burn, as the pioneer woman said. Maybe a fire will help get rid of the awful stink in here. And see about Amy, too. I'm not about to go back into those vines if I can help it."

Footsteps in the hall brought her around to see who was coming. Giles stopped in the doorway and looked in.

"I opened it. It was the only door I could find downstairs. The windows won't open."

"I know, I know," Sherwood answered irritably. "Come with me and let's get something to build a fire with, and get the things brought in. You there, Red. You make a list of what we need."

"You mean groceries?"

"I mean what we need! Go upstairs and see if there's any beds and things like that. Maybe we need blankets and things too. You go make a list. Go with her, Fox."

If Eldon went with her, Tara thought, he would want to stop for necking somewhere, and she was getting to the point where she couldn't stand the man at all. She didn't intend to ever be kissed by him. "No," she said. "I'll make the check alone, you just go see if Amy is okay. I'd go myself but ..." There was no point in mentioning again her fear of snakes hiding in the vines.

A look of amusement crossed Sherwood's face. "Yeah," he said. "Maybe you ought to at that, Fox. I don't think there's any danger of Red sneaking off through them snaky vines. You see about Amy instead."

Tara watched them go out, Sherwood in the lead, Eldon following reluctantly. He looked back longingly at Tara, but Tara held her head high and kept her eyes unyielding.

When they were gone the cricket began to saw busily and loudly. "Me you don't mind, eh? Them you don't like," she said in a low voice. The cricket paused, then continued. And Tara turned her attention to the doorway into the hall, and the upper stories she was to investigate alone.

CHAPTER 4

A timid feeling gripped her suddenly when she faced the dark length of the hall. The smell there was worse than it was by the fireplace, and she glanced at dark edges of the floor for the dead rats Sherwood had spoken of. None there, of course. Nothing but gray-green mold and years of accumulated dust and debris.

The hallway looked endless. The walls and ceiling were of the same, narrow, grooved wood, and in some places drooped, showing cracks and leaking cotton-like debris. She made a mental note to avoid walking under those places so that the stuff wouldn't fall into her hair. She had an increasingly strong feeling that the house wasn't really very safe.

She walked lightly for a little while, testing the boards under her feet. They seemed as solid as they looked; wide, rough boards that contrasted with the narrow paneling. She thought perhaps they had once been covered by rugs, or, since this would have been the servants' quarters, left as they were. She noticed doors then, here and there along the hall, sunk unobtrusively into the dark walls, dwarfed by the high ceilings. But she wouldn't have opened one for anything. Dead rats. Dark rooms without windows, Giles had said. Let Sherwood open them and clean out the dead rats himself.

At the end of the hall she found a small square room, to the left of which stood a large open door. To her right was a steep, open stairway with railing on one side, wall on the other. She hesitated, then went to the door and peeked through. Another hallway, wide, and lighter, leading to the open front door. She noticed the floor: the boards were smoother, once varnished. Against the wall lay rolls of rugs.

She turned back to the stairway and with her hand on the newel post looked up toward its landing. There seemed to be about a hundred steps. She began to go up, watching ahead for broken steps or railing. She watched for other things too, just what she wasn't sure, but the smell of death and rotting was stronger on the stairway than in the lower hall.

She eventually came out on the top and paused to look back, feeling an accomplishment equal to having climbed a mountain. Going down it again, she thought, would take even more nerve. She'd probably have to get down on her knees and go backwards, like a crawling baby. And that reminded her of Amy. How on earth would Amy ever manage those stairs? There must be other, better ones in the front of the house.

The hallway she stood in was another small, square room with several doors. She hadn't noticed how dark it was, she had been so preoccupied with the stairway. To her right another, very similar stairway went on up into the third story, its top lost in the increasing darkness of another small closed room. She saw though that part of the steps had broken through, and part of the railing was gone. Well, that eliminated the third story as far as she was concerned. She might wish to explore it sometime, but not enough to tackle the crumbling stairway. She turned her attention to the closed doors that faced her.

A door would have to be opened this time, and she would have to open it because she would not go running back for one of the men to do it for her. She might be scared of snakes, but she'd be damned if she'd be scared of anything else, even dead rats. What could a dead rat do? Poor thing. Just stink, that was all.

One of the doors, though, had to open onto the upstairs hall. She figured out that the rest of the doors probably concealed more servants' quarters, bedrooms possibly, or linen and housekeeping closets and things of that nature. Logically, the door straight ahead would be the hallway door.

She crossed the small room to the door, placed her hand over the white knob and turned it, reminding herself that she wasn't afraid of anything but snakes. As she suspected, the door squealed and squeaked on rusted hinges, but it opened easily enough. The space behind it though was darker than ever, and cold goosebumps moved along her arms. Instead of a hallway she had found a large closet. Vague outlines of shelves were all she could see in the darkness.

She closed the door quickly and moved to the left, paused, and then went back to the head of the stairs and looked down. The location of the hall door down there might possibly correspond with the hall door up here. The third to the left. She turned back and opened the third door to the left.

A second accomplishment. A bit of light, a lot of roominess, and a hallway that led somewhere to a window. She walked gingerly again, looking down, testing the floor. It seemed to be sturdy enough, yet there was an undefinable feeling of something wrong.

She stopped and looked around. More doors, many of them open, revealing portions of furniture here and there. Halls branching off farther down, and at the other end of the main hall one stairway, going down, directly under a long, narrow window. Hopefully, a stairway which Amy could use.

She looked again at the floor, puzzled, trying to decide what was wrong with it. Was it slanted? It seemed to be. Tilted, as if the part where she stood had sunk a few inches. Surely it hadn't been built that way. She would have to ask Giles about that. He might know.

The bad odor was much fainter, she noticed, or she was beginning to get used to it. She walked slowly along, not entering any of the bedrooms, but noting from the doorways that each had beds with springs and in some cases mattresses. At least there were plenty of those. Amy and she could take one side by side, or, if Amy wished, together. The others could make their own choices. There was no point in trying to go on to the third story.

She began to look for a room for herself and Amy, and when she found the fireplace she crossed the threshold. It was a very large room, with a huge bed. The mattress was still there, and probably wasn't as old as most of the furniture. At least it looked as if it might hold up.

An old carpet, or Oriental rug, covered the floor. Many chairs sat around, as many tables and chests, and even a few old books, green as gourds with mildew. She wanted suddenly to get brooms, mops and dust cloths and clean things up. The fireplace, around which everything seemed to center, wasn't like the one in the kitchen. It was smaller, built of brick, faced with a dark wood of some kind, and needed only a small fire to make it seem less lonely. Above the mantle hung a large, ornately framed painting. But it too was mildewed and covered with dust so that she could only make out that it was a portrait. Man or woman, she couldn't tell. She wondered if it might be valuable. Probably not, or it would not have been left. She had not seen another painting anywhere, now that she thought of it. Nowhere in the main halls, either downstairs or up.

Anyway, she had found her room, and she was prepared to fight for it.

She looked at rooms on both sides, for Amy, and found them both small and unattractive. And no fireplaces anywhere. Not even in the room across the hall. Well, she thought, she would leave it up to Amy.

She went on to the front stairway to see if Amy could use it. She was ready to make her list, and when she got through with it Sherwood would probably wish he hadn't asked her, because the things the house needed would be enough to discourage any man.

The front stairway was, as she had expected, less steep, less narrow. It curved down to the lower hall in a sturdy but graceful way that was almost pretty. Under her feet the boards complained and groaned more than the rear stairs had, but she went on without hesitation. When she reached the kitchen they were there, all but Leda. Amy, pale, sat on the bench by the table.

"Feeling better?" Tara asked the miserable-looking girl.

Amy smiled faintly. "Yes. I think I can make it now. I wonder what on earth smells so bad?"

"Dead rats," Sherwood said. "You ready to make that list?"

"If you're so sure it's dead rats, why don't you go pick them up and throw them out while I write the list?" Tara said. "Give me a pen and notepaper."

Sherwood dug into his shirt pocket. "You tryin' to boss me around or somethin'? I ain't about to carry out no dead rats. You, Giles, Fox, you go clean them out."

They didn't move until Sherwood shouted, "Hear!" Slowly then, they went toward the door.

Tara took the notebook and pen from Sherwood, trying to avoid the touch of his fingers. "And what do you intend to do?" she asked, "sit around and look pretty?"

"I'm aiming to do your shopping for you, goddamnit."

"Well, I'm not ready yet, so you go out and bring in some wood for a fire."

His face darkened, but it only increased Tara's irritation with him. "Hear!" she said, trying hard to mock his way of saying it. "Go get some wood. I'll have the list ready when you get back."

He glared at her, looking again as if he were thinking of knocking her down and letting it go at that. But he said, "We put wood by the garage."

"I want it here. No wood, no food. Either I get a fire, or I don't cook. Now suit yourself."

He turned and stomped out, and Tara smiled with satisfaction. She hadn't really thought she could make him do it.

Amy said, "Gosh, Tara. I don't know about you. I've never seen Sherwood take backtalk before."

"What does he usually do?"

"Nobody has ever tried but Leda, that I ever knew, and he hit her so hard it cut her lip and it bled for a long time. I wouldn't dare try it myself."

Tara looked at her. Frail, helpless, small Amy. "No," she said slowly, for the first time feeling that Sherwood might be dangerous if provoked enough, "I wouldn't either if I were you, Amy."

"Of course I don't really want to," Amy said quickly, "because he's good to me. But I wish you'd be more careful, Tara. I have a bad feeling about it. I'm afraid—he'll really get mad at you someday."

"Well, I don't intend to be around long enough to get on his nerves too much. As soon as the baby is born, and I see that you're going to be all right, I'm leaving."

Tara was afraid she might protest, but Amy only looked up at her, large blue eyes sad but relieved. "I hope it happens that way, Tara. You don't belong with us. I can see that now."

Tara wanted to change the subject before Amy burst into tears so she said quickly, "I found a very lovely room upstairs, Amy. All it really needs is a good cleaning. There's no other like it, and I'd rather like to have it while I'm here and turn it over to you when I leave. There's only one bed, but it's very large, and I wondered if you'd like to share it with me."

Amy looked more relieved than ever. "Oh yes. I'll have to admit I was kind of scared about sleeping in a room alone in this house. And I can't sleep with any of the men, you know, until—until this is over. Of course then I'll have my baby to keep me company."

"Well, that's settled then. Later, when you've rested and eaten, I'll take you up and show it to you."

She began to write in the notebook: brooms, cleansers, dustpans—and suddenly paused, her pen still.

Amy asked, "What is it, Tara?"

"Water," Tara said. "I was just wondering about water. We seem to be surrounded by the stuff, but I'm sure it's not fit for anything. So what do we cook with and drink? There's no water in this house, no bathroom, not even a kitchen sink. No faucet."

"No," Amy agreed, looking about the kitchen. "That is odd, isn't it. Inconvenient. There are two old, old toilets out by the garage. One for women and one for men, I guess. This is a very old-fashioned kitchen, isn't it?"

"Yes. I'm surprised it isn't out by the garage too. Seriously, it is a wonder that it's connected to the house. They weren't always, you know. Still, people drank water, even in those days. So there has to be water around here somewhere. A well, probably."

Amy shuddered. "Oh. I saw one of those once. It was deep and black, lined with stones that looked as if they might fall, and it was at least six feet across. What if it's out there covered by those vines? Golly, Tara, you better be careful if you look for it."

"Ha! You won't catch this child out in those vines looking for anything. We'll send Sherwood." She giggled softly. "Maybe he'll fall in."

Amy smiled, but only because she was humoring Tara. "Shhh. What if he heard you?"

Tara shrugged and went back to her writing. She went through a long list of groceries that would be easy to cook over the fireplace and wouldn't need refrigeration, and then she paused again.

"What now?" asked Amy.

"It just occurred to me that this place isn't habitable at all, Amy. There's not even any electricity. So what do we use for lights?"

"Oh, Tara, candles! How cozy and romantic."

"Romantic." Tara sighed. "Somehow, they don't strike me as exactly *romantic* in this house. But okay, candles it is. I'm sure if I ordered anything else Sherwood wouldn't know how to get it. Is there anything special you'd like to eat, Amy?"

"Yes. Hotdogs and marshmallows. We could roast them over the fire, couldn't we?"

"Sure. Why not. Sounds like an easy meal to get. Main dish and dessert too."

They laughed together, just as Sherwood came in. He passed by without glancing at them, his arms cupped around a load of broken boards, sticks and small limbs that had fallen from trees. Tara wrote on in silence while Sherwood built the fire.

Sherwood was squatting on his heels on the wide stone hearth, watching his fire catch and burn, when Giles and Eldon returned from their tour of the house. Sherwood twisted about to face them.

"Well? How many did you find?"

"None," Eldon said. "They must be back in the walls." Slowly, Giles added, "We couldn't get into the third story—"

Sherwood didn't wait for him to finish. "Why the hell not? They're probably up there."

"Well—"

Eldon interrupted, talking hastily, "The stairs didn't look safe."

"Didn't look safe!" Sherwood mocked. "So? Go up anyway."

Giles started to go again, but Eldon didn't move, and then Giles too paused. Eldon said patiently, "They're broken. And there ain't any front stairs. Half the steps are gone in the middle, and the railing too. It might be possible to get up them, but I don't see why we just can't let it go for today. There's plenty of bedrooms on the second floor anyway. About seven. One of them has even got a fireplace."

"About? Is there seven or ain't there?"

"Not counting the little rooms without windows and the rooms without furniture, there are seven. I don't know what the little rooms are unless they're big closets."

"Okay, we'll let it go for now." Sherwood got up, brushed the front of his trousers and directed his question to Tara. "You got that list ready?"

"Yes. But what about water?"

Sherwood looked downright stupid for a moment. "Water?"

"Yes. You know, that stuff people drink and take baths in and cook vegetables in? It also falls from the—"

"Okay, okay, you don't have to be so goddamned bitchy about it." He turned to Giles. "Where's the water supply? Or do you drink swamp water?"

Giles too looked stupid. It took a long moment for him to answer. "I don't know. We didn't stay here, we just came out. And then Aunt Rita got nervous and said to hell with it. She didn't like the house."

"So you don't know nothin' about water?"

"No."

"Well then, go look for it!" Sherwood snatched the notebook from Tara, and then the pen, and kept walking on toward the door. His voice echoed against the fireplace. "Find drinking water. Bring in some more wood. Have a pile of it there by the fireplace when I get back. And find that water! We sure as hell don't want to have to run to town every day and haul it out in buckets. We'll use swamp water first."

Giles started to say, "Dangerous to use—"

But Sherwood was gone, and Giles hushed, licking his lips with a long tongue that had nothing else to do at the moment.

Tara decided to give him another job. "How about bringing me some swamp water to clean with first, Giles? It will do for that, won't it? I want a towel or two from the car, too, so hurry before he leaves."

"But what'll I bring the water in?"

"I don't know. Look about and maybe you'll find an old pan somewhere. Or bring me the cooking pot from the car. I've ordered new ones anyway. Go help him, Eldon." After they had gone she remembered that she had wanted to ask Giles about the floor of the upstairs hall. Well, she could ask later. It wasn't that important anyway.

Amy had gone to the fireplace to get warm, and Tara joined her. She heard the trunk lid of the car slam down, and then the car back out and drive away, a very faint sound in the space of silence left by the frogs.

The men returned in a few minutes with very murky-looking water in the black cooking pot, and a couple of not-very-clean towels. Tara took them and looked into the water.

"It's awful. But I guess it will help wipe the dust away. I'm going upstairs, Amy, to clean up our room a little."

Eldon said, "Whose room?"

Tara smiled at him over her shoulder. "I was there first, so that means I get first choice."

Giles was headed out again. "Come on, Fox, we'd better hunt up that water before Sherwood gets back. You know how fast he is when it comes to buying something. He never looks at a price or a label."

With another questioning look at Tara, Eldon followed Giles. And Tara, with her pot of dirty water, the dirty towels over her arms, followed them as far as the kitchen door.

"Tara," Amy said, close behind, "can't I come too?"

She sounded like a lost little girl, but Tara looked at her belly and thought of the stairs. "Wouldn't you rather wait until I clean it up a little?"

"No. I can help you."

"I can manage that. I think you should rest. But come along, if you want. We'll have to go to the front stairs." Tara walked behind Amy up the stairs, going slowly, prepared to let go of the pot of water and catch her if she stumbled, though she didn't know what would happen after that. Probably they'd both fall.

But Amy made it all right, though she was out of breath by the time she reached the top. She paused for a minute to catch her breath, and to look curiously about her.

"So dark, isn't it, Tara? And such a big house. I wonder why they didn't put in more windows."

"Maybe whoever built it didn't like windows. Come on, you can sit down. Our room is way back, the second on the left from the back-stairs doorway. The only one with a fireplace, they said. Though I didn't go through all the rooms to find out. I liked it because—well, I'm not sure why, unless it was because it seemed so occupied. A mattress on the bed, loads of furniture and things sitting around as if nothing had ever been moved."

"Is everything antique, you suppose?"

"Possibly. I wouldn't know."

She preceded Amy into the room, put the pot on the hearth and dampened one of the towels. The first thing she dusted was a rocking chair that stood at the end of the fireplace.

"There. Sit down and rest, and I'll see what I can do. What I need is a vacuum cleaner and a place to plug it in. Or at least a broom and some other things of that nature."

"What is this, Tara, a real painting?"

"Yeah," Tara answered without looking. She wiped the headboard of the bed, and the footboard, both solid carved wood, and moved on to a table.

"Ik," Amy said in disgust. "It's awful dirty." And a moment later, "Why, it's a picture of somebody."

"Yes."

Tara wiped the pitcher and washbowl on the table, and silently admired the cream-colored beauty of the porcelain.

"Do you suppose," Amy said after a while, "that it's a picture of the person who lived in this room?"

"It might be."

"I can't reach it very well. But look, Tara, here's a name—Sam-Sam-a—how do you suppose that's pronounced? And look, Tara, a peace sign! That's what I call a good omen, right, Tara?"

Amy's growing enthusiasm and interest drew Tara and she looked to see Amy using one very dirty forefinger to wipe away the dust on the bottom of the painting. Tara refolded her towel to a cleaner, unused spot, and went to look over Amy's shoulder.

"I'll be darned," Tara said. "It is a peace sign, isn't it?" Amy's finger wiped again at the name printed beside the tiny horizontal mark with the inverted V. "How do you think that's pronounced?"

Tara looked at the name for a moment, then spelled it aloud. "S-A-M-A-E-L. Sam-ael? Samail? I don't know, Amy. If they'd meant it to be 'Samuel' they would have spelled it that way I expect, rather than this. Names can be so difficult because people can do whatever they want with a word when it comes to names. It looks rather like the printing of a child, so maybe it's simply misspelled."

"Can you reach the face? Let's see who it is."

Tara stretched full length and managed to reach all but the-upper fourth of the painting. She carefully uncovered the face of a young boy.

"It is a child, Tara!" Amy cried. "Oh, that *is* a good omen. A child's room, and a peace sign. What a perfect place for my son to be born."

Tara stood back and looked at that which she had uncovered. The paint had been piled on heavily in places, especially on the face of the child, so that dust was still in the depths and crevices, but his features came through prominently. The eyes especially. They were a strange light yellow-green and not very well done, it seemed to Tara, because they didn't look like the eyes of a child. They held an intense, baleful glare that made her want to pull away. She lowered her dustcloth and stared back at the eyes.

"I think the painter must not have been very good," she said musingly. "Did you ever see eyes like that on a little boy?"

"They are kind of glary, aren't they?" Amy replied happily. "But the background is pretty, don't you think?"

"Purple velvet?"

Tara looked back at the huge bed, the elaborately carved wood, and the dark velvet that draped like curtains, drawn back on each side, from the ceiling above. She had thought the material was a faded pink, now more gray than pink, but when she approached it and touched its dusty folds she saw the deep purple still there within, hidden from the faint light that came through the vine-shrouded window.

Amy's voice, breaking into her formless thoughts, was subdued. "He must have been sitting in that bed, Tara. Leaning back on a pillow. See how the velvet is draped down on each side of his head. Do you suppose he was sick?"

Tara looked back at the painting. From the bed, so far across the room, the dust didn't show except as shadows on the child's face. It was a very thin face, forehead tapering to a sharp and pointed chin. The mouth was only a small, pinkish, nearly lipless hole in the white face. The eyes were the outstanding feature. Large, fiery, glaring yellow at her like the eyes of something from an old horror movie.

Slowly Tara answered, "He might have been. I wonder who he was?" She wished she hadn't uncovered it.

"I don't know." Amy was staring up at the face, and her voice was an absent whisper.

Tara's concern went suddenly to her. "Hey there, don't let it get you down. Maybe he just had a spell of pneumonia or something. In those days you know people had a lot of things, and maybe he was a little rich boy and wanted his portrait painted just because he had to stay in bed awhile and was bored to death. You know how it is when you're a lively kid and have to stay in bed."

"Oh sure. I guess, anyway." She turned away and sat down in the rocking chair. "I wish somebody would bring some of that wood up here so we could have a fire, don't you, Tara?"

"I'll bring it up myself," Tara said quickly. Anything to get busy for a while and make Amy happy again. "You sit tight and I'll have a fire going in no time."

She went down the back stairs, holding on carefully to the railing, but when she went back she went up the front stairs, both arms filled with wood from the kitchen hearth.

Amy was still in the chair, and it squeaked slowly and lazily as she rocked.

"Don't I sound just like an old-fashioned mother rocking her baby?" she asked Tara, smiling. "I like this room. I'm going to like it very much. And I will keep it after you leave." Anxiety flitted across her face, wiping away the smile. "You will stay awhile to help me, won't you, Tara? I've never taken care of a baby before in my life."

"Well, I have, and yes I'll stay until I can safely leave you. It won't take long. The main thing is lots of love and cuddling."

Tara bent to place the wood and to check to see if the flue were open, and then she struck a match to the broken kindling on the bottom.

"Tara," Amy asked bashfully, "you've never had a baby, have you?"

Tara laughed. "No. I worked as a helper in a hospital on my day off from my job as librarian. I don't know much about nursing, but I did pick up a little. Enough to know that you should go to a doctor. How about it, now that you're settled in your new home?"

"Tara, please. I'll be all right. Just please don't keep asking me. I have to do this the natural way. Okay?"

Tara drew a long breath and sat back on her heels to watch the kindling catch and begin to burn in a tiny bit of fire-life. Perhaps, she thought, it would be that way with the baby and Amy. Despite swollen ankles and eyes that looked tired and ill, perhaps the spark of life would catch and carry them on into strong life.

She stood up and dusted her hands and knees and used the towel to brush the hearth. She liked things clean and neat and had a feeling that this huge old untidy, hard-to-clean, falling-apart house would get to her before she could get away from it. Just trying to clean the thing would be enough to keep her mind, or at least her hands, well occupied for weeks to come, so that Amy and the baby would not be such a distressing situation to her.

"I think it's going to burn and you'll be as cozy as the proverbial bug in a rug."

Amy stopped rocking. "As what?"

"You know, a bug in a rug."

Amy laughed, and Tara saw that her face, in its delight, was truly beautiful. "I never heard that before. Tara, that's cute."

"Well, I didn't make it up, it's old as the hills. And that's another cliché. I'll bet this old rug has plenty of cozy inhabitants, don't you?" Tara said casually on her way to the door, following it immediately with, "Tell you what, you just sit there and rock and dream and watch the fire and when Sherwood comes back with food I'll bring yours on a tray. Yes, I even ordered a tray. Just for you. So you won't have to come down at all during your confinement. And another thing I ordered ..." She stopped in the doorway for just long enough to give Amy an impish glance. "A potty. We'll let Sherwood empty it."

She went on, laughing to herself as she thought of Sherwood emptying Amy's pot when the baby was born. Good enough for him, she thought. Let him know what life is really all about. Something besides sex and being top dog and humming along with rock music.

The stairway seemed darker than ever, and she knew she would have to get a light up to Amy before long. She heard the silence in the big house and, halfway down the steep back stairs, she heard the sound of cracking, splitting timbers somewhere above. She hoped it was on the third story.

Her heart speeded in sudden alert and she instinctively looked up at the ceiling, and saw with relief that it wasn't falling. Not yet. She hesitated, thinking of Amy. But the girl didn't call out, and the house became quiet again, so after a moment she went on down the stairs and through the darkening hall to the kitchen door.

Firelight from the burning wood sent long, dancing figures of light and shadow across the floor. They looked beautiful and friendly. She went to the fire quickly and sat on the rough little stool at the side of the hearth.

The frogs outside seemed louder than ever, but Tara began to feel her aloneness and even wished for Eldon and Giles to return. She twisted on her stool to watch the door, and as if in answer to her wish she heard the mumble of approaching voices, and then footsteps in the hall.

"We found it," Giles said, pleased as a little boy. "After I got to thinking about it I remembered that old well. It was covered over by a round lid of wood planks and had a handle you pulled up on. There used to be a top, I guess, but it had fallen. Anyway," he came close to the fire and squatted, and Eldon did the same, leaning his elbow on Tara's knee, "we found it".

"Then where's the water?" Tara asked.

"We have to have a bucket. The old rope is still there, but there's no bucket."

"Oh sure," Tara said. "As Leda says all the time, *dumb*. Of me."

Eldon said, "It's a good strong rope, looks a century old, but it will still draw water. Did you order a pail?"

"Yes." Tara moved slightly, as if the fire had gotten too warm for her, but mainly to slip Eldon's arm off her knee. She got up to walk to the window. "I wish he'd come on, it's getting dark."

"Not really. The sun has gone behind the trees is all," Giles said. "Twilight lasts awhile here."

"Anyway, the house is dark. Oh, Giles, I forgot to ask, but there's something about the upstairs hall." Tara came back from the window to stand looking down at Giles. "Does that floor slope or is it my imagination?"

"Slope?" he repeated, in the almost stupid way he had at times.

"Yes. You know. The front part looks definitely uphill to me, as if the back of the house is sinking. Or was it built that way?"

"Gosh. I don't know. I hadn't noticed."

Eldon was looking at the kitchen floor. "If that one is sinking then this would also sink, right? It doesn't look off to me. Let's test it."

He went to the cupboard side of the kitchen, took a coin from his pocket, bent and set the coin carefully on its edge. It slowly began to roll toward the other side of the room. After a couple of feet it fell to its side and lay still.

"It is a little off," he said. After a moment he picked up the coin. "It might have been built that way, or the back could be settling."

He didn't sound very concerned about it, and came back to the fire to sit cross-legged in front of it. Giles was still looking at the floor, and Tara could see that he was disturbed. There was something about Giles that was childlike, she thought, and though she didn't approve of his life-style, she felt he was somehow not totally responsible.

"It's probably nothing," she said, and thought of the falling third story. But she kept that thought to herself. And then she heard the abrupt silence of the frogs, and the soft murmur of a car.

"Sherwood," she said. "At last. At least I hope it's Sherwood. You guys go see, and he'll be wanting you to bring stuff in. In fact, he'll probably be so mad about all the stuff he had to buy that he'll be more like a grizzly than ever."

They went out hurriedly, and just as she had suspected, Sherwood came in looking like a storm cloud.

"What the hell did you want, the whole town?" He dropped three sacks of groceries onto the table. "To get the stuff you ordered I'd have to have a truck. Or a whole fleet of the damned things. Cook now, will you?"

He went out again and Tara began to dig into the bags of groceries. She saw with satisfaction that he had at least gotten part of what she had ordered. When they brought in the large iron skillet she settled it on the metal frame over the fire and put the steaks on to cook.

Giles stood behind her, loaded with blankets. "Where do you want these?"

"I'll show you in just a minute."

The three men stood waiting while she placed candles in holders and lighted them. On top of the blankets she lay several unlighted candles, and their holders, and cautioned Giles to not drop them. With a lighted candle in each hand, she started to lead the way out of the kitchen.

She noticed that Leda was still not among them.

"Where's Leda?" she asked Sherwood.

He snorted. "Where do you think? In the car. Says she's not coming in this house."

"Not even to eat?"

He shrugged and nodded impatiently toward the door. "Just move it along, all right? You're too damned bossy and nosy to suit me. I'd like to get some rest before I eat. I've been on the damned road for several days and nights."

"Who hasn't?" Tara retorted, turning on to lead the way up the back stairs.

The minute he came out into the upper hall Sherwood spotted the faint light from the fireplace in Amy's room. "What's that? I thought you didn't have any lights."

"That's a fireplace. That is Amy's and my room."

Eldon demanded sharply, "Whose?"

To Tara's surprise Sherwood laughed again, as if Eldon's disapproval was the only thing he could find funny about any of it. "You heard her. Hers and Amy's."

"What about me?" Eldon asked.

"There's about forty bedrooms," Tara replied angrily. "You take your choice. You can light your own candles, too, and make your own beds. Don't expect me to do it for you."

She had intended to help them, but Eldon's attitude, plus Sherwood's vicious enjoyment of it, changed her mind. She went to the door of the room where Amy was. They came crowding behind her.

Eldon began grumbling. "I don't see why you have to—"

"Oh, shut up," Sherwood said. "So they got the best room in the house. You didn't need a fireplace anyway."

Tara went on in, ignoring them. Amy was still rocking, and the firelight touched her face with pink on one side and soft shadows on the other.

"Hello, everyone," she said. "Isn't it a lovely room?"

Tara placed the two candles on the mantle, on each side of the painting, and then reached for the blankets in Giles' arms.

"You'll have to get more blankets for yourselves," she said. After tossing the two blankets onto the mattress, she held the rest of the candles to the tiny flames, lit them, and lined them neatly along the mantle. She had expected from the men an explosion of sorts about the blankets, but heard nothing. Puzzled, she turned to look at them. All three stood looking up at the painting.

Amy began to talk in a voice soft and pleasant. "See, isn't it a lovely place to have the baby? It was even a child's room. And look, Sherwood, there's the peace sign on the bottom of the painting. That's a very good omen, isn't it, Sherwood?"

Sherwood acted as if he hadn't heard her. Slowly he went closer to the painting, a scowl deepening between his heavy brows. Tara saw uneasily that it was not an expression of disapproval, but something else. Intense concentration. For a long while he looked at the name on the bottom of the painting, and at the horizontal bar with the inverted V. Finally he picked up one of the candles, held it close and with his finger rubbed the mark.

"That's no peace sign," he finally said.

For a reason that was unfathomable to Tara, no one spoke. She realized that she was holding her breath. It seemed as if everyone in the room was holding his breath. As if the whole house had grown still and ceased to breathe and move with the changing world. Listening now. Just listening.

"That sign," said Sherwood, withdrawing his finger, "has no circle around it, and it was made a long time ago. That's no peace sign, Amy, that's the sign of the devil."

Still no one breathed. Then after a moment Amy drew a long breath and began to rock again. The chair squeaked slowly and lazily, and somewhere in the upper part of the house a faint sound of groaning wood sounded like ancient, evil, satisfied chuckles. Tara shivered. It had listened, and it had heard, and it was pleased.

"That's ridiculous!" Tara said, speaking as much to her own thoughts as to Sherwood. "Signs are signs, they don't really mean that much. If Amy sees in it a peace sign, then it's a peace sign."

Amy didn't say anything, nor did Sherwood. He had moved the candle so that the name was clear and black in its small print.

"Samael," he said aloud. "Do you know what Samael means?"

Tara guessed he was speaking to her since no one else answered him, and after a wary hesitation, she asked, "No. What?"

"It's one of many names for the devil. Satan."

Tara glanced quickly at Amy, and saw that she was sitting very still, staring up at the painting.

"Well, whoever painted that," said Tara, "had some twisted sense of humor, I would say." She didn't want it to upset Amy, but so far the girl was showing almost no reaction. A kind of quiet curiosity, perhaps. She kept looking at the painting.

"No," Sherwood said in the same strange voice that had all at once lost its domineering quality. "It wasn't the painter. See, it's done in some kind of black ink."

Eldon asked, "Somebody playing a trick, maybe?" Sherwood walked toward the door, carrying two of the candles. He snorted, going back to his natural bullyish sarcasm. "Maybe. But I can tell you for sure I ain't fightin' for this room. The girls can have it, and as long as they stay in it they're sure as hell safe from me."

Tara looked at the doorway through which he went, watching the candlelight fade as it flickered on the opposite wall. The other men moved quickly, took candles and followed him. Tara attempted a laugh, and it sounded quite normal even to her own ears.

"Well, that might be worth something."

Amy still didn't speak and Tara turned to face her and saw that the girl was staring at the bottom of the painting, her mouth open, as if she had become entranced. Tara started toward her, but then Amy sighed and began to rock again.

"He could be wrong," she said softly, her voice lowered almost to a whisper. "Couldn't he, Tara? It could be a peace sign."

"Yes, of course." But suddenly Tara wanted to get out of the room too. "Say, I'll bet the steak is done, if not completely burned, so how would you like to come down and eat in the kitchen?"

Amy's face was calm and composed. "But you said you'd bring it on a tray. Don't you want to? If it's not too much trouble I'd really like that. Just this once. It makes me feel pampered."

"All right, Amy, if you'd rather. I don't mind at all."

She took one of the candles and held it carefully, her hand cupped over the flame to keep it from blinking out and leaving her stranded halfway down the stairs. When she reached the kitchen she saw the three men sitting at the table, and over by the hearth, on the stool, was Leda. Tara put down her candle and very deliberately smiled at Leda.

"What brought you in?"

Leda gave her a quick, sullen glare, and turned her eyes back to the fire.

From the table came Sherwood's voice in squeaky imitation of a woman's. "Them little bitty frogs out there might just gobble her right up."

Tara saw that someone had turned the steaks and that they had about reached perfection. She didn't ask for help. Doing it herself kept her busy, and she didn't stop to eat until she had taken a tray up to Amy. By then, with help of a lantern Sherwood had thought to buy on his own, the men had brought in water, clothing, and the rest of the supplies.

After the others had gone upstairs with their bedding, Tara took a brief warm bath. When she went up to bed she took a pail of warm water for Amy, washcloths and towels, but Amy was already sound asleep, rolled in a blanket on one side of the bed.

Tara started to put out her candle, changed her mind and placed it on the mantle instead, and then followed Amy. She wrapped a warm blanket around herself and lay down on the other side of the bed, her back to Amy, her face toward the door.

The painting was in sight, its strange eyes, lighted by the candles, glowing into the room—directly at her, it seemed. She knew just enough about portraits to have heard they often seemed to follow you with their eyes, no matter where you were, and she was almost directly in front of it anyway.

It occurred to her suddenly that Sherwood must have been right about the sign, and it had not been intended as a peace symbol after all. The peace sign was a recent symbol, and the mark on the painting was very, very old, dating probably from the middle of the last century.

The thought was surprisingly disturbing. She snuggled down into her blanket, cold, wishing she had gotten another, heavier one. Then, to get her mind away from the face and the small black print beneath it, she turned onto her stomach and closed her eyes.

CHAPTER 5

Eldon twisted on the saggy smelly bed in the room next to Tara's, tried to get comfortable in the blanket, and wished he had something he could hit. The bitch. The impudent, beautiful, sexy *bitch.* Always on the move. He hated women who were always busy, always cleaning, or walking, or talking, or, if nothing else, sleeping. Women you couldn't catch with a fishnet, unless you resorted to rape. And sometimes the idea was a pleasant one. Make her yell. Get some kind of emotion out of her, anyway.

He wished he hadn't put out the flame of his skinny little candle. What window he had was covered with vines and the room was so goddamned dark he couldn't see the end of his nose. If he had a match he'd get up and light the candle, but Sherwood had a thing about smoking, so Eldon didn't even carry matches. Hell.

He turned over and wondered what Tara would do if he went into her room and pulled her by the hair of her head out of bed and down the hall and onto his saggy mattress and ... The thought nearly choked him. He pounded the mattress with his fist, and smelled the dusty, musty stink of it. In his mind he could see the small cloud of dust rising into his face.

He turned his back to that spot, flopping over with anger and frustration, kicking at the tight roll of blanket. The room wasn't all that cold.

Under him the rusty old springs sounded like something from another world, screaming in agony. He gave them a good hard bounce, just to hear them complain. And he hoped Tara heard it and was scared. Scared enough to come running to him. Ha.

Yeah, ha, ha. Some chance.

Laughter came through the noise of the squeaking springs, a kind of soft, faraway, fine-voiced laughter. A woman messing around with a man? Say like Tara and Sherwood? Sometimes, the way Sherwood looked at Tara, and the way he let her boss him around ...

He listened harder. The laughter came and went, so hard to hear, mixed in with another sound, like the splintering of a board, and it didn't come from down the hall, it was above, on the third story. Maybe it hadn't been laughter at all.

It was gone then, and he knew that it wasn't Tara. And it wasn't the others, either. Not Amy, not Leda. There was someone else in the house.

He threw back the blanket and stumbled a few feet in the darkness, pausing to curse under his breath. He didn't even know which direction the goddamned door was in. He had never been any good at directions, anyway, even when the sun was up and shining he couldn't tell east from west.

And where was Sherwood? Somewhere down the hall. With his lantern, the stingy sonofabuck.

Something creaked above, as if someone walked on old loose boards, and Eldon knew he had to find his door if he had to crawl over every square inch of floor because Sherwood had to know they were not in the house alone. Who the hell was up there?

He found the wall after banging his shin against something that hurt like crazy, and finally, by walking his hands along the wall, he found the door. He stood for a moment, trying to remember whether Tara's room was to his right or left. It had to be to the right, because his had been the first one along the hall. He was the closest one to the back stairs, which was probably why he heard the sounds on the floor above and no one else seemed to.

He began to move along the hall to the right, found Tara's door—closed, of course—and went on walking as softly as he could on the wood floor. Locating Sherwood then was no trouble. Snores guided him. But of course he had to be about forty feet away, and across on the other side of the hall as well. As he left the wall and felt through the darkness with his hands he wondered vaguely if Leda and Giles were both with him. It didn't matter. The important thing was to find out who was upstairs. Of course he would probably catch double hell for not going up in the daylight to investigate the third story, but ...

He found the door, and opened it.

"Sherwood!" he hissed through his teeth, feeling toward the sound of the snores. "Sherwood! Wake up, damn it!" Snorts, sputters, bedsprings squalling, and finally voices, too loud. Too nerve-wrackingly loud. "Huh? What?" And even Leda. "What's the matter?"

Eldon hurried toward the sound of their voices, his own voice hissing at them again. "Shut up, for God's sake!" He found the bed and felt around. Sherwood's hand flung his away.

"What the hell you doin', man?"

Giles' voice came sleepily from the other side of the bed, "Huh?"

"*Listen,*" Eldon whispered. "There's somebody upstairs."

A moment of silence, and then Leda murmured, sounding scared, "Sherwood!"

Sherwood asked in an undertone, his voice calm and awake, "How do you know?"

"I heard it. Them. My room is at the end of the hall, by the back stairs, and I heard someone—what I thought was someone laughing up there. And then I heard someone walking. I think someone's been up there all this time. Spying on us, probably."

Just as he had expected, Sherwood asked furiously, "Well, why the devil didn't you check that out this afternoon?" He began getting out of bed, and the scratch of a match was followed by a faint glow of light.

The most welcome sight Eldon had ever seen. He watched Sherwood get out of bed, long and white in his nudity. He watched him light the lantern, and then pull on jeans.

Sherwood turned toward the bed and gave a sharp, low command. "Giles, get your britches on. You're the one who knows this crazy house, not me."

"I'm not going up there!" Giles replied. "Not alone! No sir."

"You will if I tell you to. Anyway, I didn't say *alone*. All three of us will go."

Leda scampered out of bed on all fours, as if she had been stung on the rear. Looking at her, not as desirable as Tara, but at least available, Eldon wished to solve a couple of problems with one whack. But he didn't know if Sherwood would take to it or not.

"Uh—" he said, "I'll stay here and keep Leda from being scared. She can't go up there."

Sherwood gave him a sideways glance and a one-sided smirk of a grin. "You can screw her when we get back. Come on, you're not gettin' out of this."

Eldon sighed and followed Sherwood and the lantern toward the door and the hall. Behind him came the soft, bare steps of the other two.

In the hall Sherwood stopped and held up the lantern. The light showed dark walls and a high ceiling and the faraway dark end of the hall. Sherwood's voice came in a whisper.

"Listen now."

Frogs outside, singing even more than in the daytime, it seemed, and other sounds that came from the swamp. A cry, far far away. An animal caught, or a bird calling, dying.

Giles whispered, "Bobcat screaming."

"Shh," said Sherwood. "We don't care what's outside. I don't hear nothin' inside."

Neither did Eldon. The house was absolutely silent. Too silent.

Still whispering, Sherwood asked, "Did you really hear something or was you dreamin'?"

"I hadn't even gone to sleep, so how the hell could I be dreaming?"

"With your brain that'd be easy," Sherwood answered, but immediately asked, "Did you check to see if Red was in her own bed?"

"No."

"Well, why didn't you? It was probably her, trying to get something started, if I know her, and I think I do. That woman's not satisfied to leave anything alone. Let's see if she's in bed."

They went quickly along the hall and without hesitation Sherwood opened the door of Tara's room. The fire on the hearth had dwindled to a small pile of coals, but on the mantle two candles still burned. The first thing Eldon saw, as he looked over Sherwood's shoulder, was Tara, sitting up, leaning on her elbow, looking at them, blinking, obviously bewildered. And the second thing was the eyes of the painting by the candles. They glowed brighter than the candlelight and were looking straight at him. He felt them like the darts of a physical pierce, and he backed into the hall, pushing Leda and Giles behind him.

Sherwood too backed out, and shut the door.

"That creepy room," he said. "First thing I'd do is burn that picture with them creepy eyes. Where you sleepin', Fox?"

"Here. Next door."

Sherwood led the way again, passed the room Eldon had indicated, and went through the door into the vestibule of the stairway. He started to go up, went three steps and stopped, looking up at the middle of the steps, broken, and at the railing, broken too for at least six feet before it again went intact into the darkness far above.

"Steps broke clear through," Sherwood said. He looked up toward the top and was silent for a moment. Then he asked softly, "Where's the front stairs, Giles?"

"I told you, there aren't any."

"No front stairs to the third floor?"

"No. Just this one is all."

"That's crazy as hell." Sherwood twisted around to look down at them. "Then there's nobody up there. If there is, how did they get there? They didn't use these stairs. Fox, I think you got bugs in your head."

He came down and was on his way out when Eldon came to and hurried after the light. He hadn't thought about how whoever it was had gotten up there, and now he was wondering if the sounds he had heard had come from somewhere else, or if it had been an animal of some kind in the walls and in the rooms above.

He caught up with the group at his door, where they stopped.

With unusual consideration, Sherwood asked, "Fox, you want her to sleep with you the rest of the night?" Then he smiled and Eldon saw that the consideration had its usual maliciousness behind it. "Since your sexy redhead won't?"

He had hit the sore spot, as he had been aiming for. Eldon replied angrily, "No thanks. I'll wait for my own girl."

Sherwood went on down the hall, laughing, followed by the two who shared his bed. And after a moment Eldon realized that he was being left in the dark.

Calling Sherwood every dirty name he could think of, but safely, under his breath, he felt his way into his room, slammed the door, hand-walked around the wall until he came to his bed and then, tense with fury, fell on it.

Aloud he said, "Damn Amy for getting herself knocked up!" And damn Sherwood for that crazy fool idea of his that a pregnant woman shouldn't be touched when she got so big you could see the baby kick.

Finally Eldon went to sleep.

He woke in the morning feeling like a misplaced polar bear. But then, above the stink of the house, came the smell of coffee and frying bacon.

He got out of bed, pulled on yesterday's clothes, and stumbled out and down the stairs. And nearly fell. He grabbed the railing, cussed the steps for being so steep, heard the railing crack somewhere along its length, patted it tenderly and murmured a couple of words of encouragement, and went on down. Carefully.

Everybody sat at the table, even Amy. Tara was luscious and beautiful in a green outfit that set to perfection her copper-bright hair and faintly freckled clear complexion. She smiled at him, and his spirits leaped.

"The man of leisure," she said.

He gave her a pointed look which he hoped she caught and understood. "I didn't exactly sleep too well last night."

"Well," she replied, "I wish you had, because you just about scared me to death."

Sherwood sneered. "He was hearing boogymen last night. Or witches or something."

Tara, still smiling, raised slanted brows. In contrast to her hair and skin they were a dark brownish-black, as were her lashes. It was the rain on her lashes that he had noticed first about her, and on looking twice, and three times, he had decided the lashes were natural. A rare thing.

She said, "Was that why you were all looking for me? Do you think I turn into a witch on the stroke of midnight or something?"

Sherwood said, "I wouldn't be a bit surprised."

Tara laughed, her head tipped back, her white teeth showing for a moment. It only made Eldon want to kiss her. To sink himself into her smoothness and beauty.

His voice came out a growl. "How about some coffee and food for me? I'm the one who didn't sleep." He glared over at Sherwood. What was the bastard trying to do, take his woman? Once upon a time this share-and-share-alike business had seemed just the thing to him, but now, where Tara was concerned, he felt he should have first rights.

He'd have to talk to Sherwood about that.

There was another thing about Tara he liked, he discovered after breakfast. She didn't ask anyone to help with the dishes, sweep the floor, or anything but to get water and wood. "Get water," she said. And the way she said it made everybody know they'd better do it or else.

Sherwood, of course, just sat there, repeating what she had already said, "Get water. Get wood," looking at Eldon and then at Giles.

That was the part Eldon didn't like. He didn't mind getting the water and wood for Tara, he just was getting fed up with being ordered about by Sherwood. "It doesn't take two of us," he said. "You get it, Giles."

And Giles got up, saying in his slow, mild way, "Where's the buckets?"

Eldon watched Tara as she moved about the room. With a soapy, wet rag she stretched to wash the higher window panes, and finally, unable to reach the top, and without asking for help, she got the hearth stool and stood on it. When she stretched her blouse separated from her slacks and the midriff of her body was white and smooth. His hands trembled to grab her and pull her down.

He noticed that Sherwood was staring at him. And then Sherwood nodded toward the door, a silent command to accompany him outside. For a moment Eldon refused to move. What was eating Sherwood? Couldn't he sit and look at his own woman, for Christ's sake?

Another, jerkier nod from Sherwood brought Eldon to his feet. He went without speaking toward the kitchen door, and on out into the sunlight.

The air was a little fresher, anyway, though a lot warmer. And he did have to go to the toilet somewhere. There were a couple of old two-hole affairs built onto the back of the garage, but Eldon didn't bother to go in. Let the girls fight the spider webs if they wanted to hide in a stinking building. Though he had to admit it didn't smell as bad as the house. He saw that someone, probably Giles, had hacked a path through the vines to one of the toilets.

Sherwood was right behind him, his boots crunching the vines as he walked.

"Get rid of her," he said.

Eldon forgot everything else. "Huh?" Sherwood's eyes were narrowed and serious.

"You heard me. Get rid of her," Sherwood repeated.

"Why?"

"You know why, damn it. She's not one of us, and she never will be. Do you know what will happen if she finds out where that money come from? Do you know? She'd turn you in so fast you wouldn't know what hit you."

"No, she wouldn't, Sherwood." Eldon found himself pleading, approaching Sherwood with both hands out, practically ready to cower on his knees and beg for her life if he had to. "She's not leaving. She's not going anywhere. She likes the house, you can see that yourself! She's a natural homemaker, Sherwood, and we need her. What the hell would we do without her? You want to eat Leda's cooking again? Come on, Sherwood, give her a chance. We can keep her here. She's my woman."

Sherwood snorted. "She's your woman like a wild stallion is your tame little horse. You ain't bedded her down once, I'll lay you ten to one. Have you?"

"Uh—she takes time, that's all. I was about to get her when this all come about. Look—give her a chance. I'll make her, if I have to break hell out of her, but I'm not going to kill her."

"You're a fool. I always thought so, now I *know* it. If you ain't got the guts to do it, I will." His narrowed eyes looked toward the black water of the swamp. "Gettin' rid of her body'd be a cinch here. Nobody'd ever know she was gone."

"But she doesn't even know, Sherwood!"

"Fox," Sherwood asked without emotion, "you want to spend the rest of your life in prison?"

Eldon grimaced, remembering five years of that hell. Bars before his eyes, like something in a nightmare.

Sherwood coldly continued, "You been in and out all your life, ain't you? Orphanages, detention homes, jails, prisons. You remember that, old boy, and think if you want her more than you want your freedom. And when the day comes that she tries to leave here, for any reason, if you ain't got her tamed, you'd better stick that knife of yours in her back, because if you don't, I will."

Eldon returned Sherwood's stare for a moment, and then dropped his gaze to the deep green of the vines. Sherwood wasn't fooling around, he knew that. He meant exactly what he said. If Tara didn't come down off the pedestal she had put herself on, if she didn't marry herself into the group, she was through. If she tried to leave, she was through. And he knew if he had to make the choice it would be in favor of his own neck, not hers. His freedom, not hers. His. That meant more to him than anything in the world.

He watched Sherwood walk away, without really seeing him, and left alone he too began to walk, going through the vines and evil-looking weeds behind the garage. The forest of the swamp was there, so near, and the ground began to feel mushy under his feet. He stopped, looking ahead at the water reflecting green foliage above, and floating green and brown and blackish plant life, and animal life too, obviously, from the noise of the frogs. They sounded so close, yet nowhere were they visible. Something about it, this place that was so alien to anything he had ever seen, was wrong. Reversed. Invisible creatures that made a racket that reverberated through your brain until you felt like pounding it with your hands, and other, visible things that stood as silent as death itself. Sherwood was right. A body pushed into that black world would never be found by anyone.

Eldon turned back toward the house. The stink of it was easier to take than the strangeness of the outdoors.

HE SAT on the bench and watched Tara wash dishes, wash one portion of the cupboard, and put the dishes away. He would have liked to talk to her but she seemed unaware of his presence. Besides, Sherwood sat on the floor, leaning back against the wall, part of the time playing a kind of tickling game with Leda, and part of the time also watching Tara. But his ears were tuned full blast, Eldon knew. They always were. Farther away, Giles also sat, but his nose was buried in a magazine. There was no danger in Giles hearing anything when he was bent into a mag. It was that way with Giles. Sometimes Eldon wished he could lose himself in a mess of words the way Giles did, but he couldn't stand the things.

Tara washed the cooking pot and then began to wash vegetables. And finally she began looking through the cupboard again, into the drawer where she had put the flat-ware. She stood back, her hands on her hips.

"I'll be damned," she said, and Eldon felt a touch of surprise. Though she could get hot and heavy with the words, they were always of a very proper order. Victorian proper. Even Sherwood and Leda stopped playing around and looked at her. Only Giles seemed not to hear.

"Do you know what I forgot?" she asked, looking at Sherwood. "I forgot to order a paring knife, and I can't peel potatoes with one of these. Is it okay if I run into town with the car and—"

Sherwood interrupted that one in a hurry. "Boil 'em in their jackets and I'll get you a knife the next time."

"I don't want to boil them in their jackets," she said firmly, her hands still on her hips, her voice emphasizing each word clearly. "If I did, I would have. I'm making a decent stew, and I want the vegetables peeled for a change! I see no reason why—"

"Okay!" Sherwood yelled. "Peel the bastards. Fox, give her your knife."

Eldon pulled his knife out of his pocket and tossed it across the room at her just to see if she could catch it. She moved quickly, and caught it. He laughed.

"Good catch, Flowerchild."

Sherwood said, "Don't call her that. I told you, you sound like a goddamned hippie."

Tara was looking at the large, slightly bowed knife. She turned it, puzzled. Her attitude amused Eldon and made him feel good. For the first time in several days he felt a touch of superiority. She was only a woman after all. Not like Leda, who knew knives forward and backward too.

"Just push the button," he said. "But watch it, or you might stick yourself."

She touched the button with her thumb, gingerly, and jumped when the blade shot out. Everyone laughed at her then, and even Giles looked up.

"Good grief," Tara said. "I'd be afraid to carry that thing around in my pocket if I were you. What if you accidentally pushed it?"

"Well," said Eldon, "you'd have a hole in your pocket, for one thing."

She was still looking at it, and her small, self-amused smile disappeared. "I'm supposed to peel vegetables with this? It's rusty. You sure don't take very good care—" With her fingernail she scratched at the knife blade, and quickly she said, "Why, that's not rust, that's dried blood!"

Eldon felt the warmth leave his face, and he knew he had turned as white as the tee shirt he wore. He remembered now, for the first time, that he had forgotten to wash it. He had only leaned down and wiped it off on the woman's dress where she lay on the plush carpets of the den. He could feel Sherwood's eyes on him as if they were twin blades of another knife.

Leda said softly in disgust, *"Dumb!"*

And Tara, still looking at the knife, made a face. "What on earth did you cut with it?"

Eldon couldn't answer. Thoughts stuck in his brain, and words somewhere in the middle of his chest. He looked hastily at Sherwood, and saw the fury there. But only for a brief moment. Sherwood looked at Tara then, got to his feet, took from his pocket his own knife and went to Tara.

"Here," he said. "I'll trade you. Mine at least is clean. Fox here's not very neat sometimes. He cut some meat for the pot once."

Sherwood didn't bother to close the knife Tara gave him but turned to face Eldon and with one short, deft movement of the wrist sent the knife through the air. Eldon sat paralyzed. The knife went into the floor at his feet, barely an inch away, and stood quivering, only its tip sunk into the old, hard wood of the floor.

In a low, controlled voice, Sherwood said, "You oughta know better than to offer our cook a dirty knife."

Eldon pulled the knife out of the floor, released the blade and got out of the room as quickly and unobtrusively as he could. His hand shook so hard that he missed his pocket on the first try. The second try pocketed the knife safely. Without planning he went down the hall to the stairs and climbed them, and then shut himself in his room.

For a while he sat on his bed, brooding, searching for excuses to clear himself for not cleaning his knife. Sherwood wouldn't forget it. Not likely to, at any rate.

A sound above, a low groan of old wood moving, brought back to his mind the night before and the laughter he had heard that had sounded so human. And the footsteps. If someone really were there, hiding, and he could prove it to Sherwood, smell them out, Sherwood might forget the knife business.

He sat straight, considering. There might not be anybody there at all, and if he called Sherwood to help him look it would only make Sherwood madder. If he could manage to get up there alone though ... He wasn't afraid of people. Not when he had that knife ready in his hand. If he took off his shoes he could sneak up on whoever was there, and prove a few things.

At least, there was no harm in trying, and nothing else to do in this place anyway.

He got out of the shoes quickly, and shut the door when he left his room. That was so Sherwood wouldn't pass by and wonder what the hell his shoes were doing there when he wasn't.

He stepped onto the stairs as lightly as he could and looked up into the semidarkness of the third-story vestibule. The middle steps were gone completely, or so it seemed from where he stood. He moved upward, pressed against the wall, testing the second, third, fourth steps. They held, and he climbed slowly until he could look down into the black hole of the broken stairway. Boards fallen, too far down to pull up. But part of the stairs, a support of some kind about the size of the end of a two-by-four, was still solidly nailed to the wall about four feet away. If he was careful, and if the next solid step above would hold him, he could make it.

With his back pressed to the wall and his arms spread and held tightly, his palms grasping at the bare wall, he stepped forward onto the end of the two-by-four. And there he stood. In order to get the other leg around he would have to turn completely, which was impossible.

He backed up, feeling as stupid as Sherwood had always said he was, and tried to figure it out. One *bleeping* place to put one foot between there and hell. The whole thing made him want to quit and go back and say to the devil with it.

But there was the fact of the knife.

He tried again, facing the wall, and twisting his right leg awkwardly past his left so that he could manage to set his heel onto the top of the board. Then, hanging to the wall, he moved his other foot and stretched desperately for the next step. And made it.

Barely.

He hung insecurely against the wall, his right heel on the board, and the toes of his left foot grasping the edge of a step that could easily go down under his weight.

He thought about it for a moment, then decided what the hell, all that would happen was he'd fall down into the pit of the broken stairway, and if he did fall all he'd have to do was yell and they'd come and help him out. Out of the frying pan into the fire, maybe, but at least out. It was a chance worth taking.

He made a one-sided, slithering leap, and went face down on the rising stairway. His fingers grasped the edge of something, and for a moment the whole stairway sounded as if it were going down, but then it stopped shaking and was still.

With satisfaction he rose to his feet.

A glance backward showed him what he had missed, and from the higher elevation the hole looked dark and treacherous. And much too close for comfort. Walking lightly, shaking the unsteady stairway as little as possible, he went on up.

The small room in which he stood was almost identical to the one at the bottom of the stairs, except where the third-story stairway had risen there was only a door. Closed. All the doors were closed except one, and it hung crooked on its hinges, about six inches open, and through it came a bit of filtered light in which floated specks of dust rising from his own steps.

There was silence, but he felt a sense of impending disaster, as if at any moment the roof would cave in. Specks of lint floated down from cracks between drooping ceiling boards.

He looked down, and his heart skipped and then began to thud in excitement. Footprints, other than his own. Instinctively he pulled his knife from his pocket and flipped out the blade. Crouching, he looked closely at the footprints.

They led toward the partly opened door, and had been made by someone wearing shoes. Quite large shoes. A man. Another set of prints came back toward the stairs, but they were obscured and spaced farther apart, as if the man had been running. He looked for other, smaller steps, but found none. There had to be a woman. Or was the man a crazy nut of some kind? A maniac?

Eldon slowly straightened, cautious and on guard, the knife blade held before him, ready. The laugh last night, yes, it could have been caused by a crazy guy. And what other kind would be hiding up in this hole?

He moved silently toward the door, and touched the knob to lift it, to keep it from making a racket. It squealed like a human with a knife in his belly.

He stopped, listening. No sound. Just a kind of soft moving of the house, as if it had settled again in another position. Eldon crept forward and peeped into the twilight-lit hall. It was just like the one downstairs, except all the bedroom doors stood open and there were no branching halls. The dust on the floor was disturbed everywhere by the footprints leading in and out of every room.

There was no way to tell which room the man was in, or what kind of weapon he had while he stood waiting. Listening.

Waiting.

Eldon had never been a coward. Not when he had his knife. He had cut his way out of more fights than he could remember, but in all that time he had never felt so defenseless. He almost backed up to go back downstairs and tell Sherwood someone was there. But that would mean he had lost his nerve.

He swallowed the funny knot that gathered in his throat and went slowly on, walking through the first door on his left. One swift glance, and then a long, deliberate look around showed him that the room was occupied only by an old iron bedstead with springs. No mattress, no tables, no chairs. One narrow window let in enough light to reveal that the man with the shoes had walked in, circled, and come out again. Eldon backed up and went to the next room.

The same. The man in the shoes had walked in, farther than Eldon did, circled, and come out again. And it was the same in the next room, and the next, and the next. Some rooms he skipped, and so did Eldon.

At the end of the hall Eldon faced a surprise. A banister, and over the banister, a pit. And in the pit, to his growing wonder and bewilderment, a curved stairway, lighted by a long window above it. He leaned over, looking, and saw why there had seemed to be no front stairway. It ended against a wall. A solid wall of dark boards. He drew back and faced the way he had come, puzzled.

The footsteps. It almost looked as if the man had done the same thing he was doing. As if he too had stood leaning over the banister. As if he had simply gone through the rooms, looking for someone.

He had covered the rooms the man had gone into, and found them similar. He still had the ones on his right.

He started forward, then hesitated, noticing from this new perspective the direction of the steps that had gone before him. They had gone into almost every room on one side of the hall, but into only one on the other side. The first room. The prints went in, and came out running.

Eldon stared at them, confused, uneasy, one big question stirring in his mind. Why? Why hadn't the man looked into any of the other rooms?

Another thought occurred to him then. If the man was there at all, he was in the one room on the right, this last room into which he had walked and out of which he had run. Yet how could that be?

The house moved again, timbers cracking somewhere above and to the left, and Eldon stepped aside just in time to miss being struck on the head by a large wad of something gray-black. It floated to the floor and settled, like a gigantic dust mote, and the house groaned softly into silence.

Eldon looked at the thing on the floor, half expecting it to look back at him. But it was only dust, dirt, mold, or whatever gathered in and between ancient old boards.

He walked on his toes around it and looked into the room.

The difference was immediately apparent. It was a nursery. Ragged, rotted lace curtains still hung at the windows, and in the corner stood the cradle, the lace that had once covered it also hanging in gray-green strings. Eldon almost laughed. A nursery, and the man had run from it?

He stepped across the threshold and went boldly into the room. Tall bureaus, tables with lamps, even a mother's rocking chair. Nothing to run from.

He noticed then that one corner of the ceiling had dropped low into the room, and its debris was still spilling, slowly, like black snowflakes from a dark sky. Oddly, a rope hung from one of the falling boards, its end lost in the heap of boards, old clothing and trash that lay in the corner. Somebody, he thought, hadn't kept the nursery very neat. But then somebody had also closed up the front stairway.

He started to look away, to go on with a natural curiosity to investigate the room, when his attention was abruptly drawn back to the ceiling. It was moving. And the floor was moving under his feet. And the thing that scared him and turned him cold with sweat that stood out on his skin was the silence. The room was moving and there was no sound.

An earthquake! The whole goddamned house was tilting, sliding, going down, slowly, its silence changing into the groan and splinter of tearing apart, of ripping of boards somewhere in the depths of the house. He turned and grasped the door frame to pull himself away from the falling room, and saw the hallway slanting away from him, and knew he had to get out, now. Now.

He ran, his breath caught in his throat, fighting at the debris that was thickening in the air. He reached the vestibule at the top of the back stairs, saw the steps still hung to the shaking wall, but he didn't have time for caution.

He crouched briefly and tried to leap across the black hole in the stairway. A chance. Just one chance to get out.

And he missed.

He knew for a second that he was falling into the black hole, and then he knew nothing.

He heard them from a long way off, soft voices close by, but the pain in his head made him want to scream. He raised one arm, and touched someone's hand. Consciousness returned suddenly and he opened his eyes and looked up info Tara's face.

"He'll be all right," a man said.

Sherwood.

They were all there, looking down at him, and Tara was trying to put a cold cloth on his forehead. He pushed her hand away and sat up, looking in amazement at the room. "Are we still in the *house*?"

"Sure," said Sherwood, and added, "That crack on the head got to him."

The pain screamed in Eldon's ears, but he shouted above it, "The house fell! There was a goddamned earthquake, didn't you feel it?"

They didn't even answer, they only stared at him. Then Tara moved toward him again, the cloth in her hand. Her voice was so soft and low that he could hardly hear it above the pain.

"Lie back, Eldon, and let me bathe your forehead. You've got a lump on it, that's all, and it will be all right in a few minutes."

Sherwood asked in his disgusted tone of voice, "What the hell did you fall into that stairway hole for? Couldn't you see you couldn't get up them stairs? Couldn't you see them steps was gone?"

Eldon held Tara's wrist in his hand so that he could see Sherwood.

"The upstairs fell!" he shouted. "The house is falling! We've got to get out of here!" He looked around, saw that he was in his own saggy bed, in his own bedroom, and it looked just as it had when he'd left it. They all thought he was lying. Or else they were lying to him. "Didn't you feel the house falling? Didn't you—"

He stopped, cut off by Sherwood turning away to leave the room.

"Oh, hell," Sherwood said. "Leave him alone awhile, maybe he'll come to. Anybody fool enough to walk head first into a big hole in the stairs ain't got no brains anyway."

One by one they followed him. Leda. Giles. Amy. Only Tara stayed. But she had drawn back and was looking as if she didn't know whether to go or stay. Eldon reached for her.

"Stay," he pleaded. "My head hurts so damned bad." She came back and began to bathe his forehead again.

He lay back on the sagging, stinking mattress, his eyes closed, and her fingers touched him, soft, smooth, tender.

He turned, pulled the rag out of her hand and threw it aside, then jerked her down upon him. "Now," he whispered against her mouth. "Now. It's got to be now. I need you." He threw her over onto her back and flattened himself against her belly, his mouth grasping for hers, and missing, missing, missing as she kept turning her face away. The groans that began to escape from her throat were like the groans that had come when the house was falling, only softer. She began to claw at him, then she was fighting. He held her, forcing her legs apart. Suddenly she relaxed, and even her mouth was there, silent and soft. He forgot his pain as he became lost in her submissiveness.

All at once she turned, throwing him, and he was left groping the mattress and pulling the empty blanket. Her voice came at him low, but boiling with fury.

"Don't you ever, ever try to force yourself on me again, *Fox*!"

And the way she said "Fox" was as if she had spat in his face. But he was thinking mostly of the trick she had played on him—pretending to give in only to throw him off guard and get away.

"I don't want you," she was saying. "And I'll tell you another thing, Fox, I'm staying here only for Amy's sake, and your baby's sake! Do you get that? Only for them! As soon as the baby is born, this chick, this stupid flower child, is leaving!"

The pain and the anger throbbed through his head like the sound of the falling house. Screaming back at her impulsively, though he tried to laugh, he struck as he could. "Leaving! Why, you stupid bitch, how far do you think Sherwood aims to let you get? He'll stick you so fast you won't know what hit you! Stupid bitch. Get out. I don't care. I was a fool to pick you up in the first place."

Her face had changed. The fury and disgust were gone. That he could see. His head hurt like nothing he had ever felt before and he moaned and held it in his hands, digging his fingers into his scalp. It didn't matter what he had told her, he thought to himself. She was going to find out anyway, the minute she tried to walk out.

"What do you mean by that?" she asked. And when he didn't answer she took his wrist and tried to pull his arm down to uncover his face. But he held against her, refusing to give in to anything. "What do you mean *stick* me?" she demanded.

He was silent, but he was beginning to think. Sherwood wouldn't like it because he had told her. He would say it was a warning, that Sherwood. And she might sneak away in the middle of the night, snakes or no snakes. And when she reached town she would turn them all in to the police. It wouldn't take long for that to happen. She could make the walk to town by sunup, if she left the house at midnight, even without her damned broomstick. Sherwood wouldn't like it, and he was mad enough now.

"What'd you think!" He tried to laugh, to make a joke of it. "Screw you. He's been trying to take you away from me all the time. Well, now he can have you. So why don't you just go on and leave me alone?"

For awhile there was no sound, then he heard her light steps going toward the door and out. He rolled over, groaning, holding his head. The pain was killing him.

Killing him.

CHAPTER 6

Tara's body still trembled when she reached the stairway, and she paused, remembering the awful scream they had heard from downstairs when Eldon fell into the other stairway. She looked back, and up the gloomy lift of the sagging, half-collapsed stairway. There had been no really sensible explanation for why he had attempted to go up those stairs, or what had happened, and a kind of ominous chill moved over her. She only wanted to get away, out of the dim light of the vestibule, as quickly as possible. Holding tight to the banister, she started on down to the bottom floor.

And paused again when she heard her name called.

"Tara?" It was Amy, back somewhere on the second floor. "Will you come here a minute, Tara?"

Tara went back up the stairs and returned to the hallway to see Amy standing in the open door of their bedroom. Tara quickly passed Eldon's door without looking in, and entered the bedroom. Amy closed the door behind her.

"Did you and the Fox have a lovers' quarrel?" Amy asked. But the way she asked it made it a question filled with amusement.

Tara said shortly, and without amusement, "We were never lovers."

"Oh!" Amy sounded surprised. "I thought you were. I could hear you yelling at each other—or him at you, really—but I didn't listen. What I called you for was to look at what I found."

She crossed the room and began to pull out a heavy chair from a dark corner. It rolled, squeaking on large, round wheels. "Look, Tara. Isn't this a wheelchair?"

"I'll be darned," Tara said softly. She helped Amy pull it farther into the light of the half-covered window. "You're right, Amy, it just couldn't be anything else. I just thought it was another of those big clumsy chairs. How did you happen to notice it had wheels?"

"I was just looking around." Her voice drooped, saddened. "He was sick, wasn't he? Poor little boy."

Tara's attention was firmly attached to the chair. It had a black bulky seat and strong arms where young hands had polished away some of the black varnish or paint, or whatever covered it. Then she noticed the letters, also black, set high in the back of the chair. They were faintly outlined in gold.

"Amy, look," she whispered, unable to conceal her interest. "It's a name, and it *is* Samuel." She turned and glanced once at the painting. "See, he did misspell that after all. Sherwood was wrong. The little boy simply wrote 'Samael' instead of 'Samuel.' "

Amy looked up at the painting too, but she was quiet. After a long moment she asked, "But how did he reach it, Tara? Being rich, as they must have been, don't you think he would have been educated enough to write his name by the time he was old enough to reach that? And besides, the painting shows that he's thirteen, maybe fourteen years old."

"Hey," Tara scolded softly. "I thought you didn't believe that stuff Sherwood was handing us. He was only trying to scare us out of our room. He wanted it for himself." She couldn't admit to Amy that her reasoning had been very logical. Too logical.

Amy asked, showing that her train of thought persisted despite Tara, "And how did he get out of the wheelchair?"

Tara was forced to return to the subject of a ghost child that for some reason was beginning to give her a feeling of horror. "Well, maybe it was a progressive disease and he didn't have to use the chair all the time. Anyway, let's do forget him, huh? And maybe we should change rooms after all. We can go down the hall and each take one near the head of the front stairs."

"No." Amy went to lie awkwardly down on the bed. "I came here to take a nap, so I think I'll lie down awhile. Don't run off though. Sit and talk if you'd like."

Tara pushed back her hair and twisted it into a knot that would start falling as soon as she let go of it, and looked thoughtfully at Amy. The girl had been spending most of the time in the room, resting. Tara would have thought it was because of overexertion from the trip, but Amy seemed to be hanging lower and enlarging at a noticeable rate, and Tara was afraid that it was more than overexertion.

"Amy, are you sure you know exactly when the baby is due?"

Amy murmured, "Uh ..." and no more. A look of concentration settled on her face. "Well, I was never very regular, so ..."

"Oh boy!" said Tara, turning helplessly, her hair falling down her back and across her shoulders. She faced Amy again. "And you never once went to a doctor?"

"No."

"You go ahead and take that nap, I'll be back up soon. We'll eat in about an hour. I'll call you then. Sleep now, okay?"

"Okay."

Tara passed by Eldon's door with only a glance. He was crying as if he were really in pain, lying on his stomach, his face buried in his hands. She felt a little sorry for him, and decided to speak for him too.

Sherwood was on the hearth stool as if he had settled down to watch the pot of stew boil. Giles was slumped against the wall again with his magazine, and Leda was walking the floor. Tara went straight to Sherwood.

"You—I—have to get those two to a doctor, Sherwood. I think Amy is going to have the baby any time, and Eldon really is in terrible pain. He must have gotten a brain concussion."

"He got a knot on his stupid head," Sherwood said calmly, still watching the pot.

"If you don't take them, I will," said Tara. "I can drive. All I need is the keys to the car. I have to get them to a doctor."

"All you have to do is mind your own business."

That calmness, that lack of caring, infuriated Tara. "You are the most selfish, exasperating, obstinate, coarse, obscene and I might add stupid individual I ever have seen!"

Sherwood had stopped watching the pot and turned a frown up at her. "Hold it right there, woman!" he shouted. "Don't you call me them dirty names!"

"They're not dirty, they're the truth! I wouldn't lower myself to call you what you really are. Now you get up from there and hand over those keys so I can get those people to a doctor."

He got up all right, but the look in his eyes had an intensity she had never before seen in human eyes. His voice was low, but clear. "Red, you been itchin' to get your hands on them keys, ain't you? Well, you listen to this. If you want them two took care of, you take care of them. They ain't going to no doctor, and you, woman, you ain't goin' nowhere. And I mean *nowhere*."

She could see that he meant it, and she was slightly puzzled, her anger dying as she attempted to reason it out. She remembered what Eldon had screamed at her upstairs, and her feeling that it had nothing to do with sex. It was something else. Something more serious, more dangerous. Had he meant that Sherwood wouldn't hesitate to knife her if she attempted to leave? She didn't understand. Sherwood obviously didn't like her, and if so, why would he care if she left?

She decided to be more tactful until she could find the answers to the puzzle. Amy might know something. "But, Sherwood, Fox could die."

Sherwood didn't answer. His eyes were still on hers, pushing her back, unblinking.

"Don't you care at all?" she asked, and knew he didn't. Immediately she said, "Do you realize I don't have a thing for the baby? I might be able to deliver one but—"

"Forget it, will you?" he said. "Babies have managed to be born without anyone's help. You just tend to the meals. You're a pretty damned good cook, I have to admit that myself. Ain't that stew about done?"

Tara sighed. "I'll see in a minute. But first I want to know what you intend for me to wrap the baby in."

"We got blankets."

"Bed blankets, not baby blankets. And babies wear diapers, you know, and little gowns."

"Okay, okay!" He walked across the room, and Tara thought he was going out, perhaps to town to get baby supplies, but he sat down at the table instead. "Come on, woman, serve the food."

Tara clenched her teeth in irritation and stooped to see about the stew. But she was a little tired of being ordered about, so she said, "Set the table, for gosh sakes, one of you. I'm not exactly your slave you know."

But no one moved. And when she turned and saw the look on their faces she thought that perhaps she was their slave. And she didn't intend to be anybody's slave.

With her head high she went toward the door. "You want food, you get your own." And she ran out and back up the stairs.

Tara went quietly into the room, thinking Amy was asleep and not wanting to alarm her, but she saw the girl was wide-eyed and looking at the painting.

The moment Tara closed the door behind her, Amy said, "Do you think I should name my son 'Samael,' Tara? I've been thinking about it, and it seems fitting."

Tara almost forgot her own problem. She stopped still just inside the door and followed Amy's eyes. "But, Amy! That name?"

"It was only a mistake in spelling, you said, and the way Sherwood pronounced it was rather cute. And different. I've never heard the name before, have you?"

In the back of Tara's mind a thought squirmed. She went closer to look at the word again, trying to place where she had seen it.

"My qualifications for librarian at home weren't what they should have been, but since it was such a small place no one objected." She laughed lightly. "They didn't have much choice, the salary that was offered. But I did have a couple of years of literature—and, yes, Amy, I have seen that name. It might not have been a misspelling at all. I can't remember right offhand, but I'll see if I can drag it out. Maybe if I looked around the house I could find some old books—"

"There's a couple over there."

Amy raised to an elbow and pointed to a closed secretary in the corner, a tall, moldy antique whose wood was nearly ruined. It looked almost as weird and unholy as the painting. Tara hadn't looked into it yet.

"You've been investigating again," Tara chided softly. "I thought you were going to rest."

"Rest? With this little ole thing kicking like he does? I just happened to see that bookcase—or whatever it is—and wondered if it opened. And it does, and it's loaded with little bitty drawers and crannies and doors and things. It's wild. And there are some books. And another thing—black candles. What do you think of that, Tara?"

"I think black candles would be very fitting for that painting. But probably, someone liked black candles. Don't you like colored candles, Amy?"

"Well, yes, but ..."

Tara sat down on her side of the bed. "How about coming down to eat now. Aren't you hungry?"

"Sure. I'm always hungry."

"Another thing, Amy. What do the guys mean when they say stick?"

Amy's round eyes stared unwaveringly at her, but her small, thin-lipped mouth remained closed.

Tara kept her voice soft, unconcerned. "Like, you know, when Fox says when Sherwood sticks something he sticks her good. What does he mean?"

Amy frowned slightly. "Her? Why would he want to ... well, I mean, don't you really know?"

"No, I don't know. I've noticed they use the word a lot, and I'm not very up on some kinds of talk, and so I wondered."

Amy smiled. "I can imagine. You being a li-librarian. You don't fit the picture at all. I always thought librarians had round glasses and wore long skirts."

"How long has it been since you've been in a library, Amy?" Tara answered, well aware that they were wandering too far from the subject.

"I—gosh. I really never was, I guess, except at school."

"Back to Sherwood and the guys, Amy, okay? And the word, 'stick'. "

"Well, it usually means to knife, that's all."

"All!" Tara exclaimed angrily. "Well, that's what Eldon said Sherwood was going to do to me if I tried to leave here."

"But why?" Amy asked quickly.

Tara looked into her eyes. The girl had sat up, and seemed as perplexed as she had been earlier, yet not really surprised.

Amy asked again, "What have you done, Tara?"

"You mean he would?" Tara responded irrationally. "He actually would?"

Amy turned slightly pale, it seemed to Tara. Her eyes widened, as if from fright. A thought, a memory, something, had come to her. Her round eyes wavered then, and she looked away.

"Would he?" Tara demanded. "What right does he have to threaten me?"

"I don't know," Amy cried. "Honestly, I don't know, Tara, believe me."

Amy had grown nervous under the questioning, and seemed ready to burst out sobbing, but Tara was thinking of herself at the moment. She leaned toward the girl. "Yes, you do know. You know that he would, anyway, don't you? I want to know why, Amy, and you're the only one who can tell me. Who *will* tell me."

"I can't because—I can't tell you b-because I don't know what you've done, Tara," Amy cried. Tears were shining in her eyes. "But don't do it anymore, Tara, whatever it is. Please?" She looked again at Tara, and two large tears pinched loose and hung on her lower lashes. "*Please!*"

"Has he killed someone before?"

Amy began shaking her head, but Tara saw that it was not in answer to her question, it was simply a refusal to talk.

"Amy, if you know, you should tell the police!"

"Oh no! Oh no! Only in self-defense, that's all. I know he wouldn't. Tara, please."

Tara got up and went to the fireplace, but the painting was there, looking gleefully happy about her agitation, so she went on and looked out the window. It was the first time she had looked out the window, any upstairs window. A few vines crisscrossed the narrow dust-stained panes, so that it was something like looking through Spanish grill-work, but there were places through which she could see. For a while, though, a kind of helpless anger controlled her so that she wasn't aware of seeing anything but vines. Gradually then the anger ceased, she drew a couple of deep breaths to calm herself, and made herself concentrate on the view available beyond the vines.

To her surprise she could see the garage, the faint tracks that the car had made from the road, and a bit of the road itself. On eye level were the trees of the swamp, and not too far from her window, the limb of a tree reaching green leaves toward her. They moved in a breeze stronger than usual, then she saw a slither of lightning beyond the treetops, and the dark gray of an approaching cloud.

She sighed. "A storm is coming. Do you like thunder and lightning storms, Amy, or are you afraid of them?"

"No, no. I'm not afraid. Tara, are you?" Amy sounded like a child pleading for friendliness. "If you are, Tara, I'm right here, and—and Sherwood is here, and he'll protect you, always. Really he will. But he has to keep the discipline. That's one of the rules you have to abide by. He said that. We can't be a family without discipline. So whatever you did, Tara, please don't do it again."

Instead of replying to Amy with the words that first occurred to her, Tara drew another deep, relaxing breath. It was pretty obvious that Amy didn't know what she had done either to be so threatened by Sherwood, and there was no point in pursuing it. Instead, she said, "I'm not afraid of thunder storms, Amy. In fact I find them very stimulating. I love the sound of thunder, and I think lightning is beautiful. I know it can, and often does, kill. But still I can't be afraid of it."

"Oh, I'm so glad, because if you're not afraid, neither am I."

Tara left the window and found that the room had grown much darker. "We need a fire," she said, going toward the huge old secretary in the back of the room, "but it's a little sultry for that, so we'll have to settle for candlelight. How about celebrating the storm and using those black candles you found?"

"They're right there—in one of those cubby holes."

The center of the tall piece of furniture had a flat, carved-board front and in the center a ring of yellow metal. She pulled it, and it opened into a desk that hung by slender, rusted chains. It was so nearly dark in the alcove she uncovered that the candles were at first invisible. Her fingers roved the cubby holes and finally touched the candles, and she estimated there must be a dozen.

"We'll save most of these for really special occasions," Tara said. "So I'll light only one, okay? We'll use it to go downstairs for dinner, and light the regular ones on the mantle to brighten the room. It must be much later than I thought it was, because the storm isn't close enough yet to cause so much darkness."

"It's just a plain old dark house anyway, but it doesn't bother me, does it you? It makes me feel—well—protected, I guess."

"And it makes me feel smothered. I prefer sunshine. But right now I'm hungry, and if we don't hurry those vultures down there will eat all the food. Do you feel like going down, Amy?"

"Yes, sure."

Tara lighted the candle with a match, and then lighted the candles on the mantle. By the time she had finished Amy was waiting near the door.

In the hallway, Tara paused, thinking of Eldon. "Just a minute, Amy, and I'll see if Eldon has gone down."

"Wait!" Amy's voice was quick and low. "Don't leave me alone without a light."

Tara smiled over the candle flame at Amy. "I thought you said you weren't afraid of the dark?"

Amy was close beside her, and clutched her arm with fingers that held so tightly they pinched. "Out here it's different. This hall reminds me of a long, dark tunnel. The kind they make for roads under mountains. They always scared me."

"All right, come along."

Their shadows, thrown by the single flame of the candle, climbed the walls like long, crooked wraiths, dancing and writhing as they walked along. Tara saw Amy looking at them, and she transferred the candle to her other hand and held it slightly forward so that the shadows were left behind. The light, though tiny, blinded her, and seemed suspended alone in the darkness above her hand, its long, tapering black body lost. She had a strange, uncomfortable feeling that it was beckoning them to follow somewhere.

Amy said suddenly, "I don't think I like that candle." Tara didn't especially like it either, but she said casually, "It drips, too. My hand will be as freckled as my face by the time we get downstairs."

That brought a giggle to Amy. Slightly nervous, but a giggle anyway. "Oh, Tara, your face isn't that freckled." Through the sound of Amy's voice came the loud, quavering moan, a fitting accompaniment to the disembodied light and the following shadows. Amy stopped abruptly, her fingers digging into Tara's arm. Tara couldn't help the chill that went up her back, though she knew the source of the moan.

"Tara," Amy whispered, "what was that?"

Tara pulled forward toward Eldon's still-open door. "It was Eldon. He must be worse, poor fellow. He needs something for the pain."

The room was almost totally dark, the window but a rectangle of gray. The candlelight danced toward Eldon, blinding, beckoning. Tara raised it high and looked down. He was curled into a knot of misery, face down, his hands holding his head. His breathing was quick and shallow and the moaning soft again.

"Eldon," Tara said, "is there anything we can do for you?"

He didn't answer.

"Would you like me to bring you a tray of food?"

Still no answer.

Tara said to Amy, feeling helpless, "I don't suppose he really feels like eating."

Amy said, "I've had headaches. They go away."

"I certainly hope so. Eldon, would you like us to light a candle for you?"

He moved then, turned and glared up at them with eyes nearly as wild as the eyes in the painting. "No!" he screamed. "Get out! Get out with—with—" He sat up and crouched away, his eyes raising to the light of the candle above Tara's head. "What's that? What is that?" he cried, his voice high with a kind of hysteria that caused Tara to move back toward the door. "Get out of here!"

Amy released Tara's arm and ran into the hallway. Tara brought the candle down and cupped her hand to protect its flame, then followed Amy and closed the door softly. She stood for a moment, unnerved, hearing the sobs from the closed room behind. They had a new sound, one of wild fear.

"My God," she said softly.

Amy whispered, "Tara, he's crazy! Really he is!"

Tara shook her head, not in disagreement, but because she didn't understand what was happening. "Something is wrong. But what can we do for him when Sherwood won't let me have the keys to the car, or won't take him to the doctor—"

Amy interrupted, "Was that what you been trying to do, Tara? That's why Sherwood is mad at you! He doesn't believe in doctors! He says they're all just after money. He believes in the natural way."

Tara felt like saying a dirty word, but she squished it back by pressing her lips tightly together. "Okay," she said. "We might as well go on and let the poor guy suffer through it. We'll just hope he gets better."

As they went down the long hall toward the front stairs she thought of Sherwood and his strange, unreasonable treatment of his people, and decided that she had better not cross him so much that he was tempted to cut her throat and be done with her. That was hardly the best way out of her predicament.

They entered the kitchen to find the three seated at the long table, eating. In the center of the table was an opened loaf of bread, a jar of pickles, and two white candles. The lantern sat unlit in the corner by the fireplace.

"Hello, everybody," Tara said in false cheerfulness. "Amy felt like coming down to join you. Sit down, little girl, and I'll bring you a bowl of stew."

From the cupboard, along with the two bowls, Tara brought a candle holder. She carefully placed the black candle in it and set it on the end of the table.

"Where'd you get that?" Sherwood demanded, his voice high pitched and sharp.

Tara glanced at him and saw that he was looking at her candle with much the same expression that had been in Eldon's crazed eyes.

Amy answered quickly, her eyes darting from Sherwood to Tara and back again. "It was in the room, Sherwood. And we needed a light."

"Get it away! Put the thing out!" He was starting to rise from the table.

"Why?" Tara asked. "It's only a candle. Don't you like black?"

Where Eldon's fear had disturbed her, Sherwood's only amused her. She smiled at him over the flame of the candle.

He pointed a finger at her. "For you, maybe, for you! If you don't know what that is, you ain't very damned smart. And if you do know, you'd just better keep away from me, and I mean it!"

Tara frowned. "What on earth are you talking about?"

Leda spoke up suddenly, her voice filled with curiosity, her mouth with food. She mumbled slightly. "What's wrong with it, Sherwood?"

"Don't none of you stupes know? That's a witch's candle! That's what they use in black magic, and you better believe it, they're evil. Evil!"

Tara found that she was looking at the candle too, but then she began to laugh. "Come on now, Sherwood, you surely don't believe in black magic! That's ancient superstition, that's all."

"Hah! That's all you know about it, or so you claim." He leaned over and with a wide swipe of his arm knocked the black candle far across the room.

The holder broke and the candle rolled, circling to finally lie still, its flame gone.

For a moment the room was very still, its occupants as wordless as the walls. From far away came the sound of thunder.

Sherwood crossed the room to the black candle and with the toe of his boot kicked it toward the fireplace. Tara and the others watched him in silence. It required several kicks to get it into the small fire on the hearth because it kept rolling in a circle and Sherwood danced around it in a comical way. Beside him, his shadow danced grotesquely on the wall. Tara wanted to laugh, and finally did, but very quietly. And when he turned, the candle pushed into the fire, and followed his long shadow back to the table, Tara busied herself with serving Amy's dinner.

She got her own bowl of stew and sat down on the end of a bench and said conversationally, "There's a storm coming."

Sherwood sat taciturn and grumpy-looking over his food.

Amy responded to Tara, looked up, eager and large-eyed in the pale candlelight.

"Yes!" she said, looking around to include everyone. "A real one, with thunder and everyth—"

Leda interrupted with a caustic, *"Dumb."*

And Sherwood shouted, practically screamed, across the table at her, "Shut up! Shut up! Eat your suppers and go to bed, damn it anyway."

No one said a word then. Tara watched them, thinking how like an old-fashioned, iron-hard father he was, and how like obedient children they were. She watched Sherwood settle back to lower his face near his bowl of stew, and she too remained quiet. She didn't mention that it seemed a bit early to go to bed because the thought of lying in her blanket and listening to the thunder was comforting.

She and Amy were the last to leave the kitchen. After the other three had gone they sat on for a while, watching the fire die down on the hearth, listening to the cricket strike up his song, listening to the frogs. The storm was still far away, and seemed to have little effect on them.

When Amy began to yawn they took white candles from the cupboard and went along the halls to the front stairs.

The upper hall was as still and deserted as if no one had ever walked there, and Tara thought to herself that she had no idea where the others' rooms were. Only Eldon's. And she didn't go near his closed door.

The candles in their room had dwindled to half their original size. Tara started to add the others to them, to keep the light through the night, but on impulse blew them out instead.

"Let's not have light, all right, Amy? I like to watch the lightning."

"Okay," Amy answered sleepily. The girl was already curled in her blanket, her eyes closed.

Tara changed quickly to pajamas, and hung her one robe over the foot of the bed. It was a long white cotton and polyester blend, with long sleeves gathered with lace at the wrists and a high, small neck that tied with a ribbon. But it was light and cool.

She blew out the candles on the mantle, and kept one to take to her bedside table. A small box of matches was there, in case she wished to light the candle. She was quite sure she didn't want to be caught wholly in the dark in this house. When she blew out the candle though, and lay down in her blanket, the dark was a welcome enclosure, keeping the painting from staring at her all night long.

From Amy came soft snores.

Tara turned onto her back to watch the soft touches of light that came occasionally to the window as the lightning drew near. The walls of the house trembled faintly under the following thunder.

She slept, but only for a moment it seemed. She woke quickly and completely, tense and listening. Something had awakened her, but she wasn't sure exactly what. She wasn't even sure if it had been a noise. In fact, only the thunder was there, sporadically, much louder, much closer. A long flash of lightning illuminated part of the room, and the vines on the window stood out like black, irregular grillwork.

The silence. It was the silence.

She sat up, listening hard, her body alert with cold fear. Suddenly then she realized the source of the difference. The frogs were not singing. They had become voiceless in the night.

She relaxed, smiling with relief and amusement at herself. Only the frogs. Afraid of the thunder?

Then, piping like a lonely wayfarer in a half-bright, half-black world, one frog began to sing. Another joined him, and another, and the chorus was back again, in full swing, as loud or louder than ever, and the thunder continued to toll and the lightning washed the window brilliantly.

And then softly, very softly. Continuously.

Tara kept looking at the window, and the light that was there. It dawned on her that the soft glow of light was not from the storm, and it was not the storm that had caused the frogs to silence their singing.

She threw her blanket aside and got off the bed, careful to make no noise. On bare, silent feet she felt her way around the end of the bed and over to the window.

She had to put her face against the pane in order to see the car that was parked below, its twin beams on dim, a stranger in the dark. She watched it for a long moment, wondering who it was, what they were doing there; wondering if they were lost in this weird and dangerous area of nearly invisible swampland. It was a good thing they had turned in beside the house, she thought, instead of driving straight ahead into the water. If they should back out and decide to go on ...

She felt her way back to the bed and around it to her bedside table where the candle and matches lay. She lighted the candle, a tiny flame that did not touch the window, and reached for her robe.

She'd go down and tell them to be careful where they drove, or at least see what they wanted.

The one candle was hardly enough to light the way along the hall. Gradually though, the flame grew larger, wavering in the stir of air created by her movement. She walked as smoothly as if she balanced a book on her head so that her feeble light would be disturbed as little as possible.

The blackness in the house did not enter her mind except as a detriment in going down the stairs. Her mind was on the person or people in the car, and what exactly they were doing on this dead-end road.

Fortunately, the night was very still. The swamp air lay heavily damp, like a fog, waiting for the approach of the storm. It hadn't yet begun to stir, so it had little effect on her candle's flame when she opened the large front door. She cringed at the squall of rusted hinges.

The car was parked slightly to her right, and she could see all but its headlights. She held the candle still, raised it high over her head and walked farther out onto the stoop.

A long streak of lightning crossed and crisscrossed the sky overhead and for a long moment the car was sharply outlined, and its occupants clearly visible. Two heads in the front seat, close beside each other, turned and looked her way. They sat like wax dolls, gaping at her, not moving.

She started to call out to them when suddenly the boy moved, the car started, roared backwards in a semicircle, slid to a stop at the edge of the swamp, and then spun forward, lost in the darkness of the spent lightning. The sound of the car was lost too in the rush of close thunder that followed swiftly on the trail of the lightning.

Tara turned to watch the disappearing taillights of the car.

A large drop of rain brushed her cheek, and she backed into the hallway and closed the door and leaned against it, listening to the increasing rain, puzzled over the actions of the people in the car.

They had acted as if they had seen a ...

All at once she began to laugh. Young lovers, out for the night, out to see the old—what had Giles called it?— Black Swamp Mansion, supposedly haunted.

"Oh my gosh," she laughed aloud into the long dark hall that stretched before her, feeling herself in that car, seeing the front door of the house open and a woman in white appear on the front stoop holding a candle in her hand.

She couldn't stop laughing. She almost blew her candle out before she took her hand off her stomach and used it instead to protect her jumping flame.

She went up the stairs laughing, delighted. She had sure given someone a night's thrill, she thought. They would probably never come near the place again. Its reputation would be cemented forever.

She went down the hall toward her room, softening her laughter, hoping that no one had been disturbed by it.

She saw the door, just one among many on her right, move slightly as she approached it. Someone was there, looking out at her. She went on, giggling softly, knowing that it was Sherwood. Watching her. Hiding in the darkness of his room.

Let him watch, yes. And let him wonder. Wonder why she was walking down the hall at midnight, laughing. She rather hoped he thought she was a ghost too, because it had been fun. But knowing Sherwood, he would probably be more positive than ever that she was a witch of some strange breed that had just come in from the most evil of black-magic rituals.

Well, let him.

She went on, laughing, and the door behind her squeaked eerily as it moved.

CHAPTER 7

Scott Yates sat in the Main Street Cafe at a small table where he could watch both the clock and the pretty waitress, Mary, and drank another cup of coffee. The place closed at midnight, which was twenty minutes away. He had finally asked Mary for a date of sorts. He was going to drive her home. He wondered what she would be like, if she would let him kiss her, maybe even make love to her. He had mixed feelings about it. He hoped for a few kisses at least, but for the other he would prefer that she make him wait. Then, if everything turned out okay between them, he might just ask her to marry him.

He had a feeling she wouldn't refuse, and he already knew about a certain house that would make a good home for his family. The kitchen was sunny and friendly, and he could visualize everything but the girl to whom it would belong. He tried to put Mary there, but somehow the cafe counter kept popping up in front of her apron. Oh well. He'd have to work on it, that was all.

The door of the cafe burst open and a wild-eyed youth came running in. Behind him came his girl, pale and trembling. They stopped just inside the door, blinking in the light, looking dazed, scared to death. Scott's first thought was that there must have been a wreck somewhere on the highway. He could hear the rain coming down like water over a dam, and saw tiny streamlets of water running down the faces of both young people.

Mary had stopped, the coffee pot in her hand. The half dozen or so people in the cafe had grown very quiet, all facing the two at the door. The roar of the storm was loud in the silence.

Scott recognized the couple then. Claude Barnes and Judy Pierce. High-school students. They had been going steady for several months. Where you saw one you saw the other.

Mary was the first to speak. "What on earth happened to you two?" She evidently knew them well. "Shut the door, will you please? I don't want to mop up a river before I leave."

The girl automatically reached behind her and gave the door a shove.

"We saw it!" Claude squeaked. "We saw it!"

"Yes!"

"What?" asked Mary.

"The ghost. The—the—" Claude came forward to a table, rubbing his hands over his quite long, wet hair. He sat down, leaving his girl to get her own chair. She joined him, biting her lip, chewing first on one side and then the other.

Mary laughed lightly, a laugh that was not really a laugh at all, but a kind of gentle *ha-ha*. "You're about as clear as this coffee."

"Give us some, will you?" Claude said. Then, "No. Bring us beer. We need beer."

Mary said huffily, going on to pour the coffee into cups, "You need beer like I need a holey umbrella. In about four years you can have beer. Tonight, coffee. You really should drink milk."

In a stronger voice Claude said, "I aged at least four years tonight. I want beer."

"You're getting coffee," Mary said firmly, putting the cups before them. "Do you want something to eat? Hot soup?"

"Are you kidding?" Claude retorted. "I'll be lucky if I can swallow at all!"

Judy said, "If you'd seen what we just saw ..."

A man at a table asked, "Well, what was it?"

Claude, clearly on the defensive, looked around at all the customers. "You'd better not laugh, that's all I've got to say, because we saw it, both of us. That's no joke. We saw the ghost at Black Swamp Mansion."

"Come on now—"

"I said don't laugh. It was there. Both of us saw it as plain as we see you."

Judy was nodding and nodding agreement, still biting her lower lip.

Scott decided they had entered his territory, and he could see that the kids were scared half to death. If they hadn't seen something, they sure thought they had. In a voice serious and loud enough to down the murmurs and smiles that were rising among the customers, he said, "You went out to the house tonight?"

Claude looked at him, and relaxed, recognizing a supporter when he saw one. "Yes, we did. We drove out there after we saw the movie—" He glanced around, saying for the benefit of some of the others, "—and it wasn't a ghost story, either, it was a western! Anyway, we drove out there, and parked. We had never been there before, and we kind of got the urge to go."

"In this storm?" asked Mary.

"It wasn't storming then. I mean, it was just coming. It seemed the best time to go. I'd heard all these wild tales, but I had never believed it, so I said let's go just for the hell of it. So we did. That was about eleven o'clock. We just pulled in off the road, by the house, and sat there a few minutes. It was a spooky-looking big old place, all dark and viney, you know. We didn't aim to stay. I didn't even turn the lights out. Then—" He glanced at Judy. She was still nodding, and she shuddered visibly. "Then—so help me God the front door opened and out came a woman. The lightning was bright, and we saw her as plain as day! She—she wore a long white gown, and she had long dark hair that fell forward over her shoulders. In the lightning it glowed, didn't it, Judy, almost as if it were on fire."

"What glowed?" asked Mary.

"Her hair!" Claude said as if she had challenged him.

And Judy repeated in a thin little voice, "Her hair."

"You're kidding!" Mary said.

"No."

"No!"

The rain beat harder against the wide plate-glass windows. Everyone stared at the kids. The grins had faded away.

Finally a man said, "You had to be imagining that." His wife spoke up. "Why? What makes everyone so sure there is no such thing as a ghost? I believe them. I believe them so much that you will never catch me going out there."

Claude said, "Boy, me neither! Never again. They can have it, far as I'm concerned. I want some more coffee, Mary."

The old-timer who always seemed to be around the cafe, or anywhere else in town where a crowd was likely to gather, said, "I never heard of nobody seeing a woman ghost there, but I heard about how everyone who lives there, or tries to live there, will die in the house, so it's probably likely that a woman is haunting the place. God knows a woman is capable of being that damned mean."

"Now wait a minute, Jake," Mary said. "You happen to be in the company of a few women, you know."

Jake said slowly, in a heavy Southern drawl, "I didn't say all women are bad, Mary, but I will say, just like my pa said, that there ain't no bad man as bad as a bad woman, and no good man as good as a good woman. They can go one way or the other."

Mary asked, "What makes you think the poor thing is bad just because she's haunting the place?" Her voice was light, and Scott knew she had her doubts about the whole thing.

"Why would she be scaring a couple of kids?"

"Maybe because it's a dangerous old place out there and she wanted them to leave?"

Scott said, "Now that's a reasonable assumption. I like it."

"Christ," Claude said. "So she gives you a heart attack and kills you on the spot just trying to do you a favor?"

Mary smiled. "What's this I see sitting here? A couple of half-drowned, half-batty ghosts? You're still alive."

"Damned right," said Claude, "and I aim to stay that way. The woman in white with the burning hair can have the place."

"She was holding a candle," Judy said.

Everyone looked at the girl then, even Claude. He asked, sounding astonished, "She was?"

"Yes. Didn't you see it?" For the first time she looked up, her eyes roving blankly, looking back to that which she had seen. "She was holding it above her head."

Scott felt himself frowning in concentration, and smoothed it away. He was inclined to be a bit like Mary— skeptical. But this was beginning to take on too much reality. "Just exactly what did this woman look like? Was she apparently flesh and blood, or more of an apparition?" Judy looked at Claude, and Claude looked at Judy. Then once again, her voice more calm and normal, Judy said, "She was ..." Her hesitation was brief, then, as if the memory surprised her, she began to describe the ghost. "She was not see-through, you know, not—not diaphanous. Remember, Claude? The lightning flashed and there wasn't anything but that big old house front with all those crawly vines, and then just for an instant it was dark, and that was when she suddenly appeared standing on the stoop with the candle over her head."

Claude interrupted in a low voice, "I wasn't looking then, I guess. I didn't see the candle."

"I did. And then the lightning came again, and she was there so brilliant it hurt your eyes. She was wearing white, and it reached from her neck to the stoop, and her hair kind of glowed. She still had her arm raised. Don't you remember, Claude?"

"No. Along about that time I was driving."

He smiled out of one corner of his mouth, but no one else joined him.

Mary moved, putting the coffee pot back on its hotplate. "I'd be driving too," she said.

Scott asked Judy, "Did she move at all? Or was she just there?"

"No. Yes. I mean, like a statue." She shivered and stood up. "I want to go home, Claude."

Claude took her out a bit reluctantly because the old-timer was beginning to talk and the boy obviously wanted to hear. The roar of the rain was loud for a moment as the door opened, then quieted again when it closed.

"You couldn't hire me to go close to that place," Jake was saying. "I never heard of a woman being seen there before. Mostly what goes on out there I hear is noises in the house, and everybody who lives there a dying, and I mean to say you couldn't hire me to live there. Ain't many people with enough nerve to go out there during a storm, so maybe there was something about the storm that brought the woman out—"

Mary was pulling blinds and locking the front door, though the chance of more customers in this town, at this hour, in this rain, was not enough to worry about. Scott watched her, and saw that the clock had passed midnight. But Mary sat down at one of the tables and gave her attention to the old man in the striped overalls and the stained and floppy-brimmed hat that could have grown on his scalp so far as Scott knew. He had never seen Jake without it.

"I know for a fact," Jake said, "that a murder has been committed in that house—and they say more than one." He paused dramatically, and looked around at his listening audience.

Scott had never heard that one before. "A murder?"

"Could of been several murders."

"Well, who? And when? I never heard of it."

Several others grunted, but Scott wasn't sure if the grunts were for or against.

"Well," Jake said, settling back as if he had all night. "I know there was a slave hanged in a bedroom—mind you right in a bedroom—upstairs in that house, way back, oh, well, back in slave days. Not too long after the house was built."

Mary cried in horror, "Hanged in the house? While people lived there?"

"Right. Hanged right in the bedroom where they said he committed the murder."

Scott felt like getting up and leaving. Jake could be so frustrating when he told his tales, because of the long pauses during which he sucked on his cold pipe and waited for someone to egg him on.

"Well?" Mary demanded impatiently, "who did he kill?" Jake paused longer than usual, and his answer was far from positively spoken. "I think it was a baby, 'cause the hanging took place in the nursery on the third floor."

"Why would he kill a baby?" Mary asked, her face still twisted into an expression of horror and disbelief.

Jake shrugged. "I don't know. It was a little before my time."

"A little before everyone's time," another man said. "But I heard tell that something awfully bad went on out there with slaves. Like the man who built the house was supposed to make his money by catching the slaves that ran away and went into the swamp. They said he'd lure them up to the house and then turn them back to their owners for the ransom."

That story was not new to Scott. He said, "I don't think there is any proof of that at all. The Civil War brought a lot of tales with it."

Jake said belligerently, as if his story had been questioned, "Well, I can prove what I know. My neighbor woman is old Aunt Betts. She's about ninety or a hundred, and her mother was a slave girl there when the man was hanged. She knows about it. She remembers. She won't hardly talk about it, but she knows."

Scott wondered how he had missed hearing that one too. "Old Aunt Betts was a slave then? I mean—her mother was?"

"That's right. And so was her grandmother, naturally. Her grandmother was the cook, and she was there. And so was Aunt Betts' ma. Ask her yourself. If you can get her to talk. The only time I ever heard her tell about it was when that man was killed there last week. They said it was an accident. Wasn't, she said, wasn't no accident. She said a curse is on that house. And I believe it."

The man who had his wife along said, "I always heard that old place was haunted too, but my granddad told me it was just to put a scare in people back in the days of the war, and it was done by the slaves that hid out there. The house was already empty then, and he figured a bunch of big black runaway slaves hid there and made all those rackets and noises to scare other people away."

"Bosh!" Jake said angrily. "It's not slaves that cursed that house. Nobody ever lived there during the war—nobody!"

Mary interposed quickly, as if deflecting a free-for-all, "It does seem a little strange, when you think about it, that it's the only pre-Civil War house left standing in this area." She looked at Scott. "It wasn't even damaged, was it?"

"No, it wasn't."

"Every other house was, if it was any good, you know. The furniture taken, the windows knocked out, and usually the whole thing burned to the ground. I know that's what happened to several of the plantation houses."

"Say, you're right!" the wife cried excitedly, as if that proved everything.

"Cursed, that's why," Jake said. "And I'll tell you what the curse is."

The pause again. Everyone waited and watched the old man, and Scott listened to the rain outside and tapped his foot lightly on the floor. Jake chewed awhile on his pipe stem.

"The curse," he said, eyeing each and all, as if he were going down a police lineup, "was that anyone who ever lived in that house would die in it."

Mary shook her head and got up. "Too creepy for me. If you all don't mind I would like to close this place for a few hours. I'll get my things, Scott, and be with you in a minute."

"Fine. Want us to drop you off at home, Jake?"

"Naw, much obliged. This here old hat of mine needs warshing anyway. I never minded a spring rain."

Mary had an umbrella, and stood at the door with it still folded as her customers filed out, like a plump milkmaid herding cattle through a gate. When everyone had gone except Scott, she opened the umbrella.

In the car, rain bouncing on the roof, Scott drove slowly, reminding himself that he should be thinking romantic thoughts about Mary, but he couldn't get his mind off what the kids had seen. With half an ear he listened to Mary talk. Small talk. Business talk. Customer talk. Just talk.

He hadn't known that she talked so much.

In front of her house he pulled her into his arms and kissed her softly, testing. Her lips were smooth and rather cool under his. She didn't raise her arms to hug him, she didn't push her body against him, or otherwise show any aggression. He tried a little harder, still testing. He kissed her neck, her cheek, her ear, and then her mouth again. He felt her soften against him. She still didn't attempt to put her arms around him, but she wasn't objecting to anything so far.

He pulled himself away from her. "Maybe we can have a regular date sometime, eh, Mary? Go somewhere?"

"Yes," she whispered.

He should set a particular time and place and all that, but it could wait, he decided, until it wasn't raining so damned hard and he could get his mind off those stupid, scared kids.

He took her to her door, kissed her again, feeling the length of her full body and not much else, then he ran through the rain back to his car.

Well, he thought as he started the car again, a lot of thrills don't last anyway. And a marriage should have something in it to last. Like companionship, and wanting the same things. He'd have to remember to ask Mary sometime just what she wanted out of life, and if she wanted to be a housewife and raise a couple of kids. That would probably settle the whole thing.

She was a good, straight, moral girl. That much he now felt was confirmed, and that was what he wanted in a wife. He wouldn't settle for less.

His mind kept wandering back to the kids like a bird to its roost. They hadn't been lying when they'd told about seeing the ghost at the Bishop place. He had a notion to drive out and see for himself. He stopped in the middle of Main Street, the engine idling, and thought about going out to that house, with the rain pouring, the night black as hell. Two hells, in fact.

And decided to wait until morning.

There was always the possibility that it hadn't been a ghost at all, and he wanted to make sure. Maybe someone had taken refuge in the storm. If so, there would probably be some sign—and not a dead body, he hoped. If someone had taken refuge he hoped they'd get out of there as soon as it was light enough to go.

He didn't bother to go to the office the next morning, or even to the cafe for an extra cup of coffee or his breakfast. He went instead to the muddy road that led out to the Bishop place. The rain had stopped, and the sun shined on a world washed so clean that it sparkled.

He checked the road a bit. It was probably passable. At least the kids had gotten through last night. But their car tracks had been washed out.

He drove the last quarter of a mile very slowly, almost as if he unconsciously were trying to sneak up on something. The frogs kept giving him away though, every inch. He felt like putting his head out the window and yelling at them to shut up and keep singing. Which made him wonder what state his nerves were in. He didn't really believe there were ghosts and curses and things, did he? No, of course not. The man had fallen down the stairs. The others had caught something contagious. Whatever the kids saw last night was—well—it could have been a ball of lightning striking the house.

He halfway hoped it was, and that it had burned the house to the ground. But of course he knew that that hadn't happened because someone would have seen the fire.

The house was still there, big and brown and nearly covered with vines, its tiny window-eyes peeping out.

He stopped the car in the road, and sat still until the frogs were fully at it again. Meanwhile he looked around. There was no sign of lightning or anything else having struck the front door. It was as solidly closed as it had been the last time he'd seen it. There was no sign of anything. Not even a car track where the kids had driven in last night.

There wouldn't be, in all those vines.

He got out of the car, but left the door open. No reason to give the frogs something to shut up about. He felt more comfortable with their melodious din going on as usual.

He went through the vines to the front stoop, and up. His searching gaze covered the door and settled on the knob, just in time to see it begin to turn.

He stared at it, his feelings suspended for a long moment, a very long moment, as the doorknob turned. It was like being in an unreal dream, seeing something move when it shouldn't be moving. He had locked that door just a few days ago.

Then, in the midst of a drawn-out, rusty squeak, the door opened and he was looking into very bright green eyes, shaded by long, thick, curling lashes. The girl was smiling, almost laughing. Red hair, the color of a bright copper penny, fell over one shoulder to her breast. She was wearing blue slacks and a short, matching top, and Scott's tongue lay immobile somewhere in the back of his open mouth.

She was the most unexpected and most beautiful thing he had ever seen.

And she was real. She even had a voice.

"Hello!" she said. "My, aren't we popular these days. I'll bet you came out to see the ghost." And then she laughed, her eyes narrowing and continuing to hold his, and the chill of it, of what her eyes did to him, jumped from his brain through his body and left him more speechless than ever.

Her laughter stopped and she tipped her head to one side. "I'm real. Honestly. I'll let you touch, if you'll watch what you're touching."

Scott's voice came from somewhere deep in his belly, with no preparation. "I'll promise to watch it carefully." As if they worked automatically his eyes followed the seductive lines of her body, down and up again to where her hair touched her breast.

"Now wait," she said, backing into the hall. "That wasn't exactly what I meant."

Scott swallowed and looked into her eyes again, stiffening himself against the impact. "Who are you?" he demanded gruffly, "and what the damnation are you doing here?"

"Well!" she replied shortly. "We aren't so popular after all. Who are you?"

"The name is Scott Yates, of the Yates Realty in town. I just happen to have the authority to rent, sell or lease this property, and I don't recall ever seeing you around the office asking about it, or even around town so far as that goes." He didn't mean to sound so crabby. But she had caused him to feel so many different things, including concern for her safety that he also was strangely, unaccountably angry with her. "So where the hell did you come from?"

The smile, the laughter, even the friendliness was gone. "I don't think I want to answer that."

Scott took a deep breath and looked up at the sky. A blue sky always helped him get his tacks together again. Gently then, he asked, "*Who* are you?"

"Tara is my name."

"Well, Tara, you sure scared hell out of those kids last night."

She laughed softly, "Yeah, I know. I can't say I'm truly sorry because it was really worth something, knowing this old house is supposed to be haunted. I expect I gave them a thrill they will never forget. Now wouldn't it be a shame to ruin it all by telling them it wasn't a ghost?"

Scott laughed a little too. "I guess it would." He sobered quickly. "But I still want to know what you're doing here."

"Isn't that obvious? I'm living here."

"*Living* here! Since when? And why?"

"Because ..." she shrugged, and raised both hands to push back her hair and roll it into a knot at the back of her head. Her eyes lowered. "Because—well—"

He saw the freckles, tanned pinpoints in a clear skin, like stars in a sky. It added cute to beautiful, and he wanted to kiss her cheek and nose where freckles clustered like dim, faraway galaxies.

The man appeared behind her magically, out of nowhere. Or else Scott had been so engrossed in the girl that he hadn't seen the man approach. He was on the tall and slender side, well built, wearing western clothes and standing with his feet wide apart. All he needed, thought Scott, was a holster with guns. He wasn't friendly. His eyes were narrowed, making them look smaller than they probably were. Behind him, coming down the dim hall, were two others. One a thin, dark girl, the other a man. A younger man, with a face that was boyish. He too was wearing western clothes.

The guy with the small eyes said, "What do you want?" Tara released her hair and whirled, evidently startled. She hadn't heard his approach. The man put out his hand, took her arm and pushed her behind him. He came on then to stand within reach of Scott.

"I said what do you want here?"

Scott automatically pulled a card from his pocket and extended it toward the man, who made no move to take it. "As I was telling the—your wife—" He paused for a correction or affirmation, but no one said anything. The disappointment was sharp and sudden. He put the card in his pocket and squeezed it into a ball with his fist. "As I told her, I have the authority to rent, sell or lease this property, and I have not had any dealings with you. So I'm asking you to vacate the place as quickly as possible."

The man with the small eyes grinned. An unfriendly, impudent thing that made Scott want to wipe it off his face. He felt an impulse to take the whole face while he was at it. Instead, he clenched the fist in his pocket and mangled the card.

"On the contrary," the man said. "Your authority has been over-ruled. You happen to be lookin' at the people who own this property, and your services won't be needed any longer. Take the place off the market."

"Now wait a minute!" Scott replied, trying to hold his temper. "The owner of this property lives in Michigan, and has not contacted me in any way. I happen to know she's a lady in her seventies—"

The man turned and motioned the other one forward. He put his arm over the shoulders of the baby-faced one. Scott glanced at Tara and saw that she was looking straight at him, eyes widened. She looked as if she were about to speak, but then her lips closed.

"Meet Giles," the man said. "Giles here is Mrs. Bishop's nephew. You can ask her if we ain't welcome to this place. She'll tell you yes."

The man called Giles nodded his head. "That's right. Aunt Rita doesn't mind if we live here. Ask her. You have my permission."

Scott looked from one face to the next. They all stared back at him, but only the bully of the bunch kept on grinning. Tara's eyes were still direct and steady, unnerving him.

"I appreciate your permission to ask," Scott said, laying the sarcasm on heavily, "and don't worry, because I'll certainly do that."

He turned and walked swiftly through the vines to his car. Driving away, he handled it far more roughly than he usually did, aware that they were still watching him. He felt his temper boiling in his throat.

Two couples.

He split through the mud holes and the frogs, and water splashed on his windshield. By the time he turned onto the highway and gunned it toward town, his car was a muddy mess.

Two couples. He wondered which of the men was the husband of Tara. Beautiful Tara with the cute freckles and the sexy figure. Well, she probably had a personality to match her hair and it was just as well that she was already married.

He didn't speak to Anna Lou or his dad either when he burst into the office and headed for his desk. While he was leafing through the address book to find Rita Bishop's number, he heard Anna Lou say, "I think Mister Scott Yates just tangled with a bear and lost. What'd you do, Scott, have to climb a tree?"

Both Anna Lou and his dad laughed, but Scott didn't. He didn't even smile as he dialed the long-distance number.

As he listened to the phone ringing somewhere in Michigan he thought of the people who had taken over the Bishop house, and remembered one thing. They had known the woman's name. So maybe the guy really was her nephew.

A maid answered the phone, and it was a while before Mrs. Bishop's voice came strongly on the line.

"Scott Yates?" she said. "You must have sold that old place!"

That was the way she was. You had to talk fast to let her know your business, and he was a Southerner, not a Northerner. She could out-talk him a mile a minute. "No—" he said, too late.

"Well, what on earth are you wasting money calling me for, then, young man? It does have something to do with the place, doesn't it?"

"I'm sorry if I disturbed you—"

"You didn't disturb me, I don't have anything else to do but talk, anyway. It was your money I was concerned about. You say it does have something to do with the place?"

"Yes. And a man named Giles. Do you know him?"

"Giles? Giles? Giles who?"

"Well, he said he is your nephew—"

"Oh, that Giles! My gracious, I haven't heard from him in years, where is he now? How on earth do you happen to know him?"

"That's why I'm calling," Scott said, talking faster, wishing she'd shut up for a minute. "I went out to the place to find that he is living there—with his wife and another couple."

"Giles is married? My gracious—well, I guess he *is* about old enough, at that. He must be twenty or more now, maybe more. The last I saw of poor Giles was when his father sent him away to a school when he was fourteen. A special school of some kind. He's my sister's boy, you know, and after dear Ellen died I kept him for a while, but then his father finally took him away for good, and I lost touch."

"The point is," Scott said, "do you have any objections to Giles living in your house?"

"My gracious no. He can live there as long as he wants. No one seems to want to buy it anyway—and between you and me I can't say I blame them. Though why Giles wants to live there is beyond me. I remember he didn't like it much when we went down there. It frightened him. We didn't even take the time to look the entire house over because he was nervous about it. And I must say, I wasn't too comfortable either. So why he wants to live there I can't imagine."

"He seems to."

"Well, do give him my love and tell him he can stay as long as he wishes."

"Yes. All right, Mrs. Bishop."

Scott hung up the phone and sat tapping the tips of his fingers together.

"What was that all about?" his dad asked. Anna Lou was waiting too, and there had to be an explanation made.

Scott made it as short as possible. "I went out to the Bishop house to find two couples there, that's all. One of the men is Mrs. Bishop's nephew, and they have her permission to live there."

Their faces looked stunned for a moment, then his dad exploded, "Live there!"

From the corner of his eye Scott could see a frown grow and deepen. He turned away so that he couldn't see that look of intense disapproval. There was nothing more to say. He was feeling thwarted enough the way it was. No one was supposed to go into that house again if it could be helped, and now ... why the hell did it have to be *her*?

His dad asked gruffly, "Do they realize the danger? Do they know a man was found dead there just a few days ago?"

"Evidently not," Scott said.

"You'd better tell them."

"The man died of an accident," Scott said stubbornly. "If they want to live there, that's their business. I can't see what good it would do for them to know about the accident."

"Then at least tell them about the rest—the poison in the house. They'd better know."

"A lot of hooey," Scott said angrily, getting up and leaving. He went to his muddy car and spun it into the street.

In the cafe he drank a cup of coffee in the corner booth. Mary was busy, and he was glad because he didn't want to talk anyway.

He was thinking. Let them live there without interruption or interference. They were young and healthy and not apt to fall down any stairs, or catch any old-time disease. Leave them alone.

The coffee made him fidgety. He kept seeing the freckles on Tara's white nose. Maybe he should go tell them anyway. At least give them the message from Rita Bishop. It would give him a good excuse to go back.

First though he drove through the car wash. Going back out there with his car a mess made him feel as if he were about to go on an important date wearing blue jeans. Just exactly why he should be sprucing up for a married woman, though, was something he didn't bring to the front of his mind, or exactly admit to himself at all. The touch of guilt he felt was easily rationalized away by emphasizing in his mind that his car did need washing. Besides, he washed it in between regular clean-ups every once in a while.

It was no big deal.

He drove carefully and slowly, in a way wishing that he hadn't come. He would have to face the triumphant sneer of the guy with the little-bitty eyes. He hoped to hell Tara wasn't married to *that* creep, but she probably was, the way he had jerked her back as if he owned her.

The guy was standing near the garage when Scott turned his car into what should have been a driveway, and stopped. Whistling, Scott went to the front of the house, pretending he didn't see a soul.

He knocked, and waited. But before the door finally opened, both men had come around the corner of the house. They stood hostile and unspeaking. The door opened then and Tara came out onto the step. She smiled at him, and then saw the two men.

And stopped smiling.

"I came to see Giles," Scott lied, looking at Tara as if he might never get another chance. Something had happened, he thought, since he was there earlier. Because she was staring at the two men as threateningly as they stared at him.

The guy Scott liked the least said, "Well, that's not him you're lookin' at, Mister. Giles is over here."

Scott turned slowly and faced them, looked them over from vine-surrounded ankles to freshly shorn heads and faces. The partly tanned, partly bleached skin gave them away, but Scott wasn't concerned with that. He decided to go ahead and let them have the facts, and maybe a bit more.

"I talked to Mrs. Bishop on the phone and she said to give her nephew her love. You're welcome to stay here as long as you like."

Giles glanced sideways at his friend, saw the beginning of the smirk, and quickly laid one on his own face.

Like papa, like boy, Scott thought. The kid had to see what the older one was going to do before he made a move.

"But I'd better warn you," Scott said in the same cool, casual tone, "about a few things that Mrs. Bishop doesn't know. Less than a week ago a man who rented this house was found dead. Long dead. He was lying at the foot of the third-story stairs. The police said he must have gone into the third story and on his way down, the stairs gave way, caved in, and he fell. His neck was broken."

The grins had gone. Giles' baby face had softened into a blob of wide-eyed attention. And from the corner of his watchful eye Scott saw that Tara had turned back and was again looking at him. He wished he could read her mind. For some reason he had certainly captured their attention.

Tara said softly, as if speaking to herself, "That's what smells so horrible in here!"

Scott had forgotten the smell, and the memory hit him with a jolt of surprise. "Why, yes, probably it is. He was dead several weeks before I found him."

The men edged forward.

"What happened to him you say?" the tall one demanded.

"He fell down the third-floor stairway."

"Christomighty!"

A long look passed between the two men. Scott found himself enjoying their agitation.

Suddenly the man barked a question at Scott. "What's up them stairs anyway? What's on that third floor?"

"I don't know."

"What the sonofabuckin' bitch do you mean you don't know? You rented the house, didn't you? You had the dealer's listin' didn't you?" His face had turned a mottled red and white.

"Yes, I have the listing," Scott answered. "And my dad, and granddad before me. But none of us, so far as I know, ever went on up to the third floor. Not many people went beyond the kitchen. Not many people ever even wanted to see that much. The place is large, the price high."

"You shoulda found out what's up there!"

Scott wondered why it should bother him as it did, since he didn't exactly look like the type to be put off by violence. "I guess you know this house is supposed to be cursed and haunted. Of course you do, because Giles was here once before, and you—Mrs.—uh—Tara, you mentioned it yourself. You obviously had heard it from some source."

Still softly, she said, "Tara. Just Tara. Not 'Mrs.' Giles mentioned it."

Scott forgot his mission for a moment. He looked into her shaded green eyes, thoughts flying through his mind. Not Mrs., yet she was living with one woman and two men, and that spelled ...

Scott pretended to clear his throat. Get back on the subject, idiot, he told himself fiercely. So what if she was a live-in broad? Why should he get so interested all of a sudden? It left her out of his life as much as if she were legally married. More so. He wouldn't be caught dead taking one of those home to meet his mother and dad.

"I thought I should warn you that the house is dangerous. Everyone who has ever lived here—uh—" He faced those freckles and curious eyes and couldn't tell her that everyone seemed to disappear or die. The psychological effect might be bad for her. And no matter what her morals, or lack of morals, he couldn't worry her like that.

"Look, man," the guy stepped forward onto the stoop, his face hard and belligerent. "Just get this straight, and then maybe you won't have to come trottin' out here no more. We ain't afraid of no stupid ghosts. We don't believe in haunts. We're living here, ain't we? And nobody's seen a ghost. So start truckin', okay?" He laughed, a sound not quite convincing. "If all we got on the third floor is a bleepin' ghost we ain't goin' to be needin' any help from you. And neither is *she*."

Giles came onto the stoop too, and it was suddenly so crowded that Scott was forced to either fight for space or back off into the vines. He backed away. The guy took Tara's arm again and pushed her into the hall, then, with a final glare at Scott, he followed. Giles went in too, pausing on the threshold for a moment to look back at Scott.

There was no attempt at belligerence in that baby face, just a kind of struggling wonder, as if he wished to understand something. Scott felt as if Giles were actually looking through him and seeing something else.

The door closed then, and Scott was left facing the ugly front of the tall, vine-shrouded house. He had a sudden, unreasonable urge to jerk open the door and drag the girl out because the door had closed behind her as if it had closed never to be opened again.

He controlled the urge with effort and stood awhile longer, but there was no sound. Not even a footstep. The frogs piped loudly, drowning out any sound of footsteps inside the house.

Scott went back to his car, and just as he was getting into it he heard the cry. It sounded faraway and muffled, and he wasn't even sure then that it had been a cry. He listened, but it didn't come again. He wondered if he should go in anyway and see about Tara, but he was sure that the sound had not been the scream of a woman. It had a deeper, wilder quality, like a long, sobbing groan.

Probably a bird somewhere back in the swamp, he decided. Or one of those peculiar sounds that came from the rotting timbers of the old house.

He got into his car, backed into the road, and drove toward town.

CHAPTER 8

The quavering moan from upstairs stopped Tara abruptly on her way down the hall. She looked up at the ceiling as if to see right through it to the room where Eldon was. Knowing now that someone had actually died falling down those stairs gave her a feeling of foreboding, a strong feeling that Fox would die also, that he might be dying now. But her feet felt glued to the spot as she listened to his cry quiver and fade.

"Well," said Sherwood, going on around her, "at least he wasn't killed when he fell down them stupid stairs, he just got a knot on his head."

Giles laughed, going around her, following Sherwood. But Tara saw that he laughed because Sherwood gave him that certain, commanding look that said *now laugh*. Tara saw the look, and hated both of them for a moment. She hated Sherwood for his lack of compassion, and Giles for his subservience.

She turned back to the front stairs and climbed, going quickly down the hall to Eldon's room. She stood for a moment, listening. But he was quiet. Suddenly she was afraid that he had died, that the cry had been his last fight against death.

She opened the door.

Eldon was sitting up in his bed, his face turned toward the ceiling. He threw his hand out toward her, as if holding her back, and said in a hiss, "Shhhh! Listen!"

The look on his face, his posture, his entire attitude, chilled Tara, and she realized that she was all at once afraid of him. She wished she hadn't opened the door. Trying to make no sound, she stepped backwards to leave, but he heard her.

His hand jabbed the air, motioning for her to be quiet and stop moving, but otherwise he was still. He continued to stare with hypnotically fixed attention at the ceiling. His voice was a harsh, loud whisper.

"Don't you hear it?"

She was thinking of him, not the upstairs. She had the uneasy feeling that he had gone insane, that his mind had entered another, alien world. "Hear what?" she asked cautiously.

"Shhh! If you don't be quiet it will hear, and know where we are. *Don't move.*"

She licked her lips, thought of Amy next door trying to rest, left alone so much up here with this man. "Hear what?" she asked again, in a lower voice, wondering if there were any way to persuade Sherwood to take Eldon away.

"It."

Pacifyingly, she said, "An—an animal perhaps? Walking, or gnawing on wood?"

"No!" he answered, as if she were both deaf and stupid. "Something that's going to kill us. Kill us all. Listen. You can hear it moving, moving, all the time. And it breathes." His voice dropped to a barely audible whisper. "It breathes. All around us it sighs and breathes. This house is its body. It's closing us in. Closing in."

"I'll go tell Sherwood about it," Tara said, and backed out of the room, closing the door gently.

She stood in the hall, her fingers pressed tightly against her lips, her eyes closed. Such a relief to be away from him. Poor guy. She would tell Sherwood all right, as quickly as possible.

She started toward the back stairs, then remembered that Amy would be left alone with Fox, and in his present state he might hurt her.

She went as quickly and quietly as possible back to the closed door of their bedroom, but Amy was not there. The dim room was dominated by the painting on the mantle, and nothing else that seemed even remotely alive. Even the heavy, dark furniture was but a background for the eyes in the painting.

The painting hadn't bothered her so much before, but it was probably because of Eldon. Fox. Just a state of nervousness on her part. She was glad that Amy had left the room. Gone down to the kitchen, probably, or perhaps out to the toilet. God knew the poor girl got sufficient exercise just going to and from the toilet.

With a sense of satisfaction Tara closed the bedroom door between her and the face of the painting that she had come to think of as *Samael*, as if he were a real person. At least she could shut him away. It occurred to her that she could not only shut him away, but completely destroy him if she wanted to. The fireplace could take care of the painting about as well as it had the black candle.

Later, she promised herself, later, after she had told Sherwood about Eldon.

She went into the kitchen to find Leda sprawled on the floor on a blanket. Giles was sitting beside her, his hands folded between his knees. Instead of reading he was looking thoughtfully at his hands. By the table, one on one bench, the other across on the other, sat Sherwood and Amy.

Tara stopped at the end of the table. "Sherwood, Eldon is completely out of his mind."

"He always was."

"I'm serious, Sherwood. You've got to get him out of here."

Leda sat up. "I think you ought to too, Sherwood. I heard him groaning and carrying on and it gets to me. It's downright creepy. It's bad enough having to stay in this awful old house without hearing that yelling and moaning going on."

"He's quiet now, ain't he?" Sherwood replied, throwing a frown at Leda.

Tara said, "Yes, he's quiet, but you should go up and look at him, and try to talk to him. He thinks there's something on the third floor that is going to kill all of us."

Sherwood snorted. "Heard what that cornball from town said, probably."

His tone infuriated Tara. "I thought Scott Yates was very nice. He's certainly no cornball—whatever that means. Or if he is, then I prefer cornballs to hippies."

Sherwood glared at her. "And who the hell's a hippie I'd like to know?"

"Cutting your hair and changing your clothes didn't change your character!"

"Hold it right there, Red!"

Sherwood placed his hands flat on the table and pushed himself a couple of inches off the bench. Tara thought of a frog about to leap, and smiled at the comparison. She had been hearing frogs so much that now she was seeing frogs in very odd places.

"You look just like a frog, Sherwood," she said sweetly. "Why don't you sit down before I turn you into one with *warts*."

He sat, and raised a poker-straight finger to point at her. "I'm warnin' you, Red, a few more smart cracks and you—"

Giles spoke up as if he hadn't heard the latter part of the conversation. "Maybe he's right. Maybe there is something on the third story that's going to kill us all."

For a moment the room was silent, then Sherwood yelled angrily, "Are you goin' out of your frickin' head too?"

"A man died here—that smell is still everywhere. They said the house was haunted. What if it really is? Fox isn't a nut. Wasn't. Why did he try to go upstairs? And the night before, remember? He said he heard something up there. Laughing, he said."

"He was too a nut! He didn't hear nothin'!"

Amy asked in a worried voice, "Who died? This stink in the house—it's because someone died?"

Tara looked at Amy, remembering that she hadn't even seen Scott Yates. Scott. She liked the name. It fit his dark, good looks.

Giles said, "That real-estate man who came said that a man fell down the stairs and was killed some time ago. They found him not long before we came. And it was him we can smell."

Leda demanded, "When did he say that?"

"Just now, when he came back to say he'd talked to Aunt Rita on the phone."

"Then I'm getting out of here myself! Let Fox stay. This dish, she's leaving!"

She was up and on her way to the door. Sherwood sat still, grinning at her back. When she reached the hallway and paused, he laughed.

"Just exactly where is that dish goin'?"

Leda didn't turn around, but she didn't go any farther. Her profile was toward Tara as she looked in a lost and bewildered way toward the open back door. For the first time Tara felt sorry for her.

After a long moment she came slowly back into the room and sat down beside Giles.

Amy said weakly, "I didn't know anyone had died here."

Sherwood yelled, "People die all over! Jesus, that's the tail end of life. If you gotta be born you gotta die. So what?"

Leda looked up. "How about the washing, Sherwood? We got to have clean clothes. Let's take it to the laundromat. Since Tara does all the cooking and cleaning I ought to do the washings."

Leda offering to do some work? Tara could see she was grasping at anything to get out of the house. "It's true," she agreed as cheerfully as she could. "If you'll go wash them, I'll gather them up, okay?"

"We have to have clean clothes, Sherwood," Leda said, begging.

"Groceries too," Tara added. "And a paring knife. We need milk." Sherwood was a milk drinker, and although there was half a gallon, he didn't know it. "Since we don't have refrigeration you'll probably have to go after milk every day." Solve two problems with one solution, she thought as Leda looked at her gratefully. It would help her as much to have Sherwood out from under foot as it would help Leda to get out of the house. "I'll get the clothes ready."

Sherwood hadn't objected, so Leda jumped up, smiling. "I'll help you, Tara." She actually sounded friendly.

They went into the hall together and toward the back stairs, and Leda said in a low, confiding voice, "Thanks, Tara. I won't forget that. I'll return the favor sometime, and when I say I will, I mean it. I keep my word."

Tara stopped and faced her, keeping her voice as quiet as Leda's. "Do you? If so, try to prevent Sherwood from sticking me in the back sometime when I'm not looking, okay? Or the front either, for that matter."

Leda looked at her in a straightforward way that showed no surprise. Then she said, "I'll do my best, Tara. But let me tell you this—and I think I can promise it—so long as you don't try to leave you'll be okay."

"Why?" Tara asked. "He doesn't like me. Why doesn't he want me to leave?"

Leda ran a red tongue-tip over her lips. "I can't tell you that. Don't ever ask again, and especially don't ask the guys. Just don't mention it."

"Then I'm not ever supposed to get away?"

"Something like that."

Nothing in Leda's face or dark, secretive eyes gave Tara a hint to the reason behind it all. Tara's eyes searched hers silently, and unproductively.

Leda touched her arm lightly with very cold fingertips. "I'm sorry," she said simply. "I think I know how you feel. I know this house doesn't bother you the way it does me—but at least I get to leave it long enough to do the washing and help with the shopping." She turned and walked on.

"We'd better hurry before Sherwood gets a bully streak and changes his mind."

Leda walked fast, and Tara followed slightly behind her. When Leda didn't pause at Eldon's door, neither did Tara.

Leda said as she went on by, "Let his clothes go. I don't want to go in there. Besides, it will give me an excuse to get out of here tomorrow. I'll tell Sherwood I forgot them."

They quickly gathered clothes from the other two rooms, and as quickly went on down the front stairs and back to the kitchen without additional conversation. Tara was thinking, wondering just exactly why she would never be allowed to leave, and coming up with nothing but fury. Not allowed to leave? Damn Sherwood to hell and back, she'd show him when the time came, if she had to sneak in at midnight and sew him up in his blanket.

"When you go to the store," she said, "bring me a big needle and some very strong thread."

"What the hell for?" Sherwood bellowed suspiciously.

Tara recalled with amusement the old tale about her eighty-pound great-grandmother sewing into his bed a recalcitrant hundred-and-ninety-pound son and then taking the horse whip to him until he was yelling for help. If Granny could do it, so could she.

"Well," she offered sweetly, "I do have to make some clothes for the baby."

Sherwood pointed a finger at her, threatening. "When you use that sugar-syrup voice at me I know you ain't thinkin' about no baby, so listen here, Red, I wouldn't bring you a needle if I had a knot on my head twice the size of Fox's!"

Tara leaned down and put her hands on the table, deliberately taunting. "Chicken."

Sherwood leaped up, but Leda hastily stepped in front of him, her arms loaded with soiled clothing. "Ready!" she cried with a large smile that trembled slightly with nervousness.

Sherwood continued to glare over Leda's head at Tara, but gradually he began to relax.

Amy asked timidly, "Can I go too? This smell is making me sick."

Sherwood gave her a quick glance. "I don't want you havin' no baby in no laundromat. You stay here. Giles, you stay too," he said as Giles started to get up from the floor.

Giles dropped bock.

But Tara didn't want Giles to stay. She felt it would be a relief to get them all out of the house. Give her a chance to *breathe*.

"Let him go," she said. "He looks like he could stand some fresh air too. I'll stay here, don't worry." She meant it. She had no intentions of attempting to leave until Amy's baby was born. Meanwhile, she was going to do a bit of exploring and find a way out, and when she did leave it would be in the middle of the night when she could walk the road without fear of Sherwood overtaking her in the car.

Leda said, "She means it, Sherwood, really she does. Let Giles come along."

Sherwood pointed his entire arm, plus stiffened finger, at Tara. "You just better be here when I get back, you just better."

"She will!" Leda promised for her. "Come on, let's go."

"All right, but, Giles, you stay. I don't trust that redhead."

Giles settled back again, and that ended it, to Tara's disappointment. Sherwood and Leda left the house, and after a moment the frogs quieted a bit and Tara knew he had started the car.

Giles was gazing at his hands again.

Tara said, "Why don't you read, Giles? Better to read than just sit there worrying about something you can't do anything about anyway, right?"

"I guess so."

"Amy and I are going upstairs. I have a couple of things to do there. You don't have to go with us."

"Don't worry, I won't. I wouldn't go in that room of yours again at all. I don't see how you can stand it."

"It's not so bad—it won't be when I get rid of that painting, anyway."

Amy cried, "Tara, are you going to take it down?"

Tara said calmly, "Come on, Amy, and we'll talk about it, all right?"

"Well, all right," Amy answered reluctantly, getting up with a soft moan.

It took forever, Tara thought as they walked, for Amy to get down the long central hall to the front stairway, up the many steps, and back along the equally long hall to their bedroom. Tara paced her steps to Amy's and talked cheerfully of whatever she could think of that had nothing to do with anything important. Having nothing on her mind was most comfortable at the moment. Just weather, frogs, birds. Small talk.

When they finally reached the bedroom, Amy collapsed into the rocking chair with short, fast breaths.

"Now then." Tara faced the painting and the harsh yellow eyes, her hands on her hips. "Would you really miss it, Amy? Doesn't it even bother you?"

"Well, it does strike me as ugly lately."

"Then you really don't care if I take it down, do you?"

"Well ..."

"I'll tell you what you can do, Amy. After your baby is born you can have a big photograph made of it—"

"Him," Amy declared strongly.

Tara smiled at her. "What if it's a her? There are two sexes, you know."

"I know." Amy didn't return her smile. Her mouth had tightened in a way that Tara had never seen. "But it won't be a her, it will be a him!"

Tara shrugged it away. So Amy was a bit cross today. She'd probably be cross too if she had a load like that and had just finished walking a half mile or so.

"How about the painting?" Tara reminded her. "Shall we take it down and get the frame ready for a new picture?"

For a long, thoughtful moment Amy looked up at the painting. "All right, if you really want to," she finally said.

"I really want to!"

Tara went farther back into the room and brought out a sturdy, ladder-backed wooden chair. She placed it carefully on the hearth beneath the painting, and then stepped onto it.

For the first time she was on eye level with Samael, and she stared for a moment into those baleful things that seemed so alive. And they stared back. She felt like looking away, but with the sudden childishness of a schoolgirl trying to stare down an enemy she kept her eyes steady. No matter where she was, it seemed, his eyes managed to be looking straight at her.

"Well, Mister," she said, placing her hands on the frame, "this is going to be the last time you'll look at me!"

Amy giggled suddenly. "You talk to it like it was a human! A man, even. It's only a little boy."

"Maybe I'm going dotty too," Tara said, and pulled. Nothing happened. Her fingers grasped the frame where it curved out from the wall, but she might as well have been pulling on a door frame that curved out. She paused, and then put more effort behind the pull. After a fruitless moment she placed one knee against the fireplace just below the mantle, for leverage, and put all her effort into pulling the painting away from the wall. The eyes looked into hers.

After watching quietly for a while Amy asked, "What's the matter, is it nailed?"

Tara stopped pulling, and drew her hands away. She panted from the effort she had used, and her fingers felt as if she had been holding sandpaper. She rubbed them together and looked at the frame.

"It must be, because it's sure there! It's not merely hanging, it's stuck to the wall tight as skin."

"I'll bet it's nailed."

Tara's eyes followed the carved frame of the painting. "If so, they are quite perfectly hidden. But of course they would be, wouldn't they? I don't see anything that's holding it. Maybe a lot of those little finishing nails, like they use in woodwork. They're invisible after the puttying and varnishing." She ran her fingers over the frame. "This isn't varnish, though, it's gold paint. Really, it feels like metal. You know, considering that this family was probably rich, it could even be gold. I would say brass, but it hasn't darkened as much as brass would, I'll bet you if I had a crowbar I could get it down."

"Or a tire tool?"

"Oh sure! Amy, you're very practical sometimes, you know."

"Well, I'm glad I'm something," Amy said. "I'm sure not very smart."

"Don't say that. Don't run yourself down."

"I'm not, it's just the truth, that's all."

"Listen, you wait here and I'll be right back. Maybe Giles could find an old tool in the garage."

She ran down the stairs, tightly holding the railing.

Giles was still sitting on the blanket, but he was reading. "Giles, would you do me a favor?"

He looked up after finishing his paragraph. "Yeah, I guess. What?"

"I wonder if you'd see about finding an old tire tool, or a crowbar, and come upstairs and pry that painting off the wall for me?"

His mouth fell open and he gaped at her. "*Pry* it off!"

"Yes, I can't budge it."

He began to shake his head. "No. No, not me, I'm not about to go into that room. That's the worst room this side of the third story, I know it is. You can feel it. Just walking by it you can feel it."

"That's ridiculous, Giles. Amy lives in it, and so do I, and we're both fine."

"I don't care what you think—you want it off, you get it off. Me, I won't even try. Not unless Sherwood helps me." He put his nose back into his magazine.

Tara sighed in exasperation and went out and onto the small back porch. And there she stopped. The path led around the garage, not into it. In order to get into the garage, she would have to wade through vines and take her chances with the snakes.

Slowly, she went along the path until she came even with the garage. She stopped and looked for a long while at the vines, and they seemed to move, as if something were waiting underneath. She couldn't help it, this fear of snakes. Weighed against the painting upstairs, the painting seemed harmless. At least it couldn't bite.

She decided to wait until Sherwood got back and then get Leda to talk him into taking down the painting.

The frogs grew silent for a moment, and she looked toward the road and saw in surprise that a car had stopped. Her heart nearly smothered her as she recognized Scott Yates. He got out and went toward the front door. Only for an instant was he in her view, and she knew he hadn't seen her at all.

She ran back to the hall, and then tiptoed quietly past the kitchen door. This time, she vowed silently to herself, Giles would not know that Scott had come, and she would get a chance to talk to him. She hoped. Also, he might help her with the painting. He probably had a tire tool he could use to pry it off the wall.

She hurried so much that she was breathless when she reached the front door, and she pulled it open under a barrage of knocks that she was afraid would alert Giles.

"Three visits in one day!" she said, low, casting a quick glance over her shoulder. Behind her the hall was long and dim, but Giles had not followed her. She had closed the door to the back hall.

Scott just stood there looking at her, and slowly lowered his fist.

She gave him a relaxed smile and leaned against the edge of the door. "It must be important."

"You know the old saying—third time charms? I guess I'm some kind of a fool. I couldn't stay away."

She knew the look when she saw it, because she'd been seeing it since she was thirteen. Scott Yates had come to see her. Just the thought of it caught her breath again. She looked up into his eyes, letting herself go, seeing the deep brown of them, the tanned skin of his finely planed face. The only thing that kept him from being downright beautiful was a square jaw and a dimple in his chin. In her estimation he came out being about as attractive as anything she had ever seen. Beneath the outward appearance was a quality puzzling and intangible that reached toward her and drew her as none other ever had.

Besides all that, he was a regular guy, and she liked him.

He said, half question, half statement, "You're not married."

She shook her head. "Are you?"

"No."

"Good." She opened the door wider. "Come in."

He looked over her shoulder, though he didn't hesitate to accept her invitation. "Sure I won't get thrown out? I mean—I'm not exactly welcome around here."

She moved close to him and whispered, "They're all gone, except Giles. He's in the kitchen reading." She took his hand and felt his fingers close tightly on hers. "We'll go upstairs. Anyway, there's something I'd like you to do."

He didn't say a word and she looked over her shoulder at him as she led him toward the front stairs, and the strange look on his face brought back to her her own words and the possible interpretation. It struck her funny and she laughed.

"What I meant was, will you take a big painting off the wall for me? You're big and strong, and, frankly, I couldn't move the thing."

"Oh," he said. "Where is it?"

"I'll show you."

She continued to lead him because there didn't seem much chance of him letting go of her hand anyway. His fingers threatened to bruise hers, and she wondered what his lips would feel like against her mouth. He must have been wondering the same thing for suddenly she was no longer leading. She was being pulled back instead, and turned, and for a brief moment his face and dark eyes were serious above hers.

She had never felt anything like it before. She weakened against him, letting the strength in his arms hold her, her own hands going up to touch his hair as his kiss burned itself into her body and heart forever. Deep in her mind the words began to form, *I love you, I love you*. She wanted him, and the urgency of it made her tremble. No man before had come close to making her feel so eager to be mastered.

Then he pushed her away and she saw that he was looking over her head down the long hall beyond where they stood near the top of the stairs. Looking at someone. Steadily.

Eldon, Tara thought in near panic. She had forgotten him.

She whirled, and to her relief she saw the vague, faraway outline of Amy instead of Eldon.

"Oh," Tara murmured, pulling at his hand again. "You'll have to meet my charge."

"Your what?"

"The reason I'm here. Come on."

"The reason you're here? I don't get it."

"Shhh. I'll tell you another time, okay?"

Amy stood just outside the bedroom door, leaning back with her hands on the wall, as if she had been there for a long time, watching them. She stared wide-eyed, with her kitten-innocent gaze.

Tara made sure to get both of them into the bedroom and then shut the door firmly before she spoke in a lowered voice. She remembered uncomfortably that Fox was next door, and stayed very quiet now, listening. And he was armed with a dangerous knife. Scott was a larger, stronger man, but she didn't know what he could do against Fox's knife.

"Amy, this is Scott Yates. You know, the real-estate man?"

Amy nodded.

Scott said, "Hello, Amy. I didn't even know you were here." He looked from Amy back to Tara. "Uh—two guys and three girls?"

Tara knew what he was asking, despite his skirting of the real question. She didn't attempt to answer him, to tell him that there were three men, because she knew what it would look like, and suddenly she was very sure she didn't want him to think that. But then Amy spoke up, candidly of course, and spilled the whole thing in a way that made it sound ten times worse than it was.

"No," the large-eyed girl said, "there really are three guys. Three girls and three guys. We're a family, you know, and this is our first baby."

Oh God, Tara thought as Scott's eyes met hers. They had narrowed and penetrated her conscience in a way that made her feel both ashamed and very guilty. Her temper flared a bit in self-defense and she lifted her chin, but before she could answer Amy was talking again.

"We live the natural way, you know. Some people call it communal, and I guess they're right."

Scott said slowly and rather coolly, "You mean none of you bother to get married, or even pair off? You all kind of—uh—live together?"

Amy smiled. "That's right. You do understand, don't you?"

His eyebrows lifted slightly. "Oh yes," he said. "I understand well enough. I've read a couple of magazines." He turned half away, looking around the room, pointedly ignoring Tara. "Where's that painting you wanted moved? The one over the fireplace?"

Tara felt like crying. He wasn't even going to give her a chance to explain. Well, to hell with him then. She had a wild desire to turn Amy over her knees and blister her bottom good, but she bit her own lower lip instead.

"Yes," she said shortly.

Scott walked over to look at it. "Samael?"

Amy went to stand at his side. "Do you know who it is? You do know, don't you, since you're the—the man who rents the house and everything."

"I guess I should know, but I'm sorry, I don't. I never really looked the house over very well because there just wasn't any use. I've never been in this room before. I don't know as much as I should about the history of the house and the people who have lived here."

Amy said, "Someone died here?"

Scott was reaching up to grasp the frame. "A lot of people have died here," he said. "That was one of the reasons I came back again—to try to persuade you all to leave. It's a dangerous house."

In alarm Amy asked, "But why? What's dangerous about it?" She looked around at the floor, walls, ceiling.

Scott's hands gripped the frame, but he paused and looked back rather tenderly at Amy. Then he said, "Well, it's old, sinking into the swamp, and gradually falling in besides. You never know when a board will fall, you know. That was the reason the renter was killed. The stairway that goes on up to the top floor broke through. The banister—"

Amy interrupted excitedly, "Fox fell there too! Will he die?"

"Fox?"

"He's the one you haven't met. He's had a dreadful headache since he fell."

Tara said quickly, "He is better though, Amy. He won't die. I was afraid for a while ..."

Scott glanced at her and then looked back at Amy. "Why didn't you get a doctor to look at him?"

Amy said proudly, "Sherwood doesn't believe in doctors, he believes in the natural way."

"Oh," Scott answered. "Some kind of religion."

Tara laughed, a mixture of contempt, anger and leftover guilt. Besides, she was feeling rejected because he so pointedly ignored her. "Sure. Religion."

Amy said, "Tara thinks we're crazy."

Scott looked at her then, his eyes searching for an answer, but Tara was mad and not about to respond. He had assumed the worst, let him go on with it.

"The painting," she said, and folded her arms tightly across her stomach. "Can you get it down or can't you?" He grinned. She saw that without looking directly at him. She kept her eyes on the painting. It was a teasing, private little grin, anyway.

"I'll see," he said, and pulled.

As she had done, he paused and looked over the frame, and then he put an effort behind it that brought the hard muscles out in his brown arms.

"I'll be damned," he said softly.

"It's nailed, I think," Amy said. "I don't think Samael wants it taken down, and I wonder if we shouldn't leave it alone?"

Scott was rubbing one hand across his chin. "All I know is it sure didn't budge. What harm is it doing?"

Tara said, "The longer I look at it the uglier it gets."

"If you want it down I'll get it down," he said. "I may have to get a keyhole saw and saw it out of the wall, but I'll get it down."

"Don't you have a tire tool? Something you can pry with?"

"Oh sure. Smart girl, aren't you?" He reached out, took her hand and pulled her along toward the door, ignoring her attempt at resisting. "Come along, we'll go get it."

Outside of saying, "The tire tool was Amy's idea, not mine," she didn't talk to him. With her head high and proud she walked beside him, not giving in to the glances she saw from the corner of her eye.

When they were well away from the bedroom, and near the front stairs, he spoke softly. "Are you part of it?"

"Part of what?" She knew well enough what he meant.

"The—family."

"I must be, I'm here."

His hand almost crushed her fingers for an instant. A mild reproof. "Come on now, tell me the truth. Do you—"

The face loomed before them suddenly, tight with fury. Tara stopped, staring at Sherwood as he came slowly up the front stairs. The anger in his face made him look ready to explode, and he was letting it build as he climbed toward them. Saving it. Probably relishing the thought of what he was going to do to them.

Tara spoke without thinking. "Are you back?"

"I ain't none of your goddamned ghosts," he answered without looking at her. His small eyes held hard to Scott Yates. "What I want to know, man, is what the bleepin' bitch are you doin' here again?"

"Well," Scott answered good-naturedly, "I came to remove a painting. I was just on my way down after a tire tool—"

"Okay, when you get down there, man, you drive, see? We don't need you around here. I told you, I ain't tellin' you no more."

Scott deliberately turned toward Tara. It was up to her whether he left or stayed, and the anger in Sherwood's eyes was beyond anything she had seen there before. Three men against one. She was afraid of what they would do to Scott Yates.

She pulled her hand out of his, and said with a coldness that successfully covered the regret deep in her heart, "You'd better go, Mr. Yates. As Sherwood said, we don't need you here."

Scott's voice, as he answered, held a note of hostility. "I can see that. What you need is more women, right?"

He released Tara's hand suddenly, walked around Sherwood and ran down the stairs without looking back. Leda stood at the bottom of the stairs. She stepped aside as he passed. The front door slammed so hard that the window high in the wall above it, over the stairway, rattled, and something fell on the third floor.

Sherwood's voice shook. "What was that all about? You givin' him the come-on or somethin'? Where the hell is Giles?"

He whirled and ran down the stairs and back along the hall, angrily flinging open the door. It bounced against the wall, causing reverberations in another part of the house, and almost closed itself again. Leda, trailing closely behind Sherwood, pushed the door back.

Tara watched them go, and something touched her back softly. She jumped and turned, but it was only Amy. A very frightened Amy. Tara hadn't noticed that she had followed down the stairs.

"We'd better go with them," Amy said, grasping for the newel post as she took the last step down. "He'll be wanting us all there. He'll be madder than ever if you don't come, Tara. Hurry."

By the time they reached the kitchen Giles was on his feet, facing Sherwood, and Sherwood was yelling so hard that his face had gone a dull red.

"You're worth about shit around here, if I can't leave for an hour without you lettin' that bastard in. What you doin', Giles? Dreamin'?"

In the brief pause Tara said, "You didn't have time to do the washing!"

Leda answered her hastily, "We were in the laundry when we saw Scott Yates' car go by."

"I knew he was comin' here, I knew it! You, Red, you're goin' to keep on till you've got us—" His anger seemed to be increasing. He stopped talking and stood shaking his head, blubbering almost uncontrollably. Leda touched his arm timidly.

"Sherwood, listen. It wasn't Tara's fault. Honestly. And it won't happen again, will it, Tara?" When Tara didn't say anything Leda shouted frantically, "Will it, Tara! How can I keep my promise to you if you won't cooperate?"

Sherwood caught his voice somewhere from the depths. "What promise?" he demanded suspiciously, his attention on Leda.

Leda, pale, shrugged. "Just—just girl stuff, Sherwood. Look, Sherwood, you know she can cook circles around me. You don't want to eat my slop, do you? He's gone now. He won't come back."

Sherwood calmed down a little. "He'd better not. He'd just better not. I've had it up to here with that snooper. Giles' aunt said this is our house, and nobody—*nobody*— comes in I don't bring. You hear that, Red?"

"I hear that, Bossman," Tara answered haughtily.

He gave her a last glare and turned away. "All right, you, Leda, and you, Giles, go back and finish that warshin'."

They left quickly, obviously glad to get away, and Tara too sought refuge from Sherwood's temper before she got into a death-to-the-finish fight, as she was tempted to.

"Where you think you're goin', Red?" Sherwood yelled after her.

"I'm going to take Amy back upstairs where she can rest. You've got her shaking like a scared puppy. Come on, Amy."

To her surprise Sherwood said nothing, and slowly Tara and Amy made their way back upstairs. Amy lay down on the bed and Tara spread a blanket over her.

But staying in the room was intolerable. Tara felt confined, closed in, faced by a smirking Samael.

"I have to be doing something, Amy," she said. "You don't need me here, so I think I'll get the broom and see if I can get rid of some of the dust."

"Okay, Tara. Just don't argue with Sherwood anymore, okay?"

"You sleep," Tara said gently as she closed the door.

She remembered Fox again, and stopped at his door. The silence in his room was absolute. She thought about looking in, and started to turn the knob but couldn't. Her hand simply refused to move, to lay herself open to what might lie beyond. She told herself he was all right. He was better. In fact, she assured herself, he was probably sleeping, gaining strength.

She went on toward the kitchen where the dust mops, brooms, dust pans and other cleaning paraphernalia were kept stacked in a corner.

Sherwood was sprawled face down on the blanket, his head on his arms, his eyes closed. Asleep, Tara thought, and was glad of it. She went very quietly past him to the corner by the fireplace and got the things she needed. When she turned back she heard a soft gurgle, a watery snore issuing from Sherwood's open mouth.

In the hallway she paused, listening. The house had never been so quiet, and having the other members of the household asleep left her feeling as if she were alone in the house. It was a strangely uncomfortable feeling, and made her reluctant to create any sound of any kind. Even the broom on the floor, when she gave a swipe at the dust, sounded abrasively loud.

She left the broom standing in a corner, took the dust mop and pan, and went quietly on toward the front stairs.

The doors on the right and left intrigued her for the first time, and very gently, hoping a hinge wouldn't squeal, she edged a door open far enough to see into the room.

It was a large, shadowed room, even more twilight-lit than the bedrooms upstairs, it seemed, and extremely ghostly with its great lumps of furniture covered with rotting gray-green sheets.

She slipped through the narrow opening and stood just inside the door. The carpet here had been rolled too, and she had no idea what kind of furniture was under the sheets. A chill crept up her back like a tiny reversed river as a thought came to her: *I'm not even sure it's furniture.*

She smiled at her own foolishness and backed out of the room. Of course it was furniture. What else? Now that she had gone into one room though, the others drew her more than ever. She crossed the hall and opened the opposite door. It was so nearly the same as the first that it could have been a twin. The only difference was that it had an old cavernous fireplace, and some of the furniture under the sheets revealed the shape of chairs. A living room. Drawing room? She didn't know what the owner could have called it, and didn't especially care. It was a puzzle though why so many rooms were needed when they all seemed to be sitting rooms, or drawing rooms, or whatever.

Maybe, she thought, it would be a diversion, later, to clean one up. For comfort it certainly would beat the kitchen.

Meanwhile though, and more important, was the dust on the stairway. It had irritated her from the first time she'd climbed the stairs.

She went to the top to work down, and then decided to go halfway back along the hall and clean forward. Then she would go and clean back to the rear stairs and down.

The dust mop made a soft sound against the floor no matter how easily she moved it. It seemed almost as loud as the broom, a scratching, splintering noise that ... She paused, and the sound continued.

Overhead.

She stood looking up at the ceiling, her hands gripping the handle of the dust mop. Gradually, like an echo of the dust mop, the sound faded. Crazy. It couldn't have been an echo of a soft little dust mop. Perhaps the house was falling in somewhere. Or a rat gnawing? Or something being dragged ...

Ridiculous, she told herself firmly, and dusted toward the top of the stairs with forced attention and energy. She wished she didn't feel quite so alone in the house. She wished she could have gone away with Scott Yates, back to a world of sunshine and reality, of music and laughter. Of love.

Laughter. It rose softly, like a child giggling when being tickled, and then rising hysterically, louder, sounding more like a woman. It had a chilling effect on her that caused her to stop abruptly and look back down the hall.

Amy? Amy laughing at something? Or Eldon!

She leaned the mop against the wall and ran on tiptoes down the hallway to Amy's room. She stopped, not opening the door, but turning instead back toward the front of the house. There was no need to open the door because the laughter, far away now, was at the front of the house, not the rear. It was not Amy, and it was not Eldon.

It was no one she had ever heard before.

A thought jerked into her mind and she grasped it thankfully. More lovers had come to the house, thought it empty, and were having themselves a giddy ball. Perhaps they had heard of the ghost who stood on the front stoop in the lightning and had come to see for themselves.

Tara hurried back toward the stairs, fully intending to go down and open the front door. But when she reached the stairway she stopped again, bewildered. The laughter, fading, going back to strange little childish giggles, came from above.

Above. The third story. And there was no way up there because the stairway was broken.

The sound was gone then, as quickly as it had come, and it seemed as if the whole house had gone to sleep.

Tara, though, was very much alert and staring at the wall against which her mop leaned. It protruded into the hallway in a way that seemed far out of proportion, and yet where the stairway joined the wall there was an odd little platform that had no obvious purpose. Just a ledge that was a dust catcher. And the dust was thicker there than anywhere else she had seen. There seemed to be no way to reach it, and it didn't look as if it had ever been cleaned.

What was its purpose?

She took the mop, held the end of the handle and reached over to the ledge and wiped at the dust. She managed to clear enough away to tell that it was made of the same narrow, varnished flooring as the hallway.

She drew back and softly set aside the mop, looking at the ledge in wonder. Why? Why a ledge, and no stairway to the upper floor?

Her attention immediately went to the first door opening on that side of the hall. It was about twenty feet back, opposite a door on the other side. She first checked the room on the other side, and judged it to be about twelve by fifteen. It was a small rather dark room because it had no front window. The front was taken up by the lift of the stairwell and a large closet. The other room, though, should be larger, since there was no stairway.

She crossed the hall and opened the door to find a room almost exactly like the other. Small, dark, dusty, with a closet in place of front windows.

She went back into the hall and looked again at the ledge, and realized what it was, and wondered that she had gone past it so many times without seeing it, because it so clearly was the landing of another stairway. A stairway that had for some reason been long ago boarded up and forgotten.

The wall looked the same as the others, a narrow grooved board that had once been varnished. With the end of her mop she lightly tapped it, and it responded with a hollow, empty ring. A ring that echoed and re-echoed somewhere above, as if her discovery and her knock had aroused a long-dead memory in the house. She drew back hastily.

But it was only an echo, she told herself, and this was only a false wall, hiding the third-floor stairway. Only that. Nothing more. Still, her knock went faintly on through the rooms above and finally died away.

She stood looking up, listening, wondering what lived above it in the third story. What, or who.

CHAPTER 9

Just wondering what was boxed up behind the hidden stairway gave her a distressing but vague sense of apprehension, as if she had just awakened from a nightmare which she couldn't grasp or recall, so she decided to dismiss the whole thing, try to get it out of her mind. She'd dust the back stairs first. To heck with the front.

She pushed the dust mop determinedly, ignoring the sounds above, trying not to hear them as footsteps following her own progress down the hall. Still echoes, surely. Or something of that sort.

When she reached the back alcove she couldn't help looking up into the dimness at the top of the broken stairway. A man had died falling down those stairs, Scott had said, and she recalled again the odor that had hung so heavily in the air when they'd first entered the house. Either she had gotten used to it, or it was finally going away. She wondered how many days it had been since the man had been taken out of the house.

She recalled too, vividly, the day before, while in the kitchen preparing the stew, she had heard the scream and the fall and had joined the others, running to see what had happened to Eldon. She had stood where she was standing now while Sherwood and Giles cautiously climbed the stairs and slowly and laboriously rescued Eldon from the black hole beneath the stairs. They had sent Leda to the garage for a rusty chain that hung on the wall there, and then Giles was lowered into the hole where he fastened it around Eldon's body and pushed while Sherwood cussed and pulled. The whole thing had taken at least an hour, and Eldon was unconscious the entire time.

But he wasn't now. He would be able to tell her if he had actually gotten into the third story, or if he had fallen on the way up.

She went quickly back to his room and opened the door, calling as she did, "Eldon, may I come in?"

This time he was sitting in the corner, staring at her from darkly circled, wild eyes as if he had never seen her before. She felt the same nervousness, as though she faced an alien being with whom she could not communicate.

"How are you feeling?" she asked gently, and very cautiously.

He didn't answer, he only hunched farther back. He seemed afraid of her, and pity melted her own fear.

"I won't hurt you," she said. "I would like to help you." *Oh God,* she thought, *that Sherwood!* Maybe if she could get him to come up and look at Eldon he would see that the poor fellow had to be taken out of the house.

"Why don't you tell me what you're afraid of, Eldon?" she prompted, wondering what to do, wondering if she could shock him out of it by bringing back his experience upstairs. "Remember you fell in the hole? And it made our head hurt. You had been upstairs, remember? You were very courageous and had gone all the way up, and you saw something."

He looked up at the ceiling, his mouth hanging open as in extreme fear. "It's there," he said timorously, "everything was falling. To kill me. Nobody lives here, nobody." He was shaking his head back and forth, back and forth, his eyes coming back to stare at her. Then he raised his hand and pointed at the opposite wall, the wall of her own bedroom where Amy lay sleeping. "And it's there," he whispered. "You can't get away from it."

"What is there, Eldon?"

He shook his head, and kept shaking it, as if once started it worked on a spring that had to run down.

"Eldon," she said, "is there another stairway up there?" She pointed up, as if talking to a child, and toward the front of the house. "A big, dark stairway that goes down to a wall?"

The direction of his head changed swiftly and he began to nod, nod, nod. "How did you know?" he cried. "You've been there! You know!" He crouched back. "Go away from me! Go away!"

"I'd like to help you—"

"Go away!" he screamed, covering his head with his arms.

She backed out through the door and closed it just as Amy opened the other one and looked out, her eyes still narrowed with drowsiness.

"Who screamed?" she asked. "Was that Fox screaming?"

"Yes."

"What's the matter with him?" Amy was waking up.

"He's sick. Really sick." Tara turned toward the back stairs. "Go ahead and rest, Amy. I'm going down to talk to Sherwood."

"Rest! No, ma'am, I'm going with you."

Tara was in a hurry. "You'd better go the front way then, these stairs are very steep."

"I don't care, I'll make it. I'm going with you. I'm not staying up here with him."

Tara slowed her own steps just a little in order to keep an eye on Amy as she descended the back stairs. The girl felt her way down, as it was impossible to see her own feet below her huge belly, but after a while she made it. Once she reached the bottom Tara waited on her no longer.

Just as she reached the kitchen door, Leda and Giles came in the back, their arms full of clean clothes. They both were talking and smiling and looked as if the trip to town had been a very good thing.

Sherwood lay sprawled on his back, his mouth wide open, snoring heavily. Tara stuck her toe against his ribs and pushed. He came up spluttering and swinging one fully extended arm toward her. She got away just in time to avoid a smashing whack across her legs.

"I'd sure hate to have to sleep with you," she said.

"What the hell do you want? What're you stickin' in my ribs, your damned broom stick? What're you doin' that for?"

"I've got something to tell you so sit up and stop snoring and yelling like a maniac."

He sat up, took a deep breath, and slumped against the wall. "I don't know why I put up with you."

"Because I can cook, and also because I know something."

His eyes popped open wide. "What—do—you—know?" he demanded in slow, vicious words.

It made her wonder briefly just what it was he was afraid she did know, but then the other took precedence. "There's a front stairway to the third story."

"Like hell!"

"Stop bellowing and listen. Eldon—Fox—is completely out of his mind with fear of something he saw while upstairs—" She paused for just long enough to see that she finally had Sherwood's full attention. Also, the attention of the others. They stood to her left, in a half-moon, listening carefully. "I was dusting the front stairs and found the false wall that boards up the stairs, and then I went to Eldon and asked if he had gone up there, and I'm sure he did."

"Goddamn," Sherwood muttered, getting to his feet.

"What are you going to do?" Leda cried, almost hysterical. "I don't like this. I don't like it at all. Why should anyone close up a stairway? What are you going to do?"

"I'm going to see what's there, that's what."

Giles said, "Do you think we should, Sherwood?"

"You just let me do the thinking, Giles." He turned to Tara suddenly. "Did you hear anything from up there?"

She hesitated, and then decided to tell it, silly or not. "Well, yes. I heard a child's laughter, or—" She frowned, trying to find words for it. "An unnatural sound, in a way. It became like a woman's after—"

Sherwood slapped his thigh, hard, and interrupted her. "Laughter! And that's what Fox said he heard. Remember, Giles? Remember, Leda? That night he come after us to go look who it was! Somebody is livin' up there, and I aim to see who it is!"

Tara recalled suddenly that someone had mentioned that before, but she had forgotten. She didn't feel so foolish if Eldon had heard it too, but— "But," she said, "how could it be people?" Something didn't fit. There was no logic to any of it.

Giles threw his armload of clean clothes onto the blanket. "But Sherwood! You heard what Tara said it did to Fox. Maybe we ought to just get out of here."

Sherwood stuck his thumbs into his pockets and looked at Giles contemptuously. "You a chicken or somethin'? Fox, he's a coward, but I'm tellin' you there ain't a person on this earth that can scare the sense out of me! I'm goin' up, and you're goin' too."

Leda said, "I'm sure not!"

"I didn't ask you."

Tara said, "I am. I want to see what's there—if anything."

"What do you mean 'if anything'?" Sherwood growled. "You heard the laughin', you said."

"It could have been—been something else. An animal? Something. Maybe even an old wind-up toy of some kind that gets started once in a while. Anyway, I want to see."

Sherwood said sneeringly to Giles, "See? She's got more guts than you have."

Tara said as she stepped over the splintered bottom of the opening, "What about yourself? You're supposed to be the leader, aren't you?"

"I broke it open, didn't I!"

Just to irritate him Tara paused long enough to say, "Yes, you did, and I'll bet whatever is hiding upstairs will remember that, too, and get you first."

Sherwood didn't have anything to say to that, he simply blinked. She smiled to herself and went on to stand in the dusky dark stairway that reached up into an upper story that had a faint aura of light, filtered through a long front window that was not quite as well covered by vines as the lower windows. She stepped to one side to allow room for the men to enter, and while she waited she looked at the difference in the two front stairways.

This one was enclosed, and a railing went up against each wall. When her fingers touched the railing near her they touched metal, and she saw a strange-looking little wheel with a handle, and around the wheel a chain. The chain was connected to the metal underneath the railing and for a moment she was puzzled, then its significance dawned on her. It was a kind of old-fashioned lift for a wheelchair. She wondered if the back stairway had a lift also, and doubted it. Furthermore, this was the only lift in the house. Neither of the two lower stairways had lifts.

The boarded stairway had something to do with the invalid boy, then. Obviously. Strangely. Uncomfortably.

Why should such an old thing bother her now, she wondered. She was uncomfortable, as if she had entered a place that was not supposed to be entered, ever, by anyone.

Giles, not to her surprise, came through next and stood close beside her, looking up. Immediately behind him came Sherwood.

They stood by her, very silent. Frightened or awed? She didn't know, and didn't feel like asking. Maybe they were feeling the same way she felt. For some reason she didn't want to break the silence, even to tell them about the lift, or to ask who was going first. There was no need. She knew if anyone went, she would have to lead.

Slowly, she proceeded up the stairway, a long, straight line of steps that had walls on both sides, and was open at the top, joining the hall that ran back into the house. A banister separated the open stairway from the hallway on one side. The long, dingy window was high in the front of the house on the left, across from the banister.

Tara stopped on the upper step, her hand on the newel post of the low railing, and looked down the hallway. She saw the thick dust, and the footprints. And felt on the back of her neck the breath of one of the men as he came to stand close behind her and look over her shoulder. She knew he must be standing on the step below, because both men were at least a head taller than she.

The breath grew hotter and stronger as Sherwood said in a near whisper, "Look at them footprints! Somebody *is* up here."

Open bedroom doors threw light on the heavy dust and fallen debris that coated the long hallway, and Tara took a step forward and up to stand where she could see more. Her earlier feeling of being a very unwelcome intruder was overpowered by her curiosity. The footprints near her, by the railing, were quite clear. Two people had walked there. One wore shoes, and one was barefoot.

"Eldon didn't have any shoes on when we found him that day, did he?" she asked aloud.

"Huh?" Sherwood answered as he followed her, looking down at the prints. Then, as if her words had finally penetrated, he said, "No."

"Then," Tara pointed out, motioning with her hand, "these are Eldon's footprints and—" Her eyes followed them back toward the other end of the hall where they were lost in darkness. In and out of the rooms both prints had gone, and into only one room directly on the left. Down the left side of the hall they blurred into a single path, mingling, the dust disturbed. "They ran, see? Out of this room on the left."

"Goddamn!" Sherwood whispered shrilly. "Keep your voice down. Whoever was there chased him out. He may still be there. Bound to be."

"No," she said, moving on to look more closely at the blurred prints. "He didn't come back. Neither of them came back."

"How do you know?" Sherwood hissed.

In the silence then Tara heard Giles draw a long, deep breath. He sounded as if he had been holding back and had been forced to take in air. She felt the cold draft against her face, and thought in part of her mind as she stared at the footprints, trying to comprehend their message, that it was odd that Giles' breath was so strong and cold.

And Giles was behind her.

She realized suddenly that the draft was coming from somewhere in front because it moved her hair, pushing it back softly, as a breeze rising from somewhere. She automatically raised one hand and held her hair down.

"Was that a wind?" Sherwood asked.

But it was gone as suddenly as it had come, and Tara didn't bother to answer.

"Must be some windows open," he said. "Where do you think that other guy is? Since you're so positive he didn't come back."

"I think he's dead," she answered softly.

"Hey! Why do you think that?"

"Because Scott said a man had died here, and I think that's who was up here, and Eldon was just following where he went." Her attention came back and fastened on the door to the left. "Whatever it was that scared them is in there."

"Hey, come on," Sherwood said aloud. "What're you tryin' to do, make somethin' out of nothin'?"

Giles begged suddenly, "Let's go. There's no one up here."

"Wait," Tara said. "I want to see a couple of these rooms while we're here."

She had begun to walk. She paused at a door on the right and looked in, and saw the twin sets of prints in the dust. Then she crossed the hall and looked into the room next door to the one from which the men had run. No prints there at all. The dust and mildew lay heavily on everything, furniture, shredded draperies, sagging bed. There was one large chair, black, that looked as if it might have held a large man. The odor in the room was musty, old, stale. No vines climbed on the window.

She backed out.

The hallway seemed to have darkened considerably. The two men looked like tall, shadowy statues at the top of the stairs. They hadn't moved.

A light, she thought, as she went slowly along the hall, she needed a light. The sun had gone behind a cloud, another storm was coming. She could feel, it, the intense stillness before a storm. The waiting silence.

She started to pass the room that intrigued her most. It could wait until tomorrow, when the sun might shine again. But when she came even with the door she stopped and looked in. Although still standing in the hallway, she could see the cradle that stood in the corner of the room. Her mind formed the words *a nursery*, and she felt astonishment. Somehow it didn't seem that Samael had ever been a baby—or had there been another baby in the house?

She stepped over the threshold, her hand on the half-opened door to push it back, and looked into the entire room. All she saw was that one corner of the ceiling had fallen, hanging nearly to the floor in places. And from one board trailed a thick, heavy rope. It was connected to the hanging board by means of a rusted iron hook.

"This room was a nursery," she said to the men in the hall, and to herself, as if putting voice to thoughts would clear the mystery she sensed. "And there's a heavy rope attached to the ceiling in the corner, and a lot of trash and stuff in the corner on the floor and—old clothes—and—" In horror she bent, and she almost touched, then quickly she drew back her hand.

And from the leg of a ragged pair of trousers, a protruding bone ...

Sherwood's voice hissed from the hall, "And what, for Christ's sake?"

And in the corner a round, whitish thing that looked like a face without flesh, a ...

In unconscious recoil she was backing out of the room, slowly, slowly backing out.

"What's wrong?" Sherwood demanded. "What's in there?"

She turned and looked at him, and whatever he saw on her face caused him to shut his mouth and stare round-eyed at her. Wordless.

The wind struck suddenly, and the thunder, and it was as if the house had no roof to keep the wind away, and no walls. It swept hard against her, pushing her blouse against her breasts and blowing her hair back. She put out her hand to steady herself against the force of the wind, and touched the wall. It moved under her hand, and as though in slow motion she saw a portion of the ceiling turn loose and fall, fall downward toward the two men who stood on the stairway. She tried to scream at them to move, because they weren't looking up, they were looking at *her*. Staring, gaping, like immobilized waxed dummies. The board swung down, one end still holding at the top, and one of the men cried out, a hoarse, deep near-scream. They stumbled backward, going down the steps, grabbing the railing for support and turning, running, falling, getting up and running again.

The board swung in the air, and black motes drifted down from the opened hole in the ceiling.

Tara's paralysis left her and she too began to run. The storm was destroying the house and if she didn't hurry she would never get out. The distance to the stairway seemed long, nearly impossible to reach, but finally her hand grasped the newel post.

She pushed the swinging board aside and ran down the steps and through the hole into the second story.

And stopped.

All four of them, Sherwood, Giles, Leda, and Amy, stood in the lower hall by the opened front door, staring up at her. The looks on their faces made her pause, and she realized that the sounds of the storm had gone. The frogs sang, a bird called, and the remains of a sinking sun cast pale light on the floor behind Amy.

"What's wrong?" Leda demanded as if she had asked it before. Her face showed bewilderment, as did Amy's.

But both Giles and Sherwood's had gone a dull gray-white like the old sheets that covered the furniture in the room behind them, and they looked at her as if she had brought with her whatever it was that had terrified them on the third story.

Tara didn't answer Leda, nor did anyone else. Tara walked swiftly on down the stairs, and the group made way for her as she went to the front door and out onto the stoop. She looked up at the sky and saw that it was without clouds except a warning, approaching black rim in the southwest.

She came back into the house, and because she had to say something, said. "There *is* a storm coming." She looked at Sherwood, defying him to say anything at all.

She saw him swallow and look at Giles.

Again Leda asked, "What the hell is wrong with you three? Did you see a ghost up there?"

"Of course not," Tara answered, going back toward the kitchen. "The place is falling in, that's all. A board came down from the ceiling and nearly got the guys. I'm hungry. I think I'll cook supper before it gets too dark to see what I'm doing. Besides, I don't like bugs in my food."

Be natural, she told herself. That's the only way. Meantime, in Leda's words, what the hell did happen up there? She didn't know.

She thought of it as she worked, and found her mind becoming more confused, as if she were trying to cram too many things into it. As if she were trying to understand the main purposes behind life and death. Whatever it was seemed beyond her. Incomprehensible.

The other four sat at the table, drooping, waiting. But not for food. Not for anything. Tara thought they too looked confused, like children pushed into a class they weren't prepared for.

Sherwood finally, morosely, said, "It rains about as much here as it does on the West Coast in winter. Worse, it thunders and lightnings and the wind blows like it was going to take everythin' along with it."

As if in agreement he was answered by a faraway sound of thunder. Tara almost dropped the pile of plates she was carrying.

She got hold of herself mentally by listening to make sure that the thunder was real this time. Physical, beautiful, real.

"I like storms," she said. "I really do."

Everyone was very quiet, and she glanced at them to see that once again the men were staring at her almost as if they were afraid of her.

"You need more fire!" Giles said, and jumped up, going to poke sticks into the blaze beneath the cooking food.

Leda got up and took the plates from Tara, saying softly, "I'll set the table."

Even so, they had to eat by candlelight because the clouds came, bringing thunder, lightning, rain, and darkness. And tiny bugs flew around the lights. Annoying. Getting in the food. Tara pushed her plate away finally when one of them sat down in her spoon.

The group around the table was quiet, each deep in private thoughts and worlds. Leda stared at the wall opposite and hardly touched her food. Amy ate, but afterwards she leaned on her hand. Giles went over and sat on the hearth stool and poked a stick into the fire occasionally, watching it burn,

Tara was the first to speak, and she had to raise her voice to be heard over the rattling of the house under the wind of the storm and the crashes of thunder. "Amy, do you want to go to bed?"

Amy looked, up. "We'd have to go up the stairs," she said. "And—and there's that open hole in ..." Her voice faded into the noises of the house in the stormy night.

Tara got up and took her arm with a valor she didn't feel. "We won't let that bother us. In a few moments we can be safe and snug in the bedroom —and much more comfortable than here."

Amy got up and allowed herself to be led, but she clung to Tara's hand like a frightened and dependent child. Tara had a hand free for only one candle, and she prayed silently that the awful draft from the third floor wouldn't blow it out.

The thought of being near that hole to the upper story, in the darkness, disturbed her so much that she paused to ask Sherwood, "Would you mind bringing the lantern and showing us the way?"

"You've got your candle," he said grouchily.

Giles moved and stood up, looking at the lantern in the center of the table. His thoughts were clear to Tara. He had been about to offer to go, and had changed his mind.

Leda said, "If we're ever going to bed we might as well all go at once. I'm cold. And I'm tired of just sitting here."

Sherwood shrugged. "Yeah, me too."

Tara said, "Why don't you take Fox's plate up to him?"

"Why the hell should I? If he wants to eat he can come down."

"I think you should go see him," Tara said. "He needs someone."

"All right! Just go on to bed, will you?"

Tara went on with Amy, and Leda came behind them with the lantern. Tara didn't look back to see if Sherwood were bringing Eldon's plate, but she would have bet that he wasn't.

At the rear stairway Leda stopped. "Let's go this way."

"But Amy can't climb these steps, Leda," Tara said. "Really, there's no harm going the front way."

"Ha! Not me. Not now."

"I don't see why not. After all, there is a stairway that goes into the third story here too, and it was here that the man was found dead, and here also that Fox fell."

Leda looked up into the darkness, her face turned colorless by the lantern light. "Hey," she said. "I hadn't thought about that. All right, then, the front stairs. One thing about them, they're easier to climb."

The hole chopped through the wall at the top of the stairs stood black and unavoidable, waiting for them. Tara heard Leda say something under her breath, and felt Amy's hand grow tighter and tighter on hers. They passed it quietly, and even Tara drew a deep breath when they were in the upper hall and away from it.

Leda said almost cheerfully, "Well, good night. I'm going to cover my head with a blanket and refuse to look out until the sun is shining again."

Amy and Tara answered her with brief good nights, and Amy's steps speeded amazingly. Tara hadn't realized that she could move so fast.

There was no sound from Eldon's closed room, and Tara didn't go near it. Even Samael, glaring at them with his odd yellow-gold eyes, seemed harmless now. She lighted all the candles on the mantle on each side of the portrait, and then, because she didn't feel like being in the dark at all, she took from the secretary the black candles and placed them in various spots around the room, lighting them all. Amy had already gone to bed, rolled in her blanket, her eyes closed. Tara didn't know if she were already asleep, but hoped so.

The boredom of the evening began to settle on her. The storm was fading some, though the house still felt slightly unsteady under the roar of the wind, and from above came an occasional tearing of wood, the sound of a falling board, and a variety of odd creaks and groans that added a definite restlessness to Tara's boredom.

Amy's breathing sounded even, and she knew the girl was asleep, though how she managed it was beyond Tara. Too tired to stay awake, probably.

Tara walked the floor for a while, and then remembered the old books. There were five scattered about on a shelf she hadn't cleaned, but they turned out to be mildewed lumps, too far gone to even be opened. She pushed them aside in distaste and wiped her fingers.

For a while longer she walked the floor, then remembered the books Amy had said were in the secretary. Hadn't Amy said they were in good condition? Or had she said? Tara went to the secretary again, wishing Amy had stayed awake longer. They could have at least discussed the books.

If she couldn't have someone to talk with though, she wanted something to read. Anything. The nineteenth century had been a great one for beautiful romances that hadn't an ounce of reality, but it might be just what she needed to weather the long, long night. She could read herself to sleep.

She found three books, all bound in black leather, and all very stiff and difficult to open, but at least not ruined by mildew. She took them to the bed, placed a couple of black candles on the table so that she could see, and found that Samael was staring at her so hard she couldn't concentrate.

She left the bed and went to the rocking chair, pushing it nearer the cold hearth in order to be out of Samael's view. The candles on the mantle cast down enough light for her to see the fine print in the old books, if she held them just right.

The first one she opened was the Bible. Saint James version, Christian Bible. In beautiful, flowery penmanship someone had written, *To Samuel from father, 1860.* And over it, as if to obscure the words entirely, someone had drawn the same mark that was on the painting.

Tara turned the book more to the light and looked again. The mark was made with a black pen, different from the writing, and drawn in heavier, deeper strokes that had cut through the thin India paper in several places.

Tara carefully turned the brittle pages, and found each one covered by the mark, drawn heavily and angrily in black ink, a horizontal bar with an inverted V.

The feeling it gave her was one of extreme aversion, as if she had touched something slimy and snaky. She dropped the Bible on the hearth and then pushed it away with the toe of her sandal. Who, she wondered, would mutilate a Bible in such a way? Even an atheist. Why bother? She had considered herself an agnostic for many years, and she had met and talked with several confirmed atheists, but she would have been surprised if any one of them would have deliberately ruined a Bible. There was no purpose behind it. But immediately she knew there was. And the purpose was, for one, hatred. And perhaps more.

Much, much more.

She was almost reluctant to open the other two books.

To her relief the next one was a simple dictionary. She glanced through it, saw not even a signature, and placed it carefully on top of the Bible.

The last book had been used a lot. The leather was cracked and worn, and the corners bent like tiny floppy puppy ears. But the contents were not innocent. Black magic. A signature, in black ink, written in dainty, neat but childish penmanship clearly read "Samael." And beneath the name was the sign again.

This name, she now knew, was not a simple misspelling. The boy had deliberately changed the spelling. Changed the name.

She read swiftly, skipping long paragraphs that made her feel ill to her stomach, pages and descriptions that filled her throat with revulsion. *Black magic.* How to curse, to kill, to sacrifice by letting blood, particularly human blood, in order to get one's wishes fulfilled. Sexual deviations that made the pornography of the Seventies seem mild. Deviations that always ended with the death of the victim.

"My God," she said softly under her breath, slapping the book shut, wishing she had never opened it. Where had an invalid boy gotten a book like that?

She stared at it, and the house over her groaned and settled with a sound similar to the laughter she had heard earlier. Or thought that she had heard. She yearned suddenly to run out of there, to risk Sherwood's knife, to run to Scott and throw herself into his arms again for protection. For sanity. She felt so alone, and so vulnerable. But she remembered Amy, and Amy, asleep on the bed, was even more vulnerable.

Tara had stood up and was on her way to the door when she stopped to look at Amy's young and helpless face. She went back to the chair then and sat down. Scott would come again, she told herself. And when he did she would ask him to get Amy out of there: The others would simply have to take care of themselves.

She didn't believe in the power of magic, black or otherwise, but when she looked at the black candles burning their wavering, dancing little lives, she recalled the gist of what she had read about their powers and couldn't stand the sight of them. She left the chair and quickly gathered up the black candles, extinguished their flaming lives, and put them back into the secretary.

The other candles, the plain white ones, lined the mantle, adding a moving light to the bottom of the painting, and the golden eyes followed her about the room.

"Old boy," she said caustically, "you just wait until tomorrow!" She'd pry the thing off the wall or know why she couldn't.

She collected the white candles, considered blowing out all of them and trying to get to sleep in the darkness, and decided that at the moment total darkness, except for lightning flashes against the vine-barred window, would be too much. She compromised by keeping one burning, and putting it on the bedside table. Then she lay down in her blanket, and wasn't even aware that she had forgotten to change to nightclothes until she was already rolled like a cocoon in its web. Too late to change now. Besides, she wasn't at all sleepy and might want to get up and go downstairs or something.

If it weren't storming so, and if the snakes didn't crawl at night, she'd consider going outside.

Storming. Did it storm every night? Nerve-racking as ... it occurred to her that there was no thunder now and no lightning, and not even the sound of rain. There was only the wind. She had never been in a hurricane and wondered if this was turning into one.

The house moved a little in the wind, splintered, a board upstairs fell, crashing against the floor overhead and making her jump and her heart pound, smothering her with its continuing heavy beat. The bed springs creaked as Amy stirred restlessly in her sleep, but she didn't wake. There followed a long, throbbing silence, as if everything were settling, and then came another faint sense of movement, like a ferry crossing a smooth, deep lake. It made her slightly sick to her stomach.

She sat up, listening. The silence penetrated her brain, her body, causing it to ache with the tension of waiting. She hardly dared breathe, dared not break the silence. Something was happening. Or something was going to happen. She didn't know, and couldn't even think without effort. Was this what happened before a hurricane or tornado struck? And what had happened to the wind?

Sound began rising then, coming from the house itself, hidden within the walls, a soft murmur, a mutter, a chuckle. Laughter. Louder and louder.

Terror chilled her body and mind yet she still sat in bed moving only to throw back the blanket, listening, looking up, straining her eyes into the ceiling, her mind crying *what is it*?

Footsteps somewhere then, loud, thudding. She realized they were in the hallway outside her door, that someone was running toward the front of the house.

The footsteps faded into a scream, a loud, frightened cry for help or release or escape. Tara pulled her legs from her blanket and ran toward the door. Eldon. *Eldon!*

Come back, Eldon!

She didn't think about a light, or even the darkness in the hall. She followed the sound of the dying scream, blindly running, with no plan of action, no knowledge of what she would find. She had to stop Eldon from going toward the front of the house.

The scream died to silence and there were only her own steps in the hall echoing back somewhere, cave-like. Her voice filled the stillness that had descended as she called, cried, "Eldon!"

She struck something solid, and stopped, and put out her hands against it. The wall.

What wall?

She saw it then. The wall of the hallway near the end. She had run against it, that was all. In relief she leaned for a moment, and then the source of the light caused her to turn, to look back down the long, long hallway.

They were all there, four shadowy figures coming behind the gaslight blaze of the lantern. Sherwood was holding it high in his hand, peering beneath it with both eyes and mouth opened to round astonishment. He stopped about ten feet away, and the others crowded behind him. They all stared at something, and it was something that was on the other side of her.

She too turned and looked.

He lay on the top of the stairs, the lower part of his body in the hall, and the upper, his head, torso and arms, hanging downward over the steps. Limp and twisted, like a huge doll thrown carelessly. The black hole chopped in the wall gaped above him.

Tara moved, running again, going down the stairway to touch Eldon's head. He lay still, his eyes open, his face contorted into a mask of terror as if he had died with the scream in his throat.

"Bring the light!" Tara shouted, feeling herself start to tremble and telling herself to cut it out now! He had fallen. It didn't mean he was dead.

The light came, and behind it, at arm's length, Sherwood. He didn't say a word. He looked as if he couldn't even get his mouth to move from its frozen O.

Tara's voice shook as hard as her body did when she cried out at the silent Sherwood, "Well, come on! Get him downstairs to the kitchen! I need water! He's only unconscious. Come on!"

Sherwood reached over and handed the lantern to her, stepped over Eldon and got his hands under the limp arms. Without being told, Giles came and took Eldon's feet. They lifted him.

Tara went down the steps sideways, looking back, holding the light so that they wouldn't stumble. Behind them, closely together, for protection, came the two girls.

The sound of the wind rose suddenly, roaring, and Tara felt it move her hair. A strong draft came out of the opened hole from the third story. It swept down the lower stairway, gaining force and, strangely, it had somehow changed direction and blew Tara's hair forward around her face. She kept one hand busy pushing it out of her way so that she could see. A door, and windows, she thought, must have blown open somewhere, creating the returning wind.

Sherwood, she saw, was staring at her, his eyes still round, fastened like glue on her face. It added to her discomfort, and her teeth began to chatter with nervousness. She couldn't hold her chin still. She turned, facing the wind, and hurried her steps.

In the kitchen coals still glowed in the fireplace, and the draft was reduced to a moving chill that reminded Tara of the ice-cold currents that lurk under the warm surface of a quiet body of water.

She put the lantern on the table, and ran for the water bucket. Water splashed as she poured part of it into a pan, and spilled when she turned.

Eldon had been dumped on the blanket and Sherwood kneeled beside him. "Don't bother," he said. "Fox don't need water, or anything else. He's dead."

Tara stopped and simply stood holding the pan of cold water. Just stood and held the pan. Part of her mind noted that Giles was looking down at Eldon, and the two girls were several feet away but still standing very close together.

Giles said, "I don't see any blood. What did he die of?"

"I'd guess a broken neck," Sherwood said. "The way his head hangs. See?" He raised Eldon's shoulders to show how the head dangled.

Tara turned quickly away. She didn't want to see. "You'd better go get a doctor," she said. "A doctor has to pronounce a person dead."

"Not this person," Sherwood replied, getting to his feet. "Giles, build up a fire and let's have some coffee. Feel like I need some booze."

Tara put down her pan and sat on the bench. Amy and Leda came and sat beside her."

"No doctor," Tara said, half dazed, hardly thinking. "The sheriff? An undertaker? You have to have somebody."

"No."

"Scott," Tara said, nearly bursting into tears with relief. "Scott Yates! Scott will know what to do."

Sherwood said in his normal, yelling voice, "I know what to do!" and poked a finger against his chest. He turned it and pointed at her nose. "You keep that out of it, hear? We'll take care of the body. We bury our own dead."

"What?" she cried. "You have to report it!"

"No, I don't! You just forget about it. It's not any of your business."

Tara drew a deep breath, and listened to the wind, and thought about Eldon lying on the stairs, and heard again his scream. The queasy feeling was in her stomach again, and she leaned her forehead against her cold hand.

She heard Leda say, "For gosh sakes do something. Get him out of here, I can't stand to sit here where he is, and I'm not going back upstairs."

Sherwood said, "In this storm? We can't take him out now. You'll have to put up with it unless you want to go back upstairs."

Just to have something to do Tara got up and went to the window at the far end of the room where the light from the lantern was dim and far away. She pressed her forehead against the cool glass and shaded both sides of her face with her hands. The trees in the swamp stood etched in black against a sky dotted with stars. She stared for a moment, then ran to the door and down the hall to the outside door and pushed it open. The swamp was filled with sound, not only the fine voices of the frogs that kept going all day as well as night, but the deep croak of bullfrogs as well.

And the sky was bright with stars that looked as if they had been there forever, and in their faint light the trees stood still because there was no wind at all.

She turned and faced the dark hole that was the hallway, and saw finally the dim light of the lantern falling through the kitchen door. Slowly she stepped over the threshold and went toward the light.

When she came to the kitchen door they were all staring at her again. She stopped and looked back at each one.

"There is no storm," she said. "The storm has gone on. The sky is clear, the stars are shining."

Still they looked at her, their faces blank.

And overhead, in the house, the sound of the wind moved, crying as wind does not. A board fell, and the entire house moved a bit, settling again into a new position, and Tara thought to herself, *one down and five to go.*

CHAPTER 10

When Scott entered the office the next morning, late because of an earlier appointment, he was greeted with a surprise. Anna Lou held up her left hand, showing off a diamond.

"Would you believe it?" she cooed, smiling all over.

Scott almost said "no," then thought how it would sound. Odd, he hadn't really thought about Anna Lou having any kind of life outside the office. She had worked there for two years, and she was practically indispensable.

Scott's father said, "What we're going to do without her. I don't know."

"I said I'd stay until you can get a replacement, provided you don't wait too long."

Scott asked, "Why do you have to quit work just because you're getting married?"

"He doesn't want me to work out and I don't want to. Just at home, thanks. I want to be a homemaker. I've got this nesting urge, see, and when a woman has a nesting urge it's time to nest, wouldn't you say?" She twisted her ring and grinned. "Besides, he lives over a hundred miles from here. Start working on it, will you please? I can't think of a soul."

Scott could. Immediately he saw a vision of a red-haired beauty sitting behind that desk where he could look at her several times a day—and then —"I'll look around," he said, "but first I've got some things to do. See you."

He drove south, not as slowly as he should have, considering that dogs dozed in the warm sun right in the middle of the road and got up reluctantly to move from his path, and chickens ran like scared, half-winged rabbits, all wishing to cross the road in front of him for some odd reasons of their own. This part of town had unpaved streets and small homes that were mostly occupied by the elderly. Black and white side by side. He knew all of them, if only to speak to in some cases.

When he stopped it was under the shade of a large oak tree that hung not only over the neat yard but the road as well. The house had three rooms, or maybe less, an uneven front porch with lots of flowers in tin cans that had once held coffee, lard, or canned meat, depending on the size of the flower, and a row of old chairs that were still sturdy enough for his one hundred and eighty-five pounds. Aunt Betts sat in one of the chairs. Scott was glad to see that she was alone. A rare thing, he knew. Those chairs weren't lined up on the porch for nothing.

"Well, Scott Yates, ain't it? How you, son?"

"Fine. And you, Aunt Betts?"

"Couldn't be better. So pretty a day." '

"Yes, it is."

He sat down. If he had waited she would have gotten up to stand until he was seated, which had always made him uncomfortable. Nobody had ever told her, he guessed, to not stand up for men. Or she had been told to stand up for all whites, women or men. As old as she was he didn't doubt it. "We've been having good weather for quite a spell now."

She nodded. "Just enough rain to make things grow. I've got a good garden this year."

"Are you still doing your own gardening?" he asked in surprise, though he ached to get on with the questions which he had come to ask.

"Of course I am. It keeps me young and healthy. I raise just about all I eat, and you ought to come around for supper when the beans get right."

"I'll do that. Thanks, Aunt Betts."

"No thanks needed. Bring your lady friend, too." Her black eyes cut sideways at him, cunningly. "You shorely have one by now."

She sounded like his mother. Next she'd be asking him if he ever intended to get married and raise a family. She had started asking him that when he was about fifteen, and had reached the sufficient height of six feet.

"I'd like to bring her," he said quietly, and the vision of Tara settled tantalizingly in front of his eyes. Why *her*, damnit, he thought angrily to himself. He didn't want to marry a girl who lived the way she did, screwing around with any bum. In his words she was a tramp. And he felt a little sick somewhere inside, but he recognized it as the beginning of severe conflict. He wondered if he'd throw out his old convictions just in order to get her, if he had to.

He tried to settle his mind back on business. But Tara was still there. He'd get her out of the house, her and her buddies, and then he'd forget her and go ask Mary for another date.

"I want to ask you something, Aunt Betts."

"What?"

"It's about the Bishop house—" The way she looked at him revealed plainly that she didn't know what he was talking about, so he changed it quickly. "The old Black Swamp Mansion."

She settled back in her chair with an ominous, drawn-out grunt, as though she'd been dreading the time when someone would come to question her about that.

"You don't mind talking about it, do you?" Scott asked in concern. If she refused, where next? "I've been told you know things other people don't know."

She nodded. "I know things."

And then the silence settled. He watched her rock. She filled the chair so solidly that it hadn't room for a squeak loud enough to compete with the faint squish of rocker against porch floor.

Just when he decided he was going to have to ask her again, she said slowly, "I heard about the ghost them young'ns seen."

"It wasn't a ghost, it turned out. There's a—a family living out there, and I'm convinced ..." He paused, watching her shake her head back and forth, back and forth.

"They oughtn't," she said. "Oh, they oughtn't."

"Why?" he urged. "I have to have some proof of some kind to convince them it's not safe. Nothing has worked so far."

"Don't ask me to go there," she said. "I've never been there in my life, but I know that house like the palm of my hand, because my mother lived there, and she knowed it like the palm of her hand, and she told me, and told me. Don't ever to go live in that house, she said. Don't even go in it, or close to it. How did she get out? She was always afraid it would get her, just to show it could, even though she got out."

"What are you talking about?" He tried to keep the frown of impatience off his face. All this bugaboo ...

"Well, there was this man, his name was Clement Bishop. Now he was the one built the house. He lived there with his family, a wife, a son, Samuel, a little baby boy. And my mother, she was a little girl then, the daughter of the cook, my grandmother. Slaves, they were. There were other slaves too. My mother was ten, and she remembered Samuel. He was sick, weak. Weak body, mean mind. Before he got so sick he had to stay in his wheelchair he'd get my mother sometimes and tell her terrible things about how he was a bad spirit from the devil whose real name was Samael, how he had the power to kill everything, and then he'd take the little frogs and show her how he could kill. That was when Mama was but a little girl, younger than ten. Before the new baby was born. But they couldn't get away, my Mama and Grandma, because they'uz slaves."

She paused and looked to see if he were listening, and then tilted her head back again and squinted her eyes toward the leaves of the big shading tree.

"The devil is real," she said. "He's as real as God, and you got to watch out for him all the time, because if you call him forth, you get him, and he'll destroy you and keep you from God forever. It says that in the Bible, and it's a fact."

Scott sighed softly. Aunt Betts was fanatically religious, that he knew. And that meant fanatically superstitious, too. The trip had been a waste so far as getting any tangible information, he could see that already.

"That stuff about the boy," he said. "Couldn't it have been just a spoiled brat trying to scare a little kid? Your mama?"

Her eyes blazed silently for a moment, then she demanded in snapping-turtle suddenness, "Was it just a spoiled kid trying to scare a littler one the night he murdered his own baby brother?"

Scott just sat and looked at her, wondering why this fact, if it were true, had never leaked out into all the tales surrounding the house. She nodded.

"Of course they hung a slave for the murder, saying he was the one killed the baby, but Mama, she knowed better. It was Samuel done it. He told her so. He told her everyone who ever lived in that house was going to die because he was dying, and the house was his, part of him, part of the devil. The body of hisself, a demon, because his folks cheated him out of a body. And that's a fact, Scott Yates. And do you know where that poor innocent black man was hung? Right upstairs on the third story, in the nursery where the baby slept and was killed. The slave died in the same room, a rope around his neck. And then the mother was hacked to death with a hatchet in her bed, just like the baby, and the father knew the truth had been spoken when the black man swore his innocence. He knew, but it was too late. Three dead then. And the father, Clement, had the front stairs closed up and made into a wall because that was the only stairs that had a pulley thing on it for Samuel's wheelchair. They boarded it up so he couldn't get upstairs and murder his own daddy too, because there was no one to take care of Samuel anymore but his daddy. And if you don't believe me, you go out there and take a look, because they made it look like another wall. But that didn't make any difference, because they all died anyway. Only Mama got away, but always she was scared it would come after her. And maybe it did, I don't know. But I don't think so, because she went to church and she worshipped and looked up to God to save her and—"

That would go on and on if he didn't stop it, and the sound of truth behind her words stunned him so that superstition or not, he wanted to know more about it. Besides, he remembered the name on the painting. Samael. Aunt Betts would have had no way of knowing about that.

"What happened to the others in the house? The slaves? The father and his son?"

"They died. The slaves began to die of a fever, it was said, and Samuel died too. And when Grand-mama died someone took Mama away and raised her in town here. But she was afraid to talk about what she knew. I don't think she ever told anybody but me. Just to make sure I never went there."

"And Clement Bishop?"

"He died too. He the last to go. When Mama left the house there was nobody but the boy and the man left. The man might have got away after he laid the boy in his grave, but he went back to the house. And it got him, just as Samuel told Mama it would get anybody who ever tried to live there. Because if he couldn't live, nobody could. That's the body of a demon out there, that house."

"The graves, where are they?"

She nodded toward the south. "In that old churchyard down by the river. The one nobody uses anymore."

He sat for a moment longer, then thanked Aunt Betts for her information and left.

The drive to the old churchyard was over an unpaved, twisting country road that had water-filled ruts and weed-crowded ditches. Farmers' fences hugged the ditches closely, and an occasional cow gazed at him over the fence as he drove slowly by. The bright sun would quickly dry the water from the ruts, and leave dust in its place as summer approached and the rains dwindled away. The frogs would cease to call and the jarflies and katydids would take over instead, with their constant buzz. But it was a comforting, lazy, summer sound he had grown up hearing, and he liked it.

The fever, that's what it was. Not a curse, just a strange kind of fever that was still in the house and got everyone who lived there. So the kid had been crazy, psychotic, a murderer, and he had scared a little girl into thinking that he had the powers of the devil. It was only the fever after all.

A fever that lasted a hundred years? He hoped to God not. Then the curse of the devil?

Oh hell.

The church was just around a corner, tucked in behind a grove of trees. The yard was overgrown with weeds and looked like it hadn't been walked upon for many years, but at least it was not swampy and covered with spongy vines. Behind the church, scattered among shading trees, he glimpsed the old, grayed stones of an abandoned cemetery. He stopped the car in the middle of the quiet road and got out to stand looking at the church.

It had a decayed, dilapidated appearance that reminded him of the Bishop house. Long unused, it seemed God had left it to fall as it chose.

He wondered if this were the church the original Bishops had attended.

The cemetery began just behind it and covered scarcely a quarter of an acre, but the tombstones were large and elaborately carved. Only the rich white had been buried there.

The first stone had a name like Clayton or something, and it had been erected in the late seventeen hundreds. Both name and date were so obscured by moss that he couldn't read them, but it was of no interest to him. He was looking for another name.

Near the back a rusted iron fence enclosed a small plot and four stones. Scott stopped at the fence and looked for a moment at the stones and saw that one was double. Man and wife. He stepped over the low fence and went toward the stone, pushing aside briers dried and brittle and briers young and green and bursting with bloom. Blackberries would ripen there one day soon and the birds would build nests among them, safe from cats and other predators, surrounded by lush food. He carefully pushed briers away from the double stone.

Bishop.

On this stone vines grew. He brushed away the vines, and the green and gray moss that had settled in the carved writing. Julia Adele Bishop, beloved wife of Clement, 1824-1861.

Short and simple. And beneath it, even less elaborately, Clement Bradford Bishop, 1820-1862.

No verse, no message, none of the sweet words that most old tombstones carried.

Scott moved over to the stone with the angel on top. He knew before he read the name and the dates that it was the baby's grave, because the last stone was small, harsh, plain. Just a marker with a name. He almost dreaded looking at that one. He was so extremely aware that it was there, waiting for him, that he felt the hair pull eerily on the back of his neck.

Aloud, and in disgust, he said to himself, "Come off it!"

He had been right about the stone with the angel, although the information there amounted to nothing also. *Died,* read the old script writing, *at the precious age of seven months, Clement Bradford Bishop, in the spring of 1861.*

In the spring. Scott found himself thinking one hundred and twelve years ago now this baby had been murdered. And the result of that murder was the reason he was standing there with his hand on the gravestone.

He moved quickly on to the last stone. It was low, and almost hidden by the vines whose growth seemed confined to the enclosed plot, as if the occupants, or one of them, had brought along something that belonged in the dampness of swampland. As Scott kneeled to push them aside the face of the stone came out at him with the suddenness of something alive. The printing was shallow and hard to read. Samuel Adelede Bishop, 1848-1862.

That was all. Scott let the vines fall back, rose to his feet and wiped his hands as though he had touched something that kept clinging to his fingers. His mind noted one thing in particular: the names. The second son, the baby, had been given the father's name. The older one evidently had been named for someone in the mother's family. The second son the favored? Or what? Something had been wrong all the way through, or so it seemed.

Age fourteen, huh? Died at age fourteen.

Scott climbed over the fence and wound his way back toward his car, wondering how long the boy had spent in the wheelchair. And why he had been in it to start with. One of the crippling diseases, probably.

Or had all this stuff been the distorted memory of a young black girl who had been teased by a sick, bored boy who couldn't get out of the house? What proof did he have that a murder had even been committed or a slave hanged?

Well, one way he could find that out for sure was to go back to the house, go into the third story and see for himself if a nursery had existed and if a front stairway had been boarded up, and if there were any signs of a man having been hanged in the murder room.

But first the facts. The real facts. The name of the first owner, and the names of the heirs. That he could get from going through the abstract. And the abstract, so far as he knew, was on record. That was no problem. All he had to do was call on an old buddy, Carl Linstrom, at the courthouse. They had met over those dusty old records more than once.

The county seat though was twenty miles away, and he didn't want to waste any more time than he had to. He felt a driving urgency to get back out to the Bishop house, to get those people out of there. He wasn't even sure why. The logical part of his brain said that there was nothing to the superstitions, the suggested curse on the house. But something behind the logic kept warning him that there was *something*. And whatever it was, was dangerous.

So he returned to the office, though he knew he would have to face questions he didn't want to answer.

Immediately Anna Lou asked, "Did you find someone?"

"Maybe," he answered to keep her quiet. He sat on the corner of his desk and reached over for his phone.

His dad said, "You got time to show a place to a man who's coming in after lunch?"

"No."

"What're you doing that you're so busy all the time and getting nothing done the past few days?" his dad asked mildly, his tone belying his words.

But Scott already had Carl on the phone. "Could you do me a favor, fast, Carl? I want to know all the owners of the Bishop place. The original owner, and the heir—first heir especially. Do you need the legal description?"

"No," the slow answer came. "I know it well enough to find it. How soon do you want the information?"

"I want it now. Right now."

"Now?"

"Yes, now. I'll hold the phone."

A pause, then Carl said lazily, "You must be in one damned hurry."

"I am. I'll hold the phone."

"Well, all right. You may have to hold it a few minutes."

"That's okay, I'll hold on."

Anna Lou and his dad had listened carefully to each word, and Scott knew he was in for an interrogation. He waited for the questions. No point in explaining more than he had to, mainly because he felt he really didn't know anything.

From his dad, who leaned back in his squeaky old chair and placed loosely clasped hands across his small beer-belly, "What the devil do you need to know that for?"

"I've got some things to check out."

"Like what?" Anna Lou asked.

"Like who owned it first—and who inherited it."

Anna Lou answered quickly, "Oh, that was sharp!"

Scott grinned at her, and winked.

His dad wasn't giving up though. "Why do you have to know that?"

"Well ..." Scott sighed. And then said simply, "I've got to get those people out of there."

Anna Lou made a big production of turning to look at the senior Yates. "Did you drop him in the mud when he was a baby? He's about as clear as. You might as well prepare to take that man out there yourself. I can see that junior here is occupied. And I'll bet you he hasn't been looking for a replacement for me, either."

"I do know a girl," Scott began to explain.

"I'm sure you do," Anna Lou said. "I doubt if any one of them could type her own name. Your reputation hasn't exactly kept your little secrets."

"I'll have you know the last girl I dated was Mary."

"Mary! At the cafe? What on earth for? She isn't your type at all, is she?"

"I'm thinking of settling down and getting married."

His dad said absently, "Your poor mother will die of heart failure." And to Anna Lou, who giggled, "She's been wanting to marry him off since he turned twenty-one, and she has about given up hopes. Said last week she guessed she'd raised a playboy and would never get herself a grandchild."

Actually sounding surprised instead of sarcastic and teasing, Anna Lou asked Scott, "You're thinking of marrying *Mary*?"

"Well, no," Scott said. "Not really." He looked at the window where the sun touched briefly through the leaves, and saw a vision of Tara. Always Tara now, everywhere he looked.

"That's what I thought," said Anna Lou. "I should run down there and warn her about you. Beware, the wolf is on your trail! Or should I say tail?"

"You do and I'll gently strangle you."

Anna Lou giggled again, and began to type.

Scott held the phone and fidgeted. After a while he began to tap a pencil against it, and kept that up until his dad gave him a long, straight look. Scott dropped the pencil and tapped his fingers instead.

Several minutes later Carl's slow voice came over the line. "You still there?"

"Hell yes! Did you go to lunch or something?"

Carl chuckled. "You're beginning to sound like a Northerner, old fellow. Got to slow down or you'll have a heart attack. Okay, here it is. First on record is a man named Clement Bradford Bishop. He built the house in 1856. The place was inherited by his brother, who lived in Michigan. His name was Bradford Benjamin Bishop. He inherited the place in 1862. It stayed in his name for twenty-three years and passed on to his son in 1885 and then to another son—"

"That's okay. The first two was all I wanted. Thanks, Carl. See you sometime."

"Okay, Scott. Come over and have a beer with me and relax a little."

"Some other time, Carl." Scott dropped the phone into its cradle and hurried out, ignoring the questions that followed him.

His dad said something about lunch, but Scott went on. A late lunch was often the rule for his dad, and Scott remembered that he hadn't eaten at all. But it wasn't long until dinnertime, and he wasn't hungry anyway. The so-called family living in the Bishop house might not like it, but they were destined for another visit from him.

His watch read four o'clock when he turned off the highway and onto the rutted, weedy road toward Black Swamp. He remembered she hadn't been very friendly there at the last, and if she still weren't friendly, and showed no interest in leaving the house, then he would be forced to give up at least until he could think of something else.

He'd also like to see the pregnant girl out of there. She didn't look a day over fifteen, and didn't act as if she knew much of anything at all. But she was so well wedded to her odd family that he had a feeling he was just spinning his wheels where she was concerned.

And Tara, the red-haired goddess. Just exactly what was she, anyway? Did she really think the others were crazy, as the pregnant girl had said?

No one was in sight when he stopped the car in front of the house. The front door was closed, the windows as secretive as ever. He noticed that the frogs were more quiet than usual, and then, as he approached the front stoop, he knew why. There was hammering indoors. A lot of it. Two hammers going like powered jackhammers. He could tell by the broken and overlapping rhythm that there were two.

He knocked, but it didn't do any good. The hammering continued. After a while he tried the door, and found it locked.

He went around to the back door then, and saw that it was standing open. The hammering sounded much farther away, definitely somewhere in the front of the house.

He entered the back hall for the first time since he had come in search of some reason for his renter's death. The odor still hung faintly in the air, but it was nothing at all compared to the way it had been.

He heard the soft murmurs of female voices, and followed the sound. In the kitchen doorway he paused, looking at the two girls who sat on the rough benches on either side of the long table. The pregnant girl on one side, and Tara on the other.

They were the only people in the room, and they saw him at the same time. Their murmurs stopped. They both looked surprised to see him. Too surprised even to move.

He put a professional smile on his face. "May I come in?" he asked, coming along anyhow, invitation or not. "How are you ladies today? Is somebody building something?"

The pregnant girl looked pale and large-eyed, but she sat still, looking up at him. Tara rose, but stayed where she was, one hand on the table.

"They're nailing up a hole," she said. "You'd better go."

"Why? I just got here. And I have important news for you."

"What?"

She still wasn't friendly, but he wasn't going to let that stop him. She had to hear him out first. There was something about the younger girl's face, though, that made him hesitate. It might serve only to frighten her, and what good would that do? Besides, he wanted to be alone with Tara again. To be close to her, and hold her again if she'd let him.

He took her arm in his hand and gently urged her toward the doorway. "Can we go outside? It's a private matter."

Tara glanced at Amy and then moved with him toward the door. "Only for a minute," she said. "Then you have to go."

"Why?" he asked, still smiling his sell-it-or-bust smile. "You're in the South now, remember? And you're supposed to be hospitable."

"Don't joke, please."

He felt the smile strain to a difficult end as he looked at her. The expression on her face was hard to read, but it was a new one. On any other girl he would have said it was fear, or worry. On this one he wasn't sure.

He saw her send a steady, searching glance toward the upstairs as they came into the hall, and she began to hurry toward the back door and the open air.

"Just what is it they're doing?" he asked. "Is the house caving in?"

"Something like that."

"Why do you stay? Why don't you all get out and go somewhere else?"

"I guess they don't have anywhere else to go."

"How about you? Would you like a job in my office? Our secretary is quitting, and we sure need a good girl to take her place."

Her eyes raised to his for the first time since they had left the kitchen. "Do you mean that?"

"Of course I mean it. You could go to work tomorrow if you wanted. How about it?"

"I'd love to!"

"Then it's settled. Come in—I'll take you in now. Get your things together and I'll take you home to my mom. She would adore you, and probably give you my old room until you can find what you want."

"After the baby is born." Her voice was very low and held a pleading quality.

"Baby?" The disappointment hit him again. The damned unexpected. Every time he saw her she hit him with something that felt like a rock in the belly. "Christ o' mighty, you're not pregnant, are you?"

"No!" she answered indignantly, motioning back toward the kitchen. "Amy! I can't leave Amy until her baby is born."

"Why the hell not?" he demanded.

"Shhh. They might hear you. You'd better go." She began pushing at him with both hands, and nearly succeeded in shoving him off the step before he penned her hands in his.

"Wait a minute! Why can't you leave the girl? Is she the reason you're here, or are you just feeding me the bull?"

"She's the reason I'm here, really, Scott. Please believe me, and help me."

"What the hell do you think I'm here for, but to help you?"

"Then leave. That's the only way you can help right now. As soon as the baby is born and Amy is okay I'll walk to town, that's all. I'll make it."

"You might, and you might not. Let me tell you this. I don't know what it's worth, but there's something crazy about this house. Things people aren't supposed to believe in. There's supposed to be a curse on it, Tara." His own voice astonished him. He didn't believe in silly stuff like that, yet he was telling her, and believing his own words. "I want you *out* of here!"

She didn't laugh at him. She didn't even smile. But she didn't seem surprised, either. "A curse," she answered almost dully.

"Yes, well, according to this old lady whose mother was a slave child here, a young crippled boy—the one in the painting, I guess—put a curse on the house. The more tangible parts are this: a man, a black man, was hanged in a third-story nursery for the murder of the baby brother of the crippled boy. But the girl said it was the boy who did the killing and not the black man. Now the only way I know to see if it's true is to find out if there was a front stairway and if it then was boarded up ..."

He stopped because she had bitten her lower lip. Her eyes, watching him steadily from under her lashes, held even more of what he knew had to be fear. When her teeth released her lip, leaving a deep dent in the softness, she whispered, "There was. That's what they're doing now— closing it up again."

"Closing what up again?"

"The front stairway. It was boarded, just as the girl said, and I found it. They chopped a hole in it, and now they're nailing boards back over it again."

"Why?" He started to push past her, to get into the house, but she grabbed his arm and stopped him. He explained. "I'd like to see if someone was hanged in the nursery upstairs."

"What if he were? What would it prove?"

"I don't know." He thought about it, and saw that she had a point. Indisputable. What would it prove?

"It really is dangerous up there," she was saying. "You're right about that. We went up and the whole roof, or attic, seems to be falling in. And it's true that someone was hanged—" Her voice lowered to a whisper again. "I saw a skeleton, Scott, but no one else did, and I didn't tell them. I don't know why. Because of Amy, I guess. I just don't know what to do.

It's only a house, Scott, and it's the first home Amy ever had, so I figured if they close the upstairs again, and never know, Amy and her baby can make a home of some kind. I don't know. Please, don't tell her, anyway. Curses and things don't really exist, do they, Scott? How can they? This is the latter part of the twentieth century we're in, not—" She glanced over her shoulder. The hammering had slowed to one dim *bang, bang, bang.* "Please go. They must not find you here."

"Oh, come on now—"

"I mean it. Please. As soon as the baby is born I'll let you know."

"You mean you're not going to take her to a hospital?"

She shook her head. "Look, you know they're fanatics about this 'natural' business."

"What I want to know is, how did you get tied up with them?"

"I wonder that too. The only answer I can bring forth is that my mother and daddy died within a few weeks of each other, and I couldn't take it. I escaped by—by running away from everything. My home—well, it was no longer a home ..." She kept listening, and the second hammer didn't begin again. "Go now. Hurry."

But he ignored her pleas. "Why are you so afraid of them?"

"I'm not really afraid of them. Not for myself. I'm safe enough, but they don't want you around."

"And I don't want to leave you here."

She gave him a direct, rather severe look. "I said I will leave here when Amy is able to take care of the baby and herself, and I meant it. But I will not leave her now. She needs someone."

"Bring her along. Mom will take her in. You can take care of her there better than here. You dumb kid, bring her!"

"Oh boy! You are the most hard-headed, obstinate, stubborn—"

"You're repeating yourself," he said, enjoying her attention. Fighting with her was better than nothing.

The hammering began again, louder and stronger than ever, but it didn't keep her from saying, "Leave!"

Scott saw Amy come into sight in the hallway, but Tara didn't, and when she was near enough that her steps were audible Tara whirled, her hand to her breast. The words, "My God," escaped her in a gasp.

Amy didn't say a word. She stared directly at Scott. Tara let go with a deep breath and when she faced him again Scott saw that her freckles stood out against a skin so pale it was nearly paper white. The footsteps had scared her deeply.

Scott couldn't understand it, but her need to have him leave finally got to him. He could try one more time, but what good would it do? He had a hunch she would stick to her word and stay with the girl until the baby was born no matter what anyone said, if she felt she was needed.

"It's nearly night," he said. "The house is worse at night."

He was guessing, because he didn't really know. Amy came forward and clutched Tara's arm. The two of them looked at him then, saying nothing. The dependent, and the depended-upon. He backed away, down the step and into the vines.

"Well, if you need me, you can find me in town. Everybody knows me and where I'm apt to be. All you have to do is yell."

Nobody said good-bye. Reluctantly he turned and walked around the house to his car. The hammering was loud at the front of the house, and he paused for a moment, wondering about the stairway that had not been uncovered before, and exactly what had happened to drive the men at such a frantic rate to box it up again. If only Tara had seen the room, what was ailing the men?

He went to the cafe for his supper that night, and sat by the window where he could watch the street. He didn't know what he expected—that she would materialize suddenly, coming for him?

He saw the glow of the sunset and the twilight that followed, and the lengthening shadows, and knew it was already dark in the big, shadowy house, and wished to hell he hadn't said what he had about the house being worse at night. He wasn't sure now what he had even meant by it.
"More coffee, Scott?" Mary asked.

"No, thank you." He didn't look up at her, or toward her. But he saw from the corner of his eye that she pulled out a chair and sat down. He didn't want company.

"What are you staring at the horizon for? Something bothering you?"

"No, nothing at all." He forced his eyes away from the outdoors and looked at her. And felt absolutely nothing. What had made him think he might want to marry her? He didn't even want to talk to her. Not now. "I guess I will take that coffee after all, if you don't mind, Mary."

"Anything you want, Scott." She touched his shoulder as she went by.

As he had hoped, customers came in, and he drank his coffee quickly and alone. Then, with a touch of guilt dragging at his conscience, he left a large tip under his plate and went out while she was busy.

CHAPTER 11

The two girls went slowly back into the kitchen, Amy's hand still clinging painfully to Tara's arm.

"I didn't mean to interrupt anything," Amy said. "I was afraid ..."

"I know," Tara answered. She had to push her feet along, she so dreaded going back into the house. Though she strained her ears to hear Scott's car, she heard nothing. The hammering. The frogs. Always the frogs. Perhaps he had not left, her heart longed on its own, and immediately her common sense prevailed against it, reminding her again that Sherwood would kill him—she had no doubt of that—if he found him around the house again. Especially if she were caught alone with him. Talking.

They sat down at the table again, and Tara looked at the small fire over which a light supper simmered. She wondered if anyone would be able to eat it. Even Leda had been as silent as a shadow all day, with no breakfast and no lunch. She had walked the floor, saying nothing, all day, and all the rest of last night, too, so far as Tara knew.

"Where's Leda, Amy, do you know?"

"No, I haven't seen her. Maybe she went upstairs to take a nap."

"Not likely. She may be with the guys though." Tara put her hands flat over her ears and twisted her face into exactly what she was feeling. "I wish they'd quit that damned hammering, it's driving me bats."

"Well, they won't," Amy said with a sigh of resignation. "And besides, you don't want that upstairs opened to us, do you?"

The statement, so calmly spoken, made Tara feel foolish for giving in to a moment of weakness. "No, but when you stop to consider it, what difference does it make?"

"Tara! After Fox died there last night?"

"It wasn't the open wall that caused it, nor the front stairway. It was actually the back, and the fall."

"That's right," Amy said, her voice lowered as if someone might hear. "I'd forgotten the back. It is open, isn't it? Whatever is up there can come down the back as well as the front, can't it, Tara?"

"Stop talking like that. I was only using an—well, this is only an old, dilapidated house. There's nothing up there but—" Her voice failed her. She remembered the room, the skeleton, the falling ceiling, the odd wind, and the feeling that the entire house was falling, and the other feelings that were beyond description. A feeling of terror, of being faced with something against which she was helpless, something black and evil, the inner workings of darkness and complete *nothing*.

"But what?" Amy asked. "You went, you saw."

"No. I didn't see anything but a ceiling that was falling down."

Timidly, Amy said, "Tara, I was listening. Was it true what he said about a nursery up there, and a man hanged? Do you think that little crippled boy did it instead of the man?"

"I've no idea. How would I know a thing like that? Besides, that happened over a century ago. It wouldn't have any effect on us."

But Amy wasn't going to let it go at that. "You saw the rooms though. Was there a nursery? Was a man hanged there? I heard you whispering. I know you told him something you haven't told me."

Tara looked at Amy and decided to tell her enough to keep her satisfied. "Yes, there was a nursery, and in one corner the ceiling was falling, and there was a large hook attached to the ceiling and from it hung a rope. But I don't know what lay in the rubble beneath it. I didn't get a chance to see. Probably some kids saw it once and made up a story."

Amy's mouth had dropped open. "It's true then!" she whispered. "Do you suppose his bones are still there?"

"I said probably some kids ...oh, Amy!" Tara saw that she had told her too much. She shuddered in revulsion, thinking of people living in the house while a man's body slowly decayed in a closed nursery. But that was a century ago. She had a duty now to get it out of Amy's mind, if possible.

"Amy, that's horrible. Let's don't think about it anymore. You'll only give yourself bad dreams, and it might even be bad for your baby."

Amy looked around, at the doors, so many of them closed, never yet opened, and at the opened one leading into the hall, and at the windows. "I don't like this house anymore," she said.

"I don't like it either. Listen, you must have heard Scott offer me a job, which I would like very much to accept, and he offered you refuge also in his mother's house. If you want to go we could leave now. They'd never know. We could drive away and leave his car in town."

"Sherwood would never leave keys in a car!"

"Then we could walk. If they came along looking for us, we could hide until they passed. Do you think you could make it?"

"I wish you wouldn't even talk that way. I belong to Sherwood. He's the father of the family. He took me in when nobody else would, and took care of me. All he asked was that I forever be faithful to the family. And, Tara, no matter how much I like you, I have to be."

"Then, I've got a notion to go by myself," Tara said impulsively. "I guess it's like Sherwood said, babies have been born before without me, you'll get along."

"Oh no, Tara. I can't let you do that."

"What do you mean 'you can't let me'?" Tara tried to read the truth in the girl's candid eyes, but they were almost blank in their blueness, like a cool, northern sky.

"I have to be faithful, and he said don't let you go."

After a moment of stunned silence, Tara said, "Funny. And I thought you were on my side. At least enough to not spy on me. Enough to let me go when I wanted to go."

"I am on your side," Amy said. "I'll do everything I can to help you."

"Help me? Help me from what? What have I done, anyway?"

"Nothing, you've been great. I couldn't get along without you, really I couldn't."

Amy looked more natural now, and even sincere, but Tara was still deeply perplexed, and yet a truth was dawning on her.

"You don't know what it is for sure, do you? I can see that. You just have this blind faith in Sherwood. But something is very wrong, or they would not simply have taken Eldon's body out this morning and left it God knows where, without a decent burial or funeral or anything. This thing—it's something that happened before we left San Francisco, isn't it? Something to do with the money, and the guy who didn't come back with them that night. They robbed somebody, and the other guy was either killed or they ran away from him. That's what it is, isn't it?"

Amy gazed at her, the blankness back again. Tara saw that Amy had no intention of answering.

"But you don't really know either, and you don't want to know. But if I got away all I would have to do is call the police and ask ... and that's what Sherwood is afraid of. Perhaps someone was killed there, during the robbery. Murdered, by Sherwood and the others." Tara paused for a moment, then whispered. "Leda! Even Leda was with them that night. Then even she would be involved in whatever they did. And that's bound to be it. They robbed and murdered someone!"

Amy had begun to shake her head. Her voice was a whisper too. "Don't ever say that where Sherwood can hear you! Even if it's not true, it would make him so mad ..."

She didn't have to finish the sentence. Tara looked around at the gloomy, lengthening shadows in the house, remembered what Scott had said about the nights being worse, thought of the vines and the snakes. For the first time in her life, no, the second time, she didn't know what to do. She felt as confused and helpless suddenly as she had when her parents died. No matter which way she turned it seemed the wrong way. She still had sense enough to know that even if she could get away in the middle of the night, and succeed in getting to a town that would be wrapped in darkness and silence at that hour, Sherwood would follow her. He would be as desperate as she. And where could she go but to Scott? He seemed to be her only friend. Her only chance. She spent a moment regretting that she had been foolish enough to think that she was doing Amy a favor by waiting with her. But what difference did it make? Once she had walked up to that campfire in the park, under the dripping tree, into a group of people she didn't even know, she had been doomed. Trapped, like a harmless wild animal reaching out a paw to touch a bit of steel and finding that it snapped shut and held forever.

Well, no use moaning. She still had a few brains, despite the hammering and the frogs and the sound of falling boards somewhere in the upper regions of the house, and she would get out if it killed her.

Killed her? She stopped, halfway across the room on her way to stir the mixture of vegetables and meat in the skillet. "Just an expression," she said aloud. Yes, just an expression. A bad choice of words, that was all.

Amy said, "What?"

Tara forced a smile. "Sometimes I talk to myself. Don't you ever talk to yourself, Amy?"

"I don't know. I never thought whether I did or not."

"It probably has something to do with me being closed up alone in a library for three years. Many times there was no one to talk with or to but the books. I don't know why I ever took that job. It really was never my idea of an exciting life."

"What is, Tara?" Amy asked, sounding childishly eager to be friends again.

"Oh, I don't know." But all at once she did know. "Yes. To work in a real-estate office where I have a very attractive boss with beautiful dark eyes and hair and a tanned complexion. Perhaps to go out with him on some of his business excursions ... and, well, then to find that he's the man for me and marry him and live in a house with magnolias and wisteria and—and yes, frogs in the swamp or pond yelling their little heads off. Perhaps then I would have a baby too, with dark eyes and dark hair—not red!" She looked at Amy and laughed. "For a moment there I really got carried away, right?"

Amy laughed too. "So did I! It really does sound great. I hope you ..." Her voice faded, the words dangling.

Left unspoken, because she knew it was only a dream. Tara saw it in her eyes, and felt it in her own heart. She went on to stir the conglomeration in the skillet. They were low on food because Sherwood had not gone shopping that morning and nothing kept for long without refrigeration.

"Why don't you light a bunch of candles, Amy? We don't want to be caught in the dark, do we?" She noticed then that the hammering had stopped. "I guess they can't see what they're doing. They'll be here soon."

Amy got up to light candles, and Tara watched her. She seemed to move better than she had the day before, seemed farther away from the hours of giving birth. But she definitely had dropped, and Tara knew it wouldn't be long. A few days, no more.

"How are you feeling, Amy?"

"All right. He's trying to kick a hole through me, though. You know they actually can make you sore?"

Tara said, "No, I didn't know that."

"Well, they can."

The footsteps came along the hall, and the lantern light jerked forward and backward upon the floor as it swung. Sherwood was in the lead, and behind him came Leda, then Giles. Their faces were tight and mute and serious.

Act natural and casual, Tara reminded herself. Pretend you're not even thinking of escape. "Did you finish?" she asked.

Giles said, "Well, it's mostly covered, anyway. It's not very pretty, but it's covered. Just a crack or two."

Leda went to the blanket against the wall and literally fell onto it. Tara, bringing plates from the cupboard, asked, "Don't you want to eat, Leda?"

"I'm not hungry."

"You haven't eaten since yesterday. You'll be sick if you don't eat."

Leda rested her head on her arm and pulled the blanket over her body. "I'm already sick."

Tara set the table and brought the skillet and merely put it down within reach of the men and Amy. No one paid any attention to Leda, but Tara kept watching her. The girl was trembling, shaking, and her teeth clicked faintly in the still room.

Tara left the others eating and went to kneel by Leda. "Are you chilly?" she asked gently.

Leda looked at her, eyes bright with fever. Tara knew before she touched the girl's forehead that she was really sick. Her skin was tight, dry, and very hot.

"You've taken something, Leda. And we don't even have an aspirin in the house." She raised her voice for Sherwood's benefit. "I don't suppose it would do any good to ask you to go to the store for aspirin for Leda. She's got a very high fever."

"Stores are probably already closed," he answered. "They close about sundown here in this place."

"How would you know about that?"

"I saw the sign on the door, damnit! Six o'clock, it said. Six! If she's still got fever in the morning I'll get her somethin' then. Leave it alone and it will probably pass." Tara sat back on her heels and looked at Leda. The girl kept watching her, a look in her eyes that seemed desperate, but she didn't ask for anything. Another trapped animal, Tara thought. No matter what Leda had done in her life, she was now trapped. By illness, by fear, and by Sherwood.

Tara started to rise, thinking of a cloth and cold water.

Leda reached for her, whispering, "Stay with me."

Tara touched her head. "I'll be back. We'll see if we can get that fever down with cold compresses. It will freeze you, but we can't let the fever go too high, you know that."

She brought water in a pan and several washcloths. Unsure of herself, hoping that she wasn't doing more harm than good, Tara put a wet cloth on Leda's forehead, then loosened her slacks, pushed them down and placed another wet cloth on her abdomen. With another she began to gently wash the girl's arms and throat. Leda shook harder, her teeth chattering audibly.

"I'm sorry," Tara said. "I know I'm freezing you. I just don't know what else to do. I do know that a too-high fever will send you into convulsions, and we have to avoid that. Hang in there with me, and we'll get it down, okay?"

Leda nodded, and Tara removed warmed cloths and replaced them with cool ones. She discovered that she had an audience. Giles was watching over her shoulder.

"Can you bring me fresh water from the well, Giles, please? It has to be cold."

He nodded and went quickly, taking the lantern and the pail, without a word to Sherwood. And Tara knew then that if anyone loved Leda, it was Giles. Sherwood sat on the bench at the table, picking his teeth and staring somewhere in the vicinity of the wall of cupboards across the room. His thoughts obviously were not with Leda.

Amy came over after a while, but Tara gave her swift orders. "You'd better stay away, Amy. I don't know if what she has is contagious, but it might be." And Amy backed away, going to sit by Sherwood on the end of the bench.

For hours they worked, Tara sponging with cold washcloths and changing compresses, and Giles quietly bringing fresh water from the well and otherwise hovering over Tara's shoulder.

Tara glanced back at the table occasionally and saw that Amy was leaning her head into her hand, her eyes closed, and Sherwood had turned from staring at the wall opposite to watching the quiet activity around Leda.

"Why don't you go up to bed, Amy?" Tara asked softly, for Leda's eyes had closed and Tara hoped she was going to sleep and that her fever was beginning to break.

Amy merely shook her head.

Giles whispered, "Is she asleep?"

So Tara's attention went back to Leda. "I don't know. When fever breaks they begin to perspire, and she isn't. Her skin feels cold in places, but her forehead is hot and dry. Let's keep on for a while."

Giles went without another word for more water, though the bucket was still half full. Tara changed compresses.

She began to have a feeling that something, or someone, was staring at her back, and she looked over her shoulder and met the direct, steady gaze of Sherwood. His eyes seemed to be as fixed upon her as the eyes of the painting upstairs were always fixed on their objects. She looked quickly away, but from then on she was aware of the eyes, the unwavering gaze, the stare that didn't stop.

They worked for hours longer, slowly, silently. Giles stepped lightly when he left the room for water, and reentered without sound, a thin, tall boy whose face in the flickering movement of the bright lantern light looked like something from a psychedelic print. He said nothing. He hovered like a shadow over the prostrate girl.

Tara was sometimes more aware of what was behind her than that which lay before her. She felt spotlighted, framed in a print of some kind, and she used all of her will power to keep herself from turning to see, forcibly turning her mind to the girl, and the hovering boy.

Slowly the difference dawned upon her. The silence in the house. Deep. Profound. She listened, and heard nothing but the girl's fast breath. What is it, she almost asked, half turning her head toward the fireplace. Then she remembered. The cricket was still. And everything outside seemed to have gone still. The house itself was quiet. No sound of falling boards far above, no creak as of a ghostly foot. No rustlings in the wall.

She whispered to Giles, "The frogs are still. Why?"

He looked at her, slow to answer. Then, "I don't know. They weren't when I was outside last."

Tara noticed that her legs were cramping from the position she had held for so long. She moved, saying, "I think I'll step out for a breath of fresh air and see what's up. They settle down before a storm, I think. There may be another storm on the horizon."

She carefully avoided looking toward the table and the eyes that were on her. She went to the door, and had reached the dark hall before she remembered that she had brought no light. She stopped and almost turned back, the darkness a wall in front of her, the knowledge of the open stairs on the left leading all the way into the strange, other world of the third story. But the eyes were behind her, and the open door was only down the hall to the right. She went on into the dark hall, and slowly toward the pale rectangle of light that showed at its end.

The moment she reached the doorway the sound of the frogs burst upon her, a welcome, comforting sound. She went out onto the stoop, looked up at a sky filled with tiny, bright stars and no clouds and wondered vaguely why the frogs had suddenly and loudly burst into voice after the long silence. And immediately her logic told her that it was not so, and eerie fingers of chills swept swiftly down her spine like lightning through a dark sky. It was behind her, the unaccountable silence, in the house. For some reason it had closed out all sound, as if it were wrapping its few helpless people away from the outside world.

She couldn't go back in, and yet she had to. But her feet took her farther on down the stoop to the narrow little path which Giles had cut for his girl, the path that led only to the toilet.

She stood in the path and looked toward the road. Darkness, everywhere. Under the sound of the frogs she spoke aloud, pleading, as though he could hear, "Scott, come back. Please. Oh, please."

It would be so easy. The walk through the vines to the road. Then out of the vines, away from the snakes, and safely toward the highway and town. She trembled when her foot touched the vines and sank into its wet, clinging depth, and against her will she envisioned writhing, crawling snakes coming toward her. It was foolish, and she knew it, but she couldn't help her unreasonable phobia about snakes. She had seen a painting when she was a child ...

It touched her, a cold damp thing on her arm, and she screamed. With shaking hands she covered her mouth and the scream and whirled to face the man who stood beside her. His hand closed hard on her arm as he pulled her back onto the path. He was only a tall, dark shadow, but Tara knew who he was.

"Where do you think you're goin', Red?" he asked, laughing a little, taunting, his voice carrying a suggestion of something else that turned her cold with another kind of dread. He was ready for her. Sexually. His body touched her as he pulled her with him. A lean, hard body. The palm of his hand, in startling contrast to the tips of his fingers, was warm and moist. And his breath against her cheek as he bent over her was warm and moist too.

"Come on," he murmured into her ear. "Don't make Papa spank. Because I like that too. My hands have been burnin' all night to spank your bottom."

She jerked away and went toward the black hole of the back door. In the hall, the light from the lantern cast a distant beam through the doorway that had no door, and she went toward it quickly so that he wouldn't touch her again.

She kneeled again at Leda's side after glancing to see that Amy was still awake, leaning on one elbow, her face cupped in her hand.

"Still no change?" she asked Giles, taking from him the wet cloth and dipping it again into cold water. The activity helped steady her trembling hands.

He shook his head, rose, took the half-empty pail and went again to the well.

Tara sponged the girl's abdomen, arms, face. The skin was cold in places, still very hot in others. The breath that came rapidly and shallowly from her open mouth was very hot. The fever seemed to be rising, not falling, and the girl had not moved. She might have been asleep, or in a coma. Tara could only think that. She wouldn't dare mention it to poor Giles.

When he came back he bent over her and whispered, "Is she still asleep?"

"Yes."

"Does she still have fever?"

"Yes, but it could break any time." And it could, she told herself. After all, she was no doctor. Nor was she a nurse. She really wasn't even a nurse's aid. She had no way of judging the extent of Leda's illness, but she could help Giles feel a little better. She smiled over her shoulder at him. "Don't worry. She'll be a lot better tomorrow. Nights are always bad."

Again, Scott's words came sharply to her: *the house is worse at night.*

To her awareness again came the silence. The almost total silence. As if nothing existed outside the house. She looked at the doorway. Two opened doorways between the people and all the sounds of the swamps, two doors within fifty feet, and yet no sound came through.

She heard a tapping behind her, a soft, rhythmic *thud thud thud,* and she turned quickly to look. It was Sherwood, sitting with his back to the table, one arm crooked back on it and a finger tapping against the wood. His eyes, dark, shadowed, watched her ...

She turned around immediately, wishing he would quit both the staring and the tapping. The sound was magnified in the deep silence. The cloths had grown warm and she changed them busily, working harder than necessary.

Eventually the tapping stopped, and only Leda's breathing broke the awful silence. It seemed a bit softer, and Tara wasn't sure if she were resting better, or going farther into a coma. She sat back on her heels and for a while watched the girl's face carefully. But she didn't know what she was looking for.

"*Is* she better?" Giles asked again, anxiously, whispering.

Tara nodded. "I'm sure she must be."

Time passed slowly again. Or quickly. Tara wasn't sure. It seemed very late in the night, and still the house had not made one sound. It could have been carved from a solid stone.

She asked Giles, "What time is it?"

He squinted at his watch and said, "Eleven-thirty."

"Is that all?" she cried, louder than intended, and behind her something thumped and Sherwood laughed.

Tara turned to see that Amy evidently had gone to sleep leaning on her hand and slipped sideways when startled and awakened by Tara's voice. She was pulling herself up, her large eyes blinking.

Giles said, "She'd better go to bed. You go too." When Tara hesitated, looking up at him, he said, "I'll call you if she gets worse."

Tara got to her feet and stooped to rub her knees. They felt crushed. "Be sure to."

"I will."

"Come and wake me when you get tired, and I'll come down."

"I won't get tired."

Amy had heard the conversation and was standing, waiting for Tara. Sherwood too rose and reached for the lantern.

"I'll take them up, they'll be afraid to go alone."

Tara found his consideration hard to swallow and almost said so before she changed it to a cool, "We won't be afraid. Giles needs the lantern if he has to get more water. We'll take candles."

But Sherwood answered, still in the changed voice, "I'll bring the lantern back after you girls are safely in your room."

Amy touched Tara's arm. "Let him come, Tara, I'd feel much safer with him and the lantern light."

Tara got two candles anyway, but said no more. She waited then for Sherwood to lead the way, as he would have a few hours ago, but he stood back and motioned toward the door, and even smiled, suddenly the gallant protector. Tara couldn't stand keeping her mouth shut any longer.

"What's with you?" she asked brusquely.

"I'm only trying to be nice," he answered, shrugging, smiling a little. "Can't I even be nice without you gettin' nasty?"

"I doubt it," she said, and walked ahead of him in her most queenly fashion, a total put-on for those lascivious eyes that kept watching her. Behind her, she heard his soft, private laughter.

"I think you insulted both of us that time," he said, but only Amy's small snicker answered him.

Tara remembered to slow her walk not only for Amy's sake but to prevent her two candles from flickering out. But she walked without looking back, into the hall, past the back stairs, into the front hall and up the wide front stairway. Her shadow fell ahead of her, long and crooked on the stairs, cast by the light of Sherwood's bobbing lantern. In its bright gaslight her candlelight was almost non-existent.

She paused only slightly when she reached the patched hole. The boards, some of them torn from the barn, didn't fit together too well but the narrow, dark cracks that showed here and there let through air, or a gentle draft, that moved coldly over her bare arms. She found the small slits even more eerie than the large hole had been.

She stepped carefully past the place where Eldon had fallen, hoping her hesitation wasn't noticeable to the others. In the long, tunnel-like upper hall she drew a soft breath of relief. There was something about that particular spot that disturbed her, and she didn't recognize the feeling. It had nothing to do with the cold draft issuing from the cracks, nor with what she had seen upstairs. Behind her Amy's steps sounded as if she were trying to run. Tara slowed again, and felt Amy's hand slip under her arm. From there on, to the door of their room, they walked side by side. But Sherwood was still behind, his light throwing their long shadows down the hall.

At their door he bowed. "Safe and sound. Keep a light goin' all night and leave your door open so I can see that you're both safe."

Tara said, "We'll leave a light going, but you can be quite sure we won't leave the door open."

Amy spoke up so hurriedly she almost interrupted Tara, "Oh please, Tara. Let's do leave it open."

"I thought you felt safe in here."

"I—did … Do. But …"

Tara decided that Amy was only fumbling with words because the great master had spoken. She turned to face him. "Just what do you intend to do, walk sentry or something?"

"I might," he said. "At least often enough to see that you're all right."

She gave him a hard, penetrating glare, trying to understand what he was up to and wordlessly daring him to try it.

Amy tugged at her arm. "He will, Tara. I told you he would always take care of us."

He reached out and patted Amy's head as if she were a cute little puppy dog. "Now there's a smart girl."

Tara whirled away so fast she almost lost her candle flames. "I still don't believe it," she said. "But all right, if Amy wants the door open, it stays open. You just get out of here so I can change clothes without an audience."

"Now why would I want to stand here and watch you undress? Have you got something special somewhere? Strip down and let me judge for myself."

Tara placed the candles on the mantle and then turned and gave him a cold stare. He laughed and went walking down the hall. There was no doubt that he went because his footsteps echoed softly from somewhere and the light gradually faded. She could still hear him laughing to himself.

Tara said to Amy, "You'd better get to bed before you fall again."

"I didn't really fall, I just sort of dozed off and lost my balance."

"Well, anyway, go to bed."

Quickly, in case Sherwood decided to come back and check to see if they were in bed, Tara got out of her slacks and top and into long pajamas. When she went to the bed and arranged her blanket for sleeping she saw that Amy was sitting, still dressed. She held a motionless, listening attitude.

"Tara," she said very low, "doesn't it seem awfully quiet to you?"

Tara hadn't planned to mention it to Amy, hoping she wouldn't think anything of it. "I guess the frogs were sleepy tonight for a change," she said lightly. "Or do frogs sleep?"

"But it's more than that. There's nothing." And she frowned, disturbed, uneasy, her emotions showing in her face. "I've never heard it so quiet. The house usually makes all those noises, and now there's just nothing."

"Why don't you lie down and take advantage of the quiet? Maybe you can sleep better."

Amy tossed back her hair with impatience, and snapped, "Stop treating me like a moron all the time! Or a baby! There's something wrong in this house and I can hear it. Feel it."

"I'm sorry, Amy, I didn't mean to make you feel that I ever considered you inferior. Young, that's all. Just very, very young. And impressionable."

"You mean that funny silence doesn't bother you?"

"Okay, I'll level with you. Yes, it bothers me. This whole thing—the deaths—the sickness—the location of the house, and the damned house itself, all bother me. I not only don't like it, I hate it, and I wish I had never —" She stopped, biting her lower lip. But Amy turned large, understanding eyes on her and finished the sentence herself.

"Met any of us."

Tara sighed. "Well, it's not really your fault. Nor Eldon's, nor Sherwood's for that matter, that I'm here. It's my own fault for losing my cool and taking off to look for something that didn't exist. I blame no one because I'm here. No one but me. But that doesn't mean I don't wish to the devil I was out of here."

"I know," Amy said. Her eyes drifted beyond Tara, covered the room, and stopped on the painting. "I wish now I hadn't let Sherwood talk us in to leaving the door open."

"I'll close it!" She had hardly finished saying so when she did, running on bare feet to the door. It was good to have it shut. "There's something about that dark hall that makes everybody uncomfortable. Maybe now we can sleep, right?"

Amy lay down without changing clothes and pulled the blanket over her bare feet and legs. "Yes. At least we'll try. If Sherwood does check on us he'll shut the door again, maybe. He really can be a very sweet man. You saw that yourself."

Tara grunted. In her opinion, Sherwood wasn't worth more than a grunt. She wasn't going to change her mind just because he had changed his tone of voice. There was a reason behind it, she was sure of that, and probably more than the one. She didn't trust him.

She was surprised to find herself growing sleepy. The unsettling silence, she had thought, would keep her from sleeping at all. But she drifted softly away, thinking that she was going to sleep because she was so tired.

Amy had been wrong, she saw the moment she woke, because Sherwood had opened the door and then not closed it again after all. It stood wide open, framing a black world that in her half-waking state looked endless and depthless.

Startled, her heart racing, she sat up and faced the dark hallway. Something had awakened her, but she wasn't sure what. The house was still very quiet.

The candles on the mantle had burned low, and the face in the painting was sharp and clear even in the dim light. Amy lay on her side, one hand under her cheek like a sleeping child.

As noiselessly as possible Tara disentangled herself from the blanket and slid from the high bed to the floor. She had only one thing in mind: close the door as quietly and quickly as possible.

She reached the door and touched it, standing on the edge of the black cavern of the hallway, and the sound came softly, bringing a fear that crawled like icy hands over her body.

Eldon. He was crying again.

Instantly her mind rejected that. It couldn't be Eldon. Eldon was dead, and besides, the sound was soft weeping, far away. Someone, somewhere in the house. The longer she listened the more real it became.

A man, somewhere.

She left the door as it was, hurried to the mantle and took a candle, then with one glance back at the still-sleeping Amy, Tara went into the hallway.

She stood there for a moment, her hand protecting the flame. The sound of the weeping was faint but continuous, and toward the back stairs. She followed the sound, aware of the open upstairs and that it might be like the laughter she had thought she'd heard the day she discovered the closed stairway. But when she reached the small room and the landing, she knew it wasn't. The sound came from downstairs, softly fading away again. But she knew what it was.

She went down the back stairs without trying to be so quiet about it, mentally scolding herself for leaving Giles alone. In some ways he seemed as childish as Amy, and sitting with a sick girl whom he loved was too much for his psyche.

She saw instantly that Sherwood was not in the kitchen. The lantern sat on the table, creating both bright light and deep shadows, and in one of the shadows Leda still lay on the blanket and Giles was lying beside her, his head on her chest.

When Tara touched his shoulder he jumped and looked up at her. Tara saw that he had been crying for a long time. She pushed him gently out of her way and kneeled.

Leda's skin was cold, colder it seemed than anything Tara had ever before touched. But she was still breathing.

"I think maybe her fever broke, Giles," Tara said, trying to cover her dread and uneasiness. Something was very wrong with Leda, but she had to get rid of Giles. "Is that why you've been crying?"

"You mean she's better?"

"She needs rest, and so do you. When a fever breaks the crisis is over, right?"

"I guess so. Yes," he said more positively, "Yes, it is. Will she be all right?"

Tara wondered if doctors felt as helpless sometimes, and as deceitful, as she did then. She knew only her own feelings, and could see the uselessness of having Giles suffer over Leda now.

"What time is it?"

"Three-thirty."

"Then you go to bed. I'll stay here the rest of the night. She's okay, Giles. Now go. Here, take this candle, and sleep. I don't want to see you until daylight. All right?"

He drew away, the candle in his hand. Trust was in his eyes when he looked at her. Then he turned and was gone, and Tara stayed alone with the girl, who seemed to be dying.

She drew a long breath and sat down on the floor, bending her knees and enfolding her legs in her arms. She sat so that she faced the doorway, with Leda beside her. The coldness of the girl's body came through the blanket which Giles had spread over her.

Three-thirty. Wasn't that the hour of death? Also, oddly, the hour of birth. She seemed to remember statistics that claimed more people died and more were born in the small hours of the morning. Around three o'clock.

She wished that she had asked Giles to leave his watch.

Leda breathed shallowly and irregularly. Tara wondered what it could mean. Perhaps the fever really had broken and the girl was merely sleeping. Tara pulled the blanket higher around Leda's neck, wishing she had wood for a fire. Had she done something wrong, she wondered, by sponging her with cold water? Had she allowed Leda to grow too cold?

Damn Sherwood for not believing in doctors.

She thought now that it wasn't that he didn't believe in doctors, it was simply, and frighteningly, that he did not want anyone to know where they were. Because, like it or not, Tara knew they were in hiding. A crime had been committed, and Sherwood was responsible for it. She had no doubt all of them had been implicated, except Amy. Even Leda had been along that night. But Tara didn't know what they had done, and to her these two helpless people, Leda and Giles, had no connection with anything beyond her own knowledge of them. There it started, and there it ended.

The night would never end. No, never. It would go on forever while she waited.

To straighten stiff muscles she got up and padded about the room, and noticed for the first time that she had forgotten to put on her sandals before she left the bedroom.

She looked down at Leda and saw that the girl had not changed position, not once. But she was still breathing. Maybe she would make it through the night.

A sound split the silence then, muffled but close. Thunder. And suddenly the house creaked somewhere.

She had never thought she would welcome the creaking, moving, splitting noises of the house, but at the moment it seemed almost like a friend walking into the room. She said aloud to the fireplace, "It was only the stillness before the storm after all. Thank heavens."

But that was not true, her mind instantly played back. The house was an evil, living thing, in some unnatural way, and had another reason for its periods of silence.

Well, no matter, it was over now.

Lightning illuminated the windows eerily in a beautiful way and the thunder followed, and within minutes it seemed a constant explosion of sound and light with heavy blasts of rain against the windows, tearing at the vines, weighing them down.

Upstairs, far above, something fell. A board? Perhaps even a limb from a tree, or the whole ceiling in the nursery? She didn't care. She felt that she would welcome a tornado if it would sweep the house away and be done with it. Just so the others could get downstairs before it struck.

She noticed that the light in the room had changed. A grayness was competing with the lantern and easing out the shadows. Daylight, at last, dimmed by the heavy clouds that hung over the land.

Amy stood in the doorway as still as an apparition or hallucination, and Tara screeched softly, smothering it behind her hands.

Amy came on in, saying, "I'm sorry. I never thought I'd scare you."

Tara attempted a laugh, but it failed. "You don't scare me. You've no idea how good you look to me. It was just that all of a sudden you were there, you know."

"The storm woke me. I guess that's why everything was so quiet last night. Everything quiets down before a storm. Even the frogs, I guess."

Tara almost told her that the frogs had not been quiet, but held her tongue on that one. "I guess so," she said. "I don't know what we'll have for breakfast. Since there's no wood we can't even have coffee. You didn't happen to see a man on the way down, did you?"

"No, I didn't. How's Leda?"

"She's—well, she's resting."

Amy was bending as best as she could over her stomach to look down at Leda. For a long while she looked.

"Tara!" she cried after a period of silence. "Come here!"

Tara ran. Even as she kneeled beside Leda, before she reached under the blanket and pulled out a limp wrist to take the pulse, or before she reached under the blouse to search for a heartbeat, she knew that Leda had died. The open mouth and the half-open eyes spoke their wordless message.

Amy began screaming, on and on, crying and screaming and walking an erratic circle. Tara got up and followed her, turned her around and held her.

"Stop it, stop it, Amy!"

Amy stopped screaming as suddenly as she'd started and stood gasping, looking wildly about the room.

Footsteps on the stairs and in the hall, running, faded into the crash of thunder as Giles appeared in the doorway. He ran straight to Leda and fell to his knees.

Tara turned her back to him and pushed Amy down on a bench by the table. "Calm down," she said severely. "You're only doing damage to yourself and the baby, you're not helping Leda."

Sherwood's voice bellowed out, quite normally, "What's goin' on? Who's screechin', anyway?"

Tara only looked at him, then went back to Leda. Giles was rubbing her hand, hard. When she didn't respond he reached over her as if to turn her. His hand pressed against her heart, released, pressed again.

Tara gently pulled at him. "Giles, please. You can't bring her back."

He jerked away, turning his back to all of them, going to stare into the fireplace.

Tara stood looking down at Leda, and thought of Eldon, and thought also, "Two down and four to go."

But she didn't realize she had spoken aloud until Amy cried, "What do you mean?"

Tara looked around, and the walls, the gaping fireplace, the door-less door, even the closed cupboards seemed evil and menacing. "This house is eating us," she said.

Sherwood yelled, "That's a damned crazy thing to say!"

"But she's right."

The words had come from Giles. Quiet, positive, accepting. He turned and looked at them all, and no other word was spoken.

CHAPTER 12

Giles sat down on the stool by the fireplace, his elbows on his knees, his head in his hands. And there he sat, as silent and still as if he too had died. Tara watched him for a moment, sympathy aching in her heart. But she didn't know what to do. Restlessly, she began to walk.

"What do we do now?" she asked no one in particular. "What do we do? Like with Fox—I suppose it's useless to mention anything about funeral—"

Sherwood interrupted sharply. "I'll take care of it." Tara stopped and watched him, watched him go to the girl on the floor and roll her in the blanket as if she were a package to be wrapped. In a growing horror Tara watched him. He picked Leda up and carried her in his arms across the kitchen and out the door.

The other time Tara hadn't watched. What they had done with Eldon's body she didn't know. This time the same mute horror with which she had watched him carelessly bundle her up took her to the window to peer through the dripping vines.

The storm had moved on, that she vaguely noted, and only a gentle rain was left. A moment more and Sherwood came into sight, going down the path by the garage.

Where the path turned toward the hidden toilets he went on, straight ahead, toward the black trees of the swamp. When he reached the swamp he picked each step carefully, as if he walked on stones, or protruding roots.

"He's going to just leave her in the swamp," she cried. "Just leave her there!" She whirled to look at Amy, sitting sober and silent and white at the table, and at Giles, still on the stool with his head down. "Is that what happened to Eldon? He wasn't even buried? And Leda ..."

The visions came to her like a nightmare, things that lived in the swamp eating flesh that might be dead but to her was still the girl who had been alive yesterday, and though she knew she was losing control of herself she couldn't seem to stop it. The nausea rose to her throat, nearly strangling her, and she ran to the door. But the thought of following in the path where Sherwood had gone was too much, and she ran instead to the stairway and up, and down the dim second-story hall to her room.

She slammed the door as she went through and flung herself across the bed. Chills pervaded her body. She couldn't stop trembling. She wondered briefly if she had caught Leda's fever, and didn't much care. But after a while the nausea left.

Eventually she sat up, thinking. Tears seemed to be beyond her. There were too many emotions involved, and growing strongly among them was a fear such as she had never imagined. Her mind kept asking *what is happening here*? But there was no answer.

Whatever was happening she couldn't take any more of it, and she wondered at her stupid reluctance to try to escape when she safely could. Of course she hadn't known, she reminded herself, she hadn't known. Known what? She still didn't know. Except one thing—she had to get out.

Now. While Sherwood was taking Leda into the swamp.

She went into the hall and down the rear stairs, and drew back quickly. Sherwood was standing in the doorway at the end of the hall, leaning at ease against the opened door, looking out sometimes and then down at his hands at other times, his glances casually going up and down. With his knife he slowly cleaned and pared his fingernails.

He hadn't seen or heard Tara.

Quietly she backed out of sight and stood against the wall. To get to the door to the front hall she would have to risk being seen by him, should he happen to turn. The only way out was back up the stairs and down the front way.

She went slowly and carefully, hoping with held breath that a step wouldn't squeak loudly enough to catch his attention. In the upper hall she took off her sandals and carried them, and ran on quiet, bare feet to the front stairs. The cold air came through the cracks of the boarded hole, whistling a strange and eerie little tune, but it was the least of her worries at the moment. She went down the front stairs and paused by the door for just long enough to slip into her sandals.

She turned the large, ornate knob, and found that the door had been locked. Or it was stuck. Frantically she tried again and again, and then she gave it up and ran into a front room.

She closed the door and leaned against it, looking around. The room was cluttered with gray figures that could have been old, dusty ghosts in a dim, dim world. She had never looked under the muslin that covered the furniture, and wasn't even sure that it was furniture. It didn't matter. It was a window she was concerned with, and not the large gray-green lumps that nearly filled the room.

There were two windows, one in front and the other across the room at the side of the house. Brief examinations revealed to her that in order to open either she would have to break the glass. The locks had rusted in the dampness, and the grit that covered the panes, and a kind of sticky, gooey mold, came off on her fingers.

She had a sickening feeling that all the other windows, in all the rooms, would be the same. Would Sherwood hear glass breaking from so far away? But even if he didn't it was still a problem because once the glass was gone there remained a rusted, heavy screen to get through. They were not like the nearly invisible screens of today. Still, one might easily be broken through because its age might have weakened it.

It was her only chance.

The house seemed to have come awake again and was creaking and snapping as usual and the shatter of glass might not even be noticed in the back of the house.

She looked about for something small enough to handle and was just preparing to raise a rotted gray muslin covering that looked to be a low stool of some kind when she heard her name called in a cry that almost shattered what remained of her nerves. Amy. Calling from where? She sounded in a state of panic. The call came again, nearer. She was running heavily down the hall, her steps echoing hollowly as if something followed her.

"Tara!"

Tara too began to run, the window forgotten. Amy needed her—and she was afraid to wonder why.

She opened the door just as Amy reached the front stairs. The girl was holding her stomach with both arms and the fear in her face was like a reflection of Tara's own when Tara saw the blood that ran from Amy.

"Amy, I'm here. Did he hurt you?" That was her first thought. Sherwood had stabbed Amy. But Amy was shaking her head.

"No, no, no. It's the baby! The baby!" Her voice rose to a hysterical scream.

Strangely, it had just the opposite effect on Tara. Her thoughts formulated quickly as she looked again at Amy and the pool of bloody water that was collecting between her feet.

She put a smile on her face as she took Amy's arm. "Well, at last! I've never delivered a baby before, and you've never had one before, but as Sherwood said, babies were born—have been born—" She stopped, licked her lips, and asked, "Are you in pain, Amy?"

"No. But the blood! What is it, Tara?"

Amy bent forward, trying to look at the floor between her feet in a way that struck Tara as comical. With effort she controlled a nervous giggle.

"I think it must be the bag that holds the baby, that's all. It has to break before the baby can come out, you know. If you can get upstairs and into bed we'll be able to get ready for the great moment. All right?"

Amy's lips trembled, but she managed a smile and a nod, and slowly they climbed the stairs. When they reached the top Tara looked back and saw the trail of blood.

Dark red drops on the steps. They somehow had an old look, as if they had been there for many, many years, as if they marked the steps of another woman who had walked the same stairs. The little boy had struck his own mother in her bed with his small hatchet and she had come down the stairs, life dripping from her. She had run from him, run to escape the truth as much as the act.

It was but a glimpse in Tara's mind, as intangible as extrasensory perception, but as real for a moment as if she witnessed it.

Cold air from the cracks touched them, and the fine singing of the wind had dropped to a soft moan.

Amy asked, "Why is there so much wind up there, Tara? Is there a window out?"

"I'm sure there is. Several probably."

"Yes. To cause a draft like that. Tara, how long do you think it will be before the baby comes?"

Amy's voice had acquired a lift, and Tara glanced at her to see a faint smile, a shining happiness beginning there again.

"I don't know. I think it takes quite a while for the first one. Birth is in three stages. Or so I seem to remember something of that sort from my first-aid course. The first one is the labor time, the longest part, where you just have a pain now and then. That's when you're opening up to let the baby through. That can last all day, and sometimes all night too. Then comes the part when the baby starts moving through. That doesn't last so long. Then, with the baby born, you wait a few minutes for the afterbirth to come. By that time you've got a tiny person to nurse and take care of."

"Tara, that's beautiful."

"It is?" Tara answered teasingly, trying to hide the sick feeling in her stomach, her heart, her whole body and mind. Nothing was right, and she had an awful premonition that this wouldn't be right either.

Amy sighed. "Poor Leda. I wish she ..."

Tara said nothing. To think of Leda, where she might be now, increased her despondency. Slowly they went on down the hall to the bedroom.

"You just walk around," Tara said, "while I get the bed ready."

It was good to have something to do, though, she thought. It saved her mind. The birth of the baby—if it only went right—would probably save everybody's mind, make everything seem alive again. New life, new living. So important after deaths.

"It won't hurt the baby?" Amy asked, standing still.

Tara saw that the blood had stopped dripping from Amy. Noted the fact vaguely, but with relief. At least she wasn't hemorrhaging.

"No. It won't hurt either of you. Walk when you want to, sit when you want to, or lie down. It's up to you. Just try to stay in the room or hallway. Don't go back downstairs." She folded a blanket lengthwise as she talked, and lay it on the bed. Another blanket she lay to one side. "I want you to lie on that one to have the baby, because we'll have to have it washed later. This one you can use for cover."

"But what about you, Tara?"

"I won't be sleeping much anyway, and I can get a blanket from—from another room." Eldon's blanket? Leda's? She thought she would rather freeze because it would seem like robbing a grave. "I'll go down and make preparations. I'll cut another blanket into smaller blankets for the baby, and we can use the little tea towels from the kitchen for diapers. Won't that be something? I wonder how Sherwood will like having his dishes dried on the same towels the baby uses for diapers? Maybe it will spur him on to buy some baby clothes."

"Maybe."

Amy had sat down in the rocking chair. It squeaked faintly as she began to rock. At the door Tara paused to look at her for a moment.

"You hang in there, okay? I'll be back and forth."

She went to the back stairs to save time, for one reason, and for another to avoid the blood spots on the front stairs. And the cracks in the boards. And that cold, strange wind that issued from those cracks. In the landing by the broken back stairway she paused and looked up into the dim light of the third story. It looked like something from a horror movie, but there was no wind. Only in the front did that small, cold draft blow.

She wished she had Scott to walk beside her, to hold her hand. To be with her and Amy. To stay with them until they could leave.

She said softly aloud as she started down the steep, seemingly endless steps, "I wish to God I had never found that stairway." It should have stayed as it was, boarded. Boarded against the wheelchair that could rise on its cable into the third story where the insane young boy could commit his murders.

The argument came in her own mind, logic against imagination, reason against fear. *But that was long ago, long ago, and the boy is now dead, as well as the man who finally built a barricade between himself and his son, too late, too late to save the baby, the mother, the slave.* The house was falling in because it was old, not because of a boy who had once lived there, whose portrait ...

The draft in the front stairway was caused, surely, by the fallen ceiling in the nursery, and blew down those stairs because the door to the nursery was situated near the landing. That was all. Simply.

Surely.

The railing seemed sticky under her hand. Damp. Too much rain here, she thought, too humid by the swamp. That's why. She held tightly to it even though it was sticky, and went on, watching her steps more closely than usual, hearing the boards squeak as she touched them, feeling the unsteadiness of the whole structure, as if it had grown feeble during the night. The wind in the house had weakened it, and soon it would be falling too, because the house was destined to destroy every living thing that entered it and lived, as best as it could in its cold, musty, strange way. The very wood it was made of had been programmed to kill.

That's ridiculous, her logical mind replied. A house, the wood it's created of, is harmless. *And,* another source in her mind replied, *so is a child unless it's commanded by the devil.*

"Good God," she said aloud, and began to run as she reached the hall.

Debris sifted down from the ceiling as she ran, and when she reached the kitchen she paused inside the door and brushed it from her hair.

Sherwood sat at the table eating something straight from a can. He smiled at her. "What's the matter with you, Red?"

"I think I'm going crazy," she mumbled.

Though Giles was still on the stool at the far end of the kitchen, he heard her and replied, "We all will if we don't get out of here."

"Bull," said Sherwood, taking another bite from the opened can. He ate with a tablespoon, Tara noticed absently.

She crossed the room to stand on the hearth, across from Giles. "You're the only one who seems to have any sense around here, so maybe you can convince that idiot over there stuffing his big mouth that if we don't get out of here we're all going to do more than go crazy, we're going to die."

Giles looked up at her. His eyes looked glazed and half dead.

She waited just long enough to see that she had his attention. All, at least, that he was capable of giving. "Listen to this. Nobody would ever believe it, and I wouldn't have either before I came here, but there's something about that little boy who lived here, who committed those murders upstairs, that is still here."

"Still here?" Sherwood yelled around a mouthful of food. "You *are* crazy!"

Giles stood up and faced Sherwood. "Let's get out of here while we got a chance."

"You some kind of a freak, man? Where would we go? Huh? Where would we go? Our only trouble is we got us a witch, that's what." His long arm shot out and he pointed at Tara. "She puttin' all this bull in your head and makin' you believe stuff! She probably drawed that sign on that paintin' upstairs too." He glared at her. "And what's more, ain't it kind of a coincidence that it's her that was with both Fox and Leda when they died?"

Although the seriousness on Sherwood's face when that idea had come to him surprised Tara, the thing that disturbed her was the change in Giles. His mild, sad eyes turned to look at her with an expression that made her want to take a step backwards.

She controlled the desire, but she gave up on Giles and walked over to the table. "Sherwood, you are incredible you're so stupid!"

"Stupid?" he replied. "Because I got your number, Red?"

"That reminds me," Tara said calmly, realizing that nothing would get Sherwood out of the house. "Amy is in labor."

"She's in what?"

"Labor. She's having the baby."

Sherwood went back to eating. "Well, let her have it and shut up for Christ's sake."

"I'm going to have to use dish towels for diapers, and I need a knife to cut the cord and make strings to tie it."

"You ain't gettin' my knife," Sherwood said.

Tara turned to Giles. "Could I borrow yours, please?" His eyes were still distrusting, but he obeyed like a child. He pulled from his pocket a knife similar to the one Fox had thrown to her that day. She remembered the blood, and opened it to examine the blade closely, but it was clean.

Sherwood snickered. "You won't find any blood on Giles' knife."

Tara thought that the words sounded contemptuous and looked up to see Sherwood grinning sideways at Giles.

She said, "I don't think Giles is as heartless as you are."

Sherwood got up so fast that he looked as if he popped up, like a jack-in-the-box. "Now what the hell does that mean?"

"It means," she replied distinctly, knowing that she was treading on dangerous ground, "that he probably didn't go along with that killing you did."

Giles said faintly in the background, "I'm sorry I did."

Sherwood's face changed from anger to surprise, then he started to move toward her. His eyes darted down to the knife in her hand and he stopped. She realized she was holding it open, its long blade pointed toward him. And he had more respect for that open blade than for anything else, obviously. He remained where he was, by the table.

"Who told you," he demanded, "about that?"

She returned his stare without glancing away or backing down, and then topped it with a smug, cold smile which suggested that she knew all there was to know and he would never learn how she had acquired her knowledge.

"I will need a blanket," she said softly, "to cut into smaller blankets for the baby. To wrap it in."

Sherwood dropped down to the bench again, but he looked cross and wary. "You ain't gettin' mine," he grumbled.

She hadn't thought of that, and it was an idea she couldn't resist. She left the room, the skin tightening on the back of her neck and down her backbone because she expected to feel Sherwood's knife strike her at any moment. But she didn't look back, and she didn't quicken her steps. He would never know, she thought, the relief she felt when she crossed the kitchen threshold and was out of his sight. Holding the knife carefully away from her, she ran again, to the steps and up.

Amy was still sitting in the rocking chair, looking comfortable and relaxed.

"No pains yet?" Tara asked, gingerly placing the knife on the bedside table.

"No, nothing."

"Damn! I forgot those towels after all. And I didn't want to have to go back to the kitchen." She stood with her hands on her hips and looked down at the one item she had managed to bring with her. "Not even any water. And nothing to eat. Are you hungry, Amy?"

"No."

"Well, I'm not either, so we'll wait awhile for that. When I go down for water I'll bring up something to eat and the towels. Right now I have to go get another blanket and get ready for the baby. I'll be right back."

"Don't worry about me. I'm okay."

Tara went into the hall and turned toward the front. She went easily and quickly at first, but her steps slowed and became lighter and more hesitant as her eyes sought and found the clumsily nailed boards on the hole at the head of the stairs. The fine wail came to her ears, a singing wind, rising in pitch and falling, on and on, and she thought it had the voice of a child. A child who sang a wild song with a strange delight.

She stopped, forced her attention to the bedroom doors along the hall. She couldn't remember which room it was.

Well, of course it had to be the only room that had blankets in it, she decided, because the three had always slept together, hadn't they? And the room was across the hall, that she knew for sure. And quite a way down toward the front.

She crossed to the other side of the hall and tried to keep her mind on her business, but the singing of the child kept getting her attention, and several times she stopped to listen. She tried to hear it only as wind, but could no longer. It was Samael, singing, singing, singing. Knowing something she did not know. Something that made him want to laugh as he sang.

Tara put her hands over her ears and ran, looking into bedroom after bedroom until she saw the bed with the blankets. She went into the room and slammed the door.

Too late she saw that there was no window. She had closed herself into darkness. And overhead the house moved, a board fell, and the ceiling sounded for a moment like it too was falling. If the slamming of a door could do that, she wondered frantically as she jerked it open, what small storm would it actually take to cause the collapse of the entire house?

The light from the hall, though not much, was beautiful despite the increased sound of the singing little voice of the wind down the boarded stairway.

She went to the bed and saw two blankets. Giles, she remembered, had brought one down to cover Leda. So one of those that remained was Sherwood's. To be sure he was irritated sufficiently, she gathered up both and returned to the hall and walked along it swiftly, not pausing to look back but feeling every step of the way as if fingers were reaching for the back of her neck. She was almost running again when she reached the bedroom and closed the door behind her.

"Is something wrong?" Amy asked.

"Nothing new," Tara answered. "Just a general depression from—you know."

"Yes," Amy said "Leda. I keep thinking of her. She could be kind of mean sometimes, but I miss her anyway. I don't like for people to die, do you, Tara?"

"No, I don't." Tara put the blankets on a chair, got the knife and began to hack, saw and cut them into squares that were about the size of baby blankets. "That's one of my marks of immaturity, I guess, Amy—my inability to face death, the death of others, and accept it. I've tried so long to understand it that I finally just quit. I've gained a kind of philosophy about it: if we understood it, perhaps we wouldn't want to live, perhaps we would prefer death. Otherwise, why is the understanding of it kept from us so completely? Maybe life is simply a preparation for the attainment of death after all, just as Jesus said. Maybe—" She looked up to see that Amy was engrossed in what she was saying. Too much so. Tara forced a smile. "Ah, come on, what are we talking about? Life is the natural order of things. Life is beautiful. That's why we like it so well. And that's what we're getting ready for here, right?"

"Right," Amy said. But she still looked thoughtful, as if she had glimpsed something she had never seen before. She had stopped rocking. Tara saw her steady gaze go up to the painting and remain there. "Samael," she said. "Maybe that's why he hates so much—not because he couldn't live, but because he couldn't really die. Do you think there's a heaven and a hell, Tara, and some people are really in hell? Like Samael?"

"Not really. Only when I'm feeling low. I'm a naturalist, and by that I mean I believe only in what I see. Like the trees and the sky, and spring, and flowers that bloom to create their seed and then die to make room for the seed to grow and produce its own seed. The continuous, depthless spiral. Nature in itself is—"

But Amy wasn't listening. She said, "He wants out, you know, he wants *out*."

"Amy," Tara said, holding up a ragged square of blanket and hoping that it would get her mind off the other thing, "do you think this is big enough?"

Amy looked at it and giggled. "I don't intend to have an elephant, Tara."

Tara laughed. They looked at each other, smiling over the top of the blanket with the jagged edges.

"Shall I make them smaller?" Tara asked. "They'll probably weigh more than the baby."

Amy opened her mouth to answer, but leaned forward and gripped the arms of the chair suddenly and the gasp that came from her open mouth became a low cry.

Tara dropped the blanket on the bed. "A pain, Amy?" She felt all at once very helpless. There was nothing to do, she decided, but just stand there.

After a moment Amy relaxed and drew a long breath. She closed her eyes. When she opened them again she said, "Wow! Maybe it's going to be an elephant after all. How long did you say the pains last?"

Tara shrugged and turned the palms of her hands toward the ceiling. "I don't know. I think it depends on the woman. Do you want to lie down?"

Amy got up from the chair as if she were afraid that she might break something. "Yes, I do. I feel so tired all of a sudden."

Tara hurried around the foot of the bed and smoothed the bottom blanket, although it was already as smooth as she had been able to make it.

"I sure hope you're not as nervous as I am, Amy," she said, trying to laugh again and make it sound like a joke. "I feel like I'm the one who's having the baby."

"I can guarantee you you're not," Amy said as she sat on the high bed and twisted her body up and around so that she could lie down on her side.

Tara removed the sandals from her feet, and noticed that Amy was still in a maternity dress. "Amy, you have to undress and get into a gown. Sit up and I'll get your gown. Didn't you ever undress last night?"

"No." Amy, groaning again, pushed herself up. When the pain was gone she began to get out of her clothes.

Tara found a large, untouched nightgown in a drawer where Amy kept her clothes, and brought it to the girl and held it until Amy reached up her arms to allow Tara to slip it over her head. She fell back onto the bed as if the act of changing to the gown had exhausted her. Tara wondered if the pains should be so hard so early, but said nothing. She drew one corner of the other blanket over Amy.

"Do you want anything? Food? Water?"

"I sure don't want anything to eat, but I'd like to have a drink."

That meant another trip down to the kitchen, Tara thought, but then it had to be done sometime. They couldn't remain upstairs until the baby was born and Amy able to get out of the house, with nothing to keep them alive but a knife and a few blankets.

"Okay, I'll go down and back as fast as I can. If you should need me before I get back just scream as loud as you can."

"Don't worry, I will."

When she reached the kitchen she was surprised to find it empty. Both men were gone. Even the cricket no longer occupied his small part of the fireplace. She had dreaded seeing Sherwood again, and she hurried toward the water bucket, hoping there was enough.

It was only half full, but it could be divided for drinking and washing. She opened the cupboard to look for a container for the water, and heard the mumble of Sherwood's voice, somewhere outside the kitchen, coming closer. He was talking to Giles, obviously, and they were coming back into the house.

She left the cupboard, took the water bucket and ran with it. Just as they stepped upon the back porch she ducked out of sight at the foot of the stairs.

Only then did she remember that she had forgotten the towels again.

She sighed in disgust. The baby had to have the towels. Something soft against its small body. But, she told herself, the baby wasn't born yet, and maybe by the time it came Sherwood would take interest in the baby and forget her. At least enough to allow her to do the things that had to be done without keeping that eagle eye crooked in her direction all the time.

She went on up the steps, careful to avoid making them squeak too loudly and give her away.

By mid-afternoon Amy was rolling restlessly in labor, but though she moaned softly at times, she was otherwise silent in her pain. She seemed hardly aware that Tara was in the room.

There was nothing for Tara to do. She roamed about, as restive as Amy, going from closed door to window, back to the secretary to look through drawers she hadn't touched, and finding them all empty. Sometimes she stood at the foot of the bed wondering if everything were going the way it should or if something were wrong. She had no way of knowing. There was nothing to do but walk the floor and wait ...

She remembered, when dusk fell and she had to light candles, that the knife must be sterilized. She remembered it with relief. At least it was something to do. The knife was still on the bedside table, and she placed a candle near it and then held the long blade over the flame.

Amy's moans became almost continuous, and more desperate. Tara's hands trembled as she held the knife, moving it slowly, ever so slowly over the tiny flame, careful to heat every bit of it. At last she lay it carefully on the table so that the blade touched nothing.

Occasionally, as night came darkly in, other sounds penetrated Amy's moans—sounds of falling boards far above, and then the *creak creak creak* of someone going down the hall outside their door.

Sherwood, thought Tara, on his way to his room.

And then again, *Sherwood*! Gone on to his room, gone from the kitchen. It had to be Sherwood, because Giles would not come up alone in his fear of the house, and the steps had been the steps of only one.

Now was her chance to get down to the kitchen and bring up other things she needed.

She looked at Amy, and decided to say nothing. The girl was in such misery that she wouldn't even know she had been left alone.

Tara took a candle and quietly opened the door, looking out and down the hall. All was dark, which meant that Sherwood had already gone into his room. She wondered what he would think when he found no blankets. Fortunately, the night was sultry hot, so perhaps he wouldn't even notice.

She closed the door behind her and hurried toward the back stairs, her hand cupped protectively around the candle flame so that she could hurry without losing the light.

The moment she reached the hall she saw the light that fell through the kitchen door, the white light of the gas lantern, dulled to a greenish-gray on the hall floor. She stopped, looking at it, puzzled.

Had Sherwood gone up without his light? Had she been wrong about

Giles—could it have been Giles instead of Sherwood? She almost turned back, but Amy's time was growing near, now she was sure, and she needed the towels. Besides, she was hungry. She'd take some canned beans and tomatoes and a can opener up with her. Enough to take care of both of them until they could get out of the house.

That problem, getting out, could be tackled when the time came. Right now she needed to get into the kitchen. Where had her courage gone? She was afraid to see which man was in the kitchen, but she was stunned and surprised to see that both of them were.

Giles lay stretched out on the blanket where Leda had died, and Sherwood sat on a bench at the table, using the table to lean back against.

Tara forgot her fear of him. "Did you just go upstairs?"

Sherwood said blankly, "Who me?"

She could see in his face that he didn't know what she was talking about. "It sounded like footsteps in the hall.

But had it been like that? She was no longer sure of her senses.

"Wasn't me," said Sherwood. "And wasn't him. He's been snorin' for two hours. What're you wantin', honey?"

Tara gave him a swift glare. "What did you say?"

"I said what're you wantin'?" he replied sociably.

It seemed too good to be true, but it looked as if he intended to let her get in and out with no trouble. "I came to get some things," she said, going to the cupboard.

"Here, let me help you."

She thought of the footsteps in the hall and decided that maybe in this case Sherwood was the lesser of two evils. At least his way of killing was swift.

"I could use some help," she admitted, "but I thought you were afraid of our room."

"Afraid? Who, me? Don't misjudge me, honey. I may be cautious, but I ain't afraid. I'll go as far as the door." That was good, Tara thought, and said aloud, "That's far enough. I can take it from there."

She got six cans of beans and six of tomatoes and put them in his arms. He shifted them about and got them settled on one.

"That's enough," he said. "I got to have one hand free to take the lantern."

"All right."

Into her own arms she loaded towels and on top of the towels she lay two more cans of tomatoes and the can opener. They cradled against her like a baby, and suddenly a feeling of optimism struck her. For the first time the reality of the baby was with her, and she felt an eagerness for it to hurry now and be born so that she could hold and cuddle it.

Quickly she went back to the table and took the candle in her free hand and led the way toward the door. When she turned to see if Sherwood were following her she thought of the darkness they were leaving behind, and how Giles might respond if he should wake up before Sherwood got back.

"Shouldn't we leave a light for Giles?"

"Him? He's asleep. He'll never know I was gone."

He was too close behind her, and he made no effort to move back, and his voice was sultry and hot as the night. So he was getting sexy again. That explained his nicer attitude toward her. She turned uneasily away and hurried into the hall and toward the stairs.

He stopped her in the small room at the foot of the stairs by pushing his body in front of her and forcing her back against the corner angle of the wall. His body pushed in against hers and his mouth brushed her cheek as she turned her head away from the kiss that was aimed somewhere toward her nose. It settled on her neck beneath her ear.

She twisted against him, trying to remember that her candle must not go out, but he only pushed harder, pinning her in the corner. He mumbled something obscene as he bit her earlobe.

"Let me go, you filthy queer!" she replied angrily. "I wouldn't *service* you if my life depended on it!"

He muttered something else and she thought about biting him, but the mere thought was sickening. She tried then to raise her leg and mangle his foot if possible, but he only took advantage of the move to burrow himself between her thighs.

She twisted violently sideways and struck her candle against the wall, knocking out its feeble light. Anger so filled her that she couldn't contain it. "You're a bastard, you, Sherwood—whoever you are—" She stuttered, stammered, and then felt his revenge in the heat of the lantern as he pressed it to her leg. She threw the candle—it was doing her no good anyway—and dug her fingers into his neck, clawing, fighting to hurt him as much as she could.

His curse was lost under the loud crash that came from somewhere upstairs. Wind roared along the front hall, blowing open the door and banging it against the wall. It blew down the steps from the upper stories.

Her hair was swept back from her face and her blouse flattened against her.

She forgot Sherwood as she looked up into the wind and the darkness above, as she cringed and waited for the top of the house to fall upon them. Then she heard his cry, faint under the noises of the crashing doors and timbers and the wind, and she turned to face him.

He was backing away from her, across the small room, toward the hall to the kitchen. "What did you do?" he cried, his voice high pitched and strained in terror, his eyes bulging in his gray face. "How did you do it?"

She said, "I didn't do it, you fool!" But her words were lost in the brain-crushing sounds that surrounded them.

He was still moving back, faster, and his lips moved, and twice she caught a word before he ran. "Witch!" he sobbed. "Witch!"

With him went all light, and she was in darkness that seemed total and forever. She reached behind her and felt the wall, and squeezed herself into the corner. Into the sounds that filled the house then came a scream; a long, frantic scream from upstairs.

"Amy!" Tara whispered to herself, and ran forward, feeling for the banister. She found it, felt it tremble under her hand, but she clung to it and climbed, forcing her way through the wind that roared down the stairs.

The other sounds, of falling roof or whatever it had been, drifted to silence and left only the sound of the wind and Amy's scream.

Tara reached the landing and felt her way blindly through the darkness to the hall door, and then down the hall past the first door and on to the second.

Only the sound of Amy's voice guided her, because darkness was everywhere, intense, complete.

"I'm here, Amy," she called. "I'm here!"

She felt for the bedroom door and slammed it shut, closing out the wind in the hall. Amy's screams for her dwindled to sobs.

"Tara! Tara—the door blew open—Tara! It blew open and all the lights blew out. Tara, are you here?"

"Yes, I'm here. Don't be afraid, Amy, it's all right. I'll find the matches and the—the candles—"

She felt through the darkness for the mantle and the box of matches. The candles had fallen and rolled but two still lay on the high shelf. She took them and bent to the hearth, dropping the towels as she stooped, her arm aching from her desperate, unconscious hold on them.

The small light seemed the most beautiful thing she had ever witnessed, bringing them from the darkness that had been too much to bear. She turned her face upward for a moment, saying, "And God made light ... thank You." Amy was weeping, pleading, "Please don't let it go out, Tara, please. Light them all. Even the black ones. Light something in the fireplace. Burn the books."

"Good idea," Tara said, and reached for the book that still lay on the hearth, where she had left them.

She tore the pages and their brittle edges cut her palm, so she quickly set fire to them and got up to light the rest of the candles.

The door banged open suddenly and the wind sucked at her, taking the tiny flame of the candle. But the books only flamed higher.

Tara ran for the door and pushed it shut again, and then dragged over a chair and propped it under the knob. "That should hold it," she said as she hurried to light candles before the books were gone into ashes, "at least until I can push something heavier against it."

She lighted every candle available, even the black ones, and placed them all around the room so that if the door blew open again the wind hopefully wouldn't get them all.

"What is it, Tara?" Amy asked, still weeping, her voice catching in a child's sob. "What is that wind? It's here in the house, something here in the house! Tara, I'm so afraid. I want to get out of here—"

Her words ended in a scream of pain, and Tara rushed silently to stand beside her. And then to bite her lip in frustration because there was nothing she could do.

For hours thereafter, hours that seemed unending, in a night that went on forever, Amy cried out in pain, again and again, while Tara stood by.

The wind stopped gradually, and the house was still, as if a storm had spent its energy and was moaning its life away.

Tara waited at the foot of the bed and counted candles. Twelve white and twelve black.

She dampened a cloth and wiped perspiration from Amy's forehead, then went for the dozenth time to look out the window, looking for dawn.

Back at the foot of the bed she counted candles again. Twelve white and twelve black. Some of them burned faster than others. The black ones lasted longer.

Twelve. But there was one downstairs in the fireplace where Sherwood had kicked it. And that made thirteen.

"So what!" Tara said aloud to herself, and looked up at the glowing eyes in the painting.

"Tara!"

Tara turned back to Amy and saw the beginning of the birth.

"Help me, Tara!" Amy screamed.

Tara put her hand on Amy's abdomen. "Take a deep breath," she said, her voice shaking, "and push! Bear down on it, Amy!"

Amy resisted for a moment. Then, with an effort that brought the blood veins out like tubes in her throat, she pushed, and all at once the baby was there.

A nearly paralyzing nervousness seized Tara as she looked down at the tiny, squirming, bloody thing between Amy's thighs. Then she forced herself to reach for it, picked it up and placed the slimy little body on the far side of Amy. She hurried around the bed, took two of the strings she had cut and quickly tied off the cord. Then she reached for the knife.

Blood squirted when she sliced through the cord, and at the same time the baby let out a gasping sound that was more mewing than crying.

Tara turned her back to the bed and dropped the knife. For a while she was desperately sick to her stomach. She swallowed, and swallowed again, before she was able to reach for the towels.

She gently wiped the baby as best as she could, wrapped it in a clean towel and lay it near Amy's arm. It had stopped its birth cry.

Blood covered Tara's arms nearly to the elbows and she spent a couple of minutes washing. Again she swallowed the nausea that kept rising in her throat.

The silence seemed profound once Amy's suffering was over, or nearly over, and a gray dawn was turning the candlelight into little bits of heat without purpose.

Amy's voice suddenly broke the stillness. "Tara, what is it?"

The tone, more than the words, caught Tara's attention. Amy sounded as if she were speaking of something alien and strange that had entered the room.

Tara dried her hands and arms. She didn't look around at Amy and the baby. "It's a girl, Amy."

There was no answer. The baby was as silent as Amy.

Tara turned and nearly dropped the towel. Amy had drawn back from the baby and was staring at it in revulsion. It squirmed in its towel like something struggling for freedom.

Tara hurried over to the bed. "Amy, you can't reject her just because it's a girl! She needs you, Amy."

Amy continued to draw back, shaking her head. "No," she said, her lips trembling. "No!"

"Amy!" Tara said severely. "Stop acting like a child! Just exactly how do you think this baby will live without you? Take it and nurse it. You'll like it, really you will." Amy finally gave in and lay still and let Tara push the infant to her. Slowly, she raised her hand and opened the top of her gown, but her eyes continued to stare at the baby as though it did not belong to her.

Tara left them and went to blow out the candles. She went to the door and moved the chair, and looked into the hall. There seemed to be nothing out of the ordinary. No ceilings down, no extra debris scattered about. There was no sound from anywhere.

No sound at all.

Tara went back into the bedroom and softly closed the door, remembering the other silences in the house. The silences that had every time preceded a death.

Who now, she wondered, and went back to stand at the foot of the bed and watch Amy nurse the baby.

"She's a strong, healthy baby, isn't she, Amy?" Tara asked. "Doesn't she seem strong to you?"

"Yes," Amy answered. "Yes, she does."

Tara saw with relief that Amy was acting more at ease with her new daughter. "And you, Amy. Are you feeling all right?"

Amy closed her eyes. "Yes. I'm just worn out, that's all."

"Would you like a drink or some food? Nourishment to bring up your strength?"

"Later. Now I just want to sleep."

"But the baby is all right and so are you," Tara said again, to reassure herself.

Though Amy's eyes were closed she smiled. "We're fine, Tara. We're just fine."

There was in Amy's voice a new maturity, a new quality that was soft and accepting. The birth had changed her from a girl to a woman, Tara thought.

It was going to be all right after all.

She stood at the foot of the bed and watched them both relax in sleep.

CHAPTER 13

Scott had lived alone for three years, since his return from the university. His gentle mother had said, "But, Scott, darling, how can you move away without a wife? If you were getting married I wouldn't mind so much. You really should be married, Scott. Look at all the lovely girls in town." She was small and slender and seemed always to be working in her flower gardens and worrying about whether or not he would ever marry. Mostly not. Scott, laughing, had assured her, "I can live without a wife at this time, Mom, don't worry. What can a woman do that I can't do?" And his mother had answered amiably, "Cook?" He had given her a hoarse laugh and a kiss and hadn't even bothered to answer. What was there to cooking?

Glumly, he remembered that conversation as he ate his breakfast-lunch at the Main Street Cafe. One week of trying to cook an egg right had been enough for him and since then he had either eaten his meals out or sneaked home "accidentally" right at dinner time. Of course the welcome was always enthusiastic, even though he hardly ever went a day without seeing his mother for a few minutes anyway.

When the crowd thinned out Mary brought a cup of coffee and sat down at the table with Scott.

"You're having a very late breakfast today," she said, scarcely concealing her curiosity. "Were you out late?"

"No. I just couldn't sleep. Had another one of those floor-walking nights. And then the minute I hit the office I was faced by three land buyers. I just now got away. What is it, about twelve o'clock?"

He hadn't needed to ask the time. The clock was on the wall, and a watch on his wrist. But making conversation with Mary seemed oddly difficult. He realized he was feeling slightly grumpy and introverted. He wanted to be alone. He could have gone on down the road to another cafe, but here he could watch the street that led out of town, toward Black Swamp. Watch every car that came through, and every girl who walked by. She might come looking for him.

"More like one-thirty," she said. "It was after twelve when you came in."

A girl walked by on the other side of the street and for a moment he watched, wishing to hell the cars would get out of the way so he could see ... But then she came in view and it wasn't Tara. He sighed and settled back in his chair.

"What's the matter with you, Scott?" Mary asked, stirring and stirring her coffee. "You haven't met that ghost the kids saw, have you?" She was grinning, teasing.

"Odd that you should think of that, Mary. Actually, I have." He saw her frown. She stopped stirring her coffee.

"There really is one? I thought they were just—well— just—"

"No, there's no ghost. At least not a visible ghost. Actually, Mary, that's why I couldn't sleep. You know I'm responsible for that Bishop house ... ?" He waited until she nodded, her attention fixed on him. "Well, I went out there and found—uh—some people living there."

"*Living* there!" she said, sounding like his dad. "But how? I mean, since when? It was just last week that man was found dead there, wasn't it? Were they there then?"

"No, of course not. They came in not long after that, though, evidently. I haven't talked to them much. I—"

She interrupted, eager to know. "Who on earth are they?"

"That's the drawback, the reason I can't get them out. One of the men is the nephew of the owner and she said to let him stay as long as he wanted."

"Oh my goodness."

She stirred her coffee.

Scott said, "Yeah."

After thinking awhile she asked, "Is it a family? Are there any children?"

"Uh—" Why not tell her the truth? Why not tell her it was one of those kooky communal deals? "Not really. I mean, there's a couple of guys and three girls." Well, she didn't have to know about the other guy. "One of the girls is just there to kind of help out another one that's pregnant, that's all."

He took a long breath and looked out the window, and was hardly aware of the penetrating gaze of the young woman across the table.

"She's going to leave as soon as the baby is born," he said dreamily after a bit of silence.

"And when will that be?" Mary asked.

"I don't know. It's a young kid who's having the baby. I mean she looks like she's carrying a barrel under the front of her dress."

"That doesn't mean anything. Some people get big as early as six or seven months. Have you told them the danger of living there? The rumors can't all be false, Scott. Did you tell them?"

Angrily, he answered, "What the hell do you think I've been doing running back and forth between here and there? And walking the floor all night!"

"And taking it out by yelling at me?"

"Oh, I'm sorry, Mary." He touched her hand lightly to apologize. "I just can't seem to get through to anyone, no matter what I do or how much I talk."

"Maybe the house is all right after all. They *are* living there. If you go out and tell them it's weird, that strange things happen there—well, deaths, at least—and it turns out to be all accidents, which can happen in any house that old and dark with long steep stairs, why would they really be concerned if they wanted to live there?"

"I couldn't even get the men to listen."

"But the girl? The one who's staying there just because of the baby?"

Her voice was too soft, and he felt that she knew exactly how he was feeling. He paid close attention to his cold coffee, taking up her habit of stirring it vigorously.

He said, on the defensive, "She's going to leave as soon as the baby is born. She's going to take Anna Lou's place at the office, working for Dad and me."

"But what if there really is something to that stuff Jake told and she doesn't get out before the baby is born, Scott?"

He didn't answer. He couldn't. Once again he was seeing the renter lying on the steps and the ants crawling in and out of his mouth. Nervousness gripped him again, and the frustrated feeling that he had to get out there with her. He twisted in his chair, and looked at the street and the sidewalks. No pedestrians now. Not even a car. The street swam lazily under a shimmer of heat waves.

"You're in love with her, aren't you?" Mary asked, so low he almost missed her words.

He nodded, but he said, "How can you love a person you just met?"

"I don't know, but I've heard it can happen. Just *boong* and it's there. Why don't you go drag her out, Scott?"

"She won't leave that pregnant girl, for some reason. She thinks the kid needs help because they're the kind of people who don't believe in doctors and hospitals."

"Good heavens! You mean the girl is just going to have the baby like a hundred years ago?"

Scott shrugged. "I guess."

"Well, doesn't she know the death rate of mothers at that time? So many died in childbirth!"

"I guess that's why Tara insists on staying."

"If I were you, feeling as you do, I'd go get both girls. And if they didn't come with me I'd tell those men of theirs—"

He interrupted, "*Hers*. Tara—"

Mary ignored him. "—that if they didn't let the girls come to town until that baby is born I'd take the sheriff back out there and see that something happened."

"I couldn't charge them with anything just because the girl wants to have her baby without a doctor's help, Mary. You can get into trouble by siccing the law on people who haven't done anything."

"Oh. Well, then I'd go, and I'd stay right there and see to it that the girl I loved was safe. And if something weird started to happen in that awful old house, I'd drag her out and let the rest of them go—if that's what they want. But I'll bet you they'd get out in a hurry then, too."

He looked at her long and steadily, then he got up, took her chin in his hand and gently and gratefully kissed her lips. His last kiss for Mary.

He didn't look back as he went out the door.

A great load had been lifted from him and he sang as he drove. He had stopped at his apartment just long enough to pack a few bare essentials, like the toothbrush and a change of clothes, and at a drugstore to buy a razor that didn't need electricity. If it was communal out there, then he'd join it.

Thank God for Mary after all. He had been so eaten by worry and wonder that he hadn't been able to think clearly about anything. Moving in with them would never have occurred to him.

He parked in front of the home and got out, leaving his suitcase in the car. Better let the men know his intentions first because he might have to bat a few eyebrows down, though he really didn't think Mrs. Bishop's nephew would give him any static.

Knocking on the door was not part of his plan, but opening it and walking in didn't work. He found it locked. And then he remembered something he had failed to get. House keys.

Well, around to the kitchen door. He jumped off the stoop into the vines, humming. They didn't look so boogery today.

She was probably in the kitchen, he thought as he went around the house, as she had been the last time he was there. He hoped so. He wanted to get at least one long look at her before he tackled the men. It might pay to let her get a look at him too, so she could remember what he had looked like once upon a time.

He approached the back porch in the same good humor and was still humming when he started in the door.

The guy with the little eyes stood a few feet back in the hall, in the middle of it, like a sentry on guard.

Scott stopped just inside the door, his song ended and forgotten. The smell was still there, he thought vaguely as he watched the man. What had they called him? Some kind of wood ...

"Sherwood? Your name Sherwood?"

The expression in the man's eyes had changed in a way that puzzled and disturbed Scott. What was with him, anyway? He was staring as if he had never seen him before, and he was holding something in his right hand.

A knife. It was nearly concealed. Only the blade glistened dully as it caught a bit of light from the door behind Scott.

Scott decided that he had better be friendly, under these conditions. His professional smile was almost genuine and hard to tell from the real thing. For him the smile was easy to come by because of the long hours of practice with difficult buyers and sellers. It was hard to keep both pleased without a smile of some kind. He eased it on, slowly and cautiously.

"I'm Scott Yates. I guess you remember me."

The man did not reply, nor did he move. The knife at his side was as still as his eyes, but even in the dim light of the hall Scott could see that the grip was death-tight.

The sounds in the house penetrated his consciousness. Or rather, the lack of sound. Something moved in a wall, rustling, crawling against wood, but otherwise the house could have been empty of all life.

"Where is everybody?" he asked suddenly, moving his gaze from Sherwood to look beyond him, and then toward the open doorway to the kitchen. He took a step forward, and Sherwood moved swiftly, one step. Crouching. The blade had twisted back over his hand so fast that Scott hadn't seen it move.

Scott stopped. He had seen a knife thrown a few times in his life and knew by the way the man had moved that he was prepared to throw it at any instant and he was professional enough so that he wouldn't miss any mark he chose.

Scott's brain clicked rapidly, finding a suitable excuse for digging into the whereabouts of the others.

"I've got a message for Giles—whatever his name is. From his aunt. Very important."

The man didn't relax or say a word. He wasn't going to be tricked by anything like that and Scott didn't dare move. The guy looked like he had lost his cool for damn sure. His eyes, closer to him and easier to see now, had a crazy look that beat all he had ever seen.

Softly, warily, smiling, Scott said, "You can give him the message if you like, but Mrs. Bishop wanted me to tell him in person." He paused briefly for effect. "She's coming down to see you all. She called to see if she's welcome, but said to get ready because she's coming anyway."

"Tell her to stay away! Giles ain't here no more. Everybody's gone."

Scott wasn't surprised, but his stomach hardened as he wondered where Tara and the other girls were. Maybe he could lead him out on that one too.

"Oh," he said, raising an eyebrow slightly. "What'd he do, run off and leave you? Take your car and your girls too? Left you stranded?"

"Yeah. Now get out," he said. "Get ... *out*."

Scott watched him closely, his ears strained for the sound of a voice.

Still cautiously, but loudly enough for Tara to hear in case Sherwood was lying, Scott said, "This house is a killer, you know. It's dangerous. You'd better get out of it. I'll give you a lift to town if you like."

Sherwood drew his wrist back just slightly, and Scott quickly held up a hand.

"All right," he said, backing slowly toward the door. "I'm going. I just had a message to deliver. I'll call Mrs. Bishop and tell her that her nephew is gone. I'll be sure to call her as soon as I get to a phone, so she won't come on down."

He turned, whistling, and went out the door. And to his surprise got away with it. He could thank Mrs. Bishop for that.

Maybe the guy was right and Giles and the girls had pulled out. But would Tara have gone without telling him? Well, maybe she had tried and couldn't reach him. If they had gone it would account for this bully, Sherwood, being so crazy mad. Mad enough to kill anyone who happened to get in his way.

At the corner of the house Scott looked back, but the man hadn't followed him. He went on to his car, wondering what to believe, and what to do about it.

When he got into his car he glanced at his wristwatch and saw that it was almost four o'clock. He sat still, thinking, looking up at the house.

Nothing in the windows but vines and dust and mold. No face looking down for him. But the house, the whole roof, began to make him feel as if he were at the foot of a hill, looking up. He leaned over to get a better look at it.

The house appeared to be sliding backwards into itself, closing in, going into the ground at the rear. Had the swamp moved in underneath it in some-way? He hadn't noticed the ground being any more spongy than usual. He hadn't even noticed much of a slant in the back hall.

Curiosity, mixed with a feeling of disbelief, that he was seeing crooked, that it was he who was mixed up in the upper story and not the house, spurred him on to start his car and drive around to the side of the house to sit under the tree. Looking. The bottom back window in the house was a bit lower than the front, all right, but not enough to account for the lean in the roof. His gaze ran up to the roof line, and there he found it. The roof had settled far below the front. At least two feet. And that was crazy, he almost said aloud, because how the hell could it, without it showing at the bottom? Of course the bottom was sinking too, there was no doubt about that, but ... "

The corner of his gaze caught the chrome shine of the back bumper of the car parked in the garage. The door wouldn't close, not even the good one, because the car was too long. The garage had been built for buggies or carriages, not cars—especially models from the Seventies.

So Sherwood had lied. Giles had not taken the car and left at all.

He looked at the house again as if his eyes could penetrate the walls and see what had happened there, and a cold anxiety began to grow in his heart.

He had reason enough now, he knew, to bring the sheriff out. But knowing the sheriff and the time in which he had to do nothing, he would probably be down on the river at his favorite fishing hole, which he kept carefully concealed. Besides, if Tara were still in the house, he didn't have time to go back to hunt for the sheriff, even if the man were taking a simple nap in one of his two little jail cells.

The car, Scott noticed then, had an out-of-state license plate, but though he leaned out his window and strained to see what it was, it remained blurred by the distance and the shadow cast by the leaning, broken garage door.

The best thing to do, he decided quickly, was to make the man in the house think he had gone back to town.

He roared the car unnecessarily as he backed out, turned around and drove off down the road.

After a quarter of a mile he slowed the car to a crawl and watched the road behind through the rear view mirror. The forest had closed the house from sight, but that didn't mean Sherwood wouldn't follow him. However, he knew a road, a thin, nearly overgrown trail into the forest about a mile away that Sherwood probably had never noticed. When he reached it he drove in, easing the car over soft soil that threatened to bog the car down.

Once the road was out of sight Scott pulled his car onto the exposed roots of a tree to keep at least one wheel from sinking, and got out.

As he walked swiftly back toward the road, frogs behind him set up a din that rang in his ears. The frogs though, thankfully, were as good as watch dogs to locate cars on the road, and so far the only silences he heard from them were caused by his own approaching steps.

A mile and a half back to the house. He didn't dare walk on the main road, but he walked within sight of it so that he would be able to spot the car if Sherwood should happen to drive by.

He approached the house on the side opposite the garage, and stopped where trees still grew thickly. The house was but a huge, vine-covered wall. Although the ground had grown mushier under its continuous ground cover, the swamp had not worked its way this far and he had no worry about stepping into water unexpectedly.

For several minutes he stood still, waiting until the frogs accepted him as just another part of their world, and then slowly, hoping they wouldn't notice, he moved forward, keeping out of sight of the back door.

He was within forty feet of the house when he stopped again. Beyond the tree which he stood behind, the entire side of the house was visible, but it was the side he had never seen before. The back porch was there, its roof drooping at an angle he had not noticed from the other side, and the wide, very high stone chimney rose under its slimy mosses toward the sky. No windows at all broke the broad expanse of the rear half of the house from ground to roof, or if they did they were entirely camouflaged by vines. Toward the front half of the house a few narrow panes peeped out.

To imagine anybody ever really living in that house, and liking it, was beyond him.

After a while he sat down against the tree, checking first to be sure he didn't sit on a snake. But that one brief glance down into the vines as he pushed them apart with his hands was the only time he looked away from the house.

The minutes seemed like hours. The house seemed utterly without life in a world of sound. As the evening moved in and the sunlight disappeared from the roof the bull frogs added croaks that made Scott want compulsively to try to clear his throat for them, and the whippoorwills poured forth their loud calls that rang from one dry section of forest to another. And from the house nothing. Still nothing. No one had come out or entered. No voice penetrated the walls. No smoke rose from the chimney from a dinner being cooked there.

Scott began to wonder if he were wasting time. Perhaps he should go back now and gouge the sheriff out to see what had happened. But it—

The sound from the house froze his thoughts and brought him scrambling to his feet. Board upon board crashed down somewhere within, and as he watched he saw the entire back portion of the roof tremble and drop a few inches. As suddenly as it had started then, the sound drifted to silence. The frogs nearby had hushed for the long moment, and gradually took up again as if nothing had happened after all.

"What in the devil ... ?" Scott muttered to himself, moving onward slowly, looking down from the roof, watching the back door. Surely the fool wouldn't stay in the house with it falling right on him.

But no one came out.

Darkness had crept in like a fog, and although it gave him the willies to see the old house in this strange, dull, gray light, it did have the advantage of making it possible for him to move nearer to it.

He was wondering if the man had taken the car and left and he somehow had missed it. Sherwood could have gone by while he was intent on concealing his own car.

He warily approached the windows of the kitchen, looking for a faint light, a suggestion that someone was within, but they were only blank, reflecting, black holes in the green-black walls. He ducked under each one, just in case Sherwood was keeping some kind of lonely, silent vigil somewhere in the room beyond the windows.

Scott hesitated near the small back porch, trying to make up his mind whether to go in or not. There were two things that concerned him and made him pause. If Sherwood were still in the house he had the knife and Scott had only his hands. And the other was his lack of light. He would be feeling his way through a nearly dark house with only a small box of matches in his pocket.

A noise within came faintly to his ears. It seemed to come from upstairs and at first sounded like a human voice, a fine cackle of laughter, but as the sound grew, swelled and became a roar the human quality vanished. Scott's skin, all over his entire body, tingled with warning. He listened, incredulous that something like that, something to which he could put no name, no previous knowledge or experience, actually existed. The sound died away as it had come, with human-sounding chuckles. And a board fell, and another and another—or the echo of the first carried onward into the darkness and depth of the house.

There was nothing more but faint creakings and groanings of a house that seemed to be coming awake as night fell, a part of the primitive nature that slept in sunlight and roamed its own private world in moonlight.

He took his hand away from the wall, not aware until then that he had leaned against it. From his pocket he pulled a white handkerchief and vigorously wiped the dampness from the palm that had touched the oozing moss beneath the vine growth. He felt as if he had handled something filthy.

Still there was no sound of footsteps, but in his mind he saw the room where Tara had been living, the room where he had tried to remove the ugly painting. He felt the need to go there and see for himself that she was safely gone, overpowered all other feelings. He knew the way up. When necessary he could strike a match. And if he happened to meet the madman with the knife he could simply extinguish his light and step aside. Not even the most expert knife thrower was likely to hit his target in the dark.

He stepped onto the porch with no concern about the squeak of a loose board. With all the noises going on in the house no one inside would be apt to notice one more groaning board.

To his astonishment he found the door closed and locked. He pushed and turned the knob without result, for a moment wondering how the man had managed to lock it without a key. Then he remembered that the front door had also been locked, without a key, and that both doors had been locked when the group arrived. Nevertheless they had managed to enter. So he had probably locked the doors by the same method he had once unlocked them.

But why?

Had he locked himself in, or out? Why would he bother to lock the doors if he intended to leave? "And," Scott mumbled under his breath, "why the hell are you standing here trying to figure out what goes on in the mind of someone else, when you ought to get back to town for a cup of coffee to clear the fungus out of your own mind ..."

He was already on his way around the house, almost sure now that they had left, that no one at all remained in the house. A sickness settled in his heart. She had said she wanted a job in his office. Then why had she left without saying anything?

A new thought entered his mind and it raised his spirits so intensely that it nearly shocked him for a moment. Maybe she had gone to town, rented a room, and had already contacted his office! After all, he hadn't even checked in since sometime before noon.

He began to walk faster, then on impulse decided to check the garage to make sure the car was gone.

The darkness there was complete, unbroken, black. But he could see the outline of the hanging, lopsided door and its position seemed not to have changed. He touched it for guidance and cracked his shin against metal. Stooping, he felt the bumper of the car.

The cold, cold tingles moved over his body again and his thoughts hung suspended for long heartbeats, coming back to him finally in bits and pieces.

One car. There had never been more than one car. And the pregnant girl could not have walked to town. How many miles? Seven? Six? Hell, he couldn't remember.

He turned to run, run to his own car a mile and a half away and get back to town as fast as he could and see if he could locate the fishing-nut sheriff. Or his house keys. Or to hell with his house keys, he'd get the state patrol.

Wait, he told himself sharply, don't panic like a damned fool. Get that license number.

It could mean something.

He felt his way back to the car and then ran his hands over the bumper until he located the sharp edge of the bottom of the plate. Then, knowing he was leaving himself wide open to disclosure, he took the box of matches from his pocket and lit one.

A California license. With a long number he would never be able to remember in his present state of confusion.

The match burned out and nearly took his thumb before he dropped it. From his shirt pocket he dragged a small notebook and a pen, put one foot on the bumper, balanced the notebook on his knee, and struck another match. He held the match between two fingers of his left hand, like a cigarette, and carefully wrote down the numbers. When he dropped the match it sizzled faintly in the damp vines.

CHAPTER 14

Tara sat in the rocking chair, in the rapidly increasing darkness of the room, unwilling to move or make a sound. She tried not to look at the bed, the bed on which the two of them lay. So still, so very still, as if both of them were dead instead of only one.

It hadn't been long since it had happened, or at least since she had noticed that it had happened. She had spent the morning trying to think of a way out, of how she could manage to get both Amy and the baby out before another night came and the house had a chance to fulfill another promise. And then in the afternoon, when she thought them both asleep, she had gone again to look down at them, and ...

The chair she sat in was really Amy's chair. This was the first time she had sat down. An hour ago—two hours ago—when she had seen that death had come again.

She leaned her face into her cupped hands and shut out all light and tried not to think because she was afraid that she would be unable to think at all. There was too much. Too much.

No one had approached their door all day. Not Sherwood. Not Giles. The men might have gone for all she knew. And yet she knew Sherwood hadn't. He wouldn't leave her alive, never.

Her thoughts went back to the morning and the birth of the baby. After Amy nursed the baby she had gone to sleep, worn out, exhausted. And the baby slept too, warm against Amy's arm. The rejection wouldn't last, Tara had assured herself then. In a few days Amy would accept the baby and love it more than anything.

They had seemed so normal, so well, in this room, this house where nothing else was normal or well. They were life instead of death.

What had happened? Death did not come without a reason. What had she done wrong? Or what had she left undone? What could she have done to save her?

She raised her face finally to see that the room had gone so dark that the bed was lost somewhere in the blackness. Only the soft breathing of sleep came from that direction.

The dark didn't bother her. She leaned back in the rocking chair and closed her eyes, thinking, *I'll rest too until she wakes up, and then I'll ... try to think of something.*

Foremost in her mind, more important than anything else, it seemed, was that Sherwood must not know of the death. Above all he must not know. She couldn't bear the thought of seeing that small body carried into the swamp too, like so much garbage, to be eaten by the things that lived beneath the logs in the black water.

She had to find her way out of the house, to go, to bring back someone to help, but how could she leave them lying there?

The sound of chuckles rose as if from her mind, it came so gradually into her awareness. Someone laughing somewhere, in a nonhuman, maddened way. It drew her thoughts toward it, away from the bed, the darkness, away from herself. Laughter, that wasn't laughter, somewhere in the house above. As before.

She leaned forward and gripped the arm of her chair, tense and listening, terror freezing her into the chair as the sound grew into a conscious-crushing roar. All about her in the house the sound rose. In her mind she again could see the lake, beneath so that the house moved, barely, hardly at all, like a ferry crossing the body of black water.

She clung to the chair, holding her breath, waiting. There was nothing else to do. Her mind was as frozen as her body, unable to question the source of this sound that was not a natural part of the world she had known before.

As it came it went, and only the sounds of a ceiling falling in its wake remained with the echo of the other.

When she could she swallowed and closed her eyes. If it should come again she wouldn't be able to stand it. Her senses, her mind, her sanity would go.

She left the chair and reached through the darkness for the mantle. Her fingers touched a candle, still upright in its holder. She grasped it as if it were a life rope to a safe shore and turned, one hand held out in front of her, to walk slowly through the darkness to the bed and around it to the table where she had left her box of matches.

They wouldn't light. Dampness had taken them. The heads brushed away like soft bits of cotton. Her hands trembled as she tried match after match, and dropped them. When it seemed as if nothing would ever work for her again and few matches were left in the bottom of the box her fingers touched a firm head. She held it, too desperate even to pray. Holding her breath, she scratched it quickly and it sizzled into a tiny flame.

Afraid to breathe, to allow her breath to touch it, she moved it to the wick of the candle and watched as it caught.

The light became a creature of comfort, small but sufficient. She sat back on the edge of the bed and let the tears flow for a while. Some of the tension left her body, allowing her mind to absorb reality. She wiped her eyes and looked at the door.

It was still closed, thank God. A long dark hall lay between them and escape—but if they could get past Sherwood, once outside, the darkness would be a blessing. Snakes? They didn't matter anymore.

She left the candle on the table and turned to face the bed, saying softly, very softly, "Amy, I have to leave you now ..."

Her voice caught. A need to let go, to sit down and weep for the dead young girl held her immobile as she looked upon the pale child's face. It occurred to her that she had never known how old Amy really was. In her death-sleep she looked no more than twelve years old.

The baby moved in its towel. A silent bit of life, it had hardly stirred during the whole day. Tara reached for it, handling it gently, and lay it near her side of the bed so that she could prepare it for going out into the night.

The towel fell away from its face and its eyes, hazy blue, looked steadily up at her. Steadily, ever so steadily.

Tara drew back, chills running cold fingers over her skin. She returned the baby's stare hypnotically, feeling as if she were looking into the eyes of a knowledge she herself could never grasp.

Quickly Tara turned her back to the baby, to reorient herself and take control of her situation. The baby had its eyes open. So? Babies usually opened their eyes. That was quite natural enough. How could she read into that newly born gaze anything so ridiculous?

Under her breath, to explain and understand, she said, "It's the house, that's all. The whole damned, stinking house and everything that has happened. That's all. Don't be a stupid fool."

But when she turned back she tried not to look into the baby's strange waking eyes. They had looked, she couldn't help thinking as she wrapped it tightly and snugly in a towel and then spread a blanket square to place it on, like deep, distant, angry pools which fog had veiled. Then in disgust she reminded herself that it was only her imagination.

She picked up the baby and placed it on the blanket and turned the bottom corner up to cover its tiny feet, and the sides over to lap across its body. When she reached for the top, to pull it down over the small face the eyes drew her again and held her still. Suspended in movement.

What is it thinking, she wondered, and quickly pushed the thought away. She should talk to it, but she couldn't. She just couldn't.

The eyes though. They were taking on a look that was vaguely familiar and she wondered who the baby resembled. Not Amy. No, not Amy at all. Nor Sherwood.

She pulled the top of the blanket gently over the baby's face.

Her thoughts turned to plans to get out. With the baby in her arms the back steps would be too dangerous to attempt in the dark. She would have to take the candle at least until they reached the bottom of the stairs. Then if Sherwood and Giles were in the kitchen, for instance, she could probably go unseen by the door if she extinguished the candle. From there on she had nothing to worry about. The creatures of nature would accompany them through the long miles to town.

She picked up the baby, settled it against her breast with one arm, and took the candle in her free hand. For a moment then, a very brief moment, she looked down at Amy.

"I promise you, Amy," she murmured, "I'll get your baby to safety and then I'll be back for you. Sherwood will not do to you what he did to the others."

With the baby tight in her arm, she went to the door.

Opening the door with a candle in her hand was awkward and slow, but finally it swung slowly back. She went forward into the dark hall, and stopped abruptly as the pale yellow light of the candle outlined a white face against the opposite wall.

Sherwood.

They stared into each other's eyes, and she watched him move away from the wall and raise the knife so that she could see it. He grinned in triumphant malignity.

"I been waitin' for you," he said. "You had to come out sometime. You had to." The knife blade turned toward her, and its point glistened with a silver glow.

Tara conquered a desire to step back. To retreat from Sherwood now would be like retreating from a threatening animal. He would attack.

Her voice quivered slightly. "Where's Giles?"

Giles would help her, maybe. Just maybe. Because she had helped Leda all she could.

"Giles!" He spat the name like a filthy word. "Giles. He ain't got no more guts than one of them frogs out there. Scared of the house. Scared of everythin'."

"Where is he?" Tara demanded, strengthening her voice.

"Gone. Back there." He tipped his head slightly toward the swamp and laughed. The sound echoed from both ends of the hall, but he seemed not to notice. "Went to be with Leda. Crazy as Fox. Crazy. But you, baby, you ain't goin' nowhere. Not on your feet anyway. Me, I got to get out of this place, but first, you've got to be fixed so you can't."

He started moving slowly toward her, and the knife came higher as he raised his arm. He would take his time because she couldn't fight the knife, and the look on his face showed an anticipated delight in what he intended to do.

She moved swiftly, backing into the room and slamming shut the door between them. The candle wavered and nearly went out, but settled back to burning evenly as she leaned against the door.

In the hall outside she heard him laugh, and keep laughing.

The baby stirred in her arms. She bit her lower lip, looked at her small candle, and tried to think of what to do. Stay here and wait and pray that Scott would come back? Would he ever come back since she had sent him away?

And the baby—how long would it take the baby to starve to death with no milk? She hadn't so much as a spoonful of sugar to make sugar-water for it.

The laughter in the hall stopped, and his voice came dully from beyond the door. "I'll wait. I can wait longer than you can. Whenever you're ready to leave that room, Red, I'll be here."

But he wouldn't enter the room. She remembered that suddenly. He wouldn't enter because he was afraid of the witchcraft, the black magic that had once been practiced there. Beneath his callous attitude lurked that superstitious fear of the supernatural.

And he had called her a witch. More than once.

The black candle had frightened him. He had thought she possessed supernatural powers because she had held it.

She hurried to place the white candle on the table and the baby back on the bed, then went to the secretary and removed the twelve black candles from their cubbyhole.

She would have to make it seem as real as possible. She would have to look like a witch, approach him with confidence, and take her chances. She had no black clothing, so the white robe would have to do.

Nervously she put it on, over her old blue jeans, the only clothes she possessed that were really her own. Then she carefully lighted two black candles, placed them upright in holders until she was ready, and put the other ten into the pockets of her robe. Their weight dragged it down, making it feel clumsy in front, bumping against her thighs as she walked about the room, getting ready to go out. It didn't matter. Nothing mattered but getting out.

She combed her hair long and flowing and pulled sections of it forward over each shoulder.

Two candles in her hands, held straight out in front of her, toward him ... She remembered the baby. How could she carry the baby and both candles?

The answer came readily: a sling on her back. The baby would be safer that way, too. And her old shawl was soft enough to tie easily and cradle the baby safely.

Her hands shook nervously, but she made the shawl into a sling, settled the baby in it and, by sitting on the bed with her back to the baby, brought the ends of the shawl up and around her neck and tied them in tight knots. She slipped one arm through so that it wouldn't choke her so much, and stood up, testing it. The baby lay heavily but securely against her back.

She took a deep breath to raise her courage, picked the two black candles out of their holders and went to the door. She stared at the knob, but not because turning it presented another problem. It simply was the most important object in her life at the time—to turn it or not to turn it.

She glanced back at the bed once more, and then her eyes drew from habit to the painting on the wall. "Goodbye Sama—" she started to say softly, and stopped. There was something different about the painting, but she couldn't think what it was. Then it struck her. The eyes were flat, looking straight ahead, just globs of yellowish paint.

Strange, she thought, and instantly remembered the baby's eyes. Now she knew who the baby resembled. Samael.

She frowned and lowered her head, looking down at her feet. This was nonsense, all nonsense, she told herself, but the weight of the small, warm body on her back penetrated her consciousness and made her aware that her instinct cried *run, run away as fast as you can. Run from the baby.*

But she couldn't run. She closed her eyes tightly and moistened her dry lips with her tongue. Then she straightened, opened her eyes, looked ahead and turned the doorknob as she had the first time, slowly, and easily, careful not to disturb the flame on the candle.

With her foot she shoved the door wide. And stood there, facing Sherwood, her head high, both black candles raised arm's length in front of her.

Whatever he had started to say was cut short and his eyes darted from one candle to the other, back and forth, eyes and mouth three round holes in his pale face.

Low and rapidly, so that he couldn't hear exactly what she was saying, she began to chant as her eyes held his face without wavering, "Our father which art in heaven, hallowed be thy name, thy kingdom come, thy will be done, in earth as it is in heaven ..."

"What are you saying?" he screamed, backing away. "What are you trying to do to me?"

"... give us this day our daily bread. And forgive us our debts, as we forgive our debtors. And lead us not into temptation ..."

"Stop it! Stop!" He had backed against the wall, as far as he could go. His arm jabbed the knife forward, but he did not throw it.

She continued toward him, slowly, coming into the hall. "But deliver us from evil. For thine is the kingdom."

She had reached the center of the hall, and stopped and turned her back toward the front stairs because it was a safer way down, going as she would have to—backwards. She didn't move her eyes from his face. "And the power, and the glory, forever ... Our father which art in heaven, hallowed by thy name ...

She chanted on, low and fast, as she moved slowly backwards toward the front stairs.

He had cowered, staying tightly against the wall, but his screaming voice called out at her, "You can't get out! You can't get away! Both doors are locked ... His eyes, the quivering of his chin, the drooping of the arm that held the knife, belied the confidence in his voice. She saw his fear and hoped it remained until she was downstairs, where she could break a window.

Break a window? With the baby on her back and the heavy screens that covered the windows? She almost faltered, her voice giving in under the feeling of hopelessness that seized her. But if she did slip, if he even suspected that she might, she would be at his mercy.

And he had no mercy.

She had paused slightly, but then resumed her chant in a stronger voice to keep his attention. "Our father which art in—"

Something struck the front of the house, again and again, growing louder as wood splintered. Her voice was drowned and again she stopped, and by instinct she almost whirled about to see what was happening.

She caught herself in time, and continued to face Sherwood. He wasn't watching her now, though. His eyes sought something beyond her.

The house was falling again, she thought, but it was not above, it was on the floor below. And it sounded like chopping. Rhythmic chopping on the wall. Or the door! She forgot Sherwood as a faint light entered from somewhere behind her. The chopping continued and the light grew stronger, and then she heard voices.

But the voices suddenly were lost under the crashing of falling timbers. Behind Sherwood she saw the ceiling giving way, slowly, board after board. Debris drifted down upon him, but he didn't seem to notice. His attention remained glued to something that was far behind her in the hallway.

A light spotlighted them, a round, bright beam that made her turn at last. But all she could see was the light suspended in the air at the top of the stairway.

A voice, behind the light, called out, "Police! Drop that knife, Sherwood!"

The floor began to tremble under her feet and she looked again toward the falling ceiling and saw Sherwood whirl and run back into the depths of the house.

The voice was calling again, shouting, "Don't go in there, you damned fool!"

The floor slanted suddenly backwards, and Tara was thrown against the wall. Both candles dropped from her hands as she reached for something to hold, to keep from losing her balance and going down with the house.

Strong arms caught her, lifting and pulling her toward the front stairs and down.

Several men had clustered on the stairs and in the lower hall, and the voice that shouted in her ear was beautifully familiar. She knew then whose arms were around her waist. The policeman with the light, the one who had called for Sherwood to stop, came behind them. Shouts, confused in Tara's mind, passed from one man to another. Finally, amidst the confusion, they all got through the hole in the front of the house that once had been a large, heavy door. They were standing in the damp vines several feet away from the house.

Lights from half a dozen cars, including spotlights on the cars of state police, poured out upon the house. Shivering from a nervous chill and cool night air, Tara watched the house tremble and settle backwards. And stop, for the moment, leaning far back into itself.

Silence commanded the night. No one said much, and then only mutterings. Tara was aware of the weight of the baby on her back, and its wiggling little movements. She was also aware that every face in the crowd stared wordlessly at the house. From somewhere in the swamp a frog that was a trifle more brave than the others began a tentative piping. Another, and another took it up.

Tara said tonelessly, "He's dead now, too."

"How do you know?" Scott asked.

"Hear the house? It's settled and quiet now. She's in there. Please get her out."

One of the policemen turned his light-flushed face toward her. "Who's in there?"

"Amy. The little girl. The mother of the baby."

"Good God!"

They were running again, three of them, to go back into the hole with their strong flashlights piercing the darkness. No one but Scott heard her say, "But she's dead too."

His arms pulled her closer, and touched the tiny burden on her back. Astonishment was in his voice. "What on earth—?"

"The baby. Could you take her, please?"

With his help she carefully removed the baby from her back. A man whose badge read SHERIFF had come close to watch.

"A baby," he said tenderly.

"Yes," Tara answered. "It's a girl. She was born this morning, and it's her mother who is upstairs still on the bed. She died about noon. I don't know why. I thought she was all right, but then I looked at her again and she was gone. And I had been thinking she was asleep."

In a kind voice the sheriff asked, "Do you want me to take the baby? Is it a relative?"

"No, not a relative. Amy was only a friend. As far as I know the baby has no relatives."

"Then this is a job for the child welfare people." He had pulled back the blanket and looked down at the small face. He smiled. "The way she's stirring around I'd say she's hungry. We'd better get her to town."

Tara asked, "What will happen to her?"

"Oh, she's not going to be such an unlucky baby after all. There's lots of nice young couples in this county who'd love to raise her as their own."

"She'll be taken care of then," Tara said, her voice low, competing now with the far-off wail of an ambulance siren.

"You can count on it, Miss—Miss—"

Scott said, "This is Miss Tara." And under his breath, he said close to her ear, "What is your last name anyway?"

The sheriff said, "Glad to meet you, Miss Tara."

She forced a smile and nodded at him, murmuring a reply, then to Scott she whispered, "I'll tell you later."

One of the men who had gone into the house appeared at the door with his light, yelling above the noises that had risen among the talking men, singing frogs and night birds and the renewed splintering of the still-settling old house. "We found her. On the bed yet. The room is still all right. But the whole back of the house has caved in. God only knows where that man is. We'll have to start digging him out when we can. Is that the ambulance?"

"Yeah!"

The siren had reached an ear-splitting crescendo on the road to Black Swamp, for a few minutes obliterating most other sounds. Its light appeared through the trees, spiraling like a beacon of haven in a storm. Then the headlights appeared as it spun through the ruts of the curve in the road. The siren threaded away to nothing, like a drop of sugar candy.

Not a peep came from any frog within a mile. With a grim attempt to cheer her up, Scott hugged Tara tightly and said, "They're sensitive little cusses, aren't they? I'll bet they'll be glad when we're all out of here."

She leaned into his arms and put her head on his shoulder, her face turned toward the action of the men in white who, under commands from the man in the door, ran around to the back of the ambulance and brought out a stretcher. They all disappeared into the house.

Finally, she said, "I'll be glad too."

"I'd take you out of here now but the ambulance has the road blocked," Scott answered.

"That's all right. I want to wait for Amy anyway."

The minutes seemed long and dragging before the stretcher was again in the door, carried carefully between the two men, preceded by the one with the flashlight. The body on the stretcher was hardly visible under the sheet, it was so small.

Tara watched it with a deep sadness. "They're all dead. The house will go now. It has served its purpose."

"Not all are dead," he reminded her. "The baby is alive, and so are you, thank God."

"Yes, so am I."

She had not thought of herself, or considered the reason that she had been left unharmed.

"I too," she said spontaneously, words coming from beyond her conscious reasoning, "have served my purpose. I brought the baby out."

The meaning caused her to catch her breath. She saw Scott look at her. He had not understood. But before he could ask, a state patrolman motioned them back.

"Better move, folks, the house sounds like it's caving in somewhere. The whole top might go any minute. It could be dangerous even here."

The Sheriff moved with them. He was still holding the baby, and he asked Tara, "Do you want to ride in the ambulance with her?"

Tara shook her head. "She doesn't need me now."

"Well, don't you worry about this little baby, we'll see to it that she gets the best home in the county. Don't you worry about her."

Tara shook her head again in answer, and turned to Scott. "Please, let's go to your car. Do you have it here?"

"Yes, right over this way. Want to raise your robe so you won't get it wet?"

She untied the top, preparing to take it off. The black candles still lay heavily in the pockets. "I have my old blue jeans underneath. I just put it on to—to— Please, can I tell you about it some other time?"

"You don't have to tell it at all if you don't want to."

He took the robe and started to fold it.

"Could you just leave it here? Just drop it in the vines? It will rot away."

"Of course."

They walked over it on their way to his car.

The interior smelled fresh and new, a lovely contrast from the smells and experiences in the old house.

"I forgot to tell them," she said, "that the baby needs medical care. There might be something wrong with its eyes."

"Don't worry, darling, the first place it will go is to the hospital. What makes you think something is wrong with its eyes?"

Just hoping, she almost said. Just hoping they needed some little something done to make them look like other babies' eyes. But that wouldn't have sounded right. And the fears she had felt, that terrible transference of Samael to the baby that she had seen, was something she could never tell, not even to Scott. At least not yet. And perhaps not ever. She had to make herself believe that it was just the house affecting her nerves, making her see and imagine things that weren't there.

Weren't there.

She said, after the long pause, "Well, sometimes there is if they're not treated at birth, you know. I mean, I didn't have anything to put in them in case of ... anything being wrong."

His hand touched her shoulder warmly. "I think you worry too much. You'll feel better in a week or two. Meantime I want to turn you over to my mom, okay? She'll have you out picking flowers."

"That sounds lovely. Will she want to fool with me? I can go somewhere else ... a hotel ..." She bit her lip, remembering that she not only didn't have a dime now, but not even a change of clothes.

"Want to fool with you! Honey, you don't have any idea how happy she will be to have her old little boy bring a girl home at last. If you don't watch out she'll have you married to me before you can even get well acquainted enough to know if you like me."

Despite the surroundings, Tara felt a touch of happiness and a great tenderness for Scott. She looked at him, but the lights were behind him, and his face shadowed. He kissed the end of her nose lightly.

"I wanted to do that the first time I saw you," he said. "It's got freckles. That was why I wanted to kiss it."

A large head appeared at the window and a voice boomed out in their ears, "The hospital sent a nurse along, so she's taking the baby back in the ambulance. We're ready to pull out now. If you don't mind, Miss Tara, we'd like you to come into the station tomorrow and tell us what all you know about these people that were here, and what all happened."

"Yes. All right, sheriff."

The sheriff went to his own car, and Tara and Scott wordlessly watched the ambulance turn around, laboring back and forth in its small spot. It finally got back into the rutted, narrow road and slowly pulled out, its siren quiet. Behind it went the sheriff's car. Scott was next in line. Four others were still parked in the yard, spotlights turned on the house.

Scott said, "They'll stay until they find the guy, probably. They may have to bring in a search crew to find him in all that rubble. The license plate on his car was illegal—no current registration. Even so, they think he may be connected with a bunch of robberies and murders in California, and no telling where else."

"Yes. He's buried in that house. I don't believe the house would let him out."

Tara looked out at the dark forest as they drove slowly along the road behind the taillights of the sheriff's car.

They had reached the highway before he spoke to her again.

"Are you always so quiet?" he asked.

"Hardly ever."

"What are you thinking? Are you still worried about something? The baby?"

"I was just wondering about the family that will get it."

"You don't need to let that disturb you. They'll take great care of it. The baby will be okay."

"Yes, I'm sure it will."

But what about the family? The parents? What about them?

Tara watched the spiraling ambulance light in the distance, taking its passenger through the night to her ultimate, unknown destination.

OTHER NOVELS BY RUBY JEAN JENSEN

1974 The House that Samael Built
1974 Seventh All Hallows' Eve
1974 House at River's Bend
1975 The Girl Who Didn't Die
1978 Child of Satan's House
1978 Satan's Sister
1978 Dark Angel
1982 Hear the Children Cry
1982 Such a Good Baby
1983 The Lake
1983 MaMa
1985 Home Sweet Home
1985 Best Friends
1986 Wait and See
1987 Annabelle
1987 Chain Letter
1988 Smoke
1988 House of Illusions
1988 Jump Rope
1989 Pendulum
1989 Death Stone

OTHER NOVELS BY RUBY JEAN JENSEN

1990 Vampire Child
1990 Lost and Found
1990 Victoria
1991 Celia
1991 Baby Dolly
1992 The Reckoning
1993 The Living Evil
1994 The Haunting
1995 Night Thunder
Pending Bear Hollow Charlie
Pending Cry of the Soul
Pending Pride of Bella Terra
Pending Animal Backtalk

CPSIA information can be obtained
at www.ICGtesting.com
Printed in the USA
BVHW091826111121
621363BV00014B/366/J

9 781951 580629